AMERICAN POP

ALSO BY SNOWDEN WRIGHT

Play Pretty Blues

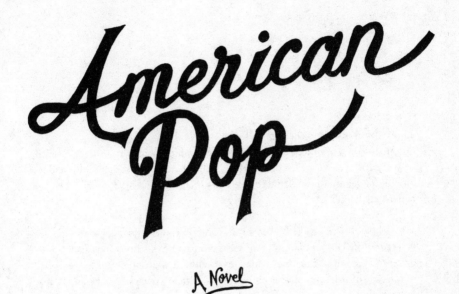

American Pop

A Novel

SNOWDEN WRIGHT

WM
WILLIAM MORROW
An Imprint of HarperCollins*Publishers*

HarperCollins books may be purchased for educational, business, or sales promotional use. For information, please e-mail the Special Markets Department at SPsales@harpercollins.com.

FIRST EDITION

Designed by Bonni Leon-Berman

Library of Congress Cataloging-in-Publication Data

Names: Wright, Snowden, 1981– author.
Title: American pop : a novel / Snowden Wright.
Description: New York, NY : William Morrow, [2019]
Identifiers: LCCN 2018032678 | ISBN 9780062697745 (hardback)
Subjects: | BISAC: FICTION / Literary. | FICTION / Family Life. |
    FICTION / Historical.
Classification: LCC PS3623.R5648 A85 2019 | DDC 813/.6—dc23
LC record available at https://lccn.loc.gov/2018032678

ISBN 978-0-06-269774-5

19 20 21 22 23   LSC   10 9 8 7 6 5 4 3 2 1

For my grandfather
Fred Snowden

Families are always rising and falling in America. But, I believe, we ought to examine more closely the how and why of it, which in the end revolves around life and how you live it.

—*Nathaniel Hawthorne*

Southerners need carbonation.

—*Nancy Lemann*, Lives of the Saints

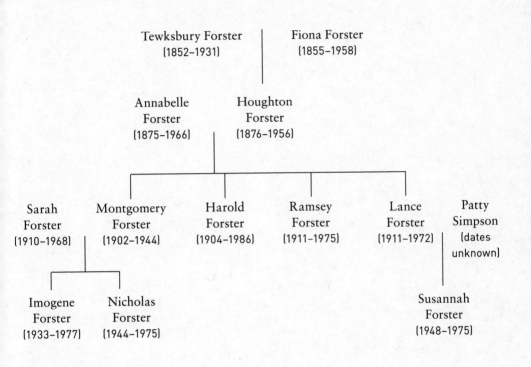

AMERICAN POP

PART 1

1.1

The Famous Panola Cola Dynasty—
Piece of Time, Piece of Ass—
Will H. Hays Rolls Over in His Grave—
Cold Duck—The Prey of a Cola Hunter—
All Happy Families

How far would he go? Montgomery Forster asked himself that question as he stood on top of the Peabody Hotel. The answer was obvious to everyone but him. Recently elected lieutenant governor of Mississippi, a graduate of Princeton University with honors, and a decorated corporal in the First World War, Montgomery's prospects were considered limitless, especially in light of his relationship to the Panola Cola Company. Political columnists said he would someday take up residence at the White House. Corporate insiders said he would expand the family business all the way to Timbuktu. On the roof of the Peabody Hotel an hour from midnight, however, the heir to the Forster dynasty was not thinking in such terms. He was calculating the number of stories and windows he would pass, the distance in yards, feet, and inches he would fall, if he took a step off the ledge.

Not far enough, Monty told himself. Gravel crunched beneath his shoes as he walked to the other side of the roof. Shortly after he rang for the elevator it arrived. The operator, Edward Pembroke, a former circus trainer who later that year would be named "Duckmaster," a position he was to hold until his retirement decades later, welcomed his new passenger. At the start of their descent Pembroke turned to Montgomery and said, "Getting some of our Memphis fresh air?"

"That's right."

"Nothing like our Memphis fresh air."

"Superb."

The air in northern France had been different. There it had been the literal humanity rather than the figurative inhumanity that shocked Monty. When he first arrived at the Front, he expected to be overwhelmed by the cordite smoke he'd read about in novels, the mustard gas he'd learned about during basic, and the kerosene vapors he'd heard about from veterans, but what he noticed more than anything were the excretions, some overflowing latrines and others staining armpits, from thousands of men living in such proximity to one another. So many bodies suffocated the scent of war. Less than a month after arriving on the Continent, though, he met a British officer, a man he would come to know, care for, and even love, whose features proved a welcome distraction: the glistening sight of the brilliantine he combed into his mustache, the exotic sound of his accent refined in public school, the smooth feel of his cheeks from the sandalwood oil he used as aftershave, the sugary taste of the hard candies he kept stuffed in his pockets. Monty managed to focus only on those sensations even when the smell coming from the bodies of his fellow soldiers was that of their decomposition as they lay scattered on the ground throughout No Man's Land.

"Lobby floor, sir," Pembroke said to Montgomery. "Watch your step."

For a moment, the tableau of the New Year's Eve party in the lobby—the drumfire of champagne corks and the salvo of foil horns, the report of toy ratchets and the detonation of confetti poppers—sent a tremor down Montgomery's forearm that he quickly dispelled by clenching his fist. GOODBYE, 1939, read a banner hanging from the mezzanine promenade, HELLO, 1940. At the center of the eighteenth-century South Italian decorative scheme of the lobby, five ducks swam in a fountain carved from black travertine marble, oblivious to the frequent explosions of flashbulbs. Floral arrangements scattered throughout the lobby lent it the atmosphere of a greenhouse.

Monty brushed against tropical orchids as he went looking for a cocktail. He advanced through the hundreds of guests his family had invited to their gala. It was held every year in honor of whoever happened to be president of the United States at the time, and though the honoree had yet to attend, each year the other guests agreed he'd missed out.

In his book *God Shakes Creation*, David Lewis Cohn writes, "The Mississippi Delta begins in the lobby of the Peabody Hotel and ends on Catfish Row in Vicksburg. The Peabody is the Paris Ritz, the Cairo Shepheard's, the London Savoy of this section. If you stand near its fountain in the middle of the lobby, where ducks waddle and turtles drowse, ultimately you will see everybody who is anybody in the Delta." This evening was no exception. Lucien Sparks Jr., heir to the fifth largest parcel of farmland in Mississippi, sat on the shoulders of Lucien Sparks Sr., owner of the fifth largest parcel of farmland in Mississippi. Sequins on the dress worn by Florine Holt, Miss Birmingham, Alabama, of 1939, reflected polka dots of light onto the face of Delmore "Hotcakes" Johnson. Delmore's wife, Wilhelmina, stood in silent agony while listening to the four Knapp brothers, founders of Knapp Family Snacks, expound on the virtues of cheese combined with peanut butter in their most successful product, Cheese Crackers and Peanut Butter. Perhaps most notable of all, on a cabriole sofa near the front desk lounged two of the evening's hosts, Lance and Ramsey Forster, both younger than Monty by nine years, fraternal twins whom people from their hometown of Batesville, Mississippi, referred to as the infernal twins.

Lance, the ends of his black bow tie hanging loose against the bib front of his tuxedo shirt, rattled the cubes in his lowball glass of Four Roses, and Ramsey, whose silk lamé evening gown coruscated whenever she moved, corked an opera-length holder with a Gauloise. Each of them held their favorite accessory, a glass of bourbon and a cigarette, in the opposing hand, such that, both yellow-haired and fine-featured but Lance a few inches taller than Ramsey and with a complexion one shade darker, they seemed fun house mirror images of one another. The siblings had always been a striking pair. Both possessed an elegant ranginess that a gossip columnist once described as making them look like feral cats with monocles.

Once he finished his drink, Lance turned to his sister and, breaking their silence of the past ten minutes, said, "Define *expatriate*."

"What?"

"Okay, I will. An expatriate is someone disappointed by the American dream because she tries too hard to buy into it. She might, for example, marry a Hollywood mogul, a man who both exemplifies and sells that dream. A man who is also, I might add, a complete dullard. So she flees the country she thinks failed her. Maybe goes to France. Ribbit, ribbit. Then the Krauts march their little Kraut boots into Poland. Oh, my. The expatriate has to scamper home for safety. Suppose that's how America and family are alike. We always welcome back our own. Don't you agree?"

"You're such a shit."

Despite her brother's claim, Ramsey did not consider herself an expatriate during her time in Paris. The term seemed better suited for intellectuals and artists, those more deserving of its cachet. Nonetheless she had to admit Lance was half right in his assessment. Throughout her courtship with and engagement to Arthur Landau, president of Vantage Pictures and the man her brother had called a "complete dullard," Ramsey had harbored fantasies of a glamorous life in Los Angeles, ordering a round of desserts at the Brown Derby after a party that went late, gossiping with starlets, hobnobbing with directors, whispering into the ear of Clark Gable that he had a little something on his chin. Those fantasies, for the most part, became reality. PRINCE OF CELLULOID WEDS PRINCESS OF SODA ran the headline in *Variety,* followed weeks later by MULHOLLAND DRIVE WELCOMES MISSISSIPPI DELTA. Tallulah took her shopping on Rodeo. Zukor took her sailing to Catalina. Marlene took her dancing at the Troc.

In his assessment Lance had misunderstood the reason for Ramsey's departure. She had not been failed by America but rather by her own body. Four miscarriages in half as many years had left her in a depression no amount of phenobarbital could fix. Every night before bed she tried and failed to stop dwelling on a litany of her favorite names. Each day after waking she reached for but could not find the gibbous curve of her belly. Worst of all was that the last had been twins. She forbade those around her, out of pride or a lack thereof, to send word to her family. Although her husband meant well with his various efforts to help—a medical pamphlet he once brought home, "Not Being Gravid Is No Reason to Be Grave," evoked her first genuine laugh in months—Ramsey refused his suggestion of a long stay at their house in Palm Springs. Being in a new city didn't make a difference. She needed a whole new continent. One thing she most certainly did not need, Ramsey thought while sitting in the lobby of the Peabody three months after her return from Europe, was to be picked at by her very own brother.

"Don't you mean, 'You're such a *merde*'? I thought life out west would have cleaned up your language. What with the Hays Code and all." Lance held up his empty glass and tapped it with his signet ring until a nearby waiter got the message. "But tell me something. It's a question been on my mind lately. Was your Creole in France tastier than our Creole cuisine back here at home?"

At those words, casual but venomous, Ramsey exhaled a stream of smoke over the cocktail table, clouding an untouched bowl of black olives. How did he know? In 1937, during her first few months abroad, Ramsey had met the star of the Folies-Bergère, Miss Josephine Baker, who at the time was often called the Creole Goddess. The two of them began what Parisian sophisticates labeled a friendship. Every moment of those years she spent with Josephine, their elbows in a daisy chain as they walked home in the early morning, their hangovers on the mend as they drank coffee in the late afternoon, helped Ramsey forget her reasons for being in a new country. Soon enough she no longer felt as though her insides had been shucked.

In Tennessee at a quarter after eleven, thousands of miles away from France, Ramsey could still remember the smell of Jo on her fingertips. She looked at her brother, sussing out his question, the implications of it. If he was privy to her secret, then who else might know? Ever since Ramsey's return a few months back, Arthur had not once visited her at their pied-à-terre in New York, making her acclimation to the States a solitary one. His secretary called each week to say, between snaps of chewing gum, that he regretfully could not make the trip. "Trouble with the dailies." Ramsey knew enough about her husband to understand the power structure at Vantage. He considered dailies beneath him.

With a congenial tone Ramsey said, "The cuisine was excellent over there. Bit too refined for your taste," thinking that ought to shut Lance up.

It did. Lance sat in silence, seething at his sister. He despised being even fractionally outwitted by her. Over the years, from their childhood in Batesville running barefoot through cotton fields to their young adulthood in New York appearing as blind items on the society page, Lance had been jealous of Ramsey. She had always been the more attractive of them. He just knew it. The lovely Miss Forster performing a perfect St. James Bow at her cotillion. The stunning Mrs. Landau entertaining guests in her Beverly Hills manor. Often Lance thought of himself as the Forster runt. That his whole family was known for its looks did not help. Monty was the kind of handsome that people had taken to calling all-American. Their mother, Annabelle, possessed a nearly flawless beauty guaranteed by the expensive diet and limited sun exposure of an aristocratic lineage dating back to the Louisiana Purchase. Their father, Houghton, gave off the accurate impression of someone whose rugged exterior had been buffed by hard-won professional success in the way so often described by Horatio Alger. From the moment of his conception, Lance figured, he was destined for relative inferiority. Even Haddy the half-wit, his older brother, had a lantern jaw, broad shoulders, a cleft chin, and incongruently bright green eyes.

Despite Lance's self-doubt, which morphed his nose, ears, and mouth into grotesques, such disfigurement was visible only to himself, as though a smudge of sleep constantly blurred his vision. Photographs from throughout his life reveal him to be just as attractive if not more so than the rest of his family. Nonetheless he compensated for his supposed ugliness by flaunting his intelligence. Ramsey's zygote may have gotten all the beauty, but Lance would be damned if his hadn't gotten the brains. He considered the point of life not to be clever but for other people to know he was. That belief influenced most of his interactions with other people, including a cigarette girl in the hotel lobby, whom he flagged over to regain, subconsciously, the advantage he had lost to his sister.

"Good evening to you," the girl said. "Filtered or unfiltered?"

Lance chose the former. On taking payment the cigarette girl offered him a light. "Thank you, sweetness," he said, pocketing the pack, "but I don't smoke."

"Then why'd you buy them?"

"Maybe I'll tell you later."

Because of the natural arch to Lance's eyebrows, a trait he shared with his sister, people often wondered if his comments were intended to be wry. The answer was almost always yes. With a slight curl etched into the corner of her mouth, the cigarette girl, turning to walk away, showed absolutely no confusion at his tone.

Lance admired how her shoulder blades flexed from the cigarette tray's weight as she walked through the crowd. He rested the ankle of one leg on the thigh of the other, finding a perch for his wrist on top of the raised knee. His new watch, a Rolex Oyster with Feuille hands, caught the light. To his sister Lance said, "How does she look to you?" He nodded in the direction of the girl.

"Expensive."

He turned to Ramsey. "What the fuck is that supposed to mean?" Lance's cheeks bloomed red.

"Your timepiece. Looks like it cost a lot. What'd you think I was talking about?"

The last few swallows of Lance's bourbon went down in one.

His sister knew damn well what he had thought she was talking about. He could see it in her face. Ramsey had expressed that same lack of affect, judgmental by not evincing judgment, the night in New York when she'd spotted him leaving a sporting house on Christopher Street. It was the first time he'd paid for it. Lance would have sworn that to her if only she did not immediately get into a taxicab. Just one time, God's honest! Ever since that night almost five years ago Lance and Ramsey had barely spoken to each other. He had to find out from their parents that she'd gotten engaged. He had to find out from her husband that she'd left the country.

Tonight was their first actual conversation in what seemed forever. Lance glared at his Rolex. Its hour and minute hands pointed at the eleventh and fourth markers while its second hand slowly denounced all of the markers in between. "Never mind the matter," Lance said to Ramsey. "Must have misheard you."

From the bowl on their cocktail table he plucked a black olive. He popped it into his mouth and hulled the meat with his teeth. Once he had swallowed all that was edible, Lance pursed his lips, leaned back, and exhaled with force, launching the pit into flight through the lobby, over the heads of city councilmen and state senators brokering deals, over the shoulders of country singers and songwriters trading compliments, until it landed in the marble fountain, on the edge of which sat Harold Forster, the second oldest of the four siblings.

His laugh lines deepened by a bemused smile, a smudge of rémoulade on the sleeve of his tuxedo, Harold did not notice the olive pit as it sank to the bottom of the fountain. He was focused on naming the ducks. All five of them circled the gurgling water. The itsy-bitsy one with a white ring around its neck he named Callie, and the one whose pretty little head was all black he named Suzette. The one that kept dunking under water he named Alma, and the one with spots on its beak he named June. Each of the names orig-inated with the people Harold considered his best friends while growing up. At various times over the years Callie, Suzette, Alma, and June had been housemaids for his family.

Now he just needed something to call the fifth duck. Although there was one more maid whose name he could use—his favorite of those best friends—Harold had been taught by his sister to never, ever think about her. It would be too much for him.

To distract himself from the noise in the lobby Harold dipped his fingers into the cool water of the fountain. The feel of wetness reminded him of swimming as a child. Back then Ramsey used to tell him he was like a turtle, slow on land but fast in water, a com-ment to which Lance, if he heard it, would invariably respond that on land wasn't the only place he was slow. Although he was still fo-cused on the ducks, Harold knew, without looking, that the twins were sitting on a sofa not far away. His family often said that Har-old had a compass inside him with any Forster as its interchange-able north. They thought his ability stemmed from a need for the safety of their presence, but in truth he kept track of his family so he could protect them. Because of this special skill, Harold wasn't startled when the crowd at the Peabody unbraided at what he knew to be the approach of his mother.

"Don't touch those things, Haddy. You want to catch a disease?" Annabelle Forster said to her thirty-five-year-old son. "Don't make me regret letting you stay up late tonight."

"Yes, ma'am."

Annabelle's stark black lace gown and porcelain skin moder-ated her effulgent blond hair and French-blue eyes. She clutched her slender wrist in the well-moisturized palm of her other hand.

At the get-up-now twitch of his mother's fingers, on which she wore only her wedding band and a modest diamond because, as the entire family knew, she considered excessive jewelry "low," Harold stood for inspection. His mother ran her hands down the lapels of his jacket and resituated a stray lick of his side part. "Do me a kindness," she said to Harold.

"Okay."

"Tell me where I can find your brother."

"Which one?"

"Monty."

"At the bar."

On the far end of the lobby, accepting clasps of the arm from people who'd donated to his campaign and from those he assumed wished they had, Monty stood in line for a drink. Some old woman, her gray hair shot through with teal, dress ten years out of fashion, and neck an avalanche of wrinkles, had spent the past five minutes arguing over the proper garnish for a sidecar. The wait didn't bother Monty. He was too busy trying not to think of his best friend from the war, Nicholas Harrington. More than twenty years had passed since they first met. "Name's Nicholas. These chaps call me Nick, but to my friends I'm Nicholas." Monty could still remember the thrill he'd felt at the implication that he was immediate friends with Nicholas. He was meditating on those three syllables—*Ni-cho-las, Ni-cho-las*—when the bartender jarred him from his thoughts.

"What's your pleasure, sir?"

Where only moments ago Montgomery had faced the back of the belligerent old lady, he now saw a clean-shaven, tan, dimple-cheeked man wearing a silk bow tie and burgundy sleeve garters. The bartender must have been in his midtwenties. A spit curl jutted like a broken bedspring from his shellacked hair, and a stray eyelash stuck like a comma on the edge of his jawline. The sight of his Adam's apple caused Monty's own to bob. "Not sure what I want. Any recommendations?"

The bartender squinted at him in the manner of a gypsy reading tarots. "I've got just the thing." He paused a moment for objections before making the drink.

Despite his proficiency behind the counter, flipping a Boston shaker through the air and spinning a Hawthorne strainer in his palm, the bartender's future was not in mixology. He would eventually gain one kind of exploitative success in Los Angeles, and then another when he moved to New York City decades later. On August 12, 1975, Knopf would pay him a reported six-figure sum for the memoir of his experiences scraping hundred-dollar bills off the nightstands of Cole Porter, James Whale, and Rock Hudson.

"Give this a try," the bartender said, pushing a glass toward Monty. "I call it a four-one-five."

"Why's that?"

"Four parts gin, one part vermouth, five parts delicious. I'll be having one myself when my shift ends in twenty minutes."

"Interesting."

Montgomery accepted the drink, whose ingredients sounded an awful lot like those of a martini, and walked back into the crowd, where he immediately encountered a swarm of glad-handers. The distraction was a welcome one. During the campaign Monty had grown used to his assigned role—that of the upstanding, honest family man, husband of a beautiful wife, father of a brilliant daughter—to the extent he now actually felt good when playing it. The cocktail didn't hurt either.

"Mr. Sparks, great to see you." Sip. "How's tricks, little man?" Sip. "Hi there." Sip. "Likewise." Sip. "Thank you." Sip. "The beautiful Miss Holt." Sip. "Hotcakes, pleasure as always." Sip. "Who let this guy in here?" Sip. "Hello, Mother."

Those unblinking, dispassionate eyes, that surgical slit of a mouth: his mother was the person Monty least wanted to see. All the cheerfulness he had begun to feel, from politicking with the crowd and chatting with the bartender, withered in her presence. Still, taught from birth to be conscious of appearances, Monty kissed his mother on the cheek, its temperature in scale to her disposition.

She had been unnervingly cold with him ever since the incident in Ecuador. On the train ride home, after she'd traveled to Quito alone to pay the $15,000 in blackmail, Montgomery's mother said only one thing to him. "Your father can never know what you are." Now, so many years after that train ride, Montgomery managed not to flinch when his mother again mentioned the one Forster whose approval mattered to him.

"He wants to see you."

"About what?"

"The senator showed up after all," she said. "They've scheduled a meeting for tonight."

"When?"

"Half past."

"Where?"

His mother gave him a look, pursing her lips and tilting her head, that meant, *You know your father well enough to know where.*

Montgomery arrived at the Presidential Suite two minutes after eleven thirty.

He did not bother to knock. Two-storied and balconied, with taupe wallpaper filigreed in gold, the suite warranted its name, authoritative but warm, judicious in its opulence, democratically regal. Oil paintings overlooked a baby grand. Kaleidoscopic shadows from a spiral staircase scored the hardwood flooring. Silk drapes framed a view of the river. On the Chesterfield sofa next to a mahogany Bornholm clock, Houghton Forster was lighting a cigar for Edmund Ainsworth, a Massachusetts senator (D) in the Seventy-Sixth U.S. Congress.

Even though both men were in their sixties, Monty's father seemed younger than Senator Ainsworth, not only because of the senator's gleaming bald spot and wrinkled sack suit, in contrast to Houghton's thick gray hair and trim tux, but also because, whereas the senator had an air of complacency, Houghton had one of hunger. If a portrait of his father were to be painted at that moment, Monty thought as he wished both men a happy new year, the inscription would likely read, "There's still more to be taken—H.F."

"So glad you could make it," Houghton said with a tone that was decidedly not glad his son had cut matters so close. Montgomery wanted to say he'd gotten there as soon as he'd heard about the meeting, that maybe next time he should be given more notice. Instead, he apologized for his lateness and situated himself in a club chair across from his father. Such a dynamic was typical of them. At seven he had remained silent behind a stream of tears as his father took a switch to him for earning poor marks on a spelling test. At twelve he had gotten frostbite of the pinkie toe when his father ordered him to chop a load of firewood in the middle of an ice storm. "They say if someone is raised by wolves, they either develop sharp claws or get torn to shreds," writes Rebecca N. Leithauser in "Fortunate Scions," a discursive essay on the children of affluent patriarchs. "Montgomery Forster never developed claws, and luckily he was too big to get torn to shreds." His notable size allowed for Monty's only act of parental defiance. Although his father had forbidden him to enlist, saying he was too young, in terms of the law and plain common sense, to fight for his country, Monty left home late one night with that goal in mind. The recruitment officer had no doubt that a six-foot-two, one-hundred-ninety-pound young man was of proper age to join the army. So at fifteen years old Montgomery Forster became a doughboy. For most of his time overseas he exhibited the lack of aggression people from home had considered a permanent aspect of his character. He followed orders. He stayed quiet. He kept to the back. Then came the evening in April 1918 when a German sniper, after spotting Nicholas fifty yards away, relaxed his upper torso, squinted, exhaled, and clenched his trigger hand. Monty sought retribution a month and a half later in the Battle of Belleau Wood. "He killed more Germans than ten of us could have combined," one marine said, concluding his assessment with an analogy that, if it had been on record at the time, might have given Leithauser second thoughts about her metaphor in "Fortunate Scions." "I've never seen anything that savage. He looked like a rabid wolf out there."

In the hotel suite Monty declined a cigar and asked what he had missed. The senator said, "Your father was just telling me," between puffs.

"We were talking about going to war."

"The *possibility* of going to war," the senator said. "Official stance is still no intervention."

"Fine, fine. But if your boys in Washington are right and Hitler does decide to make do with Poland, a piano will jump out of my ass playing 'Who'd A-Thunk-It?'" Houghton tapped a hunk of cigar ash into a tray on the coffee table. "Never mind that for now. What I want to talk about are the reasons for going to war. As you may know, my son here, Montgomery, my firstborn, fought in the Great War. Boy was only fifteen when he enlisted." Houghton tilted his head back to fill the air with a column of smoke. "The morning he left I shook his hand. I was damn proud of the boy. Tears came to my eyes, I was so proud of him. Tell the senator, Monty."

"Tears came to his eyes," Monty told the senator, "he was so proud of me."

"The only day I was more proud of my son was the day he came home. He'd been awarded a Distinguished Service Cross for extraordinary heroism. My question for you, Senator Ainsworth, is what allowed my son and all those other boys to fight so gallantly? Pride. Except this was not the pride of a father for his son. Somewhat the opposite. This was the pride of a man for his country."

"Brass tacks, Houghton. Why am I here?"

"If our boys go to war again, we need to make certain they're reminded, three times a day, of their pride in America. Three times. Breakfast, lunch, dinner. Now, unless we plan on creating a Corps of Grandmas, have them baking apple pies by the boatload, I ask you, what product represents wholesome American values more than a bottle of PanCola?"

Senator Ainsworth harrumphed. "Still doesn't answer the question of why I'm here," he said to both Forsters.

In response to that and each subsequent question, Houghton adjusted the proportions of art and matter in his talk. Montgomery listened as his father tried to make himself plain. Two months ago at the family's estate, Houghton told Ainsworth, he'd gone quail hunting with the quartermaster general. Aside from proving himself a damn fine shot, the general had suggested a few logistical tips, hypothetically speaking, on how to set up bottling plants along a front. The general expressed enthusiasm in the idea. More recently Houghton had heard from his man in Washington that there were rumblings of a new Senate subcommittee. Although the official purpose of the subcommittee would be "peacetime war efficiency," specifically how to prepare the public for the rationing that might become necessary as international trade routes deteriorated, an unofficial purpose would be to plan for an "efficient transition" from peacetime to war. Included under that rubric was the preliminary drafting of contracts for supplies other than weaponry. Houghton told the senator that competitive lobbying during a crisis, for cig-arettes and toilet paper, for shoe polish and chewing gum, would hinder more important preparations for the second Great War.

"Which brings us to why you're here talking to me twenty min-utes before the clock strikes 1940. The only matter still under de-bate is who will chair the subcommittee. And I have it on authority that the choice will be none other than Edmund Ainsworth."

At those words Houghton put the heel of one leg onto the knee of the other, glancing at Montgomery without turning his head. So far everything had gone in accordance with their plan. Monty knew what the senator would ask next.

"If what you say is true, and I'm not saying it is, but let's assume for conversation's sake it's true," the senator said as he perched his cigar in a crook of the ashtray, "then the first question that comes to mind, regarding your suggestion, is what incentive do I have to contract PanCola?"

Houghton said, "Ever heard the old saying 'An eye for an eye'? The same applies to favors."

"I'm listening," said Ainsworth.

"Someday my son here may very well be in a position of even greater power than his current one."

"Such as what?"

"This isn't the *Governor's* Suite we're sitting in."

The senator retrieved his cigar from its perch, saying, "Suppose you're planning on buying that election, too," before screwing it back into the ashtray unfinished.

"You can only buy something," Houghton said, "with what you've earned."

Since the beginning of the conversation Montgomery had con-sidered it best to remain quiet. That was no longer the case. He could see his father was getting hot. It was understandable why.

Montgomery knew that people such as Senator Ainsworth, a Boston Brahmin, considered themselves superior to the *nouveau riche,* of which Monty had to admit the Forsters were a part, even when those like Senator Ainsworth were no longer *riche.* Neither that hypocrisy nor his father's anger, however, were the reason Monty decided to speak up. He just wanted to get out of the room sometime this decade.

"Senator, all due respect, but nobody's buying anything," Monty said. "Johnson and I both ran honest campaigns, and when we're inducted two weeks from now, it will be with a clean conscience. I'll be second in line for a position that would put me in line for a run at the presidency. Understand? Fact of the matter is Paul's not in the best of health." Governor Paul B. Johnson Sr., "Champion of the Runt Pig People," would die in office on December 26, 1943, shortly after which—and for an unrelated reason, despite the headlines—Monty would tell his family he was going to "look for arrowheads" near the old barn on the Forsters' estate. "But forget potential tragedies. Let's get back to old sayings. Have you heard 'You scratch my back and I'll scratch yours'? You won your last election by only ten thousand votes, and support from your constituency is even weaker now. Added to which, your indiscretions with one Polly Cheswick of Red Hook, Brooklyn, aren't a well kept secret," Monty said. "So it would seem, *Bunny,* you have a very itchy back."

If it weren't for his father sitting there, the grin on his face so wide his eyeteeth showed, Monty would have immediately apologized. The bully was not a role he enjoyed. How could he have used Paul Johnson like that, a man who'd done nothing but right by him?

Houghton, as though sensing the misgivings of his son, said, "Couldn't have said it better myself." He stood. "Tell you what, Senator. How about you take the night to think on it?"

"I think that would be best." Senator Ainsworth gained more composure with each step toward the door of the Presidential Suite. "Certainly is getting late."

"We've got you set up in one of the finest rooms in the place. You should have no trouble getting some rest," Houghton said, one hand on the senator's back, the other on the doorknob. "Know what I like best about staying in hotels? The chocolate on the pillow. Am I right? There's just something so pleasant about finding your sheets pulled back, your pillows fluffed, and this little piece of candy to help you drift off to sleep."

"How true."

The door clicked shut. Houghton walked back across the room, sat down, and lifted an eyebrow at Montgomery. On arriving in his room, both father and son knew, Senator Ainsworth would find, placed on his pillow, $20,000 in cash. "Think he'll take the turn-down service?" Monty said.

"Of course I do. He's a man of integrity," said Houghton, unaware that at the same moment, ten stories below the suite, his daughter, Ramsey, still sitting on a sofa in the lobby except now by herself, still clutching a cigarette holder but without a cigarette, was approached by a man of similar integrity.

A briefcase dangled at his side, its leather buffed to a high shine, brass locks clouded by a patina. The man wore a black suit rather than a tuxedo, which made him both stand out from and blend into the crowd, a sore thumb on a broken hand. Ramsey felt as though she'd seen him before tonight but couldn't for her life recall where.

"Mrs. Landau."

"Yes?"

"Paul Easton."

The man reached into his briefcase and, with a cheerful clip to his voice, said, "I'm here to serve you divorce papers on behalf of

Vantage Pictures." He set a stack of documents on the table and pushed them toward her with his pinkie.

Ramsey's realization of where she had first seen this guy—at the Christmas party three years ago in Arthur's office—caused a delay in registering what he had just told her. Then it came. Of course the studio president known for producing lavish musicals such as *Catch a Tiger by the Toe* would be so theatrical as to inform his wife that he was divorcing her on New Year's Eve twelve minutes before midnight. The bastard did not even have the sand to give her the papers himself. Ramsey could have killed Arthur. God but she could have wrung his spineless little neck.

She lit a cigarette just to see the fumes. To Paul Easton, still standing in front of her, Ramsey said, "You tell that no-good, chicken-shit, heartless son of a cunt—"

"Mr. Landau said you might get colorful."

"—that he can take these goddamn papers and shove them up his dick hole."

During the few seconds of quiet following Ramsey's outburst, Paul Easton stared at her down the bridge of his nose. "My but you're good at revealing yourself as nothing more than country come to town," he said at last.

Ramsey clamped her jaw around her cigarette. *Tou*-fucking-*ché*. She blew smoke toward the skylights of the lobby. Over the years Ramsey had grown sensitive to intimations that she was some bumpkin from Mississippi who had married up. The origin of such vulnerability was the time her roommate at Miss Porter's had asked if it felt odd to wear a uniform instead of overalls. This prick from the studio knew exactly where to squeeze. As Ramsey tried to think of a suitable retort, something eloquent, something vicious, she heard a familiar voice behind her say, "My but you're good at revealing yourself as nothing more than a bagman for the flicker business who isn't even worthy of kissing my granddaughter's feet."

Fiona Forster, wearing a chinchilla stole in spite of the heat in the lobby and a necklace with an amethyst pendant big as a magnolia fruit, walked around the sofa, took a seat, and gently squeezed her granddaughter's knee, never once letting her gaze stray from the man she had addressed. "You have my blessing to leave now." She flicked her hand at Paul Easton as one would a speck of lint. He swallowed audibly, gripped his briefcase, and, without a word, walked away.

Ramsey smiled at Fiona. Even in old age her grandmother from her father's side of the family brooked no guff. She was eighty-four. All of her features except her eyes had shrunk over the years, so that she seemed the Owl of Minerva come to life in the lobby, wise and vigilant and never without a gin rickey.

"How are you?" Ramsey asked.

"Just a feeble old woman. Yourself?"

"Fine. Gettin' divorced."

Fiona shrugged. "Screw the bastard."

Despite the rage she had felt just a moment ago, Ramsey, thinking of the distance between apples and trees when one falls from the other, managed to enjoy the end of her cigarette. At least someone was on her side. While putting the butt into an ashtray Ramsey noticed her brother Harold standing by the marble fountain. He was doing that thing with his ear again. Every time Haddy became upset, whether because of something he had done or that had been done to him, his hand would latch onto his ear, tugging and pulling and twisting it raw. *Look at him over there,* thought Ramsey, *about to yank it right off. What could be the matter?*

Light from the chandelier overhead flickered along the ripples in the water fountain, and from across the lobby drifted the chipper opening chords of "Baby, Buy Me a Teddy Bear." Harold, tugging on his ear and rocking side to side, didn't notice either of those things, because he was now a capital-*M* Murderer.

The whole thing was his fault. If only he had minded his mother, none of this would have happened. She had told him not to touch the ducks. All he did was pet one of their feathery little heads, just a teensy bit with his finger, and five minutes later, after getting some cake from the dessert table, the poor thing was floating upside down.

Harold's hand clung to his ear and his lips were speckled with frosting as he paced in front of the fountain, trying to decide what to do with the body. Any minute someone would notice those life-less feet splayed in the air. He was about to scoop out the duck with his dinner jacket when he was interrupted by the screams of a man nearby. "Oh dear God, no, it can't be! No! Please God, no, it can't be!" Still in his uniform, Edward Pembroke, the elevator op-erator, jumped into the fountain, soaking his maroon flannel pants trimmed in gold braid. He lifted the duck from the water, cradled it in his arms, and sat on the marble edge.

"Everything's fine," Pembroke said, patting the duck's head as one would to wake a sleeping child. "I'm here now."

Harold watched from a few yards away. He had not even had a chance to name that one. *Can you get into heaven without a name?* he wondered, tears making his vision go wobbly.

On the edge of the fountain, with his back to the crowd so Harold could not see what he was doing, Pembroke searched for a cause of death. He used the skills from his time as a circus trainer, the same skills that would soon lead to a promotion. Nowhere on the duck could he find evidence of a puncture wound. Its keel was not distended. Its shanks were not discolored. At last, Pembroke checked the duck's neck and noticed, close to its white ring, a small obstruction. He massaged the obstruction through the neck, like squeezing out one last brush's worth of toothpaste from the tube, until it plopped into the palm of his hand.

Due to the presence of Pembroke in the lobby, where he was currently holding something hard, wet, and round that he mistakenly thought was a cherry pit, Montgomery was alone in the elevator. It took him a moment to realize he was the only one there. He pressed a button on the grid panel and pulled the lever to the down position. With each floor of his descent from the suite Monty mentally recited his three favorite syllables. Ten, nine. *Nicholas, Nicholas.* Eight, seven. *Nicholas, Nicholas.* Six, five. Over the years that name had become a sort of mantra to calm him down at times of disappointment, with himself or others, times during which he was overwhelmed with the question, first asked during the war, of whether he was in hell or simply doomed to it.

He reached his floor. Monty pulled back the lever, opened the gate, and walked out of the elevator. He had to stop thinking this way. He had to focus on something else. Monty knocked on the door to room 415.

Slowly it opened to reveal a figure in silhouette. Montgomery stepped forward and kissed the bartender, who tasted like four parts gin and one part vermouth. The door closed behind them.

A tightrope of spit connected the two as Montgomery briefly drew back from the bartender. "I don't even know your name."

"Simon Spicer."

"Really?"

"Stage name," said Simon. "I'm moving to L.A."

Although Spicer's memoir of "being out and going down" in Hollywood is no longer in print, the incendiary bestseller elicited, upon its release, devotion and litigation in equal measure. Activists for gay rights upheld the author as an iconoclast. Religious conservatives denounced his book as pornography. At the hotel that night, however, the man who hoped to have a career in acting had not yet sold his secrets or himself. Simon wrapped his arms around Monty. They stumbled through the room toward the bed, tripping over a footstool and bumping into the dresser and knocking over a lamp, until they were interrupted by a rhythmic clanging sound.

"The hell's that?" Montgomery said. He looked into the moon-lit room, trying to figure the source of the noise.

Simon's lips curled into a sly grin. He nodded at a pipe near the radiator and whispered, "Must be the heat."

He was correct in a sense. The pipe making the noise in room 415 ran vertically through the hotel, past the lending library and notary public on the mezzanine, past the cigar stands and phone booths around the lobby, past the drugstore and stenographer in the basement, all the way to the boiler room, where at that moment Lance was having sex with the cigarette girl. Each thrust caused the table on which she was positioned to ram against the pipe with a heavy clang.

Lance stood with the girl's legs straddling him. He found he preferred such a method, how it allowed for ease of access. Escape was also made easier. There in the boiler room, the girl was moaning just the right amount, not too loud and not too quiet, a Goldilocksian fit. The only problem was that she kept talking to him between moans.

"But this is only a temporary job for me." Pant. "I was thinking of maybe opening a hair salon." Sigh. "Or nails." Whimper. "I think there's a lot of growth in nails." Purr. "Ha-ha. Growth." Trill. "I'm interested in anything involved with the beauty industry." Gasp. "Mark my words. Beauty industry. It's got a future."

Trying to keep the girl quiet, Lance slid his hand up her neck and let his thumb dip into her mouth, but the move brought little result.

"You taste like cinnamon. Bet you get that a lot in your family." The girl sucked on his thumb. "That you taste like cinnamon. Do you hear that a lot in your family?"

The hell was she babbling about? Lance had heard his share of dirty talk that was actually the opposite—one time a woman he brought back to his place told him, "I'm as wet as a dog's nose," after which he sent her home with her tail between her legs—but something about this girl seemed more than awkward. Midthrust he realized why.

"I should have known," he said, their motion halted. "You're a cola hunter."

The press had given them the name. Around the time PanCola first introduced its "secret ingredient" ad campaign, Houghton Forster mentioned in an interview that his children, all four of them, were the only people he would ever tell, come the right time, the truth of the ingredient. He said it was their birthright. He said the ingredient had been with him so long, ever since his own childhood, that it was a bond among his family as strong as blood. Due to those comments, "cola hunters" began traveling to the various locales of his youth, attempting to "pan" for Panola Cola's secret ingredient. Some cola hunters avoided where the ingredient had begun and instead went searching for where the ingredient would end up.

Lance felt himself not unsheathe so much as shrivel out of the girl. He watched her face turn into that of someone who gave neither hoot nor holler about the beauty industry. "I bet your father hasn't even told you," she said before standing from the table and resituating her dress. "Knew I should have gone with the important one."

"The what?"

"Where is Montgomery anyway? Haven't seen him all night."

"I," Lance said, "uh."

"God, you really don't know anything, do you?"

Without waiting for a response the girl told him to never mind and wended her way out of the boiler room and back to the lobby. Lance stood by himself, his rib cage shrunk by her words. *Should have gone with the important one. You really don't know anything. I bet your father hasn't even told you.* Not only was he the ugliest Forster but he was also the most unnecessary. A drop of moisture trickled from Lance's cheek all the way to his jawline. Sweat from the humidity, he thought, walking toward the exit. Whoever was in charge really should do something about the humidity.

Back in the lobby, Lance tried to compose himself. He looked around the whole scene, at the women in evening gowns of mauve, saffron, vermilion, and carmine, some backless and some sleeveless and a few daringly both; at the men in obsidian-black and midnight-blue dinner jackets, their collars heavily starched and shirts as crisp as newsprint; at the waiters in uniforms the same shade of white as PanCola's label, arms laden with trays of deviled eggs, oysters casino, angels on horseback, cucumber cups with pimento cheese, stuffed kumquat, crab rangoon, and boiled shrimp fresh from the Gulf.

Lance could not find Ramsey. He needed his sister right now. She was the only person who would understand. They had too much history for her not to know the right thing to say.

He could still remember the Whippet Roadster they had shared as teenagers. To their father's chagrin, Lance and Ramsey had nicknamed the car "Volstead," a nod to the congressman whose machinations inadvertently caused the increase in soda sales that helped pay for the car's broadcloth upholstery, mechanical brakes, and pyroxylin finish. Both of them took pleasure in more than the irony whenever they drove the car to one of the speakeasies across town.

Lance needed that Ramsey right now—Ramsey his friend, Ramsey his conspirator. Why had he needled her so much earlier in the night? It was petty to wound her simply for having a life of her own. The absolute truth was Lance cared about his sister. All he wanted was for her to be as safe as she had always made him feel. That was why he had recently paid a mayor's ransom for the managing editor of the *Daily Herald* to kill an article on "Ramsey-phine." That was also why, after hearing from his investigator that Arthur had somehow learned about the affair, Lance had caught the earliest flight to L.A., hoping to convince his brother-in-law that a scandal, even just a divorce, would reflect poorly on all parties involved. The bastard had refused to meet with him.

"How close are we?"

The appearance of Montgomery at his side startled Lance from his thoughts. He had to repeat his brother's question in order to sound out its meaning. After a slight pause, Lance looked at his watch and said to Montgomery, "Two minutes away."

With each second closer to midnight the crowd seemed to grow more effervescent. Men checked their pocket watches and then loosened their semibutterfly, rounded, pointed, or straight bat-wing bow ties, while the women who'd worn their hair up let it down, petals falling from their wrist corsages to the floor with the turbulence. After the Peabody Hotel jazz quartet ended its rendition of "What's the Sweetest Thing Around? (Panola Cola, I've Found)," the screech of blowout horns erupted from distant corners of the lobby.

"And how is my big brother this evening?" Lance asked, trying to appear as carefree as everyone else.

Monty straightened his gig line, a habit since the war. He wondered how to respond. *Oh, I'm doing fine. Just got back from almost sleeping with some bartender,* he considered confessing, repercussions be damned. *The poor guy was not happy when I told him I couldn't go through with it. Called me a tease and a coward.* The bartender may have been right about the first insult, Monty would admit, but he'd been completely wrong about the second one. His decision to leave the room was not an act of cowardice but rather one of fidelity. All the blame lay with that damn pipe. The clanging noise had reminded Monty of distant gunfire, rat-a-tat, pop-pop, pop-pop, rat-a-tat, which in turn had reminded him of Nicholas. That was why he'd told the bartender he couldn't go through with it. "Just a little tired is all," Monty said to Lance. "It's been a very long night."

"You're telling me."

Midnight was thirty seconds away. The two Forster brothers looked out at the assemblage of what would be described the next day as the bon ton of the American South. Both men fell quiet at the sight.

In the *St. Louis Dispatch,* editorialist Rufus Terral once wrote, "Mississippians . . . are said to believe that when they die and go to heaven, it will be just like the Peabody lobby." It seemed as though everyone at the gala that night would have agreed. Near the elevator bank Lucien Sparks Sr. held his sleeping son, small head on large shoulder, thin arms around thick neck, a trickle of drool at the corner of the boy's mouth garnished by a smudge of peanut butter, the result of a present he'd been given by the Knapp brothers of Knapp Family Snacks, each of whom had been intrigued when the boy, Lucien Sparks Jr., mentioned he liked to sprinkle salted peanuts into Panola Cola. At a table behind the bandstand Wilhelmina Johnson slapped her husband, an action brought about by what she had caught him doing with Florine Holt, whose sequined dress had made her exit with Delmore, known as "Hotcakes" for a reason, all too easy for everyone at the gala to notice. And on the mezzanine overlooking the lobby, Harold Forster, his cheeks traced by dried tears and his brow striated with thought, sat alone at a small table, oblivious to the screams of "Three! . . . Two! . . . One!" from below.

He was playing solitaire. The game helped keep him from dwelling on the duck. Harold, who could never remember the actual rules, set down a queen, then a six and seven, then an eight and nine, and finally a king, to complete his favorite design. On the table lay the same mosaic of cards that, years later, he would have arranged before him when his heart, which had always beaten with furious pride at any slight to his family, stopped.

That night at the Peabody Hotel, though, Harold's pulse held a steady count. He looked over the handrail, studying the hourglass dresses and sharply tailored tuxedos, the various boutonnieres blending into a pointillist collage of gardenia-white, cornflower-blue, and carnation-red. What the hell was everybody hollering about? Why on earth was everyone kissing each other? Harold watched confetti rise like bubbles in the air and fall on the shoulders of his family. His siblings were dispersed throughout the crowd.

Ramsey sat on a sofa near the fountain. She was reading a stack of paper, cigarette in hand, smoke leaking from her mouth. It must be a really great story, Harold figured, what with how little she blinked. Over by the bar, his brother Monty was drinking some kind of cocktail. He held the glass in one hand and tucked in his shirt with the other. If Harold had to guess he'd say the drink tasted good. Just look at the way Monty closed his eyes with each sip. In a corner near the bathrooms Harold's brother Lance stood alone with a pack of cigarettes. He was staring at them. He'd quit a long time ago, Harold remembered, because they stained his teeth. To-night had to be a very special occasion if he was tempted to pick up the habit again.

Harold took one last look around the lobby, the sight of his brothers making his chin quake, the sight of his sister making his shoulders cave, before sitting back down with tears in his eyes. He could not find a tissue. Harold put his face into his hands as "Auld Lang Syne" echoed through the hotel. He was crying because of his family. Never in his life had he seen them all so happy.

1.2

The Original Sweetest
Thing—An Indian Named
Branchwater—A Bumper Crop of
Drinking Straws—The Annabelle Constellation

The only thing Fiona wanted was for Houghton to be happy. It simply wasn't right for a fourteen-year-old boy to work so hard. "Why don't you sit down to eat?" she asked Houghton in the kitchen of the family's two-bedroom home in Panola County, Mississippi. He forked a fried egg onto a biscuit and added a few cuts of fatback. Fiona said, "Your father wouldn't mind you being late to the store."

"Like hell he wouldn't."

"Watch that mouth."

He turned away from the stovetop, grinned at her, and made a show of taking a hefty bite. "Didn't hear you," he said, voice garbled, mouth full. "Watch what now?" Pieces of biscuit scattered on the floor.

He wasn't in want of humor; that much was for certain. Fiona was nonetheless worried about Houghton. Ever since he was a child, he'd shown an uncommon sense of industry, taking up house duties before he was assigned them. What kind of boy *volunteered* for chores? She could see him now. In the field, chopping wood, at age eight. In the barn, milking cows, at age five. His work ethic had only increased since he'd reached puberty. During the week, Houghton worked twelve hours a day at the drugstore, and on weekends he tended to his own business enterprise, collecting scrap metal from around the county, tin from barn roofs, iron from anvils, brass from doorknobs, and selling it to a foundry just south of Memphis. Fiona hoped he knew his hours at the store would have to be cut once school started back up in September. She was about to remind him that morning, but he had already clomped out the door. She watched through the casement window as he saddled his horse.

Although he would never admit it to anyone, especially not his own mother, the reason Houghton worked so much these days was circumstantial. Work was the best means he could come up with to distract from the awkward, unwieldy erections that had begun to plague him most every second of the day. It seemed anything would trigger one. Glancing at the exposed ankle of his school-teacher held him at his desk until matters had subsided. Catching a whiff of perfume from a churchgoer forced him to use a hymnal for sacrilegious cover. One time the feminine whinny of a dray horse sent him crouching to hide what had been sprung loose.

After reaching town Houghton relieved himself of such thoughts by readying Forster Rex-for-All for the business day. He ran the tumblers through a mechanized washer. Less than three weeks later those tumblers would tipple with the soda concoction made possible by the secret ingredient he would soon discover. He swept the wide-plank pine floors. Less than two years later those floors would creak with the footfall of over a hundred daily customers who had heard tell of a delicious new drink. In conclusion to his morning routine Houghton wound, dusted, polished, and set the Willard banjo regulator hanging on the wall.

The time was two minutes till eight. Because his father was away on his house calls—every month he made a trip around the county medicating the ailments of farmers too busy to come to town—Houghton was responsible for opening the store. Today, the simple act of hanging the OPEN sign would have a lasting effect. In front of the door, looking through its wobbly glass pane, Houghton noticed a girl, yellow haired and pale skinned, walking down the street. She rendered all his efforts at distraction for naught. None of his morning routine at work, not the sweeping, not the washing, not the dusting, could stop his reaction, in body and in mind, to what he decided was the sweetest thing he'd ever seen.

. . .

Since her mother's death in 1882 of scarlet fever, Annabelle Teague had doted on her father. The relationship between parent and child was the reverse of typical. She packed his lunch in the morning and asked after his day in the evening. He let her feel his brow for fever and heeded her advice on sensible attire. Owner of a shipping business based on the Mississippi, resident of New Orleans for all his life, and special adviser to the governor of Louisiana, Royal Teague never took another wife because, in addition to simply not having the time for courtship, he already had a woman in his life off whom to sound business ideas and from whom to beg for a second helping of dessert. It was due to such aspects of their relationship that Annabelle told her father, laid up with gout, to stay in his room at the Batesville Inn while she went in search of a druggist.

She came across Forster Rex-for-All around the corner. It looked to be the only pharmacy in town. Despite such a modest exterior, whitewash hatched in brown, tin roof blotchy with bird droppings, windows fogged by pollen, Annabelle found the store, judging by its interior, comparable to those scattered throughout the Garden District, a testament to modernity. On shelves lining the back wall sat an array of mercury glass, cruets next to ewers, flagons next to vases, each of them placed beneath a nameplate inscribed in Latin. Steam from an alembic wafted toward the ceiling. An elaborate show globe filled with water dyed white hung from a brass chain at the center of the room. Rattan stools leaned against a mahogany counter. Next to a soda fountain, one of the largest Annabelle had ever seen, stood a boy about her age. He seemed to be having a rather difficult time situating an apron around his waist.

"Welcome to Forster's, miss. What can I do for you?"

As he spoke those words Houghton immediately forgot them. The presence of such a beautiful girl was a breath blown against the dandelion of his thoughts. He became a fragile, bare stem in front of her, his capacity for reason scattered to the wind. "Is the druggist in?" the girl said.

"At your service."

The girl crossed her arms in a pantomime of impatience, as though to say, *That's not a satisfactory answer, and I will not repeat the question.* Houghton wouldn't have been surprised if she had started tapping her foot, lips curled, one eyebrow raised above an unwavering stare. This obnoxious brat was, undoubtedly, the most adorable person he'd ever met. He set his bite to hold back a smile.

"My father is the senior druggist of the store. He's not in at the moment and is not expected back for another day or so. Rest assured I am a more than competent proxy."

"That so?"

His pace deliberate and his manner steady, Houghton walked out from behind the counter, situated a stool in front of the girl, and motioned for her to take a seat, all while making a point of letting her notice him studying her appearance. "By the scent of your hair I take it you're from New Orleans. The apothecaries down there commonly derive sodium laureth sulfate from coconut oil to use as a surfactant. Despite a complexion that indicates a primarily in-door life, you have no signs of a deficiency in vitamin D, which tells me you take a daily supplement or have a diet with high levels of it. Either way requires a certain financial means. Your sleep patterns have not been regular of late, but you haven't treated the problem medicinally. Also, judging by the slight redness of your nostrils, I'd say you recently had a cold. What did you use to get over it? Rose hip tea, I'll conjecture." Houghton walked back around the counter. Without taking his gaze from the girl he wiped down its varnished top with a rag.

"How'd you know about my lack of sleep?"

"Even a beauty as great as yours can't distract completely from those bags under your eyes."

Although she did not realize it yet, the feature Annabelle admired most in other people, no matter her relationship to them, was guile. This boy had plenty. She could tell by that sly grin he was trying so hard to hide beneath a more somber expression. The faint line curling into the corner of his mouth, in contrast to his tightly wound bow tie and hair parted so cleanly the warp and woof of each strand was distinct, made the boy, however uncultivated and inferior his ancestry, seem liable to do anything next, whether beg pardon, snap a playing card from thin air, or remain quiet. Was he being modest in regard to his deductions, or was he pretending to be modest in regard to his deductions? Annabelle couldn't decide.

The latter was correct. Yesterday a customer had pointed out to Houghton the caravan of wagons arriving from New Orleans. The customer said only a wealthy man could afford such extrava-gant means of transport. Houghton combined that knowledge with what, over the years, he had learned working at Forster Rex-for-All. He knew the common ingredients for shampoo. He knew ex-pensive foods such as mushrooms were rich in vitamin D. He knew long trips disrupted sleep patterns. The only genuine deduction he had made about the girl was the one that involved her recent cold. To break the silence, as well as to divert any suspicions, Houghton said, "You still haven't said how I can be of use to you."

"Use?"

"Assistance."

"Oh. Assistance. Yes, of course," she said. "It's my father. He is prone to gout and has recently come down with a particularly severe case. Back home his doctor gives him—"

"Colchicine, extract of the meadow saffron."

"Yes."

"That's a fine place to start. Most pharmacists shy away from going any further in their curative." Houghton retrieved three bottles from a shelf and arranged them on top of a workbench nearby. "But I am not the type to abide the majority." He mixed liquid from one bottle with powder from the other two. "I've found that colchicine is most effective when accompanied by lime extract. With just a touch of turmeric."

Because the boy's back was to her, Annabelle could not see the details of his operations until, with a mildly theatrical air, he turned around, shaking a small bottle of brown liquid. He placed the bottle on the counter. Without fully admitting it to herself Annabelle was disappointed at such efficiency. She had wanted to hear more from this boy who, despite most likely having grown up bathing in a barrel half, acted as though he were of a station equal to hers. Such the shame. His wit had to have been a studied ploy. His game had to have been a sales tactic. Just as Annabelle concluded the boy was nothing but a parlor trickster Houghton spoke up.

"That takes care of your father. Now let's take care of you."

Annabelle managed to ask, "Excuse me?" more confounded than upset. *Take care of her how?*

"Rest assured, miss, you have done nothing offensive enough as to warrant excusing of any kind, especially from myself." Out of a trough behind the counter Houghton pulled bottles stoppered with spouts. "We'll remedy the dregs of that cold of yours. Just need the right medicinal syrups. And, of course, some help from the Mockingbird."

"The what?"

Three years earlier, Houghton's father, Tewksbury, had decided it was high time to replace the store's soda fountain, a basic gooseneck model. He hoped a more luxurious one would help cater to the carriage trade. Rather than purchase the fountain from one of the country's four largest manufacturers—Charles Lippincott & Company, James W. Tufts, A.D. Puffer & Sons, and the John Matthews Apparatus Company, all of which, in 1891, would combine to form the American Soda Fountain Company—Houghton convinced his father to let him build it himself. His side business in scrap metal came to be useful. Overall the project took two months to complete. A cottage design with Victorian gingerbread on the roof and bas-relief scenes in each tile of its Brocatelle marble, the fountain was a paradigm of aesthetic beauty as well as pneumatic chemistry, featuring innovative pump pistons, stopcocks, and block-tin coils. Houghton had bought the gold-plated figurine that provided its nickname from a retired sutler in Olive Branch. Once a decorative feature on a Pullman car owned by a textile magnate, the small metallic bird was actually a bald eagle, but after the man who stole it from a Nashville depot clipped its wings to pay a gambling debt, the piece more closely resembled the state bird of Mississippi.

The figurine from which the Mockingbird got its name has for years been one of the most sought-after pieces of memorabilia among PanCola enthusiasts throughout the country. It was officially declared missing when the company entered receivership on March 4, 1978. In *Mythic Trinkets,* a detailed compendium of Americana that are now considered lost, Timothy Hamish writes, "Those bullies of life—time and chance—conspired, by way of family neglect, corporate theft, or sheer public disregard, to hide the Mockingbird somewhere in the world: that yard sale down the street, a corner of your friend's basement, the landfill across town, or maybe your very own garage." Those words proved fateful in more ways than one. In addition to predicting the circumstances for how the Mockingbird figurine would eventually be found, they also mirrored, unbeknownst to their author, a moment of philosophical revelry in Houghton Forster's mind as he told Annabelle Teague the story of how he'd built the soda fountain, concluding with the namesake ornament that Hamish would later describe as the victim of two bullies. Houghton stared at the beautiful girl before him, decided it was love at first sight, and, wondering about the thousands of seemingly inconsequential events that must have led to this introduction, formed a theory: fate is nothing but chance plus time.

He brushed aside the thought to focus on mixing a drink for the girl. With his back to the fountain, its marble splotched in red, brown, yellow, white, and three shades of blue, Houghton combined a similarly varied range of ingredients: tincture ginger and Seidlitz powders, bromo-caffeine and bromo-seltzer, ester gum, bicarbonate of soda, and pepsin. Into the mix he poured a dose of apple syrup for taste. Houghton said over his shoulder, "This should be plenty invigorating enough to treat your cold," while filling the glass with soda water. Foam bulbed the rim as he set the drink before her.

"What do you call it?" Annabelle asked.

Houghton answered, "Apple of My Eye."

Of all his facial expressions, the boy knew from a smirk. None-

theless Annabelle wanted to see how easily it could be wiped clean
of this Mississippi ragamuffin. She drew on her knowledge of the
soda trade to say, "Apple of My Eye. Hmm. I've always preferred
a virgin."

That surely did put him in a pet. His face lost its color and his
shoulders caved in and his smirk became a frown. "I'm sorry, miss."
The boy gulped onomatopoetically. "But did you say—"

"That I prefer virgins? Yes. Isn't that what soda jerks call it
when they add cherry flavor to a drink? Make it a virgin?"

"Around here we say, 'Make it virtuous.'"

Despite the brief moment of crisis, his thoughts forming an in-
ventory of how the girl could have known, Houghton quickly re-
vitalized, grabbing the bottle of cherry syrup and adding a pony's
worth to the drink. Something told him she had simply been toying
with his composure as a means to justify her own snobbery, to re-
store the natural order as she understood it, and to see, perhaps, if
he would stand for such treatment. Houghton was trying to think
of a sufficiently playful way to call her on the move when a voice
came hollering from the back of the store.

"The ice man's in the alley, Houghton. How many blocks we
need today?"

Into the front of the store walked an Indian larger than any
Annabelle had ever had occasion to glimpse when passing through
the French Quarter on the way to her weekly piano lesson. Still, in
spite of his size, shoulders as wide as a wagon axle and each hand
as big as a lettuce, he appeared to be of the civilized sort, black
hair held down by an elegant trilby, tab-collar shirt laundered to a
crisp white. The Indian paused on noticing Annabelle. "My sincer-
est apologies for the interruption," he said, surprising her with his
elocution. "Did not realize we had a customer on the premises."
Have mercy, but he even bowed like a gentleman.

"Branchwater, I'd like you to meet"—the boy turned to her—"what was your name again, miss?"

"Annabelle. I mean, Miss Teague."

The situation, Annabelle thought while being greeted, again with impressive manners, by this fellow named Branchwater, was strange. Why was she being spoken to so frankly? Why was she still there in the store? And most perplexing of all, why did she feel so at ease? These people were beneath her. She was a Teague!

"Such a peculiar name, Mr. Branchwater. Might I ask its etymology?"

"He's genuine Cherokee nation," said the boy behind the counter. "Isn't that so, Branchwater?"

Mr. Branchwater squared his stance, raised the palm of his hand, and solemnly said, "How." Annabelle was not sure if he was joking until she heard a snicker from Houghton.

"I love it when he does that."

Despite Thomas Jefferson Branchwater's tribal heritage, his friends liked to say he'd gotten his last name because, whenever any of them were drinking bourbon, he made for good company. His people skills were just as deft when put to other use. "Send Branchwater to have a talk with them," Houghton, throughout the years ahead, would often say in regard to troublesome distributors, merchants, or contractors, who, after the meeting, would explain the ring of black around their eye or the new sedan in their driveway, the wad of hundreds in their pocket or the cast around their forearm, by saying, "The Indian came to see me."

The heat in the store, increasing each minute, was starting to get to Annabelle. "How much do I owe you?" she asked, the taffeta at her neckline damp with sweat, the glass on the counter jeweled from the humidity. Appearances, she reminded herself. The world was always watching.

"Dollar for the medicine," Houghton said. "Soda's on the house."

"That won't be necessary. Send the bill in its entirety to the hotel. It'll be paid promptly."

Behind the counter, watching this Annabelle Teague walk away, Houghton knew without looking that she had not touched, let alone sipped, the virtuous drink. He wanted to see her again. He needed to see her again. Houghton called out to Annabelle and, attempting in vain to keep his tone casual, asked about her plans for the rest of the day.

"That's hardly the affair of some tiller boy."

The door screeched shut as she departed. In the silence that followed, Houghton tried to convince himself that he had misheard Annabelle, because of the rusty hinges. He might have been successful in doing so, if only Branchwater had not, at that moment, broken down into a raucous fit of laughter.

. . .

On his third attempt Houghton persuaded Annabelle to go on a date. She had been in town a week because her father's gout, despite a variety of treatments, still hadn't shown a single sign of being on the mend. "Man must eat a beefsteak at each meal," the doctor said, "such for his foot to get swoled that big." Every time Annabelle came by the store to pick up more medicine she turned down whatever social activity Houghton proposed. She did not want to watch the sunset. She had no interest in going for a stroll. What finally caused her to acquiesce was an invitation to help with the monthly harvest of drinking straws.

Houghton handled the wagon reins while he sat beside Annabelle. Above her head she held a parasol even though the tree canopy provided adequate shade. The image tickled Houghton. A parasol in Panola County! Just the same, he did appreciate the collateral breeze made by her other accessory, a silk folding fan. The morning had grown into a scorcher. He now considered it a mistake to have tried to pretty up for Annabelle by wearing wool trousers instead of the overalls typical of him. He found it difficult to fathom the notion that all of society's upper crust went about their lives sopped in sweat. No wonder they cherished their fancy sunshades.

Throughout the four-mile trip on county roads, Mississippi's flora and fauna varied between its pastures and woodland, the honey locust, sycamore, and mountain laurel as frequent as the papaw, wisteria, and buckeye, pink Cherokee roses growing next to green Virginia creepers, an occasional hooded warbler flitting above a cow pond. Houghton pointed out the most distinctive scenes as they passed by them. A dog of indeterminate breed climbing a ladder perched against the gable of a barn. A yard full of Plymouth Rocks clucking away. A bullfrog hopping from red to black on an abandoned game of bottle-top checkers. Houghton held a hand over each smile brought about by each of those he saw on Annabelle.

"Would it bother you if I asked a frank question?" he said, already braced for a pert response.

"I'll assume you're being rhetorical."

Hoping that was the extent of it, he asked, "Why did you finally say yes to letting me see you outside the store?"

Annabelle side-eyed Houghton. She knew what he was really asking and she knew the genuine answer to it. There certainly was plenty to like about him. His tongue was of equal speed to his wit. His fettle appeared to be in fine condition. Yet, more than those two obvious attributes, a body fit for the proscenium and an ability to handle a quip, Annabelle liked that Houghton, who probably did not know a dance card from the stag line, would even consider her a possibility.

"The tiller boy would like to know why I agreed to this little excursion," she said to the horse team, and then looked at Houghton. "I suppose it had to do with just how pathetic you seemed asking."

In a trice Houghton flicked the reins, bringing the wagon to an abrupt stop. Dust unfurled around it from back to front. Annabelle said, "Oh, come now. It was only a joke. Don't be upset."

"I'm not upset."

"Then why'd you stop?"

"We're here."

The meadow in front of them, Annabelle noticed on hearing those words, was covered with wild rye. Gusts of wind sent ripples through the field, as though invisible sailboats were cruising by, parting the yellow stalks of grain like water.

"It's beautiful," Annabelle said, "so Edenic." At the time, while being helped down from the wagon by a boy who would one day be her husband, she did not know the meadow sat on the southeastern perimeter of land that years later would become their home, nor did she know the estate would be called "Eden." The first of their four children, Montgomery, was responsible for the name. Prior to the Forsters, those twelve hundred acres outside Batesville, Mississippi, had been owned by the bankrupt descendants of a second-son Welsh aristocrat who, in homage to the public school where he'd first dreamed of making a fortune all his own, had named the property Eton. That word turned biblical when spoken by a child only five years old. Due to the same reason, the family's first dog, a yellow Labrador named after an Anglo-Saxon epic poem, became known as "Bear-Wolf."

From the back of the wagon Houghton grabbed two empty feed sacks and handed one to Annabelle as they walked toward the field. "Usually farmers plant rye to feed their livestock," he said, "but this here is just growing natural on its own." Once they were within those wild plants, he pulled a small pair of shears from his pocket and knelt down next to the stalks adrift in the wind, motioning for her to do the same. "You've got to cut them down here where they're still green. See? I like to cut them at an angle. Let's our customers know the drinking straws are handmade. Not cut by some machine." Houghton gave another pair of shears to Annabelle. "Let's see you give it a try." He took each of her hands in his own, guiding the empty one to clutch at a stalk and guiding the one holding shears to snip its base, and then dropped the rye into her feed sack. "Back at the store I'll set them out in the sun. When they're dry, I'll peel off the outer covering and bundle them by diameter and length. And that's it. Homemade sippers ready for service." On her own Annabelle began to harvest the natural drinking straws, so intent on the process that she didn't notice Houghton watching her.

He couldn't help it. Something about this girl compelled him to ogle. Houghton didn't know why exactly. She was such a sight. Freckles on her elbow, ankle, earlobe, and wrist constellated her figure against the trees, air, grass, and clouds of the summer afternoon. Annabelle became a sort of astronavigation that distracted rather than guided Houghton. Only a little did he notice the bumblebees bumbling, and hardly at all did he notice the roly-polies rolling. Was this how love felt, he wondered, like being lost with a map?

They'd filled their sacks by three o'clock. After putting them in the wagon Houghton retrieved the picnic supplies and walked just ahead of Annabelle to a walnut tree across the meadow. He set down the basket in a spot of shade, spread out a throw, and picked up a halved nutshell from the ground. While he organized the food, uncovering a plate of cold fried chicken and polishing two apples with a checkered rag, Houghton asked Annabelle, "What animals prefer walnuts on their banana split?"

"Don't know."

"Monkeys," he said, holding up the walnut, the cross section of its kernel shaped like a simian visage.

"Soda-jerk humor?"

"Something like it."

Whatever kind of humor it was, Annabelle thought, it was fairly close to adorable. She would give him that much. One thing she most certainly would not give him, however, was the sight of her gnawing on a greasy drumstick. It was impossible to keep up a lady-like appearance in this heat. Why on earth did she wear a whale-bone corset in high summer? Annabelle made do with an apple.

"A nice touch," she said, glad for the breeze drying the sweat from her brow. "The apples."

"What do you mean?"

"You brought them in reference to the first drink you made me. The Apple of My Eye. Didn't you?"

"Actually, I hadn't thought about it. We just had a lot of apples back at the house. Interesting coincidence, though."

"Must be fate."

Beneath tree limbs heavy with foliage, Houghton considered those words from Annabelle, how they reminded him of something. The thought occurred to him with a ping as distinct as tobacco gleet hitting the inside of a cuspidor. "I was thinking about fate the first time we met," he said, repositioning himself a few inches closer to her.

"That so?"

"I was thinking about how us meeting that day was fate. I was thinking about how fate is simply chance plus time."

"You know what the only thing stronger than fate is?"

"Tell me."

"Will."

Houghton was now close enough to feel each breath from Annabelle. In that moment, before he could convince himself otherwise, he decided to prove her point.

He kissed her.

Decades later, over drinks at The Brook one evening, William K. Vanderbilt II would jokingly ask, "What gave you the nerve to even try to land a Teague?" to which Houghton answered that it was the same thing that let their ancestors think about leaving the old country, the same thing that helped those first settlers wrest farmland from the wilderness, the same thing giving their waiter that look of defiance tempered with envy, but on August 6, 1890, the smell of honeysuckle flowers in the air and the taste of apple pulp on his lips, the most profundity Houghton could muster while kissing Annabelle was the thought, *Thank God this happened sometime before I die.*

Both of them leaned back on the blanket. With the palm of his hand Houghton buffered Annabelle's head from the hard ground, and with the fingers of his other hand he traveled the stars. He touched her freckles, the faint smudge where her earlobe curled in on itself, the tiny circle of brown above the pulse in her wrist, the dark nebula showing through the fine hairs of her elbow, all of which constituted what Houghton had come to think of, since he first noticed them in the rye field, as the Annabelle constellation. Those freckles, he could have sworn, radiated celestial heat.

The world around the two of them seemed to grow more alive the longer they kissed—flowers had heartbeats and clouds had friends, trees had dreams and puddles had families—to the extent that, for a brief moment, Houghton thought the train whistle in the distance was the hoot of an owl.

"Is that the four twelve?" Annabelle asked.

"I suppose so."

All in a single motion, she pushed Houghton off from her, sat up, and laced the front of her bodice. "If we aren't back when my father takes his tea, he'll start to wonder where I've been all day." With the blanket she balled up what was left of their picnic, as though to hang it from the end of a stick, and then shoved the whole clattering mess into the basket. Annabelle began to hurry through the stalks of rye. To catch up Houghton had to sprint.

"You didn't tell him where you were going?"

"Of course not."

"Think he'll be upset?"

"He certainly won't be delighted," Annabelle said, already halfway to the wagon. She left out the part about how her father wouldn't care where she had gone so much as with whom.

. . .

Royal Teague declined the offer of a cigar from Tewksbury Forster. He was in no mood. On the porch of Forster Rex-for-All in the early evening, the two men sat opposite each other, one rubbing his sore foot and the other striking a match as they waited for their children to return.

"Houghton is always back before nightfall whenever he makes these trips," Tewksbury said. "I'm sure there's nothing to worry about. Houghton's a good boy."

"We'll see about that."

Born into wealth, privilege, and class—his parents were diagnostic rather than prognostic in their naming of him—Royal had been raised to believe that "blood tells." He expected his daughter, Annabelle, to follow the same axiom. She was meant to be courted by men who could one day be governor. She was meant to give birth to children who could one day be president. Given such high expectations, Royal had been dismayed to learn from the hotel manager that Annabelle had ridden off sub rosa with some local boy named Houghton, the runt son of a nostrum peddler.

"Mind if I sweep past y'all?"

Out the front door to Forster Rex-for-All walked the biggest Indian that Royal had seen in all his life. Tewksbury said, "Go ahead," to the Indian. Despite the permission for him to sweep off the porch, the giant Indian stood still, broom in hand, spine straight, and feet planted firm, a stance so wooden and statuesque that Royal mused, amid the cigar smoke, whether this was a drugstore or a tobacconist shop. Then he followed the Indian's gaze down the street.

The wagon had just rounded a corner and was trundling slowly toward the store. His daughter was sitting far too close to the boy. Even worse, however, was that the two of them, in the plainest of sight, were holding hands. Royal felt liable to faint from anger. What had happened to his little girl? His propriety was dyed in the wool but hers had apparently died on the vine. As the wagon drew up to the store, its bangboard thumping a racket and its horse team chuffing heavily, Royal limped down the porch stairs and reached toward his daughter, saying, "Get down out of there before you make yourself into even more of a disgrace."

"Here, let me help you, Mr. Teague," Houghton said, hopping from his seat and running around the wagon. "You shouldn't be up on your sore f—" The blow from Annabelle's father bloodied Houghton's bottom lip.

"Address me as 'sir' until we're introduced."

From his position in the street, keeled over with one hand on his mouth and the other hanging onto a wagon wheel, Houghton managed to see Branchwater reach for the Bowie knife that, according to stories, had unburdened some forty-odd men of their receding hairlines, bald spots, and touches of gray. Houghton shook his head so subtly, like plucking a guitar string, that only Branchwater noticed. The blade disappeared back into its sheath.

Houghton straightened just in time to be grabbed at the back of his neck by Mr. Teague. "I could bring you up on charges," the man said. "Kidnapping, attempted molestation." Even though he was still conscious, the severe pain in Houghton's neck caused him to lose track of the different voices, a deep one whispering further allegations, a high one screaming to please let him go. Through the din, however, he recognized a voice, calm but stern, from on the porch.

"This evening has been spoiled enough, Mr. Teague. I'll have you kindly unhand my son."

On a farm somewhere outside of town a dinner bell rang. Neither that sound nor Tewksbury's words, however, were the reason Royal let go of Houghton. He let him go because of the stricken look from his daughter. Years earlier, Royal's wife, only a few hours before she succumbed to the fever, had given him that same look, mouth twisted in pain, brow smoothed by thought, eyes wide from trust, when she made him promise to raise Annabelle to be a lady with superior, untroubled prospects.

"Come along. Let's go back to the hotel."

"But, Daddy."

"Didn't you hear the bell? It's time for dinner."

With that, as though it were dawn instead of dusk, the Annabelle constellation vanished, all the lovely freckles on her elbow, wrist, ankle, and earlobe hidden by the encroaching dark. Neither father nor daughter looked back as they walked away from Forster Rex-for-All. They did not take a final glance at Branchwater holding his broom, Tewksbury smoking his cigar, or Houghton putting his hands in his pockets, where, unbeknownst to him until that moment, Annabelle had placed a card with her mailing address. The card marked the beginning of a courtship via post. Over the next few years, the two of them would correspond regularly, often several times a week. Each handwritten description of their daily lives reaffirmed a future in which those lives would be entwined. "I invented a new drink that is selling well," Houghton wrote in his first letter to Annabelle. "Customers have nicknamed it Panola Cola."

1.3

A Soda by Any Other Name

Word spread fast. During those first couple of months following its invention, the house soda of Forster Rex-for-All remained a local treat, known only to the genteel citizens of Batesville proper. Soon enough the county farmers and field hands discovered the drink. In the evenings they would cool down with a glass on their way to deliver a wagonload of hog shorts. In the mornings they would perk up with a glass while eating a drop biscuit made for them by the missus.

How that popularity went national could be described as the old college try. At the University of Mississippi in Oxford, roughly forty miles east of the drugstore, students became fond of the soda, not only for its adaptability as a mixer with various liquors, rum and whiskey and gin, but also for its restorative properties when consumed the next day. The graduation of those students scattered them across the country. Because of such fortunate circumstances, they spread their taste for the soda from one coast to the other, seeding it as if in some patriotic folktale. Stockbrokers going out for a quick bite on Fulton Street asked their coworker if they could try a sip. Housewives living in suburban Chicago exhorted it as a cleaning agent. Doctors practicing in downtown Houston prescribed it for the gripes. Regulars at blind tigers all throughout the Tenderloin begged their bartenders to order the syrup. None of

those things could happen, however, until one deficiency was recti-
fied. The drink needed a name.

The day after he invented the soda, Houghton, not yet realizing the import of what he had created, asked his mother to sample
it. He said, "Just tell me the first words that come to you."

"Delicious," Fiona said with a shrug, her smile turning into a
frown when she saw her son wanted more. "Fizzy?"

Houghton figured that would suffice. What he did not figure
was that "Forster's Delicious Fizzy" would prove too much of a
mouthful. Over the first few weeks the drink was served at the
store, most customers referred to it by the size they wanted, a tall,
a regular, or a short, rather than by its given name. Some called it
the good stuff. Others called it the new thing. Then one customer
used a handle that stuck. On a particularly crowded afternoon, a
stevedore from New Orleans came into the store and, by the seren-
dipitous fluke of an accidental rhyme, asked for "that Panola cola"
he'd heard so much about.

Even the surname was a matter of chance. Despite the etymology of *cola*, its taste, as can be verified by anyone who has chewed
a kola nut, possesses no real cognate in nature. Cola tastes like its
namesake as much as ketchup tastes like tomatoes. Houghton referenced the fruit on sandwich boards outside the store because he
thought it sounded intriguingly exotic. "Made from the finest kola
nut in all Panola County." Back then, he could never have foreseen
how that seemingly exotic term would soon morph into one of the
most domestic in the country, comparable to apple pie, baseball,
jazz, and blue jeans.

In order for Panola Cola to become as nationally known as cola
in general, though, Houghton hired a consultant, Seymour Chessman, best known for his book *The Democratic Market*.

"What's the one thing a business strategist does not want to hear? 'Let's keep it regional,'" Chessman said to Houghton. "This isn't just a drink for southerners. This drink deserves to be known the world wide."

The result was PanCola. Although the company itself remained The Panola Cola Company, its signature product became known primarily by its abbreviated name, one that could soon be seen painted on barn sides, stamped into tin sheets, and lettered in flash-bulbs throughout the United States. The soda-water habit grew, as the century turned, into the ten-cent tradition. Despite the in-creasing number of competitors—a man named Pemberton sold a cola that was popular in Georgia and a man named Bradham sold one that was popular in North Carolina—PanCola was the leader not only in sales but also in what, decades later, would be described as brand recognition. The company achieved that rare linguistic feat of a specific product integrating with its general category. In the Northeast, carbonated drinks were called "soda." In the Mid-west, carbonated drinks were called "pop." Across the Southeast, however, they were called "Pan."

At the same time as that word became synonymous with cola another one became synonymous with wealth. "Forster" had con-notations similar to "Astor." That was why Houghton worked so hard. He wanted to make a name for his family so his children could more easily make a name for their own. His ultimate goal was the cultivation of a lineage that embodied the twentieth century in America. It has been widely agreed he was successful in achiev-ing that goal, though discord remains on what respect, the ascent or the descent, connected his family most to the trajectory of its country.

PART 2

PART 2

2.1

The National Centennial—
Sweets for the Sweet—The Malediction—
Betsy Ross's Legacy

Tewksbury Forster chose not to celebrate the Fourth of July, but the decision had nothing to do with his patriotism. Ever since he had arrived in America less than a year earlier, an immigrant from the Scottish Highlands hoping to start a medical practice, Tewksbury loved nearly everything about his new country, regardless of its refusal to issue him a license for anything but pharmacology. He paid every cent of his taxes without acrimony. He put his marker in voting booths with pride. The reason Tewksbury was not marching in the parade down Main Street was that his wife was in labor with their first child.

The year was 1876. In a cottage three miles north of Batesville, Mississippi, which her husband had designed himself based on her specifications, Fiona lay on the floor, dress hitched up to her knees, sweat crowning her brow. She counted the rafters in the ceiling to avoid thinking of the pain. The cottage had been a belated wedding gift from Tewksbury. "Are you right-handed or left?" he had asked when drafting the plans. "I'll put our bedroom on the east or west side, depending." Fiona's surprise that her husband did not yet know which hand she favored was supplanted by the question of how he'd build a house by himself. She received both an answer and an additional surprise when their neighbors offered to help. Back in England, the country she doubted she'd ever stop thinking of as home, people tolerated, at best, the occasional interloper from distant outposts of the empire, with their strange accents, their strange attire, their strange customs. Now here in these United States she was the stranger. But instead of making hurtful comments, asking Tewksbury where his kilt was or telling Fiona to go bow to her queen, the people of Mississippi had offered to help them build a house. How truly remarkable, this southern hospitality!

Yet, when their neighbors had offered to help, it turned out, they had meant they would loan out their "help," the people Tewksbury, trying to avoid the more aggressive terms preferred by the locals, sometimes called "those dark lads."

One, two, three, Fiona continued counting the rafters, each number somehow increasing rather than decreasing the labor pains. *Four, five, six.* Tewksbury was in the kitchen, looking for his medical kit. He had barely used it since their arrival in the States. During their courtship, Fiona had been proud, even boastful, about the fact that Tewksbury was a doctor, but since the Forsters' trip to this country, taken a week after their nuptials, she had never seen him practice medicine other than to prescribe, sell, and provide drugs to rural farmers with only a pittance to spare. Had he ever aided in childbirth? Could he be trusted at her side? Handsome but mysterious, charming but distant, Tewksbury had wooed her into their engagement with promises of a new life in America, untold riches around every corner, limitless opportunity, elegant culture, a land of boundless splendor.

Once they'd reached America, they had to travel through Europe all over again, encountering Irish immigrants on their stop in New York, Spanish when they rounded the tip of Florida, French while docked in New Orleans, and German as they departed in Tennessee. Fiona and Tewksbury had spent the entire voyage interacting as though they were but a touch above acquaintances. Not once did he mention his kinfolk. Rarely did he speak of his childhood. Only after their arrival in Memphis on a steamboat named *Fortune's Hostage,* as they traveled south by stagecoach to the small town in Mississippi where they planned to settle, did Fiona question whether Tewksbury really was an honest man. The thought occurred to her as they secured the curtains of their private coach and, with the steady creaking of the wagon axles their only distraction from the awkwardness, finally summoned the nerve to consummate their marriage. The act hurt more than she had imagined.

"Don't leave me here alone," she called from the pine floor. "The pain's getting worse."

What was Tewksbury doing back there in the kitchen? He confounded Fiona so often these days. True, he had built her a house. True, he made a living with his vials. True, he had kept to a gentle nature. Still, despite such qualities, Fiona harbored an indeterminate suspicion of her husband, perhaps a result of his Scottish brogue, which had begun to devolve into a southern twang. He'd adopted trouser galluses for fashion, taken to spitting chaw, and declared intentions to farm. His behavior confused her as much as the peculiarities of their new homeland. America guaranteed its citizens life and liberty, for example, but also promised that happiness would always be out of reach, a thing to be forever pursued. It didn't make any sense to Fiona. Sometimes she wondered if she had made a mistake in moving to a country she barely understood with a man she barely knew.

One rafter, two rafter, three rafter, four.

. . .

In the kitchen, Tewksbury was busy not being able to find his black leather medical pouch, which had been given to him years ago by his mentor, Dr. Phillip McAllister. Tewksbury had been a twelve-year-old orphan when his acquaintance was made with the good doctor.

The brethren at the orphanage had told him his parents had died in India. Tewksbury's father had been counselor to Governor-General Lord Canning, explained the brother to whom he was closest, and based in Fort William during the years leading to the Uprising of 1857. "Both your parents died valiantly at Her Majesty's Service after the Curry Mongers chose not to bite cartridges dipped in bacon grease." Tewksbury took their word for Gospel. Born near Inverness but later moved to Bristol, he had been especially naïve as a child, considering the roads and cottages of Ashley Down to be the center of the known world, accepting Director Muller as a saint, and believing it a miracle when the No. 2 House received fresh milk and bread by mere serendipity. "The baker's cart broke down at our door," one of the brethren said to him, "due to the cobblestones placed there by God!" Tewksbury was so green to all forms of duplicity that at the age of twelve, while being led away from the orphanage carrying a tin trunk with two sets of clothes, he asked his new guardian's name, to which the strange man who had taken over his supervision said, "I'm your uncle, fool," causing the young boy to mistake the nominative of address for the given name of Dr. McAllister.

Tewksbury gave up on finding his medical kit and went to check on the condition of his wife. In light of his missing equipment, not to mention the sheer dread of making a mistake on a patient so close to him, he decided to take her to another physician. Dr. Phelps kept a small office on Main Street. Without any delays Tewksbury could get Fiona there in an hour. He lifted her from the floor, carried her through the house, and placed her in the wagon.

It grew near impossible for Tewksbury to overlook the ire in how his darling Fiona muddled through her pain. She called him a scoundrel for having put her in this wretched state. She said he was a fraud who could but hardly fix a sore thumb. Even though he worried she may have been correct in the first accusation—"Damn near ruffled my heart," he would tell his granddaughter—Tewksbury knew she was wrong when it came to the second. His uncle of no genuine family relation had taught Tewksbury well enough throughout his time as an apprentice. Together they had toured Europe as traveling physicians. During the half decade he'd spent assisting the doctor, Tewksbury learned all the common techniques of their trade, such as what diet to prescribe for a strain in the back and how to lance a boil at no risk of infection. He also learned that the practice of medicine was not as lucrative as the sale of it.

"Just stay with me for a little piece more," Tewksbury said over his shoulder to Fiona. "Go on clinching your toes like I told you."

Despite his claims to have been "taught the humors" at Cambridge, Dr. McAllister earned most of his money selling a bubbly elixir said to cure "all manner of malady." Seldom were the occasions for Tewksbury to observe complicated procedures. What he would have given to witness just a few seconds of open surgery! Instead, Tewksbury spent most of his time aiding in the continual improvement of the doctor's special curative, purchasing tinctures on gas-lit streets overlooking the Thames at midnight, visiting

Morocco to sample black market extracts of various foreign herbs, all the while having to listen to Dr. McAllister proclaim the virtues of effervescence.

Although Tewksbury considered such experiences the opposite of storybook, his grandson Montgomery would years later be taken with the novels of Charles Dickens, finding in them an expansion of the anecdotes his grandfather sometimes let slip. Monty was carrying his favorite of those Victorian cliffhangers inside his AEF overcoat the evening he saw his best friend's skull encounter a half-inch cylinder of German industrialism. Thereafter it became impossible for Monty to read a single word of *Great Expectations*.

In 1870, during his apprenticeship with the doctor, Tewksbury had laid the foundation of either coincidence or providence by traveling across what would one day become the Western Front. Dr. McAllister was taking him on a sales trip to Belgium. Instead of barbed wire they strolled through tulips in full bloom. Instead of artillery blasts they listened to larks at song. What made Tewksbury's trip to the Flemish provinces a toss-up between coincidental and providential was that the beauty of the area inspired him to emigrate to America, a country for which Tewksbury's grandson would feel such patriotism he did not hesitate to enlist in a war that would leave his hands shaking even as they gripped the Winchester Model 12 that would still them forever.

. . .

The wagon jostled through a rut Fiona thought seemed deep as a trench. In the back of the wagon, racked with labor pains, she rested her head on a damp sack of feed, mentally accusing her husband of deceit. Why could she not have seen it? Her gullibility, decided Fiona, was congenital. Established in 1839 by Fiona's father, Wadsworth Confections had been, in more ways than she could tell at the time, the primary influence on Fiona's early life in Yorkshire. She passed most of her childhood bagging out mixes by the pound. Fiona now supposed that her intimacy with licorice satins, Catherine wheels, tiger's paws, sugar mice, Turkish lumps, and bonfire toffee had led to her relationship with Tewksbury. Only the daughter of a man who owned a sweet shop would be so oblivious to the bitter nature in others. Under heavy breath Fiona cursed Tewksbury for beguiling her. Hindsight made it all blatant. The stories of his teenage years abroad, from what little she had been told, now seemed bred of knavish fancy. An orphan apprentice? For mercy's and heaven's and pity's sake.

Even how they first met smacked of artifice. Here in the back of a wagon, squinting down the trail at a wooden sign, BATESVILLE, PANOLA COUNTY, POP. 392, which meant her ordeal was almost over, Fiona could remember clearly the road, thousands of miles away, where she literally fell for Tewksbury. That day two years ago, she had been in a rush. At a crossing near her father's shop, Fiona, without having checked for oncoming traffic, was sideswiped by a carriage horse. The harness left a gash along her hand. On sight of the blood, Fiona grew faint, tripping to a seat curbside.

All she saw of the man at first was his medical kit stitched of black leather so old it looked as supple as cloth. From his bag the man removed a small jar of ointment, and with his kerchief he daubed the ointment along her wound. Fiona's senses returned to her right as the man finally spoke. "It's just a balm for healing. Called aloe vera. I picked it up in Egypt." He leaned toward her hand, lips pursed as though to give a kiss, only to blow on the treated gash.

If her heels hadn't been on the curb Fiona's head would have been over them. Egypt! She had never met anyone who had traveled so far. Her visualization of pith helmets brought to mind certain private aspects of the male anatomy, which in turn made her blush, a symptom that thankfully brought on further attention from the handsome man clutching his medical kit. Tewksbury had that very same look of attention now as he carried Fiona toward an office into the door of which was carved AL PHELPS, M.D. Why would one doctor need to take his wife to be treated by another, she wondered, particularly somebody who couldn't be bothered to spell out his full first name?

"She's already deep into the throes," Tewksbury said as he carried her into the office of Albert Phelps. "Help me get her up on this table."

Odds were good that Phelps had been celebrating the Fourth for a very long while. Tewksbury could smell the Speyside. Notes of cask-smoky peat and aridly sweet heather wafted among cedar tongue depressants and ether-inhalant bottles. The doctor was sufficient proof in himself. On the dusty floor he dropped a forceps, and in the dirty sink he washed a speculum. He stifled a belch with his hand. During the last few years of his life, Dr. McAllister, who had begun regularly taking his own elixir to abate the tuberculosis corroding his lungs, showed similar disregard. Often he could not even be trusted to set a bone correctly. At last the situation reached such a threshold that Tewksbury quit his appointed duties, rendering laudanum, synthesizing salicylates, processing quinine, so he could take over for Dr. McAllister in matters that required a more assured hand.

"What's wrong with him?" Fiona asked Tewksbury. "Is something wrong with him?"

She had to admit it was the strangest thing. There Fiona lay perched on the table, nether parts exposed to the room and mind reeling in pain, when her husband, who had brought her all the way into town just to be treated by this man, pushed Dr. Phelps aside. "I'll handle it from here, tosspot. You're in no condition." What on earth? The same man whose hands had shaken when she told him her water had loosed was at present handling the birth with nary a drop of sweat forming on his brow. Fiona almost had a mind to feel sorry for her recent misgivings of his character, if only she weren't distracted by another swell of pain. She gnashed her teeth. She clenched her fists. Then, through a fog, she heard Tewksbury say he could see the head.

Tiny bits of molar loose in her mouth and a row of half-moons cut on her palms, Fiona was in such agony, pushing, pushing, that she just about failed to notice, pushing, pushing, when the agony was over. Across from her Tewksbury held a tiny person. Even though she'd never believed in a higher power, Fiona, staring at her limp and silent newborn son, cursed God for taking his life so soon. It was at that moment the child lurched awake with the shrillest of cries.

Fiona's elation at seeing her son come to life was matched only by her terror from having blasphemed the Lord. That she previously had no religion did little to mitigate her belief in a curse. Her child was doomed. She knew it. Her child was doomed. Over the following decades, Fiona would be proven half correct as the supposed curse skipped her son but came for his descendants, plucking them from the world like petals from a flower, with Fiona unable to do anything but age and watch. Henceforth she called it the Malediction.

Once Tewksbury had given Fiona time to hold the baby—she certainly was acting odd, but that was likely due to the strain—he took his son back for the labor's third stage. He figured that in such a benign operation Phelps was about sober enough to provide assistance. Despite a few hand tremors while clamping the cord, Dr. Phelps performed admirably, cutting through the umbilical with a clean swipe. Tewksbury said, "Obliged." He coo-chee-coo'd over to the window, where the afternoon light was stronger. Ten fingers and ten toes, ten toes and ten fingers: he counted them twice, not for fear they wouldn't add up, but simply to dote. For a moment Tewksbury thought of Dr. McAllister on his final day. Back in their room at the public house, Tewksbury finally asked his mentor, whose entire shirtfront was caked in maroon spittle, why exactly he'd chosen him, Tewksbury, over all the other boys at the orphanage. "I asked for the smartest," Dr. McAllister told him, smiling with such warmth, "and they gave me you." Seven years after the death of the closest thing he had ever had to a father, Tewksbury, while holding his newborn son, remembered those words, thinking how, though he would never have presumed to ask for the most beautiful child in the world, he had now been given it.

Out the window he could see the aftermath of the Independence Day parade: streamer confetti, apple cores, bunting gone ragged, paper fans, and popped balloons, all the rubbish either red, white, blue, or some combination thereof. Not until he noticed the banner hanging over Main Street did Tewksbury realize that this year the celebrations were a centennial. Houghton Forster had been born on the hundredth birthday of America. That sort of thing, considered Tewksbury cautiously, must be a sign. Of what exactly, he had no clue. Perhaps it was nothing.

His gaze wandering with his thoughts, Tewksbury spotted, in a vacant shop window across the street, a cardboard placard, the letters of which were written in blue ink alternating with red. SPACE FOR RENT. On looking at those words he had an idea for a type of store that, with any luck, would net him just enough money to provide for his infant child. Tewksbury couldn't have known that the one color of his new country's flag that was missing from that placard would one day be used for the label of a soft drink that would make his son a millionaire.

Tewksbury carried the child back to Fiona. He didn't want to think about business ventures right now. He didn't want to think about omens. He didn't want to think about his mentor. A celebration was in order! Tewksbury turned to the doctor and said, "Got any more of that whisky?"

2.2

The Littlest General—Soda Walkabout—The Pride
of Quito—"Spare a Fag?"—A German Sniper Takes a
Deep Breath—The Candy Wrapper Solution

Toward the end of his speech the CO's voice cracked on each word. He almost seemed about to cry. "Everybody eats shit from the man above them. You know I have a man above me?" Colonel Frank Duluth said to the Ninth Regiment. "I eat his shit every goddamn day. What I'm asking is for you to eat my shit. And I'm not asking."

Once the colonel had finished, it was clear that his men, standing in formation, were moved by such candidness. Some of them clenched their jaws. Others stared at the ground. A few wiped tears from their eyes. On March 5, 1918, in Lorraine, France, only one of the "Manchus" of the Second Infantry Division, AEF—America's expeditionary forces in the War to End All Wars—appeared unmoved. Instead of evincing awe Montgomery Forster was trying not to giggle.

He had nothing against Colonel Duluth. Since the regiment's transport across the Atlantic—twelve days at sea without cigarettes because they'd been ordered to give up their matches, the only light coming from tiny blue bulbs because all portholes were closed—the colonel, similar to what the dramatist Samuel Foote once said of a dull associate, was not only calm himself but the cause of calmness in others. The men respected him so much they didn't even complain when forced to cross the French countryside in 40-and-8 boxcars so cramped they'd have been considered a cruel means of transit for livestock. Monty was on the verge of laughter not because of the colonel but because of the French children. He could see them behind a shed. Led by a nine-year-old boy whom Monty had begun to think of as the "Littlest General," the group of children stood at attention, just like the regiment was now, listening as the Littlest General gave a speech that, though they were out of earshot, Monty felt certain was a verbatim copy of the one Colonel Duluth was giving at this moment.

With one last salute the men were dismissed for their evening chow. The tight lines broke into haphazard clusters as everyone wandered back to their billets. On his walk through the village, Monty wasn't looking forward to another night of washing out his mess kit in the street, trying to ignore the *fumier* heaped in front of each house. He lit the last cigarette in his pack, its gray smoke hardly distinguishable from the gray sky, a sight typical of the past month. *Whoever came up with the term "Sunny France" knew from snake oil like nobody,* he was thinking as someone approached him, draped an arm over his shoulder, and, in the clipped warble of a blueblood at least a quarter in the bag, said, "I've come down with a horrid case of Americanitis. Medic says the only cure is to relent to it."

Monty leaned into Nicholas. "What'd you have in mind, you stuck-up, drunk Englishman?" His friend's breath smelled of the local vintner's finest.

"There's this little place in a village just outside of Gondre-court. Been meaning to take you. The food's magnificent, despite being French. What do you say? I'll understand if you prefer to eat lukewarm gruel from a Marmite can."

"Got any more wine for the trip?"

During the half hour it took to reach the village, the two of them finished one bottle, both hiding it in their saddlebags between gulps. They had first met near "Washington Center," a trench complex meant for realistic training, built by the "Blue Devils" of the French Forty-Seventh Division. That day Nicholas had shown Monty how to reload his Chauchat rifle. "Be careful should the damned thing overheat," he'd said. "There's more than one way to skin a Chauchat." Since then, their friendship had become a welcome distraction from the circumstances that made it possible, allowing them to focus on each other, making jokes, trading stories, instead of what they would encounter at the front lines soon enough.

"Be a good boy and look after your brother and sister," Monty had written to Harold, fourteen years old, in his first letter home, and in his second, he'd written to Lance and Ramsey, both seven years old, "It's up to y'all to keep our Haddy safe." Monty avoided contacting his mother and father until he was out of the country, protected by an entire ocean from any chance his parents could have their sixteen-year-old son removed from the military service he'd unlawfully joined. "I hope you understand why I left under such surreptitious circumstances," he finally wrote them. Rather than describe his training in weapons and marksmanship, Monty told his parents about the more innocuous elements of his time in the Plattsburgh camps, how he could buy stamps and stationery at the Y hut, that his favorite thing to do was watch movies at the liberty theater. He never once told them about the twenty-year-old man he'd come to think of as his best friend and with whom he was at the moment finishing a bottle of unsurprisingly good Alsatian Riesling.

Nicholas tossed the empty bottle into a woodbine-choked shrub as he and Montgomery rode up to the tavern outside Gondrecourt.

A modest building of two stories, timber framed with stucco in-fill, the tavern appeared similar to the other farmhouses in the area, except its hitching post was crowded with horses bearing the insignia of many nationalities, British and French and American. Nicholas unwrapped a hard candy, put it in his mouth, dropped the wrapper, and offered one to Monty. The man certainly loved his sweets. Throughout the time Monty had known him, Nicholas seemed to have an endless supply of hard candies, pulling one after another from his pocket, untwisting the wax paper, and placing the sugary lump on his tongue, a Eucharist of butterscotch, cinnamon, horehound, and peppermint. "No, thanks," said Monty.

"One day I'm going to convince you to try some of my candy," Nicholas said as they walked into the tavern. "You'll be so sad to learn the wonders you've been missing."

The scene inside reminded Monty of the paintings some families in the Delta had commissioned, where the artist placed the family members, attired in modern clothes and groomed in modern fashion, into the Old World milieu of a Renaissance portrait. That evening the tavern could have been mistaken for Flemish Baroque were it not for all the men in military garb eating dinner. Beneath the shining black leather of boots lay a floor covered in dirty straw. Next to the elegant flower garlands hung campaign hats stained with gun oil.

Just as Monty and Nicholas sat down, a group of soldiers at the other end of the banquet table began to sing, with varying fidelity to the actual lyrics, "We'll Hang Kaiser Bill to a Sour-apple Tree!" Nicholas smiled and winked at Monty. "The Allies do enjoy giving a rouse. If only they could carry a tune." Although Monty, a corporal, had initially felt conspicuous among so many commissioned officers, both the drunken song and the wink from Nicholas, a second lieutenant, set him at ease.

The barmaid placed a carafe of wine and two pewter goblets in front of them. In fluent but too formal French, the proficiency of a man who'd studied up to the sixth form, Nicholas ordered *gougères* to start and quiche as the main course, noting afterward, "I suppose that when in Lorraine one calls it simply 'quiche.'" He and Monty started in on the wine, toasting, over the next few hours and with only partial irony, General Pershing, Woodrow Wilson, Archduke Ferdinand, the Marne, the Somme, and His Majesty King George V. For most of the evening, their conversation bore a lightness that belied its subject matter, which was usual for them. Monty liked this about Nicholas. It was such a Dickensian way to behave. Late in the night, however, Nicholas broke the pattern by asking, "You're scared, aren't you?" the sudden intimacy of his tone made manifest by his fingers grazing the inside of Monty's wrist.

"Of course not." Monty pulled his hand away. "Scared of what?"

Nicholas's facial expression, malleable as unfired pottery, shifted from coy to wry. "Of going to the Front. I want you to know it's okay to be afraid." He drained the last of his wine. "What is it they say? A man without fear is a man who cannot love."

"I don't think they say that. I think you made it up."

"*C'est la vie,*" said the tipsy Brit just before the French barmaid asked, "*Encore du vin?*" He told her no but thank you, that they had a war to fight, had she not heard, as he handed her a stack of coins.

Outside, where the air had turned crisp, Nicholas and Monty stood beneath a rare starlit, cloudless sky. They faced each other while putting on their jackets. "You're off by one," Nicholas said. "Let me show you." He pulled Montgomery toward him. Alone in front of the tavern, both men swaying from drink, Nicholas unbuttoned Monty's jacket, realigned the lapels, and, like a parent would a child, began to button it again. What happened when Nicholas reached the collar Monty did not register at first. In the moment it merely seemed as though their faces had accidently bumped against each other.

That Nicholas did not acknowledge what he had done only confused Monty more. Whether unconcerned, carefree, or simply indifferent, Nicholas mounted his horse, not saying a word, the flickering lamp in the tavern window destabilizing the contours of his eyes, his lips, his cheeks, his nose. Monty remained on the ground, waiting for his senses to untangle themselves, sight no longer touch, taste no longer sound. As soon as they did he realized something was in his mouth. He plucked it out.

Between his fingers, glistening in the moonlight, was a hard candy.

. . .

Licorice, thought Monty. It tasted like licorice. At a terrace café in Quito, Ecuador, he took another sip of the soda. "What you think?" said the waiter who had recommended it. "Good bubbles?"

"Good bubbles."

That carbonated drink was the first he had come across in his travels to use anise as a flavoring agent. Reporters had dubbed the trip a soda walkabout. Following Montgomery's graduation from Princeton on June 12, 1924, his father had offered to pay for him to travel the world, sampling foreign drinks as a kind of R & D for the Panola Cola Company. Monty accepted the offer on the condition he could avoid northwestern France. He was given an expense account, suited with the finest luggage, and booked first class on an ocean liner. The world became not a single oyster of his but a multitude, each with a taste specific to its environment as well as to its culture. In Ireland, he drank three varieties of lemonade,

red and brown and white, some of them mixed with *uisce beatha.*
In Chile, he tried a drink made from wheat and peaches called
mote con huesillo, the origin of an expression that translates as
"more Chilean than a *mote con huesillo.*" In Argentina, he drank
the "national infusion," *yerba mate,* sipping it with a metal straw
called a *bombilla.* China had an herbal tea named Wong Lo Kat.
Italy had a mineral water named Mangiatorella. At a beachside bar
in Cuba, he downed a pint of Iron Beer, which tasted like a cross
between Dr Pepper, root beer, and PanCola. While crossing the Pacific he gulped from a bottle of homemade lightning stowed away
by a deckhand who used to work for a florist named O'Banion in
Chicago. At a roadside stand in Peru, he quaffed an early iteration
of what would become Inca Kola, whose taste could have been said
to resemble bubble gum, except Dubble Bubble, the first bubble
gum, had not yet been invented. He drank pear-flavored sodas in
Finland, guarana-flavored sodas in Brazil, lime-flavored sodas in India, and tarragon-flavored sodas in Estonia.

"You should try it with rum."

At his table in the terrace café, Monty looked up from the licorice soda named Raiz Dulce, wondering who had spoken to him. His
gaze was met by a man two tables away. Deep olive in complexion,
midtwenties, with dark hair slicked back, the man smiled at Monty
using his eyes but not his mouth, no teeth showing from behind his
closed, roseate lips. His thumb methodically rotated a gold signet
ring on his pinkie. Before Monty could reply, the man flagged a
waiter and spoke to him in Spanish. Then he rose from his chair,
straightened his necktie, and walked over to Monty's table.

"May I?" he asked.

"Please."

The man took a seat and introduced himself. "Juan Alhambra
Diaz." Once Monty had stated his own name, the waiter arrived

with another glass of the soda as well as a carafe of clear liquid, placing the former in front of Juan and the latter at the center of the table. "The rum brings out the flavor," said Juan, pouring from the carafe into each of their sodas. "As strawberries do champagne." Miniature tornados formed when the rum met the carbonation.

"You speak English very well," Monty said. "Were you raised in Ecuador?"

"Was I raised in Ecuador? That is to, how do you say, 'put it mildly.'" Over the next few minutes, as Monty decided the rum did indeed bring out the flavor in his Raiz Dulce soda, Juan spoke of his family's history in Ecuador, how his great-grandfather had fought under Antonio José de Sucre in the Battle of Pichincha and subsequently helped establish the country as an independent republic, how, throughout the following decades of instability, the Diazes had used their signature attributes, intuition and quiescence and flattery, to survive the rule of several leaders, including Vicente Rocafuerte, José María Urbina, Diego Noboa, and Pedro José de Arteta. "Not only did we survive but flourish," Juan concluded. "And now my family is the pride of Quito!"

In the tintype light of the deepening afternoon, Monty stared at this man and was reminded of Nicholas, those taut cheeks that looked as though they had been splashed with sandalwood oil, that black hair that seemed to have been combed with brilliantine. So clearly could he remember those two smells, one rich and woodsy and the other medicinal and tart, he could almost conjure his friend here now. Nicholas would have loved Quito. *Think of it,* Monty thought. The two of them, sipping coffee in the Plaza Grande on a bright morning, shoeshine boys offering a discount. The two of them, visiting the Otavalo town market to try on Panama hats, the vendors telling them how great they looked.

"Tell me of your family, *señor.*"

"Excuse me?" Monty said.

"Your family. Tell me their story."

For a moment, as though a baby transfixed by a gleaming object, Montgomery could not take his gaze from Juan's gold signet ring. He was still rotating it. "Your family is from South America," said Monty, purposefully looking away, toward the Cotopaxi volcano, snowcapped and cloud ringed, looming in the distance. "Mine is from the American South."

Juan laughed. "I like that."

"We own a soda company."

"Successful?"

"I suppose you could say that. Ever heard of Panola Cola?"

"*Sí!*" While tilting his chair back, Juan grew thoughtful, and then began to hum a jingle Monty immediately recognized. He made clicking noises with his tongue, like a drumstick tapping a hi-hat, as one does when unable to remember lyrics. At the end of the tune, however, Juan managed to recall the last line, singing triumphantly, "More cola for less moolah!"

Monty smiled. That catchphrase had been introduced a few years back as part of an effort to curb the rising popularity of Coca-Cola. PanCola had changed their bottle design from the standard 6.5-ounce model to an 8-ounce one, hoping to keep customers from switching their loyalty to the small upstart based in Atlanta. Neither company foresaw that, during the Great Depression a decade later, both would be challenged when Pepsi-Cola, bordering on bankruptcy, introduced a 12-ounce bottle.

"Do you like to dance, Montgomery?" No longer rotating his ring, Juan sat motionless across the table. An ellipsis dribbled off the end of his question, and as though in visualization of the punctuation mark, three dots of sweat formed along the brow of his curled lip.

"On occasion."

"Not very far from here is a social club. Wonderful music. Very good dancing. Would you like to accompany me to this club? I believe you would enjoy it very much."

Monty asked the waiter for his check.

Outside the café, walking along narrow cobblestone streets, the two men encountered a city winding both down and up, the sound of yawns mixed with that of laughter, the smell of coffee mixed with that of wine. The sky had gone purple with the approaching night. Monty followed his new friend through a labyrinth of passageways, alleys, and sidewalks, the predominance of bell towers, sometimes four on a single block, making it impossible to visualize their route.

They reached their destination right as the last scraps of day had vanished. With his hand at the small of Monty's back Juan led them to a brick gateway. "It is just through here, my friend," he said, pressing Monty forward. "There is a courtyard in the back." Their footsteps echoed against the walls of a short tunnel lit by kerosene lamps. Up ahead all was quiet.

Where was the music? Just as he asked himself that question, Monty felt a sharp pain at the back of his head and, as he fell to the ground, heard Juan whisper, "*Maricón*."

• • •

At the Front near Sommedieue, where his division had been sent after training camp, Monty responded to Gunner Thomas Dinsmore, RFA, by asking, "Spare you a what?"

"Americans," the gunner said under his breath. "A cigarette!"

They were standing near the fire bay, both covered in soot from their boots to their eyelids, except the gunner also had white dust on his hands, chest, and face. Monty figured he must have spent most of the afternoon covering bodies with lime. The Brits called them "wastage."

He gave the gunner the cigarette he clearly deserved. "Know where I could find Lieutenant Harrington?" Monty asked, lighting the cigarette, not worried about drawing fire while it was still daytime.

"Who?"

"Nicholas Harrington. Should be around here somewhere."

"Think I saw him earlier. Check by the gas hut."

With a tap to the front of his helmet, Monty thanked the gunner and continued down the duckboards of the British trench, searching the faces for one he recognized. It was April 14, 1918. He had been at the Front for a month. Although his experience there had not been pleasant—once on patrol, he came across a dead body emitting a fart, nauseating but mellifluous, that lasted nearly twenty minutes, the time it took for the gas from decomposition to seep out the rectum—it also wasn't the pure hell he'd been told to expect. He had not once touched the bar of soap he carried in his pocket in case he encountered mustard gas and had to scrub down quick. He worried if he would even remember how to shoot his pistol in the event of small-arms fire. Most of his days were spent digging trenches, playing cards, hanging laundry, and smoking cigarettes, all while wondering if, on the other side, they were doing just the same.

Montgomery spotted Nicholas. In front of a deflated observation balloon, his friend, squat copped, was speaking to a technician, pointing at the balloon and then up into the air. He looked so handsome with his Sam Browne belt cinched high around his waist. Monty cleared his throat when he was within earshot.

"Is that Corporal Forster I hear behaving like a civilian, making nonverbal appeals for my attention and not, as it were, showing that heralded American can-do?"

"Yes, sir, Lieutenant. Apologies."

Nicholas, after telling the technician he wanted the balloon in the air by noon tomorrow, stood and faced Monty. He squinted in the nonexistent glare. "Walk with me, Corporal."

Along the back rim of the trench, they walked side by side, their knuckles, on occasion but not on accident, brushing against each other. Monty looked out onto the shell-pocked terrain. All of the holes, growing more deeply shadowed as evening approached, reminded him of carbonation in reverse, bubbles floating down. He would have taken the thought further if only Nicholas had not suddenly clutched one of his butt cheeks. They were at the end of the trench. Nobody was around to see them.

"I've missed you," said Nicholas.

Monty smiled. "It's been one day."

The sun had almost gone down. Unlike the rest of the trench, which ran at a diagonal, southeast to northwest, the part in which they stood branched into a dogleg, running west to east for ten yards. A black-boxed field phone leaned against the southern wall. Shovels were piled in one corner, their blades caked in mud, handles rubbed smooth as ebony.

"I told the diggers to take the evening off," Nicholas said. "Don't want them reaching the Channel."

He picked up a large tarp and laid it over a short ledge. He sat down on the ledge and patted the spot beside him. Monty did as requested. "So it's just you and me, all alone out here?" he asked Nicholas.

"The cat's away."

On the ledge in the dark, cheek by jowl, the two of them kissed. The air filled with a sound like that of water lapping against the side of a bathtub. Even though they had kissed numerous times over the past month—next to the Mill bombs in the munitions shed, behind the CCS among the mounds of boots—Monty still felt, each time, not that he was doing something illicit but that, despite what the bombs could do to others and unlike the people to whom the boots belonged, he was being *alive*. Prior to joining the army it had never occurred to him that he would experience so much living in a place full of the opposite.

The first time he and Nicholas had kissed had been the first time Monty had kissed anybody. While growing up, though he'd understood the "rules" of romance the way a dropped stone understands gravity—men belong with women, never with other men—he hadn't felt conflicted, hurt, or constrained by them. Monty always knew he was different, but he assumed the difference, what separated him from his classmates worried about who they would take to the dance, lay in his pedigree. He wasn't normal; he was a Forster. Asking girls on dates and trying to sneak a kiss weren't his concerns nearly as much as living up to his family name and making his father proud. In spite of the rare occasions when something he saw—Francis X. Bushman's aquiline nose on the cover of *Photoplay,* Jimmy Fairhope nibbling on his thumbnail in geometry class—realigned his internal compass, Monty's magnetic north pointed in one direction: leading the Forster family into the twentieth century. Then came Nicholas. On the Front, Monty's internal compass whirled between north and south, east and west, and never more so than now, sitting on a ledge in a grimy trench, ecstatically directionless, kissing the man with whom he had not yet admitted he was in unexpected, intractable love.

Nicholas pulled back from Monty. A smile on his face but a tremor in his hand, Nicholas lit a cigarette, the process of it seeming to calm him. His smile waxed and his tremor waned. In measured steps, with eyes locked on Monty sitting by his side, Nicholas flicked the cigarette away, wrapped one end of the tarp over their waists, reached beneath it, and, while a parabola of sparks faded in the night air, snapped loose the fly buttons of Monty's wool trousers.

Decades later, one great war ended and another on its way, Monty would wonder, as tears streamed down his cheeks, over his chin, and onto the barrel pressed to his neck, why Nicholas had flicked the cigarette instead of putting it out like soldiers, British and American, were taught to do in the trenches. That day on the Front, however, Monty hardly gave the issue mind, as the entirety of his attention was drawn to one thing, Nicholas's hand, pumping at a gentle pace.

Neither of them knew that the sparks from the cigarette had been seen by a sniper fifty yards away, or that the angle of the trench provided him with adequate line of sight.

No sound accompanied the shot, but its tactile effects were apparent. The bullet severed the part of Nicholas's spinal cord allowing for motor functions and plowed through the area of his brain in charge of higher cognition: his grip went slack before his face did.

Still reeling in the past moment, Monty turned to him and whispered, "Why are you stopping?" He sat forward when an answer did not come. There in the cold dark of the trench, Nicholas's face slowly drew into focus, its expression one of dazed surprise. Blood leaked from his mouth. Sweat dripped from his nose. He blinked once, twice, and never again.

. . .

On that first day, waking up suddenly in Quito with his head throbbing, Monty was shocked most of all by the fact that the gang leader spoke with a southern accent. None of the three men who had kidnapped him bothered to wear masks. They didn't even put a blindfold on him. So he knew exactly who was in charge. Nothing about the man seemed different from the other two—he was dark skinned and dark haired—except for the subtle drawl in how he pronounced his vowels.

That first day of the kidnapping, the leader, after noticing Monty had come to, slowly walked across the large, barren room, in the center of which Monty was hog-tied to a wooden chair. "Don't you look the pitiful thing," he said, his voice reverberating off the sun-dried brick walls.

"Who are you?" Monty asked.

"That don't matter."

The man wore a tan linen suit over a white shirt, no tie and no belt, with brown wing tips that had recently been shined. He held a blue coffee cup. "Here," he said, holding the cup to Monty's clenched mouth. "No? Okay." The man slurped as he took a long sip of coffee.

"What do you want from me?"

"Now you're asking the right sort of question, Mr. Forster." Insouciant as a landed gentleman taking a constitutional, the man strolled around the room, running his finger through the dust on an empty mantel, pausing to appreciate the view from a curtained window. He pointed with his cup and said, "See that big hill yonder? That's El Panecillo. Means 'a small piece of bread.' What we want from you, Mr. Forster, is a *big* piece of bread. Am I understood?"

"How big?"

"Fifteen thousand."

Despite the fact Monty's first impulse was to agree outright, something made him hesitate, as though he were back in the trenches, trying to decide if that smell was yellow cabbage weed or German mustard gas. How would he explain what happened to the money? His father would certainly notice a withdrawal that size. What guarantee did he have they would let him go?

He needed more time to think this situation through. With that in mind, Monty decided that of the two ways he'd been taught to stall a negotiation—either kiss the other guy's ass or unabashedly shine your own—the latter seemed the most appropriate here.

"Where'd you get that accent, cornpone?"

Still wandering around the room, the man stopped of a sudden, dust angels trailing behind his feet. He stood motionless for a second. Then he turned to Monty, grinned, and said, "Same place you got yours."

Harrison Oliveira, whose full name Monty would never know, was the grandchild of Otis and Pearl Ledbetter, two of the original Confederados, southerners from the United States who emigrated to São Paulo, Brazil, following the Civil War. The Ledbetters were originally from Mississippi. Ashamed of their defeat and fearful of Reconstruction, they, along with ten thousand other Confederate émigrés, accepted Emperor Dom Pedro II's offer of tax breaks, cheap land, and subsidies on travel. The couple boarded a ship named *Marmion* on April 16, 1867, and made the 5,600-mile journey to Rio de Janeiro within a month. In New Vicksburg, where they eventually settled, the Ledbetters successfully cultivated sugarcane, King Cotton of the Deepest South. Their four children grew up bilingual. Fried chicken they called *frango frito*. Coleslaw they called *salada repolho*. Despite the family's acclimation, its descendants, unvanquished and unreconstructed, exhibited not just the vocal mannerisms of their homeland but also the rebelliousness that had brought about their separation from it, to the extent that one of those descendants joined an organization specializing in theft, extortion, gambling, drugs, prostitution, and the blackmail of wealthy foreigners in town on business.

"You can call me Harrison," he said to Monty. "Cornpone's a bit too formal."

In the open doorway across the room, Monty saw Juan, wearing the same clothes as the night before, look in to check on things. Clearly they were growing impatient. "If I pay you the fifteen thousand," he asked Harrison, "how do I know you'll let me go?"

Harrison laughed, coming forward. "You're not paying us to let you go." With the back of his fingers he grazed Monty's cheek, the ring on his pinkie, just like Juan's, a cold dot of metal that took the path of a tear. He said, "You're paying us not to tell."

Bells started to ring throughout the city, their concussive, overlapping peals creating, by design or by accident, a kind of melodic clarity. If he were going to give these men the money, Montgomery figured, he at least needed a third party present, somebody to keep them in line and, more important, do just what Harrison claimed they would—not tell. Who then? He looked out the window, trying to figure as best he could the time of day, not here but back at home. Ecuador was roughly on the same longitude as Mississippi. It must be eight or nine o'clock, judging by the light, which meant the household was either being served breakfast, eating it, or preparing for the rest of the day. None of his family would answer the phone themselves that early. So, when the house servant on duty picked up, Montgomery would, in a garbled voice, ask to speak with the one person whose discretion he could trust. With the slightest bit of luck Branchwater might even answer it himself.

"Is there a telephone in this place?" Monty asked Harrison.

"Think I'd let you use one if there were?"

Regarding human nature, Monty had learned, in his twenty-three years, a few elemental truths. He knew that people who used the word *spiritual* usually weren't, for example, as well as that people who used the word *reasonable* tended to be taken as such. So he said to Harrison, "Let's be reasonable. I don't carry that much cash with me when I travel. All I have is a few hundred dollars in my hotel room. Now suppose I go to the bank. You think a withdrawal that size would go unnoticed? Uh-uh."

"Who is it you want to call?"

"A business associate who's been with my family since before I was born. Rest assured he will not do anything to endanger my life. He'll have the money wired here from the company account. Sound reasonable?"

Harrison turned to the door and said something in Spanish. From his coat pocket he pulled a red bandanna. "Wire's not long enough to reach," he said while blindfolding Monty.

His view of the exterior world now a red blur, Montgomery, as he was untied from the chair and guided through a series of rooms, grew more aware of his inner state, registering not only the conditions present, anger and thirst and caution and hunger, but also the one distinctly absent. He wasn't afraid. Monty thought of what Nicholas had once told him—*I want you to know it's okay to be afraid. What is it they say? A man without fear is a man who cannot love*—but he was interrupted by the phone receiver pressed to his ear. "Hello," he said, "operator?" Throughout the prompts for the connection, he considered what he would say, glad for the distraction from the fact that he felt so calm, so collected, so unafraid. The person who answered on the other end, however, was not the person he wanted to speak with.

"Forster residence," said Annabelle Forster.

. . .

"Hello?" The marine waved his hand in front of Monty's face. "You there?"

He was not. Ever since the night Nicholas died six weeks ago, Monty had been drifting in some liminal place, his body disconnected from his mind. He had not really been there when the Second Division received orders to help Marshal Pétain fend against a series of German attacks on a small hunting preserve to the north. He had not really been there as his regiment, driven in trucks by Annamites and Tonkinese up a dusty highway, passed crowds of refugees, their arms full of birdcages, lamps, feather beds, and clocks. He had not really been there when they reached Belleau Wood at eight in the morning on June 1, 1918, only to be told by the French that they should fall back because of overwhelming enemy forces. "Retreat? Hell," said the same marine now asking Monty if he was okay. "We just got here."

Through the haze in Monty's mind, echoing as though shouted into a canyon, the marine's question reached him. "I'm okay," Monty answered.

"Name's Randall Babb."

"Forster. Montgomery."

"What regiment?"

"Ninth."

"Guess we're both lost."

The two of them were crouched behind a boulder on the eastern rim of the woods. Shaped like a kidney, roughly a thousand yards wide and three thousand yards long, the Bois de Belleau was a tactical nightmare, its full summertime foliage hiding German encampments, its deep ravines making replenishment of supplies—zinc ointment for chemical blisters, castor oil for blinded eyes, morphine doses for bullet wounds—next to impossible. Most of the troops fell into disarray when the fighting began. Eight days had passed since Monty had seen any of his regiment. During that time, he had survived as a free agent of sorts, a mercenary with no need for payment, engaging in combat while avoiding gas barrage only on occasion running into other soldiers.

"Got any food?" he asked the marine.

"Food, yes. Water, no."

Randall pulled raw bacon and hard tack from his bag and handed them to Monty. "Beats monkey meat, am I right?" he said, referring to the canned Madagascar beef often found in AEF rations. Monty, his mouth full, grunted.

"So, listen, I'm thinking we head southwest. Gut tells me that's where the stronghold of our forces are holed up. Should be dark soon. We can head out then."

"I'm going north."

"Negative. I just came from there. You've got Wilhelm all over. I was lucky to make it out not looking like a colander."

"Thanks for the grub."

Without looking at Randall, who continued to object by saying it was suicide to go north, Monty collected his gear, a .45 automatic and a Springfield rifle, plus a trench knife, black with blood. Spare ammo rattled in his pockets as he stood. Around the boulder he peeked his head, felt satisfied that it remained atop his neck, and cautiously began to walk due north.

"You're one goddamn crazy son of a bitch," said Randall, yelling in whisper. "The hell is it you think you're going to do?"

"Punish Wilhelm."

Montgomery loaded a clip into the Springfield. Toward a field of wheat, high as his waistband and studded with poppies, he walked, a man possessed in a land dispossessed. With each step forward his mental state regressed to where it had been the past eight days. The sunset became nothing but a smear of color, and the chirping birds devolved into a remote hum. On entering a dense boscage, where he came upon three Germans digging foxholes in the dark, Monty's condition worsened, his present senses getting confused with his past ones, as though he suffered from a form of synesthesia. The cold steel gripped in his hand felt like a cheek softened by sandalwood oil. The bright blood spilled on the ground looked like brilliantine combed into hair. None of the three soldiers even managed to scream.

At such a total remove was Monty as he stood over the dead Germans he did not hear the first shot. It flew past his ear. The second bullet, which grazed his thigh, brought him back.

He collapsed to the ground. On his knees and elbows, he scuttled between the bodies, using them as a shield. More shots were fired, but they hit the dead flesh. Pock, pock. The sound was almost comforting, a stalled pulse trying to find its rhythm. Pock, pock. Judging by the reverb of the shots and where the bodies were getting hit, Monty was fairly certain the gunmen were on a hillock forty yards to the west, but it was too dark beneath the tree canopy to say for sure. Even worse, when he tried to aim, situating the gun barrel on top of a lifeless shoulder, Monty realized it was also too dark to see the sight posts of his Springfield, not the front one, not the rear one, their black metal indistinguishable from the black night. Pock, pock, pock.

How in hell could he hope to hit them if he could not even aim? Monty needed to think. He could try firing into the tree branches above him, clearing a hole for the moonlight, but that would probably use up most of his ammo. He could try waiting them out for the entire night, sending the occasional warning shot, but soon enough they would probably decide to flank him.

Think. Goddamn it. Think.

From the pocket of his shirt Monty took one of the hard candies Nicholas had on him the night he died. They always helped Monty calm his nerves. Right as he was about to place one in his mouth, he noticed how the wrapper reflected the scant ambient light, a tiny moon in the palm of his hand.

Monty pushed the wrapper onto his rifle's front sight post, letting the metal triangle tear through so it was hooked. He tried to aim. The white paper at the end of the barrel provided just enough contrast for him to line up the two sight posts. He took a long breath and relaxed his shoulders. All he needed was some movement, a shimmer in the darkness, a humming made visible, anything to pinpoint in his sights. Monty noticed a distant bush shake, just a touch, as though seen through a heat haze. He pulled the trigger, over and again, until he had to reload, which he did, over and again, until all his ammo was spent.

"Would you say you have a death wish?" Colonel Duluth asked Montgomery, who was sitting in a tent at base camp twelve days later. "I'd honestly like to know."

The two men faced each other across a small table. Both in clean uniforms, hair combed and cheeks shaved, they were unrecognizable compared to just two days prior, when a report had come through, "Woods now U.S. Marine Corps entirely." From outside the tent came sounds of celebration, men slapping each other on the back, wine corks popping from bottles, the occasional salvo of a sidearm being misused.

"No, sir," said Monty.

"For two weeks I received reports of a soldier gone rogue. But that's not the unusual thing. We were all scattered by the shit storm out there." The colonel flipped through a folder. "The unusual thing is that the rogue soldier, according to reports, repeatedly went back into enemy terrain. Always alone. Like he wanted to die."

"All due respect, but I disagree, Colonel. Sounds to me more like he wanted to win."

Inside a tent miles from what had been enemy terrain, Monty thought of the moment, twelve days ago, when his desire to die had been overcome not by the will to live, nor even by some urge to be the victor, but rather by the desperate, instinctive need to survive. He could still see the lunar surface of a candy wrapper at the end of his rifle, still hear the crack of each bullet like a syllable of *Ni-cho-las, Ni-cho-las* echoing through the dark woods, still feel the cold air drying sweat from his forehead after he shot his last round. "Never be ashamed of who you are," the colonel said, jarring Monty from his thoughts.

"Sir?"

"You're a soldier. Be proud of that."

Monty stood, squared himself, and saluted Colonel Duluth. The colonel did the same. Despite the dim light of the tent, the colonel's hand was clearly visible, the skin on its knuckles webbed with age, nails clipped, a gold wedding band on its ring finger. He sat back down. "Dismissed." Montgomery took one last glance at the gold wedding band, transfixed for some reason he could not discern, and walked outside into a crowd of triumphant soldiers, where it occurred to him, with bitter clarity, that the Allied forces, American and French and British, had a long fight ahead of them.

2.3

Tree Bear! Tree Bear!—Rocket the Miracle Horse—
A Serenade in the Moonglade—Storyville Stories—
Historical Secrets

"When a can of soda gets shaken up, let's say because of a bumpy car ride, or some kid accidentally dropping it on the floor, or it falls out of the refrigerator, or because it's been dealing with organized crime," Special Agent Phillip Johnson said to Lance Forster on August 4, 1973, "do you know what you do with that can of soda? You tap. On the lid. With your fingernail. Tap, tap, tap. Then it cracks wide open. That's what you do to a can of delicious, mouthwatering, thirst-quenching *pop*."

Decades before that interrogation, Lance, age twelve, was playing "Spot the Tree Bear" with two of his siblings, Ramsey and Harold. They were on the northeast corner of Eden. The twins ran ahead of their brother, older than them by seven years, while shouting over their shoulders. "Tree bear, Haddy! See?" "Tree bear!" "Tree bear!" "See it, Haddy? Tree bear!" With each shout, they pointed, at the ruins of a sharecropper cottage, toward a copse of pine trees, into a patch of nettles, at the old farm equipment, cow troughs and middle busters and well pumps, so rusted over as to be statuary.

The children came upon a barn that had not been used since

the year their father had a more modern one erected closer to the big house. The old barn's rusting tin roof, situated atop wooden walls the color of brick, creaked in the afternoon breeze. A bluish copper weather vane on the barn's cupola swayed from northwest to southeast.

Built by the property's first owner, the barn would remain standing for another two decades, its roof warping in the summer heat, its paint fading in the winter sun, until the day a report came from inside its walls, echoing across the hills, through the trees, and over the ponds of Eden, so weak by the time it reached the living room where the Forsters were gathered that the only reaction came from their white Labrador, who trotted into the kitchen and, whimpering, began to scratch at the back door. Houghton had the barn razed within hours of finding Monty.

"Know what's inside there?" Lance said to Haddy. "The king of the tree bears!"

"Honest?"

"The king spooks real easy," Ramsey said to Haddy. "Let us go inside first."

Tree bears were a family legend. On trips to and from town, shadowy woods reeling past the carriage, Houghton would tell his children about those elusive creatures, how their skin was the color of bark and their eyes the color of leaves, how they lived on a diet of budworms, slept curled into tree hollows, and, when standing still, could be mistaken for bear-shaped stove wood. The twins had long since realized tree bears were about as real as unicorns. Their brother had not. Outside the old barn years after he'd first been told of the legend, waiting for Ramsey and Lance to call him, Harold shifted his feet as though he had to make water, he was so excited to see the King Tree Bear.

At the sound of his brother and sister yelling, "We found it!

Come look!" Haddy sprinted to the barn and slid open its door. His jitters turned to fear quicker than the one time he'd played a game of mumblety-peg. Inside, all was quiet. Prismatic cobwebs split the daylight into circular rainbows, and organ pipes built by mud daubers speckled the roof beams. Bales of hay were strewn about in a pattern as haphazard and methodical as the fallen stones of some prehistoric monument, shafts of light intersecting them to predict equinoxes and solstices that would only come round by a coincidence of time. Dust pirouetted in the humid air. Unable to see Lance and Ramsey anywhere in the dark barn, Harold called out to them, loud enough to send an owl, hidden among the rafters, soaring through a chute into the open air. Nobody who was a person gave any more of a response. Then, right as he was about to holler this was no longer any fun, Harold saw, rising from behind one of the hay bales, the head of something that was most certainly not a person.

The tree bear looked just as he had thought it would, animate but whittled, its eyes two ragged holes, mouth a yawning slash, and ears two brown triangles lodged at the top corners of its head. Was that the king? Haddy couldn't tell. Without thinking he took a step forward. As the tree bear made like a curious dog, tilting its head from one side to the other, Haddy pursed his lips to whistle but was interrupted by Lance, who jumped out from behind a stall door and, with a growl to his voice, screamed, "Rawr!"

At the Panola Cola Museum years later, while arranging colorful kings and queens into meaningless patterns, Harold would remember not the shock but rather the confusion as he stumbled backward, tripped over a pitchfork, and fell onto a pile of scrap lumber. He would remember a rope coiled by his shoulder. He would remember how the rope started to move. Still and all, despite those sensations etched into his memory, Harold would be unable, throughout the years following the incident, to recall any sound: the rattling did not begin until after the snake had bitten his neck.

Pain spread out from the wound as steadily as a drop of iodine touched to a cotton ball. Its intensity grew. His mind collapsing into shock, Harold could think of nothing but the wave of fire coursing from his neck, down his shoulder, and through his chest, as though his veins were filled with gasoline and the rattlesnake's fangs had been a lit match. His field of vision telescoped from where he lay on the ground. Into it appeared two heads, that of his brother and that of his sister, both with mouths gaping. At the same moment as Harold began to wonder why Ramsey was holding a sugar sack, one that had three holes torn into it, Lance picked up the pitchfork and thrust it toward the ground, where, if Harold had been able to turn his head, he would have seen the pitchfork's rusted tines impale four feet and six pounds of eastern diamondback.

"Oh God, I'm so sorry," Ramsey said, falling to her knees. With the sugar sack she wiped the sweat from Harold's brow. "It was only a joke."

Although moments earlier he had shouted loud enough to scare away a barn owl, Harold, his vocal cords wrecked by the venom and his throat muscles convulsing from the bite, couldn't speak loud enough to frighten a field mouse. He only managed to muster a single word.

"Branchwater."

. . .

Throughout their early childhood, Thomas Jefferson Branchwater had been looked after by his brother, George Washington Branchwater, the favorite son of their household. Little Tommy idealized Big George. It was from his older brother he learned how to laze away an afternoon tossing a line from a john boat. It was with his older brother he got corned for the first time on a stolen bottle of busthead whiskey. George shielded Tom from anyone in their small Cherokee community who called them half-breeds or pinkskins, who whispered that their father had been working on an oil field a thousand miles away when they were born, or who swapped rumors of a circuit judge from Oxford who'd been known to socialize with their mother around the time of their conception.

Then came the morning when no one could find George. The family searched everywhere to no avail. Finally, on the second day George had been missing, Tom, while getting water for the morning coffee, heard a moan echoing faintly from the bottom of the well.

George never was the same after his sleepwalking accident. Not only did his mind go simple—sweeping his only manageable chore, vocabulary often a mush of syllables, getting dressed difficult without help—but his body seemed to freeze in time, leading many elders in their community to suspect devilry in that fateful plunge down the well. Prior to the accident, George had been two years older than Tom, and three inches taller. Afterward, as he grew older, George remained the same size, trapped forever in the body of a twelve-year-old. He became an object of ridicule in town. "Georgie the cripple," schoolchildren would taunt singsong, "Georgie the simple." On most occasions, Tom—whose size following his brother's accident had developed at twice the rate of a normal child, as though by some fourth law of motion one body's deceleration led to the acceleration of another—would protect George, usually with an action no more violent than the folding of his arms across the precut, hardwood four-by-four that was his chest.

Years later, the urgency with which he would lift Harold's slack body from the floor of the barn and order Lance and Ramsey to run home, stemmed from the one time, back when his brother was still alive, he'd failed to keep him safe.

"Who did this?" he asked George, eighteen years old, in the kitchen of their house. Using the side of his favored hand, the one already balled into a fist for whoever the answer might be, Tom lifted his brother's chin to inspect the bloody scrape along his cheekbone. George shrank away in the childish manner, his whole body curling into itself, that always made Tom ripple with both heartache and anger, a combination that resulted in guilt. He felt the same way whenever he thought of the rumors his father must have heard about his wife and children after he returned home from his stint repairing oil drills in Texas.

"Tell me, Georgie. Who did this?"

"Them boys at school."

"Give me their names."

"It's okay, Tommy. They look worse."

According to George, he had been playing jackstones when a couple of teenagers sidled up, knocked him over, and kicked dirt in his face, at which point another boy their age helped George stand up, telling the others to leave him be, an order the other boys refused, calling the one boy an injun lover, after which that boy threw down on the others until they were limping home with blood dripping from their noses. The story birthed Tom's future career. Although George didn't know the name of the boy who had helped him, nor could he provide a description more detailed than his gender, he did remember where he had run across the boy before that day.

"I seen him behind the counter at that place with the pills that make my head feel better."

Early the next morning, Tom walked into Forster Rex-for-All and, with the manners his parents had made a point of teaching him, asked Tewksbury Forster if he might have a word with his son. "Houghton!" the drugstore proprietor called toward the back. "Visitor."

Tom chose to wait on the porch with his hat in hand, a preliminary attempt at deference, but he was taken aback when joined by the boy Houghton. "Can I help you, sir?" It was not so much that he was unused to being addressed that way, though such a thing was rare in these parts, but rather that he'd been addressed that way by someone so young. This boy had to have been at least four years Tom's junior. How did he have the sand to fend off a pair of farm toughs?

"Just wanted to say thank you for helping my little brother." Tom rotated the brim of his hat like the wheel of a ship, a result of the realization he'd just referred to his older brother as "little."

"Your brother's Georgie?"

"That's him."

With a swat of his hand at a fly that wasn't there, Houghton expressed two seemingly disparate views of humanity, how some people had been given such innocence that only a lack of innocence could protect them and how other people had been born such shit-asses that only a whupping of said ass could learn them. The coupling of the sentiments, so redoubtable and frank, so droll and charismatic, engendered a loyalty Tom was not yet able to grasp and a surrogate family he had not yet met. All he could think to say was, "Consider me obliged nonetheless."

"I'm sure you'd do the same for my kin."

He would. Throughout the years ahead, Tom Branchwater, who in his last interview said that being close to "a family that rode shotgun with history" had been one of the greatest privileges of his life, treated Houghton's children as though they were his own. He taught Monty how to thread a wriggling catalpa worm on a hook so it would not fall off midcast. "They call them catfish candy." For her fifteenth birthday he gave Ramsey a Bond Arms derringer with a rosewood grip. "Helps keep the fellas in line." He showed Lance the best methods for sleeving a face card such that he could cut to royalty whenever needed. Despite his affection for those three of the Forster children, though, Tom felt the strongest bond with Harold, who, for reasons that family and townsfolk understood but did not express out loud, reminded Tom of his brother. He was, in fact, thinking of George as he lifted Harold onto his horse, situated him in his lap, and said, "Stay with me now, Haddy. You're doing great."

The boy was not doing great. That much was plain to Branchwater as he geed up the mare. His neck was swollen like a sausage casing that had just been filled. The skin around the puncture wounds ranged from purple to black. To keep his constitution about him, Branchwater set his gaze on the far tree line, toward a Negro camp named Hobson Crossing, home of the county's finest root doctor.

After twenty minutes of a hard ride in summer heat, they reached the camp, tearing into it as though propelled by the cyclone of orange dust kicked up behind them. Branchwater dismounted with a swift back kick of his leg while still carrying Harold. He sprinted through the camp, scattering yard birds, causing old men to raise their suspenders over their shirtless torsos, piquing stray dogs, until he arrived at the home of Mother Shumate. So winded was he by that point Branchwater could just barely call out her name.

In *Mississippi: The WPA Guide to the Magnolia State,* published in 1938, a chapter titled "Negro Folkways" notes, "When ill, the rural Negro has his particular methods. He discards all the stored-up information he has gathered by frequent trips to the doctor. The remedies he wants come from custom, not from science.

At these times he calls a powerful root doctor or hoodoo woman to diagnose his case for him." Mother Shumate practiced that sort of medicine on the citizenry of Batesville. Former proprietress of a hot-pillow joint two hundred miles south, she had changed her career as part of a deal to avoid jail time, taking her knowledge of venereal cures and repurposing them for all manner of sickness, be it insanity or constipation or anything between. To treat neuralgia she would hang a ball of camphor gum about the neck. As an aid for indigestion she would place a bag of tea on the ear. For nausea she would recommend a piece of cake with hair baked into it.

The first time Branchwater made the acquaintance of Mother Shumate she was preparing his brother George for burial. He had watched as she washed his skin with a piece of flannel, put on the grave clothes, placed a coin on each eye, and set a dish of salt on his chest to keep the body from purging. In the root doctor's double-shotgun cottage almost two decades after his brother's death, Branchwater could still remember her idea of condolences—"This must have been a smart boy," she had said, "if he knew to cut long-wise rather than across the wrist"—as he placed Haddy on the rug at her feet.

He looked as fragile as a cicada husk, eyes rolling behind closed lids, sweat dotting the ridge of his pale brow. Still short of breath, Branchwater explained the situation to Mother Shumate, who, sitting calmly in a Morris chair with a sampler, responded, "Did you bring the snake?"

"No."

"Why must I be the only one who knows," she said, interrupting her words with a well-formed tsk, "the best way to fight *venom* is with *venom*?"

As she tossed her needlework to the dusty pine floor Mother Shumate mumbled something about doing it the old-fashioned way.

She got down on her knees, bared her gold tooth to the wan light of the room, leaned toward Haddy, placed her lips to his neck, and, as though a character from one of the penny horrors Branchwater used to read at the general store as a child, sucked at the wound. Afterward she walked to the window and watered a box planter with a mouthful of blood.

Even mettle as legendary as Branchwater's was tested by such an image. He managed to regain a handle on his inner workings when Mother Shumate ordered him to muddle a patch of magnolia blossoms. "They're over on the shelf with all the blackamoors." From a silver plate attached to the arms of a bejeweled, turbaned figurine of some African servant, a decoration Branchwater considered a bit odd to find in Hobson Crossing of all places, he picked up a magnolia flower as big as a fist. He plucked the large white petals, dropped them into a mortar, and ground them with a pestle, releasing the smell of lemons into the air.

Back in the main room, he handed Mother Shumate the mortar, now filled with a floral paste. Haddy was still unconscious. On top of the wound was affixed a small glass cup, and on top of the small glass cup was affixed a lit candle. Mother Shumate said the heat would draw out the remnants of the venom, the logic of which seemed reasonable enough to Branchwater. Minutes later, she removed the cup and candle and, with her fingers, daubed paste from the bowl onto the wound. Branchwater said, "I didn't know magnolia blossoms had healing properties."

"It's not the blooms that have the power to heal. It's the souls trapped in the statues where I keep them."

Branchwater decided to let the logic of that last bit stand for now. He remained quiet as Mother Shumate finished her treatment. She pulled a piece of red flannel from a pecan hull, covered the wound with it, and leaned back with a slump to her shoulders. Now all they had to do, she explained, was wait until he woke. The boy would make it just fine.

"Well, how have you been otherwise, Nyva Adanvdo?" she said as Branchwater retrieved something from a chair across the room.

"Nobody calls me that anymore."

He was speaking the truth. Nearly two decades had passed since anyone had referred to him by that name. He hated it as much as the event that had inspired people to use it. On the floor of the cottage, while his pulse slowly ratcheted down, Branchwater lifted the head of the young man who as a toddler he'd bobbed on his knee, who as a child he'd carried to school on his shoulders, and, using the same care he had for those other activities, placed a pillow beneath it.

...

Ramsey took what happened to Harold that day in the barn far worse than Lance did. Of course the whole thing was their fault. She knew it as surely as the texture of cotton. Were they not the ones who'd tricked Haddy into entering the old barn? Had they not made a mask by cutting holes in a sugar sack? Were they not the ones who scared the poor boy into falling on the woodpile? Yet, even though the two of them had almost killed their brother, Ramsey was the only one of the twins to show any remorse, taking Haddy to the swimming hole after school, reading him his favorite storybooks before bed. Lance behaved the opposite, constantly mocking Harold. He behaved as if he wanted retribution for something he himself had done. None of his attempts, however, seemed to have any effect.

On the evening of June 16, 1928, half a decade after the incident at the barn, Lance finally got his revenge, the means for which was five feet four inches tall, twenty-three years old, 115 pounds, and, at the moment, walking around the dinner table with a tray of butter beans.

"Second helping, sir?"

"No, thank you, Lurlene."

The housemaid continued on from Houghton at the head of the table, next asking Annabelle if she wanted any, and then moving to Ramsey, Harold, and Lance, all but the last of whom politely refused. "Guess I'm the only one not full, Lurlene. Can't get enough of your side dishes." Lance held up his plate for a second helping of beans. He didn't make eye contact with the woman serving them.

Six months prior to that night, Lurlene Culp had arrived at the Forsters' home, The Sweetest Thing, with a haversack slung across her shoulder. That a petite woman of such innocent appearance used baggage favored by steely war veterans was only the first of many seeming paradoxes to her character. Lurlene was a sure hand at cooking southern fare despite having grown up in the Midwest. Her vocabulary was unusually learned for a person of color. In the evenings, unbeknownst to the heads of the household, she unwound with a bottle of raisin jack, cigarettes she rolled herself, and the occasional visit from seventeen-year-old Lance, a relationship that, given her propriety while serving him that evening, few could have discerned, even as Lance's hand, the one not holding his plate, breached her dirndl skirt and slid up her inner thigh, causing no visible reaction other than a slight lowering of her eyelids.

The only person at the dinner table who might have noticed was Ramsey, but she was too busy plotting how to leave before the serving of dessert. Otherwise she would be late. That evening the annual Moonglade Serenade was being held at the club. A part of her resented the fact that she even had to ask permission. At seventeen, she considered herself an adult, practically ancient. "May I be excused early?" Ramsey asked her father.

"Depends."

"On what?"

"How much you've learned this past year at school." Houghton wiped his mouth with a napkin. Only recently had his daughter arrived home from boarding school, and he had been looking forward to fresh rounds of their usual banter. Smiling, he said, "Count to twelve in Latin."

"Oneyay, otway, eethray, ourfay, ivefay, ixsay, evensay, eightyay, inenay, entay, elevenyay, elvetway."

"What were the last words of Socrates?"

"'That wine tasted funny.'"

"If a man travels by foot at ten yards per minute, starting in New Orleans and heading due north, where will he be after one day, two hours, and six minutes?"

"Lost."

"*King Lear,* comedy or tragedy?"

"A laugh riot, old man."

At that answer, Houghton lifted his hand to his chest, as though giving the Pledge of Allegiance but with fingers splayed, a parody of taking offense. "*Old man?*" His little girl still had the stuff, he could gladly affirm, despite her altered appearance. It was true, he did not wholly approve of her modern new look, an indiscreet use of paint on her lips, knees visible above rolled stockings, a small cloche hat atop her shingled hair, but thus far he had avoided the topic, trying to keep dinner a peaceful affair. Ever since Monty had been called to the colors eleven years ago, meals in the house had become a frequent place of drama, even more so after Lance and Ramsey entered puberty.

"Okay, you can go, but I want you back here by midnight,"

Houghton said to his little girl who no longer looked like one. He did his best not to think of jazz babies, champagne baths, and petting parties, what pundits on the wireless called the Problems of the Younger Generation.

"Thanks, Daddy!"

Ramsey, who knew when to use that name for her father the way a seasoned gambler knows when to play a trump, stood from the table. "You coming?" she asked Lance.

"Think I'll stay in tonight. Feeling a bit peaked."

Although she could not recall her brother ever turning down a party, Ramsey did not give it more than a passing thought, she was so eager to get there herself.

"What about me?" Harold asked. "Can I come?"

With half a weak smile, Ramsey ruffled Haddy's hair, saying he wouldn't like it. She told her twenty-four-year-old brother, "This party's just for big kids. 'Kay? I'll bring some cake home for you."

Harold didn't want to go to the stupid party anyhow. He told himself that while listening to Ramsey's heels clack through the hardwood foyer, the front door rasp open, and her roadster, Volstead, cough out a backfire as she drove away. In the following silence he tried to picture her route, which turns she would take, which bends she would round, but he could only see one long ribbon of road going nowhere, just darkness ahead, the way he remembered thinking the future must look.

The future. During Harold's childhood, the idea of the future, whenever he considered it, curdled inside him, rank, viscous, sour, because he knew the future was something that did not belong to him. Ramsey had a future. Lance had a future. Monty, Dad, Mom, Branchwater, all of them had a future, but Haddy only had the right now. While his sister got to go to boarding school, learning all kinds of smart things, while one of his brothers debated which college he should attend, Harvard or Yale or Princeton, and the other went off to war, where he got to fight for his country, Harold stayed behind at The Sweetest Thing, yesterday becoming today, today becoming tomorrow.

Years earlier, after he realized he was different, Harold decided to spend every one of his todays insuring his family's tomorrows. Doing so kept the future from curdling inside him. On the days when his mother, reading the newspaper or overseeing dinner, smiled in the strained way, keeping her lips closed, that meant she was upset, Haddy would offer to "teach" her how to play solitaire, though they both knew he had long since given up on understanding the rules. Whenever Monty acted lonesome and distant for no reason, Haddy would ask him to tell the story of Oliver Twist again, and on the evenings his father looked discouraged from work, Haddy would beg him for another clue about the secret ingredient.

If the future were a road, Harold thought while attempting to imagine Ramsey's route to the Moonglade Serenade, then he would make certain it was straight and smooth, as well lit as a doctor's office, free of fallen tree limbs and blown tires and anything that could make a Forster sad.

The road disappeared when someone snapped by his ear. "You've been staring at your plate for five minutes," Harold's father said. "Go off into one of your thought rambles again?"

"Yes, sir. Guess so."

They were the only two left at the table. All the plates but Harold's had been cleared. His father said, "I'll be in the study taking my cigar. If you're going to play with your cards on the porch, be sure to close the door when you come back in, understood?"

Glad for the suggestion, Harold nodded, asked to be excused, sprang from his seat, and grabbed a deck of Tally-Hos from the kitchen. He situated a rocking chair and side table on the porch, where mounted oil lamps, orbited by mayflies, provided just enough light. He shuffled the cards via the faro method and then cut the deck using only one hand. Over the next hour, as the candlelit windows behind him went dark in the order of his father's walk from the study on the first floor to the master bedroom on the second, Harold laid out the cards, hardly taking notice of the cicadas shrieking throughout the countryside, such was his resolve on finding a pattern.

Oftentimes it seemed the cards had personalities and his job was to facilitate the drama of their interactions. Tonight he was focused on a story developing between two numbers, the sevens and the eights, but he was having trouble figuring out the exact details. They didn't add up. With the advent of a six, laid down impulsively but which nonetheless felt right, Harold was close to understanding the cards' narrative, a feat he might have accomplished if only he had not been distracted by the neigh, pleasant and unmistakable and soothing, of Rocket the Miracle Horse.

That was not her original name. Prior to the rattlesnake accident, the horse had been known as Semper Fi, so christened by her breeder, a Kentuckian fond of reminding people he had served. Afterward, though, everyone in the county began to call the horse Rocket, owing to that was what people said she resembled on the day she blasted into Hobson Crossing, Branchwater at the reins and Harold on her back, a fiery cloud of orange dust kicked up in their wake. The additional descriptor of "Miracle" was a secret act of modesty. In the weeks following the accident, the citizens of Batesville lauded Branchwater as a hero, a reputation he found burdensome. So, rather than abide his role in the events, Branchwater deflected praise to Rocket, noting how she had run faster than any horse he'd ever known and that, neither bidden nor guided by the likes of himself, she had instinctively found her way to Hobson Crossing. Everyone loved the story, none more so than Harold. That evening, his game of solitaire cut short, he recounted the details in his mind, the rhythmic thud of unshod hooves racing across a field, the glint of sunlight in big hazel eyes too focused to blink, as he stroked Rocket's nose.

"A horse that can do miracles," he whispered in her ear, "is its own miracle in my book."

Except for the two of them, the stable was quiet, nary a swallow stirring in its rafters, nothing but hay covering its floor. Harold liked the thought of them being the only two things awake. A boy and his horse, a horse and her boy: the only open eyes in the entirety of Eden. The thought reminded him, however, that it was past his bedtime. He brushed his fingers through Rocket's forelocks one last time for luck.

Harold made certain to close the stable doors slowly enough to avoid their usual creak. On his walk back to the house, he was so intent on being quiet, keeping to the soft grass instead of the noisy gravel, he almost didn't notice the red dot, rising and falling, of a lit cigarette over by the servants' quarters.

"Want to play a game, Haddy?" came a voice across the way. Harold knew the answer before he could even see the person asking the question. Of course he wanted to play a game. Harold wouldn't turn down the chance to play a game for the whole wide world. As he got close to the quarters, a body materialized from the air gone blue with smoke, followed soon after by the smiling face of Lurlene Culp.

She wore nothing but an envelope chemise, her shoulders, neck, and ankles bare to the elements. One of her hands was pressed against her cocked hip.

Despite her attire and stature that night, Lurlene did not bring about unease in Harold, because of the extent to which he trusted her. She had always treated him like one of the grown-ups. In the mornings she would offer him coffee even though the other servants of the house automatically poured him a glass of milk, and before church service she would tell him his tie was crooked even though people in his family just straightened it themselves. "What kind of game?" Harold asked, no longer seeing her naked skin but a mental list, one full of names like tic-tac-toe, seven-up, auntie over, and tiddlywinks.

"Any kind you want."

Lurlene reached toward his collar and ran her fingers down the buttons of his shirt. Her hands slid toward the place where Haddy's mother had taught him his own didn't belong.

What happened next seemed the funniest thing. Inside him, right where this woman he had always liked so much was gripped, his body got too hot to hold its shape, melted, and then somehow grew into a new part, a puddle of wax becoming a candle. The funny thing wasn't that it felt wrong. The funny thing was that it felt so good.

Lurlene inched toward Haddy's cheek, her breath smelling of grapes that had begun to turn, her voice underscored by the clicking of a zipper. "Do you know what this is?" she asked. "An occasion." The clicking slowed and stopped. "Are you going to rise to it?"

Haddy provided an involuntary affirmation.

Her hand wrapped around Haddy's new part, tugging on it gently, and her cigarette burning on the ground, Lurlene led him into her room, which contained a bed with unmade sheets, a wall closet whose door was a set of cretonne drapes, and a desk strewn with writing implements. The ceiling was painted bluish-green, a color that Lurlene's predecessor, an octogenarian so prone to dropsy she looked made of dough, had told Haddy was called "haint blue." She'd said it kept people safe.

Near the foot of the tick mattress Lurlene began to undress Haddy as though it were time for a bath. He could no longer recall why he had always hated washing time. Once done with him she did herself. In the candlelit room, he kept his eyes open for the second it took her chemise to hit the floor, and then he shut them tight. *I'm not supposed to see such things,* Haddy thought at the same time as he told Lurlene, "I'm not opposed to see such things."

"Few men would be."

She placed her hands on his shoulders, guided him onto the bed, and situated herself astride his hip bones. All the sensations of the next few minutes jumbled together without the anchor of sight. Inside Haddy it felt as if a snowball were rolling through his anatomy, down and down, between his lungs, past his heart, over his stomach, down and down, getting bigger as it rolled, except instead of snow this snowball was made of fire.

If Haddy's eyes had been open, he would have seen that Lurlene, moving and kneading her body on top of his own in a steady and cyclical pattern, was not looking at him. She was looking at the closet. If Haddy's eyes had been open, he would have seen that Lurlene, whispering, "This what you wanted, baby?" between moans, was not talking to him. She was talking to his brother Lance.

The heavy drapes fell behind Lance as he stepped into the room, his eyebrows arched higher than usual, the grin on his face creating multiple, concentric parentheses around his mouth. He clapped a round of rapturous applause, cupping his hands so that the sound seemed to shake the gelatinously muggy air. "Bravo! Bravissimo! What a performance!" Lance said to his older brother. "Who'd have guessed you could fuck like such a champ!"

Harold scrambled to hide himself. His trembling beneath the white sheets that soon covered him from head to toe made the sheets look like the surface of a milk saucer carried roughshod on a tray. He had done something bad, so very bad, but he did not know what. His mind fluttered through all of the rules his mother had taught him over the years. Stand up straight. Look people in the eye. The greatest tragedy of the world is that people can get used to anything. Overpraise is the worst kind of insult. Address your elders as "sir" and "ma'am." Use silverware from the outside in. Sometimes the world can get so biting you have to start biting back. Napkin first.

Certain he was a disappointment but confused about which of his mother's rules he had broken, Harold raised the sheets and saw, through a crack that kept the rest of his face hidden, something that left him even more confused: his brother caressing Lurlene's cheek.

"Baby, you did good," Lance said.

Lurlene slapped his hand away. "You didn't tell me all you wanted was to embarrass the poor boy." Unconcerned by her own nudity, she got up from the bed and walked across the room and then sat down at the desk, lit a cigarette, and filled the air with smoke. She pleated her legs and laced her arms, a piece of origami going from lewd to chaste.

"Now why would I want to embarrass my sweet big brother?" Lance ripped the sheets off Harold. He lay down next to the naked, trembling knot of his brother's body. "I love the idiot. You know, Haddy," Lance said, staring at the ceiling, his hands placed on his stomach, "you didn't do anything wrong. Sex is perfectly natural." He paused. "I just worry what Mother's going to think."

Haddy began to wail and could not stop.

Over the years ahead, the next few moments would, in Harold's mind, appear as two pairs of numbers, 5–6 and 4–2, the chance appearance of which in a game of solitaire would render him momentarily catatonic. The former pair was how he pictured himself, knees touching his chest and his head bent forward, like the number five, in tandem with Lurlene over at the desk, the bottom half of her body looped into itself, a number six made of limbs. The latter pair was the scene after his sister suddenly appeared in the doorway to the room. On taking in the tableau, ceiling fan chopping the smoke of a cigarette into confetti, dipped candles sputtering flecks of beeswax, feathers poking through the seams of an unmade mattress, Ramsey glared at Lance, who had stood up from the bed and was running his hands through his hair. "The fuck have you done?" Without waiting for an answer, she grabbed Lance by his throat and shoved him up against the wall, her arm's extension, bent at the elbow, making her look like the number four, her brother's bent knees and drooping, flushed head turning him into a two.

Ramsey let go of Lance. The little shit wasn't worth the effort. She needed to get Haddy out of here quick. From the floor she picked up a sheet and wrapped it around her crying brother. Ramsey pried loose his hand latched onto his ear, coaxed him from the bed, and led him across the room's unpainted floorboards.

"Not a single goddamn word out of you," she said to Lance, coughing while on his knees, and then to Lurlene, frantically gathering her clothes, she added, "I'll decide how to deal with you later."

Outside, where the cicadas were still going strong, Ramsey fetched to a standstill. She listened to make sure there were no stirs coming from the house. Satisfied she could get him in unnoticed, Ramsey gathered the sheet tighter around Harold, whose hand was back to pulling on his ear. She grabbed his wrist and told him to look at her.

"Never think about tonight again. Okay, Haddy? It would be too much for you."

He didn't seem to hear her. Instead he mumbled, "Please don't tell Mother what I did. Please don't tell Mother what I did. Please don't tell Mother what I did," as persistent as radio static. To get him to stop Ramsey promised not to tell.

"But only if you do what I asked."

"Okay," he said.

"What was it I asked you to do?"

"Don't think about tonight ever again."

She said, "Why?"

"'Cause it'd be too much for me."

"Good boy."

That night in June of 1928, as she snuck her brother into the house, got him to his room, put him in his bed, and read from a storybook till he fell asleep, Ramsey genuinely intended to keep her promise not to tell, and for a time she did. She did not tell their parents, and she forbade Lance to so much as look at Harold. Most important, rather than have Lurlene fired for misconduct, a risky maneuver if the goal were to keep matters quiet, Ramsey had her placed on back-of-the-house duties, ones that would keep her out of Harold's sight most of the day. She also had her switched to quarters that came with a roommate, in order to ward against potential visits from inappropriate guests.

The situation, though appearing to have been resolved, was anything but. Three months later Lurlene started to show.

. . .

A key player in her family's swift rise to affluence, Annabelle Forster was once described as having the bearing of a Plantagenet and the ruthlessness of a Tudor, but people who knew her well, from either before or after her marriage, understood those two points could be conveyed in one: she was a Teague. That fact was part of the reason why, when Ramsey knocked on the door to her study, entered after being permitted, and told her the story concerning Lurlene the maid, Annabelle's internal response was, *This again?*

She had dealt with sordid affairs before that day. One in particular came to mind as she considered how best to handle the maid.

In 1893, her father, convinced by his friends at the Choctaw Club that a win was all but guaranteed, campaigned for a seat in the Louisiana House of Representatives. He ran against a candidate backed by the Populist movement, whose slogan, "I ain't in league with Teague," solidified the resentment many New Orleans citizens felt toward the Old Regulars, an influential group of conservatives. Following the landslide defeat, which hurt his willpower as much as his pride, Royal began to frequent a neighborhood adjacent to the French Quarter that, despite its future nickname, exhibited only one kind of story.

Sweetwater Grange was located at no. 137 Basin Street. On a foggy morning in early autumn, Annabelle, nineteen going on twenty, visited the "pleasure palace" and, unsatisfied with the answer to her initial request, said to the proprietor, "Tell me which room he's in or I'll have this place turned into a mule lot."

She was quickly led to a parlor in the back. There, among potted palms and scarlet curtains and decanters of whiskey, Annabelle found her father lying on a plush magenta divan, like the leftover stick in a bolt of velvet unspooled. His shirt was halfway unbuttoned, and his eyes were lacquered from booze. Next to him lay some kind of pipe fitted out for purposes other than the smoking of tobacco. Its floral stink hung thick about the room.

"Get up, Father. We're going."

In a delayed response, he lolled his head in Annabelle's direction, squinting against the dusky glow of a pillar candle. "Is that my little girl?" The parlor's chandelier threw shards of light onto his smiling face. "I do believe it is." Royal got up from the divan and lumbered across the room, somehow managing not to trip on the dozen Oriental rugs overlapping each other on the pillow-strewn floor. He made it to the doorway where Annabelle stood, and with his knuckles curled inward, as though he were holding an umbrella, he rubbed her cheek. Annabelle's mother used to rub her cheek the same way. Her touch was so gentle it was as if she were petting a baby bird. Annabelle could still see her mother's shaking, emaciated hand reaching toward her from the bed where she'd lain for days, coughing and sweating, her skin flecked in tiny red spots.

"My, but you've grown," Annabelle's father said. "Look at you," the man who raised her said. "Grown up so pretty," the man she idolized said. "My beautiful, beautiful girl."

His fingers, one of which no longer bore a ring, trailed down the length of Annabelle's cheek, along her neck, across her collar, until they reached the piping of her dress. The pressure of his hand cupping her breast was replaced almost immediately by the sting in her own hand as it slapped his face.

The following day, sitting across from him at the breakfast table, Annabelle spoke to her father in the calculating, authoritative manner of a chairperson addressing the board. "The events of the previous evening, as well as the degenerative behavior of the past year, will be forgotten, you have my assurance, if three provisions are met. One, you will no longer visit any house of assignation. Two, you will not imbibe of the amber fluid nor smoke anything other than tobacco. And three, you will give your blessing, in public and in private, to my marriage to Houghton Forster."

"Who?"

"'Son of the nostrum peddler,'" she said. "He proposed two days ago."

Several decades later, Annabelle used that same tone, calculating and authoritative, during her talk with Lurlene Culp, and she minced not a word. Due to indiscretions that would go unnamed and unreported if her instructions were followed, Annabelle told Lurlene, it had become apparent that the latter's services were no longer required of the household. She was to leave town on the afternoon train. If she did so without argument, Lurlene would be given $2,000, delivered in cash by Branchwater, who would take her to the depot. Annabelle concluded by saying, "When people ask, you are to tell them the child's father was a migrant worker, someone just passing through. You don't even remember his name. Am I understood?"

"Uh-huh."

"Am I understood?"

"Yes, ma'am."

That afternoon Lurlene boarded a train for Kansas against her will. None of the Forsters saw her again. They carried on as though she had not existed. Even after receiving word that the baby had been lost during childbirth, neither Annabelle nor Ramsey ever spoke to anyone of the reason for Lurlene's departure, a secret that most historians, present one included, believe they kept their entire lives.

2.4

Secret Ingredients, Public Biographies—
Public Biographies, Secret Ingredients

In his seminal work on corporate strategy, *United States of Advertisement: How Cars, Computers, and Cola Shaped a Nation,* Jeremy Turnbull posits that PanCola's "secret ingredient" ad campaign was the first modern use of marketing in America. "Not only did Houghton Forster provide a compelling—one might even say 'viral'—narrative by which to interest customers in his product," Turnbull writes, "but he also created, during that process, the concept of CEO-as-a-household-name, predating Lee Iacocca by over half a century." Public engagement with Forster's life story began on November 12, 1927, when *Forbes* published an interview with the inventor of Panola Cola. In the interview, he spoke of what he would leave behind, noting that his product belonged to the customers but that its creation, a singular moment alchemized into a singular taste, would forever and always belong to his family.

"I'm just a soda jerk at heart," Forster told *Forbes.* "I got to do by me and mine."

His claim later in the interview to have discovered the secret ingredient during childhood did little to narrow the range of clues by which to identify it. As a child the world for Houghton Forster was one of myriad flavors. He would cringe at the pungency of tobacco cud hocked by farmers onto the board sidewalk. He would grin at the piquancy of his own sweat dribbled from the dirty brim of his woven flop hat. Over corn bread he liked to pour redeye. Into gumbo he liked to crumble saltines. With a biscuit he liked to sop molasses. He cooled off with Neapolitan ice cream during the summer. He warmed up with Old English wassail during the winter. Beneath a walnut tree he savored his first kiss from Annabelle, those crinkles in her lips, that down on her ears, tinged with the scent of honeysuckle, mellow and cool and buoyant, latticing the damp soil beneath them. He sneezed from dandelion at age ten. He chewed on birch bark at age four. He inhaled of rosemary at age nine. He teethed with sarsaparilla at age one. Near his mother's dressing screen he could almost taste the eau de toilette, "A Smell Fresh from the Rhine," that she bought by the quart from a perfumer based in Knoxville, and near his father's medicine chest he would often smell the chicle lozenges, "Taste the Orient in Every Chew," that he ordered from a circular sent by the T. Eaton Co. Limited. He preferred banana cake to monkey bread for breakfast. He preferred hush puppies to fried catfish for dinner. With confusion he sampled a piece of saltwater taffy. On a dare he took a whiff of a lady's discarded underthings. After misspeaking he had to gnaw on a hunk of soap.

"What makes Panola Cola the sweetest thing around?" asked one of the first print ads for the secret-ingredient campaign. Under the sketch of a man glugging at a bottle of soda appeared the answer, "Our lips are sealed. Yours aren't."

Less than a year after the debut of such advertisements the initial wave of cola hunters arrived in Mississippi. Who they were varied as much as where they looked. At the schoolhouse where Houghton had been taught, a retired beekeeper made a rubbing of algebraic formulas etched into a desktop, clapped yellow dust from chalk erasers, and sifted through a pile of pencil shavings with a yardstick. A mother of five staked out the police station. A father of two cordoned off the fire department. Over an extended period of months, a team of experts, including a horticulturist, biologist, geologist, landscaper, chemist, and even an archaeologist, studied the lot where, decades earlier, Fiona Forster had tended a garden, its tilled rows of squash, collards, tomatoes, okra, and snap peas surrounded by various flowers: four-o'-clocks and verbena, old maids and phlox. The cartoonist for a syndicated gazette drew sketches of every show window in the business district. A subscriber to *Popular Mechanics* posed as an electrician in order to ransack the Avalon Cinema one town over. The coach of a champion basketball team kept a playbook of all train routes into the nearest depot. No matter who comprised the cola hunters or where they chose to search for clues, a raconteur panning a cakewalk, an asthmatic panning an orchard, a hypocrite panning a bait shop, what drove them to Panola County was the very same emotion felt by Houghton Forster on the day when, after finally discovering the sweet or savory or bitter or salty or sour taste of his secret ingredient, he combined a prototype of the syrup with carbonated water.

"Not a doubt in my mind," he once said. "It was love at first sip."

Although the concept of a secret recipe, ingredient, or formula would later be used to market everything from baked beans to fried chicken, few people realized how revolutionary it was at the time. What made the particular campaign so unique, J. Mumford Simms of Simms & Powell claims in *Mum Is Not the Word: An Ad Man Tells All,* wasn't its sense of intrigue but rather of intimacy. "Prior to my agency's work with PanCola, nothing was personal to the consumer," writes the ad man, "but after my agency's work with them, PanCola was like a part of your family." J. Mumford Simms never shied from giving credit to Houghton. He would often admit it was Forster who thought up the campaign. He would often admit it was Forster who sold the idea to his country. On May 7, 1956, the *Wall Street Journal* corroborated those sentiments by concluding its obituary of Houghton Forster with the statement, grandiose but prophetic, that PanCola's secret ingredient was "the rosebud to his entire family saga."

2.5

June 10, 1923, Weekend Edition—*Anything Goes*—
Everything Goes—Contrite and Lonesome in
Greenwich Village

CRIQUI KNOCKS OUT KILBANE. OUR CHILDREN READING PRO-BRITISH TEXTBOOKS? DELTA MAN BURIED OWN TRACTOR, INSURANCE COMPANY SAYS. PRINCESS HELENA DEAD AT 77. ROAD CLOSURE ON FRONTAGE, DETOUR VIA PANCOLA DRIVE. GERMANY ASKS FOR, DENIED, REPARATIONS. LON CHANEY'S SHOCKING IN "THE SHOCK"!

At the breakfast table, surrounded by his children, Houghton scanned the day's headlines in the *Batesville Gazette*, his face scrunched into the smile of a proud father. The impetus of his pride was not his children but the newspaper. It was free. Two weeks earlier, his daughter, Ramsey, had won the *Gazette*'s annual contest, in which a year's subscription to the paper was offered to whoever in Panola County, Mississippi, brought in the first bloomed cotton boll of the season.

"So you just spotted it in a field on your way to school?"

"Yes, sir," lied Ramsey.

The previous winter, unbeknownst to her father, she had built a small-scale, rudimentary but functioning hothouse on the outskirts of their property, and inside the contraption she had planted cottonseeds. Nobody at the paper thought even for an instant to question the twelve-year-old girl who brought in a boll two months before one should have matured.

"Well then, isn't that something," Houghton said, turning a page. "Good to know you don't need glasses."

Across the table Lance glared at his sister, who beamed at their father and said, "Thanks, Daddy!" Lance's glare sharpened, and his lips turned colorless, he was pressing them together so tight.

The Forsters, like most southern families, typically had one of two intentions when conversing among themselves: to make each other laugh or to make each other bleed. Earlier that summer, when Annabelle complimented Houghton's new hat, a straw boater with a blue paisley band, she had meant that he needed to throw the ugly thing away, perhaps even burn it for adequate measure. Any anecdotes told on the porch or in front of the fireplace—whether they concerned how John "Turtle Food" McDonald lost his pinkie while noodling for catfish, the time Houghton was almost arrested in Memphis for driving tight and the officer wrote in his report, "Suspect asked, 'Are you *sure* you want to do this?'" or Fiona's "extremely" difficult-to-bake dessert, for which, the family later discovered, she used a recipe entitled *Easy Berry Cobbler*—none of those anecdotes were ever a cautionary tale or a story of woe, and they never had a moral. A true Forster, Lance intended to strike an artery when he asked his father that morning at the breakfast table, "What's black and white and doesn't cost any green?"

"I don't know," said Houghton.

"The newspaper that Ramsey won by growing a cotton plant in a glass box she made last February over by the pond."

Houghton put down the paper. "Glass box?" he asked Lance, his gaze drifting to Ramsey before he'd finished the question. "Is this true?"

Her head lowered and facing what was left of her pancakes,

Ramsey nodded. "Yes, sir." She waited for her father's anger to detonate. To keep from flinching, she tightened the muscles in her face, held her breath, and willed herself not to blink. Across the room a kitchen timer tick-tocked like a fingernail on tooth enamel. Outside a bird started to whistle. Both those sounds, however, were soon overwhelmed by Houghton, who was laughing so hard he could barely catch his breath.

Eleven years later, while telling the story about the hothouse, Ramsey concluded, "I think he was more proud of me after he found out I'd cheated than when he thought I'd won it fair and square."

She was at a house party in the West Village, New York, hosted by one of Ramsey's friends from boarding school. In the living room of a two-story, four-bedroom apartment, its hallways scuffed by the workman boots Emma Goldman was said to have been fond of a decade back, its bathtub sandy to the touch because of a gin recipe Joe Gould had claimed would remedy the measles, Ramsey was sur-rounded by poor shades of the neighborhood's bohemian past, in particular a group of recent Bryn Mawr graduates with clambake accents and topiary hair, none of whom seemed amused by her hot-house story.

"That sounds like a very, uh, *colorful* childhood," one of them said. Then, referring to the host of the evening, she asked, "And how is it you came to know Liz?"

At Miss Porter's, Ramsey and Elizabeth Katherine Peterson of St. Paul, Minnesota, who both found it difficult to fit in with the East Coast set while so far away from their own families, bonded as first-years, often joking they hailed from opposite ends of Amer-ica's great river. They soon developed a code language as a means to deal with their classmates. One phrase was a favorite. Did the daughter of a shipping magnate mock their performance on the oral exams in French class? "*Sic transit.*" Had a girl in their dorm claimed they once got drunk on gin with some local boys at the nearby fairgrounds? "*Sic transit.*" So now, though years had passed since high school, Ramsey knew the perfect answer to the Bryn Mawr girl's question about how she knew Liz. "Through a mutual friend," she said. "Name of Gloria Mundi."

"Oh, I believe I've met her! Gloria Mundi. From Philadelphia, right?"

Just as Ramsey was about to say, "Yes, that's right, Gloria Mundi of the Philadelphia Mundis," Liz appeared at her side, saying, "Girls, do forgive me for stealing Ramsey from you. There's someone I simply must introduce her to." She handed Ramsey a martini. "Come, come, dear."

They walked cocktail by cocktail down the hall, so close one occasionally spilled into the other. "Sorry, but I had to get you away from them." Liz took a sip. "I didn't want anybody getting hurt."

"I wouldn't have gotten hurt."

"I wasn't talking about you."

Oh, thank God, thought Ramsey. It was the same old Liz. For a moment there, hearing the way she spoke to the other girls, Ramsey was worried her friend had switched sides, giving up her Minnesota scrap for New England refinement, a world of alley breweries overcome by one of swallowtail coats.

"There really is someone I want you to meet," said Liz.

"Who?"

Liz simpered. "Why, the man of your dreams, of course."

According to an interview conducted on May 5, 1986, Elizabeth Peterson, sole heiress of the Peterson Radio Network, knew nothing of what was to happen later that night. "They were two of my dearest friends. I'd never want either of them to get hurt. He did not do anything to her. Honestly I'm offended at what you're suggesting. What did you say your name was again? You don't look old enough to be a journalist."

Liz said, "Follow me," to Ramsey. She led her friend through various clusters of people at the party, most of them arranged by alma mater, Ramsey could tell by catching the frequent "What house were you in?" The number of mandarin collars on the men was matched only by the number of bob cuts on the women.

"He's a Roosevelt once removed," Liz whispered over her shoulder. "Lacrosse champion at Andover. Summa cum laude from Harvard. He loves his mother, writes poetry, and looks like Bobby Jones. I mean, *have you ever?*" With an imaginary roll of her eyes Ramsey agreed that she had in fact never.

They stopped in front of a tall man, early twenties, dressed in Oxford bags and a white pongee shirt, hair parted crisply down the middle. Liz had at least been right about one thing. He was as handsome as Bobby Jones. For a second Ramsey pictured him in the rotogravure section, looking tan somehow despite the gray scale, against one shoulder propped Calamity Jane, his famous putter.

"Nathaniel, meet Ramsey. Ramsey, meet Nathaniel."

In the living room of Liz's apartment, the yellow light from the lamps making everyone there seem not preserved in amber but animated by it, Ramsey and Nathaniel, each claiming the pleasure as their own, shook hands. Liz excused herself. Although things started rough for them—"Nathaniel," he corrected her when she addressed him as "Nate"—Ramsey soon began to warm to the guy. The unprohibited alcohol helped. Both of them exercised the Twenty-First Amendment while exchanging their bios. Born and raised in Westchester County, New York, as a third-generation American, Nathaniel Afternoon, whose Slavic family name had been Anglicized by Ellis Island officials, bore a chip not on his shoulder but in his signature. He resented the near-comic quality of his surname. What made the situation worse, he explained to Ramsey at the cocktail party, was that the success of his family's business, a chain of five-and-dimes called Good Afternoon!, owed much to their unusual name. "So I've kind of gone through life as a flagpole sitter," he said. "In an elevated position but with a constant pain in my ass."

"Nice metaphor."

"English major." Nathaniel finished his third martini. After fetching another round from the bar, he looked at Ramsey and, with the authority of the resentful, advantaged, and drunken, a medley she admired, said, "You're not like the other girls here."

"How so?"

"You're not the type to call your mother 'Maman,' just so people know you summered in France as a child."

This guy was starting to grow on Ramsey. He was such an unabashed contradiction, someone pretentious enough to insist on being addressed by his full first name but who also despised his last name, a Harvard graduate, lacrosse player, boarding schooler, and cousin of the Roosevelts with the gall to mock people for having spent their childhood summers abroad. Ramsey had always enjoyed a good paradox.

"How else am I different from the other girls here?" she asked Nathaniel, whose subsequent grin was only partly obscured by the lip of his martini glass. He pretended to think.

"You're the type who would say yes."

"To what?"

"Us finding someplace private to talk."

Although the apartment, so crowded with people, was sweltering that night, Ramsey, who prided herself on being modern minded, crossed her arms, feigned a shiver, and said, "Chilly in here. I think I need my shawl." Together she and Nathaniel found the coatroom.

On top of a bed covered with fur, cashmere, and wool, paletots and chesterfields, coverts and ulsters, mounds of car coats, trench coats, and peacoats, Ramsey began to make out with Nathaniel. He was a decent kisser. His mouth tasted so strongly of gin it felt as if she were drinking a giant martini. Through the closed door, which they'd locked, she could hear a group of people, muffled but distinct, talking about a new musical. One person loved it. Another said it was terrible.

"Hey there," she said, pushing Nathaniel's hand from her thigh. "Watch it."

Ramsey gathered the musical under discussion was *Anything Goes*. She had seen a matinee of it last week. Ever since then the lyrics of its catchy title number had been lodged in her mind. *We've often rewound the clock, since the Puritans got a shock, when they landed on Plymouth Rock.* The weight of Nathaniel on top of her began to make Ramsey uncomfortable. Coat buttons were pressing into her spine. She tried asking him to move, but he did not seem to hear her. *But now, God knows, anything goes.* The stubble of his cheek burning the skin of her own, Ramsey tried pulling away from Nathaniel, but he just burrowed his face into the crook of her neck. With one hand he held her wrists pinned above her head. The other he used to go where she had told him he could not. *If driving fast cars you like, if low bars you like, if old hymns you like.* Clanking filled her ears—the sound of belt buckles, the sound of zippers, the sound of pant buttons—as she repeated one word. "Don't." *The world has gone mad today, and good's bad today, and black's white today.* Ramsey could smell herself on the hand he was using to cover her mouth. Please, she couldn't say, stop. Focusing all of her concentration she tried to relax her body. Let it happen, she told herself. Even the voice in her head was muzzled by his grip. *Then . . . I suppose . . . anything goes.* From beneath her she noticed the different smells of coats, perfume on one, musk on another, ghosts of the people who had worn them, all of which she imagined watching her intently now, their presence worldly, ephemeral, and uncaring.

In the corner of her eye Ramsey saw her clutch on the bed. It was just out of reach. She freed one arm, straining toward it. As her fingers grazed the metal clasp, though, she heard a sigh uncouple from a grunt. Nathaniel rolled off her.

"I don't remember why I even agreed to this interview. Hear this, young man. I had no idea. It was clear she was shaken up, but how could I have known? I just supposed she regretted letting things go too far. That's still what I think," said Elizabeth Peterson, seventy-five years old, in her palatial estate near Wayzata, Minnesota. Fifty years earlier, following the tragic death of her parents in a car accident, Ms. Peterson had diversified her family's business, then a commercial broadcaster in radio, by taking a risk on a new invention from some man named Farnsworth. Residents of the Great Lakes region during the 1950s may recall that *I Love Lucy* was often "Brought to you by our friends at Good Afternoon!"

Without looking at anyone, Ramsey, hair disheveled and eyeliner smeared, walked through the crowded party, out the door, down the stairs, and onto a sidewalk of Christopher Street. It took all of her effort not to crumple sobbing to the ground.

Take a deep breath, she told herself, taking a deep breath. Everything has its place, a place where it belongs. Pain was the sensation of something being out of place. Nothing more. Disorder could always be ordered. The bean could always be put back in the king cake. Ramsey took another deep breath. The inside of her felt empty, hollowed out, an echo waiting for a scream.

Ramsey needed a cigarette. Despite the trembling of her hands, she managed to open her clutch, inside of which, next to a Bond Arms derringer, she found her pack of Luckies. Lighting one proved more difficult. The flame from her lighter kept slipping out of alignment with the end of her cigarette. Finally she got it going. Beneath a streetlamp, its light sieved by the branches and foliage of an overgrown pin oak, Ramsey slowly exhaled. Her gaze was unfocused but aimed toward the street, where, on the other side, her brother Lance stared back, the sight of him obstructed by smoke.

How long had his sister been standing there? Lance figured it was clearly long enough for her to have seen him walk out of the sporting house. Of course he would end up getting caught his very first time. He never should have come to this place.

Just as he was about to cross the street and try to explain, his sister threw down her cigarette, hailed a taxi, and sped off into the darkness uptown. Lance watched as her cab broke apart a column of gutter steam. It soon disappeared in traffic. Unsure of what had just happened, he began to walk through the Village, trying to figure why Ramsey had not spoken or waved to him or even shaken her head in disapproval. She had to have seen him. At the entrance to Washington Square, crossing the threshold of its archway, Lance decided the whole thing was typical Ramsey, a maneuver to get him riled. She wanted him to wonder if she had seen him. That way she knew he would torture himself about what he had done. God damn her. How would she have him live? Celibacy was plain unnatural. Onan's solution solved nothing. Across the street, a young woman with marcelled hair stepped out of a brownstone, followed soon after by three other women, a redhead and two brunettes, wearing clothes so tightly fitted they could have served as riding habits.

Okay, fine, all right! Lance thought. He shouldn't have paid for it. At the south end of the park, noting the laughter from tea-rooms and nightclubs a few blocks away, he decided his trip to the sporting house tonight had been his first, his only, and his last. Ramsey had won again.

For a number of years Lance Forster would stand by his vow. In May of 1947, however, he spent an evening with one Patty Simpson of St. Louis, Missouri, who surprised him the next morning by requesting fifty dollars for what he had thought were innocent, nonvocational services. Nine months later she gave him some even more surprising news. The subsequent adoption of the child by Lance's sister would, ironically and fatefully, reconcile the Forster twins after more than a decade of ill will. Ramsey came to discover she had needed a daughter in her life as assuredly as her father had wanted a new addition to the next generation of Forsters. Who else would carry on the family legacy?

2.6

Fortuneless Son—Now a Word from Our Sponsors— The Horns of a Dilemma—No More Fizz

In 1984, Ronald Reagan, fortieth president of the United States, promised voters, "It's morning again in America." He claimed that more people were employed than ever before in the country's history. He claimed that on each day that year 6,500 men and women would get married and nearly 2,000 families would buy new homes. He claimed that interest rates as well as inflation were half of what they'd been four years earlier. "Under the leadership of President Reagan," noted the television commercial that would lead to his landslide reelection, "our country is prouder and stronger and better." In September of that year, Harold Forster repeated those words in his mind as he arrived at work, duct tape securing one arm of his eyeglasses, button-up oxford from JCPenney mired with sweat prints, and leather fixative holding his shoe soles together.

The worn tires on his pickup slid a foot through gravel as its rusty gasket left a trail of oil spots on the ground. Harold was in too much of a hurry to give it mind. He was half an hour late. At nine thirty in the morning just north of Batesville, Mississippi, he started his day as proprietor of the Panola Cola Historical Museum by unlocking the doors with his key ring and flipping the light switch to reveal shelves of Forster's Delicious Fizzy, their crown caps furred with dust.

"The Forsters lost their entire fortune during the 1970s. Your brother committed suicide after investing in a Detroit venture two months prior to the fuel crisis. Your nephew saw the stocks drop 90 percent with the introduction of PanCola Too after his controversial takeover as CEO of the company," a *New York Times* reporter had said to Harold years earlier during an interview for the Business Day section. "Your sister died in a car accident on the Pacific Coast Highway with a criminally high blood-alcohol level. Perhaps most tragic of all, your older brother, once considered a presidential hopeful, died of an accidental gunshot wound on your family's estate. Have I missed anything, Mr. Forster?"

Harold wiped the countertop for dust. He turned on the overhead fan and tuned the radio to his station. He drew the venetian blinds and hung the WE'RE OPEN sign. Afterward, while eating an early lunch, Harold sat on a hickory stool behind the front desk and laid out cards for a game of solitaire. Each round he came close but never quite achieved the pattern he had in mind. Around four o'clock, he almost had the perfect composition of kings, jacks, queens, and jokers when the door opened with a jangle of its cowbell.

"Rats."

Despite his initial reaction, Harold was wracked with joy on seeing a family enter the museum, a husband and wife, Peter and Claire, as well as their daughter, Rose, and two sons, Jones and Brooks. Five visitors in one day! Such an occasion Harold could barely recall. The family was on the last dogleg of a road trip to the father's hometown of Memphis, where his aunt had recently passed away from a coronary. Formerly a failed novelist but now a successful biographer, Peter could have afforded plane tickets from the family's current city of residence, Austin, Texas, but instead felt a road trip would help him and his wife bond with their sons, twelve and fourteen, and their daughter, nine. Success for the family could be discerned on closer inspection. From Claire's wrist hung an eighteen-carat tennis bracelet from Cartier. An alligator gaped its jaw on Jones's polo, and a man rode horseback on Brooks's broadcloth. Beneath Rose's dress shone the patent leather of dance shoes bought for private lessons. Three months after Harold's death, two dozen marble-print boxes full of registration ledgers, each filed with impressive precision according to month, would identify not only this family but every child, woman, and man who had made footfall through the museum.

The Maitland children had never heard of Panola Cola. Their father, interviewed on October 12, 1989, while on a book tour, could not believe it. "About thirty miles away from Memphis we passed the sign along the side of the road. The kids go, 'What's PanCola?' Can you believe that? So I pulled off the interstate and said I'd show them what's PanCola. I mean, it was a staple of my childhood. Guess what? After that visit I actually gave some thought to writing a book on it. Is yours going to be fiction or nonfiction?"

At the museum, Peter Maitland asked Harold about ticket prices, and without a word, Harold pointed to the chalkboard sign behind him, on the cloudy black surface of which was written, "Five dollars for the nickel tour."

"Is that per person," Peter said, "or all-inclusive?"

"Five dollars for the nickel tour," Harold said in a whisper, pondering the integrity of his brogans. "Five dollars for the nickel tour."

Peter took account of his family before placing a twenty on the countertop. With an arch smile he said to keep the change. Harold rang up the cash register and placed the twenty in its slot. His father had always claimed he wasn't much for sums.

Harold stepped from behind the desk, saying, "Follow me, step this way," with a showman's flourish, and situated the needle on a turntable. He led the family just two feet before stopping in front of the nearest wall. At the start of Harold's speech, memorized through years of repetition, the record player issued the first of six commercials that had once borne proof of PanCola's sponsorship of WMAQ's *Amos 'n' Andy* program from 1929 to 1934. *Welcome to our program, folks. Know what Amos and Andy enjoy before going on air?* In the first photograph, a group of field hands, sweaty from a long day, sat on the back of a wagon as it lumbered forward, each of them clutching a glass bottle, and in the next photograph, three more well-to-do men, hatted and suspendered and groomed, stood in agrarian gentility before the arcade of a Forster Rex-for-All, shaded from the late-afternoon light of a warm southern day. "This is where it all began for the company," Harold said, "planters and clodhoppers alike cooling off with a cold soda pop." The third photograph featured an extravagant ballroom. Foremost in the picture stood Montgomery Forster, dressed in a tuxedo identical to those of the state senators flanking him, while in the background, clutching the midriff of a cigarette girl, sat Lance Forster beneath a banner for New Year's Eve of 1939. "Things were flying high for the PanCola dynasty. At least till America entered the war a couple of years later." In the next five photographs, a veritable flip-book of hard-won capitalism, billowy pillars of gray soot reached for the heavens from smokestacks atop a newly built factory, caravans of shipping trucks held back traffic on a long stretch of highway, a deliveryman refilled a vending machine, a laundry woman chugged at a dripping bottle, and thousands of pennants at a football stadium bore the logo for one of the most internationally recognizable brands. "Everyone the world over wanted a can of Pan," said Harold. A photograph of the Avenue des Champs-Élysées, most likely taken in Paris well before the occupation, featured two famous celebrities, an actress black and expatriate and a socialite white and affluent, embracing in the shadow of the Arc de Triomphe, a handful of pedestrians near them marveling at the spectacle of one, the other, or both. Harold said, "Miss Ramsey Forster was a special friend of the Creole Goddess." In the last photograph, whose caption penciled at the bottom, "Panola County, Mississippi, September 1914," has never been verified by historians, the Forster family posed before their home. They were a handsome bunch. Going gray at his temples, Houghton, thirty-eight, kept an arm on the shoulder of his blond wife, Annabelle, thirty-nine, while their children, Montgomery, twelve, Haddy, ten, Lance, three, and Ramsey, three, sat at their feet, each dressed in white linen. "The Panola Cola Company was still private at this time," Harold told his guests, "but the family had just the wealth to build their new home." At those words, the record on the turntable began its last commercial—*That's all from Amos and Andy this evening, folks, but sit tight for a word from our sponsor*—as Harold Forster led the Maitland family to the Panola Cola Historical Museum's second floor.

"What happened to those people in the pictures," Rose, the youngest, asked, "the mommy and daddy and the brothers and sister?"

Harold said, "They're long gone."

"That's sad."

"Yessum."

On their climb up the rickety stairs, Peter and Claire, ignoring their two boys roughhousing with each other, exchanged a look that conveyed the question *What's wrong with him?* Peter drew circles with his finger around his ear, prompting Claire to give him a slap on the shoulder to stifle her laugh. Jones wet-willied Brooks.

The Attic of Advertisements contained all kinds of memorabilia for PanCola. Across the room, Frank Sinatra stood beside

Elvis Presley, one-dimensional and corrugated-stock, both hold-ing an open bottle of "The Sweetest Thing Around." Five "Panola Heat Wave" clocks read the time as "A Hair Above Thirsty!" A calendar from 1972 showcased a bottle of CitraPan, and a calendar from 1948 pictured a bottle of Mr. Pan, and a calendar from 1966 depicted a bottle of DietPan. On one wall, an original oil paint-ing, commissioned from Norman Rockwell during his prime, por-trayed a 1950s housewife playfully withholding a tasty treat from her daughter and son, their one line of speech, written in an air bubble, the soon-to-be catchphrase, "Can of Pan, Please!" while on another wall, the headline ONLY THE BEST FOR OUR BOYS floated above a scene, its design reminiscent of the WPA ads prevalent in years past, of American soldiers finding a surprise beverage in their GI rations. The two brothers had themselves a fine time. In front of the shelving, Jones fiddled with the ceramic figurines of the "Pan-Cola Tooth Fairy" until one of them shattered to pieces against the floor, and next to the window, Brooks left smudge marks on a rare cutout from *Photoplay* in which Jean Harlow "Dares You" to try a glass of Panola Cola. Harold Forster found himself at what his mother used to call the Horns of Dilemma. He liked to have had a fit. These were paying customers, but they were ruining his legacy. At the funeral for Imogene Forster, whose death, as with all the others that had preceded it, Harold considered his ultimate failure to keep his family safe, a team of lawyers had informed him that, despite the family's once great fortune, all that was left of his birthright fit easily into the two-story house built by Harold's grandfather. "Mostly trinkets of little worth," one had said, "but maybe of sentimental value." Since that day so many years ago, Harold had managed to renovate the house, arrange each of his family's artifacts for effect, and found the Panola Cola Historical Museum. And just look at how these boys were treating it.

"Now, after years of tragedy, you, the only Forster never to sit on the board of your family's company, you, the only Forster left alive after your niece passed of cancer, you are all that remains of a family that used to be spoken of in the same breath as the Hearsts and Rockefellers," the *New York Times* reporter had said to Harold Forster. "For the past few years you have been the proprietor and sole employee of a museum dedicated to your family's company. You work as a handyman for your apartment complex in exchange for discount rent. Not to mention, you have never been married and do not have any children. So I guess my real question is a very simple one. Was it worth it?"

Only the littlest of the Maitland children, Rose, showed any respect for the PanCola history. Harold appreciated Rose. She reminded him of his sister, but he didn't enjoy thinking of her. It was too much for him. At the conclusion of the tour, Harold told the Maitland family, "We enjoyed having y'all as our guests on this fine day. Please tell your friends." Peter and Claire took that as ample sign to lead their children down the stairs, through the main level, and toward the door.

"We appreciate it," Peter said, thinking this guy really meant his bit about the nickel tour. It hardly seemed worth that much. "See you next time."

Either Brooks or Jones asked to try a PanCola, to which Harold replied there were no more left. One of the boys said, "What a gyp," but Harold couldn't tell which. On the way to their station wagon, Claire Maitland told her son to watch his mouth, secretly glad that somebody had the nerve. Harold flagged Rose.

"I think you got something stuck in your ear," he said before performing the only magic trick he knew. "Would you look at that?" Harold handed Rose a magnetic bottle cap labeled PC SODA. "For your refrigerator. Good to hold up drawings."

"Thank you, mister."

"You're so welcome."

"Bye-bye."

"Have a safe trip now."

Harold went inside and then came back out. On the front porch of the Panola Cola Historical Museum, he watched as the dust kicked up by the station wagon caught the glow of September twilight. The evening air had grown sepia as blood. He held on to a cold bottle of PanCola, one from the last shipment made before the company filed for bankruptcy, the rest of which he kept in a cooler out back. Harold took a seat on the porch steps, his view of the countryside a picture show of grackles perched in beeches, horses grazing, cows lowing, water turkeys swimming amid water oaks, and lightning bugs like holes punched in a stage backdrop. He pried off the bottle cap, making less the sound of a sneeze and more that of biting into an apple, and took the first sip. Sweetness. Frost. Vapor. Memories. He loved these moments more than anything else left in his life. At another dusk of another day, Harold sat on the porch of his museum, alone, drinking from a soda long gone flat.

PART 3

3.1

Histor in the Greek—Breakfast of Champions

At seven in the morning on March 12, 1985, Robert Vaughn, while sitting on the toilet, thought, *If everyone's life has an arc, then all of history is a story, in hindsight or in foresight but never in both.* It could be an okay line, he figured, with a little teasing out. A scholarship student, frequent dean's list honoree, and philosophy major at Millsaps College in Jackson, Mississippi, Robert had a paper due tomorrow for his class "The Machine in the Ghost: Antiquity and Infinite Regression." He had finished a draft, but it still needed work. Should he note how those two words, *story* and *history,* share the same etymological root? Robert couldn't decide. He balled some toilet paper, reached between his legs, and wiped himself clean.

His breath grew visible in the cold air as he walked into the living area of his trailer. Every witch in the county had put on her brass brassiere. Robert folded his arms around his chest, upset he had forgotten to fix the heater.

He'd inherited the singlewide when his father died of a heart attack last year. Prior to his death, Jimmy Vaughn had been a racist, a womanizer, a drunk, and a card cheat, in other words, as his only child was sometimes known to say, a Mississippian. The Fleetwood sat on a half-acre pecan grove in Yazoo County. Although Robert did not know the specifics, his father told him the land had been left to their family by Henry Vaughan, a distant relative, wealthy plantation owner, and namesake of Vaughan, Mississippi, the nearby town where Casey Jones, "right high-wheeler of mighty fame," had ridden his train to the end of the line.

More than just a vowel in his last name separated Robert from that withered branch of his family. He would be the first to admit as much. Just look around. A dented can of Charles Chips on top of the refrigerator, fly tape hung from a light fixture, windows lined with rusty trinkets found in an old feedlot out back, a La-Z-Boy with holes, a console Magnavox: these accommodations were not exactly what one would expect of a man whose ancestral name graced the town charter. Robert considered it fitting that the grove on which his trailer sat rarely yielded enough pecans to warrant a single bottle of Karo.

"How's tricks, pussy hound?"

On the couch lay Hellion, an eleven-year-old golden retriever who, after an unfortunate encounter with a combine, had continually proved, every time he lapped at the face of a stranger or took a dirt bath on a sunny day, that there was no such thing as an unhappy three-legged dog. He gave up his belly for a scratch. "You be a good little gimp while I'm out," Robert said while doing as requested, the furry stump of Hellion's hind leg twitching, an invisible limb trotting along an invisible treadmill. "No wild parties. Leftovers are in the fridge."

Robert grabbed his book bag and keys from the kitchen table and left without locking the door. Outside was overcast. To either side of him as he walked through his front yard lay the dioramic detritus of his own childhood: a rusted tricycle halfway sunk into the dried bed of a mud puddle, flat footballs, flat soccer balls, flat basketballs, a jungle gym turned birdhouse, a birdhouse turned squirrel feeder, GI Joes that had been unearthed like arrowheads by a recent hard rain. Nothing gave a shadow on that gray morning.

In his car, a navy Buick won by his father in a game of Texas hold 'em, Robert turned the ignition, hoping the old girl's luck would last. The engine giddyapped to life after four increasingly nervous tries. Lukewarm air sputtered from the vents as he made his usual turn, Fugates Road onto Berryville, though he was too preoccupied to worry about the temperature. Robert was worried about Marunga. He was scheduled to meet with his thesis adviser later that day. Despite the epithet Leopold Marunga was called around school, Robert knew "Professor Cowabunga" to be far more temperamental than laid-back, the type who would have a student expelled, write him a glowing letter of rec, forget his name, or guarantee a graduation summa cum laude at the drop of a hat or the toss of a mortarboard. Who could tell how that man would react when, on asking his supposedly favorite student about a thesis topic, a thesis topic in a field that was essentially the study of thought, he received an answer of "I can't think of one"?

Robert pulled into a gas station named Campbell's. Inside the store, a clapboard affair arrayed in Golden Flake–branded racks of road food, he nodded at the attendant, half of whose face was obscured by the morning's *Clarion-Ledger*.

The attendant asked, "Borden and MoonPie?"

"Borden and MoonPie," answered Robert.

From the candy aisle he picked up a vanilla MoonPie, and from a cooler in the back he grabbed a pint of Borden milk. They were his usual breakfast. On his way to the front counter, though, Robert passed an open bin of ice, its surface studded with glistening cans of soda, Pepsi-Cola and RC Cola and Coca-Cola. He suddenly had a craving for one. After returning the milk, Robert picked up a can of Coke, ice still clinging to its lid. He figured what the hell. Today was his birthday. He deserved it.

3.2

On This Day in History—The Butterfly Effect—"Who knows what evil lurks within the hearts of men?"— As Goes General Motors So Goes the Nation—From Newton's Cradle to the Grave—Chaos Theory— Secret Ingredient?

On February 29, 1932, two years before Lance wandered through Greenwich Village, contrite and lonesome, and Ramsey rode uptown in a taxicab, trying to keep her hands from shaking; eight years after Monty sat at a café in Ecuador, sipping on a soda called Raiz Dulce; and fifty-two years before Harold gave the Maitland family a tour of the Panola Cola Museum, Fiona and Annabelle Forster were drinking hot toddies on the porch of The Sweetest Thing.

"Enjoy your leap day?" Fiona said, taking in the evening view.

"Feels strange, doesn't it?" said Annabelle. "It's like we're living in a day that doesn't really exist. A fictional day."

"An extra one never hurts."

"Or like we're trapped inside a mathematical course correction."

Steam rose from Fiona's mug as she took a sip. "I'm afraid to ask, but still no grandchildren on the way?"

"No, ma'am."

Fiona was afraid to ask not because the answer was probably no but that it might be yes. Ever since the birth of her son, she had been certain the Malediction would come for her family, if not Houghton then his children, if not his children then their children. So far it hadn't. Houghton was doing well with his fizzy water, and all of his children seemed happy in their lives. The problem was Fiona would forever be trapped on the Old World side of the nebulous juncture at which a family in America becomes an American family. She knew herself well enough to know that. Prosperity to her being just another word for liability, she had never managed to shake the belief that what rises may fall, what falls might rise, and fate could not care less about keeping a balance.

"More tea?" asked a house girl, holding a kettle of bourbon, honey, lemon, and not a drop of tea, to which Fiona answered, "Yes, dear."

Annabelle took a refill as well. "Would you be a darling and bring us some of those baked goods that came in this morning?" she said to the girl. Once they were alone again on the porch, Annabelle turned to Fiona and said, "So hard to find good help these days," then gave a nod toward the view, as though it were a testament to her standards. That evening the front lawn, overrun with hawk moths and dragonflies hovering above its flower beds and mimosa trees, was far quieter than it had been the night years earlier when, unbeknownst to Annabelle, her daughter had returned home from the Moonglade Serenade and briefly mistaken Harold's wails for the sound of cicadas. "Took us forever to find that one." Annabelle sipped at her toddy.

Despite the cheery pitch to her voice, a put-on for her mother-in-law's sake, the lady of the house was in no mood. It was Houghton again. This week he was out in California, ostensibly to visit the producers of *Amos 'n' Andy*—there had been reports Pepsodent wanted in as sponsors—but the real purpose of the trip was for Houghton to take a meeting with RKO Pictures. He hoped to convince the studio executives that the verisimilitude of their characters would be best served if those characters were portrayed enjoying the kind of beverage real people drank. What did real people drink? PanCola, of course.

Annabelle was upset because product placement had been her idea. God save the mark should Houghton give her an ounce of credit! She had even helped set up the meeting with the studio. Last month in New York, while getting a cocktail at a former speak, she and Houghton had bumped into Joe Kennedy. "Well, if it isn't the belch manufacturer," he had said, to which Annabelle, taking account of Joe's date, pretty as a Poiret model and just as young, responded before Houghton had a chance: "Evening, Joseph. How's your wife?" For the rest of the night, Joe was like a whipped puppy, docile and obedient, except instead of wagging his tail he agreed to liaise between Houghton and the contacts he'd made while brokering the formation of RKO.

So now, with her husband in Hollywood trading on her scheme, Annabelle was left at home with the exciting, glamorous job of entertaining her mother-in-law. Not that she didn't like Fiona. She admired her. Fiona was like a Norn who had quit the trade, fed up with the absurdities of Gods and Men. That night at Eden, she even showed some of her old skills, managing, it seemed, to read Annabelle's thoughts.

"Don't worry about Houghton. I'm sure he's behaving himself out there," Fiona said. "He misses you every time he's gone more than a day. That's the pure D truth."

"I know."

"How's your father getting by? There's a man I worry about."

"My father?" said Annabelle. Last she heard he was sitting in a run-down café on Toulouse Street, its proprietor, half asleep behind the guichet, pouring him a glass of Amer Picon every quarter of the hour. On the rare occasion someone he knew stopped by, Royal would claim to be enjoying a quick drink before attending *Lohengrin,* even though it had been fifteen years since the opera house burned down. Annabelle said, "He's doing well."

"Good to hear."

Even though she could tell Annabelle was lying about her father—that man had been more brined than a turkey at the wedding—Fiona decided not to pry further into the concern. The girl had always done the same for her. Ever since the day Fiona had walked into the kitchen and mistakenly thought Tewksbury had fallen asleep, Houghton had been trying to convince her to pack up, move across town, and live in one of the spare rooms at The Sweetest Thing. Each time he pressed the issue too far Annabelle would give him a look that meant stop.

The fact of it was Fiona could not leave the house Tewksbury had built for her. Memories decorated it like furniture. Between those walls she had first realized love is not a dot but a line. Under that roof she had first realized love is not a bang but a hum. She'd come to those realizations when, cleaning out the closet, she found Tewksbury's old medical bag, so covered in dust its leather was more gray than black. He had lost it the day their son was born. On the floor of the closet, where she had sunk clutching the bag in her arms, Fiona cried not because it had belonged to her husband, but that he would never hear her say, "You won't believe what I found!"

Onto the porch walked the house girl, in her hands a tray of assorted sweets, pralines and chess squares and nougat, each piece nestled in a foil baking cup. She set the tray on a small table. "We're gracious," said Annabelle, meaning, "You're dismissed."

The hour was getting late. Fiona's skin had begun to turn seersucker from the evening chill. If she didn't excuse herself soon, she knew, her daughter-in-law would insist she stay the night. That fresh nougat, though, did look delicious. Fiona's parents used to sell a special variety at their sweet shop. She had not eaten any since crossing the Atlantic.

"Just one piece. Then I have to go." The candy was wonderful, Fiona had to admit, better than the kind sold at Wadsworth Confections, not too chewy, not too soft. "Who'd you say made this again?"

"Oh, some new bakery. I don't recall the name."

Butterfly Bakery was located near a plantation called China Grove. Several decades earlier, the plantation had been won in a game of Mr. Pan poker, the story of which inspired a screenplay, *Five Thousand Acre Hand,* by a young writer with few credits at the time, Clarence Braithwaite, whose subsequent career was less than prestigious, including work on the teen sex comedies *Pay the Queen* and *Frat Daddy.* The director of *Frat Daddy* moved on to more reputable fare with *Killing Mr. Tiffee,* a fictionalized account of the Dixie Mafia focused on the unsolved murder of Larry Tiffee in Lauderdale County, a case said to have been followed religiously by the ailing, bed-prone former governor Paul B. Johnson Jr., whose father, Paul B. Johnson Sr., half a century before the murder case, secretly invited Montgomery Forster to dinner at Lusco's Restaurant in Greenwood, Mississippi, to discuss an issue Johnson described as "a private matter for a private booth." They were seated at nine o'clock in the evening on February 29, 1936.

Once the waiter had closed the curtains to their booth, the two men studied their menus by candlelight, neither of them saying a word, their shadows flickering on the booth's calcimined walls.

Johnson broke the silence without looking up from his menu. "Hear you were quite the war hero."

"That's what they say."

"I also hear you enlisted illegally at age fifteen."

Montgomery was surprised at how surprised he was by the comment. Tonight, even though he didn't know why he'd been invited, he had expected more cloak than dagger, a desperate request for a campaign donation, perhaps, in a setting that would save face. "Where might you have heard that?" he asked, honestly wanting to know the answer. Since his time in the war almost two decades earlier, Monty had graduated from college and law school, worked as in-house counsel for his father's company, run a successful campaign for public office, and, over the past three years, served as district attorney, never once being questioned about his military career. How did this man uncover what Houghton Forster had paid so handsomely to hide?

"My investigators are nothing if not thorough."

"I'm flattered by your interest, Mr. Johnson, but how about we ignore the fact I have a D.S.C. in a shoe box back home that says I served my country with gallantry in the extreme, regardless of my age on enlisting, and instead let's focus on the question of just why you had your thorough investigators look into me."

"Know what the French who fought at Belleau Wood nicknamed you?"

"Don't know, don't care."

"*L'ombre vivante*," Johnson said, unaware those same words had, a few years after the war, been used for a cloaked vigilante. Speculation remains even now as to whether Montgomery Forster's exploits in World War I inspired the character introduced in print as "The Living Shadow."

"You're not answering my question." One fold at a time Monty opened his napkin. He'd always found it calming to be fastidious in small operations. "Why did you have me investigated?"

From the other side of the curtain came the voice of their waiter. Johnson answered him by saying they were indeed ready to order. The waiter, materializing before them like a stage headliner, held a notepad, on which he wrote what Johnson ordered for them both, oyster soup to start, porterhouse for the main course, and a bowl of ambrosia.

"Step up from hoop-cheese sandwiches, don't you think?" said Johnson after the waiter had left. "As a child I used to dream of eating at a place like this."

"Me, too."

"Not to be rude, Montgomery, but that's a lie."

During the time it took for their soup to arrive, Paul B. Johnson Sr. told an abridged version of his life story, starting with his childhood in Scott County. He grew up poor. His family slept on rope beds four to a room, sharing a linsey-woolsey blanket, cedar smudge keeping the mosquitoes away. Everyone knew to check for wriggle-tails before drinking the cistern water. The boys from town, seeing his bib-and-braces and thrice-handed-down boots, would taunt Johnson. "Runty pig, runt, runt, runty pig." He never forgot those words while in law school, after being elected a circuit judge, and throughout his three terms in the U.S. Congress. To help the other runt pigs of the world, he decided to run for governor, but that sort of benevolent motive did not guarantee success. Thus far he had lost twice. In retrospect, Johnson told Monty, he felt that what his campaigns had lacked wasn't "money from someone but rather someone moneyed," the type of person who had never eaten hoop cheese, a representative of voters from the other half.

"Which is where I come in," Monty said.

"Which is where you come in."

"So in other words, you'd like me to be some kind of a stand-in for the upper crust," said Monty, to which Johnson replied, "What I need you to be, Living Shadow, is my shining diamond."

The oyster soup did little to settle the queasiness those words brought about in Monty. Ever since the incident in Ecuador, he had tried to keep a low profile, despite pressure from his father, who'd told him, correctly it seemed, that serving as D.A. would be a good stepping-stone. Monty stirred his soup. "But this is Mississippi. We won't be running on the same ticket."

"You just answered your own question. This is Mississippi. Never been a campaign in this state not made possible by handshakes in a back room. You publicly support me and I'll publicly support you. Two boats rising on the same tide."

"And you're not worried," Monty said, "reporters might find out what your investigators found out?"

Johnson chuckled paternally. "Of course not. I hope they find out! You're a war hero, Montgomery. That you enlisted while still basically a child makes you even more of one."

On the other side of the curtain could be heard the sound of sizzling meat. "Careful with the plates," the waiter said as he parted the curtain, removed the soup bowls, and placed a steak before each man. "They're hot." He set two large knives on the table before leaving them to it.

"Not to mention," Johnson said, cutting into his porterhouse, "you're a family man." He paused with a bite held midair on his fork. "How's your little girl? I heard about what she's going through. So awful. So awful."

Monty swallowed, picturing Imogene. What kind of man was he

to have gone the entire night without once thinking of his daughter? Just hearing her name made his chest curl into itself. One morning earlier that year, Imogene had been unable to get out of bed because, as she put it, a ghost was sitting on her legs. She was officially diagnosed with polio the following week. Over the past six months Monty had gotten Imogene all the best treatments, renting out a floor at the Mayo Clinic for the season, leasing a Douglas DC-3 to have specialists flown in, but none of it worked. Each of the doctors told Montgomery it was best to move on, and so now he had to watch helplessly as his little girl learned how to be unable to walk.

Even though her father would not be around to see her as an adult, Imogene Forster, indomitable and generous, pragmatic and intelligent, would grow up to be an extraordinary one. She wheeled herself to the podium for her speech as valedictorian of her class at Radcliffe. She refused to take off her glasses when being photographed for the cover of *Time*. During her relatively short tenure as CEO of PanCola, Imogene managed to increase sales through a strategy known as "cola warfare," defying not only the supposed limitations of her gender and infirmity but also the fact that, despite protests from many board members, she did not inherit a controlling share of the company on her grandfather's death. Her brother did.

That brother had not yet been conceived the evening of the dinner at Lusco's. The necessary circumstances, Monty's consumption of a fifth of whisky sent to him by a business associate in Ashbrook, England, and his wife's perforation via knitting needle of her diaphragm, were still eight years away. Known more for her exquisite beauty than for her skills of deduction, Montgomery's wife, Sarah, giving birth as a new widow, would christen the child with the name she had so often heard her husband mumbling in his sleep. She assumed it was merely a word he found comforting to hear.

Nicholas Forster was born on August 12, 1944.

"Last week they had her fitted for a chair. The doctors say she's taking to it quicker than any child they've seen," Montgomery said to Johnson, hoping the splinter in his throat could not be heard as readily as it was felt.

As a distraction Monty focused on his steak, the pat of butter melting on top of it, the cracked peppercorns and sea salt big as crumbs. Steam rose from the plate like a charmed snake. Johnson described the logistics of the campaign as both men whittled their meals down to the T-bone.

The waiter replaced their plates with bowls of ambrosia. "We'll take two teacups—empty—please and thank you," Johnson said.

"Shall I bring any ice, sir?"

"That won't be necessary."

Following the advent of teacups to their table, both men grew disinterested in the bowls of pineapple, mandarin oranges, coconut, and marshmallows. Johnson lifted a bottle-shaped paper bag from his side, unscrewed it, and filled each of their cups with three fingers of White Label.

"Your strategy sounds reasonable." Monty took a long sip. "I like what you said about runt pigs. You could even take it further."

"How so?"

"If that's your people, be their champion."

Three and a half years later, Paul B. Johnson Sr., "Champion of the Runt Pig People," would be elected the forty-sixth governor of Mississippi, a position through which he gave historically unprecedented support to the state's day laborers, sharecroppers, and tenant farmers, but at eleven in the evening on February 29, 1936, the future governor, smiling as he refilled their teacups, asked his future lieutenant, "How about you let me handle the campaign slogans?"

. . .

WOULDN'T YOU LOVE TO WALK A MILE IN HIS SHOES?

On his way out of the liquor store, Lance Forster read the advertisement for Johnnie Walker hanging above the door—an onyx-black banner with the gold silhouette of a tailcoated man in midstride—and as he made his way back to his hotel, the Jacobs-Allen, he thought that, yes, in fact, he *would* love to walk a mile in Mr. Walker's shoes. Anything to get out of this damn town.

He'd been in Detroit a week now. It hadn't been a particularly pleasant week, either, sitting in his room alone and every few days his associate calling to say that, sorry, the meeting had to be postponed. Lance despised being told what *not* to do more than he despised being told what to do. He would've left town after the first postponement if only the deal weren't so necessary for him.

In the hotel lobby, heading past the orange decor that, no matter the type of material of each part, be it the cloth of the sofas, the plastic of the light fixtures, or the wood of the side tables, seemed to be made entirely of polyester, he noticed the desk clerk, a girl in her twenties, blond and thin and dressed in a (polyester, of course) pantsuit that was just right for someone blond and thin. Lance walked over and said, "Miss—what's your name?"

"Laura."

"Laura, would you have a bucket of ice sent up? Room 1508."

"Of course, sir. Right away."

Lance shifted his package from one arm to the other. The clanking of the bottles he hoped made for a subtle invitation. "Awful busy down here." He looked around at the lobby void of anybody but one bellhop.

"That time of year. February's always slow."

"It won't be February for long. In fact, it wouldn't be now, normally. Today only comes 'round once every four years. It's a day without consequences."

"I guess."

"You could chop down a cherry tree and get away with it."

"A cherry tree?"

"If things don't pick up down here, Laura, feel free to join me. You know the room number."

For the next two minutes, as he strode across the lobby with one arm swinging and waited for the elevator, posed with one hip cocked, Lance figured the girl must be watching him, thinking, *Some people really do have style.*

Still got it, he told himself, even at sixty-one.

He did not still have it. The years had been passive-aggressive to Lance. Not quite cruel and not quite kind, they'd left him bloated, pink faced, and saggy about the jowls, but he still had his hair. On occasion, too, his face, despite the bloating, the pink, and the sagginess, caught a good light, and its wrinkles, properly shadowed, looked distinguished. His eyes remained a brilliant blue even when their whites were cracked by a hangover.

Back in his room, plodding over the shag carpet thick as the sideburns on a hippie, Lance went straight to the bar. He unwrapped and arranged bottles of Vat 69, Imperial, Windsor Canadian, Old Crow, Kessler, and 100 Pipers, all the brands that had been on sale. Lance couldn't tell a difference in the taste anyway. Once the ice arrived—delivered by the bellhop, disappointingly, rather than the desk clerk—he broke a seal, filled a glass, took a sip, and checked his watch. It was 11:30 A.M. His father always said only lushes drank straight liquor before noon. Lance added a splash of tap water to the glass.

The living room of the suite had a large window overlooking the city. Lance studied the snapshot of Detroit. From the window he could see Washington Boulevard stretching out toward the river. Beyond that lay the rest of the country. What was it the GM president had once said? Lance sipped at his drink, trying to think of the line. Eventually it came to him, but in paraphrased form, mutated by his own recall.

As goes PanCola so goes my life.

Ever since 1967, the year his nephew took over the company, Lance had been forced to watch, helpless and outraged, as PanCola's stock plummeted. The little shit thought he could reinvent the wheel. PanCola Too? That was like bonking a driver on the head, replacing his wheels with square blocks, and then betting a fortune he would win the race. Lance blamed his father for having coddled Nick. Raising his grandson had helped Houghton overcome the depression he'd fallen into after Monty decided to clean his gun, it was true, but that did not mean Nick should have been indulged by his grandfather so much more than every Forster who'd preceded him. Sometimes, when he was in a generous mood, Lance thought his nephew suffered the worst fate of any family member: unbridled privilege.

That still didn't excuse him. In the five years Nick had run the company things had gone exactly as one would expect them to go with a man in his twenties at the helm. Sales were down, and profits were low. Panola Cola had dropped to fifth place, for Christ's sake, behind that redneck drink Royal Crown. Lance had gotten out while the getting was terrible. After divesting from the business, he put all his money into a fledgling car manufacturer, Moretti

Motors, which, due to cost overruns and delays in production, was now on the verge of bankruptcy. Today's meeting was their last ditch.

Across the room the phone rang, eliciting a groan from Lance. He figured it was another postponement. "Not again, Jack," he said into the receiver, prompting his sister to respond, "Jack who?"

"Ramsey? What's the matter? You okay?"

"I'm fine. Didn't mean to intrude on you. It's probably nothing. It's just, you haven't heard from Susannah, have you?"

"Why would I hear from Susannah?"

"I know, I know. I'm just worried, is all. Haven't heard from her in a few days. It's nothing, I'm sure. I shouldn't have bothered you."

"Ramsey, I—"

She hung up before her brother could say anything else. At fifteen minutes till nine, daylight verging on sunglasses level, Ramsey stood on the balcony of her home in Los Angeles, trying not to worry over the whereabouts of her only child. She took a sip of weak coffee.

It was silly for her to have called Lance. The whole thing was silly, in fact, especially how it all started. Three days ago, on an afternoon when Susannah stopped by the house, Ramsey had mentioned that the Hannigans, who lived down the street, had seen her, Susannah, having dinner at the Tulip earlier in the week. They said she'd been with a man. "So who is he?" Ramsey asked, casually, she hoped. "Some new boyfriend?" Anger was a rare emotion for her daughter. A self-proclaimed pacifist, vegan, transcendentalist, bohemian, and clairvoyant, in that order, Susannah Forster, perpetually clad in mandala patterns and her hair always spangled with lilac, gave the lie to the notion the 1960s had ended with the Tate murders. For that reason Ramsey was surprised to see Susannah launch into a fury. Her espadrilles thumped on the hardwood as she paced through the house, and beads jangled on her gesticulating wrists. Susannah claimed her mother had sent spies. Over and again she spoke about "him" as if they both knew to whom she referred—"I want to be with him," "You can't stop me from seeing him," "I'm in love with him"—until she spoke one sentence that turned Ramsey's heart into a pair of jagged halves tottering on the floor.

"We're not *actually* related, Mother."

Three days later, after hanging up the phone with her brother, Ramsey still believed the "we" in that sentence had been Susannah and herself, mother and daughter. That was part of the reason she had called Lance. From the day she was born, Susannah had been raised thinking Lance was nothing but her uncle. Ramsey still felt that was the right thing to have done. The problem was she had also done something she now thought was absolutely wrong. On Susannah's sixteenth birthday, Ramsey had sat her down, poured them both a glass of wine, and, like a fool, told her she was adopted.

She had not said Lance was her real father. After three long days of no word from her little girl, though, Ramsey thought perhaps Susannah, somehow intuiting the relation, might have reached out to him. It was ridiculous, she knew, too much of a stretch.

In the kitchen Ramsey refilled her coffee and looked out the window, at its view of the Hollywood Hills. On first moving here, she'd grasped one aspect of Los Angeles quicker than any other, how it was all scenery and no scene, background with no foreground, a vista without a perspective. She wondered if it had been a mistake to raise a child in this city. Would Susannah have become a different sort of woman if she had grown up in the South? Ramsey's childhood had been so unique, eating pain perdu and hopping john and pear salad, getting her clothes filthy from playing all day in gumball dirt, building forts with broken locust posts and cottonseed hulls. It made her feel immune to this world of false superiority. Whenever someone condescendingly asked her to "say 'y'all' again," she happily deigned to fulfill the request.

The day was turning into a gorgeous one, Ramsey thought while sipping her coffee. Sunlight filled the house she had managed to afford following her divorce from Arthur not because of alimony, nor even with help from her father, but with royalties from *The Adventures of Catfish the Dog* (vols. 1–12), a series of children's books she had written about a French zoo full of animals that consider humans their pets. Most of the books had begun as bedtime stories she had told Susannah.

"So that's why you made Catfish an orphan," said Susannah on her sixteenth birthday. "That's why you had him adopted by the zoo. As some ridiculous way to prepare me for the truth."

"No, of course not, honey!"

"The family's always treated me different. Like I'm not even one of you. Now it makes sense. Now it makes so much sense. All of you knew I wasn't really a Forster by blood."

But honey, you are! Ramsey had wanted to scream. *You are a Forster!*

The phone sat on an end table by the sofa, next to her two framed Caldecott Medals. Even though she knew it was just as foolish an idea as it had been ten minutes earlier, Ramsey thought of calling Lance again, asking him, begging him to let her tell Susannah the truth, that she was his daughter, a genuine part of their family, a Forster by blood, flesh, and bone.

He wouldn't have picked up even if she'd called. At that same moment, half a continent and two time zones away, Lance was standing in his room at the Jacobs-Allen, fourth drink of the day in his hand, listening to Jack Moretti, CEO of Moretti Motors, describe how to launder money. None of it sank in. The Lance Forster from fifteen years ago would have dissected every detail, especially given that the plan had been devised by somebody like Jack Moretti. A former executive at Ford, youngest in the history of the company, Jack was known not for his ruthlessness and creativity but rather, as noted in a *BusinessWeek* cover story, for his "creative ruthlessness." Lance could throw the man farther than he trusted him. That was why he had insisted on being at the meet. Nonetheless, as Jack Moretti went over the venture they were about to involve Moretti Motors in, Lance only heard the last part. "In a nutshell, we put their guys on the payroll, they give us money to pay them, and we keep a sizable cut. Placement, *a partridge,* layering, *a pear tree,* integration."

Right as Lance was about to ask, *Who's "they" again?* the answer to his question knocked at the door.

Jack took the lead. Brushing a hand through his mop of hair that had been the color of oyster shells since his twenties, an effective disguise for his relatively young age in the business world, he looked through the peephole and opened the door halfway, after which he welcomed three men and guided them to the sitting area. All three men wore matching gray suits, white shirts, no ties, high starch, as though they were in some kind of band. The only difference between them was that one carried a briefcase. No member of what Lance thought of as "Pancho Villa and the Bagmen" introduced himself.

If Lance had been listening to Jack earlier, he would have known the men belonged to an outfit originally based in South America, one whose lion-esque territorialism and ferocity in cities like Bogotá and Quito had warranted its nickname, The Pride.

"Get y'all a drink?" Lance said, holding up his own. "Bar's stocked."

"Do you have any sparkling water?"

The man with the briefcase had spoken. Lance told him he thought he could scrounge up a Perrier. At the bar alcove, making the man a sparkling water and himself another whiskey rocks, Lance did not look at his own reflection in the mirror on the back wall, not the swollen eyes, not the bristly cheeks, which upset the FBI agent watching via a camera behind the two-way mirror. He was hoping to get a nice head shot from a direct angle before the deal went down.

"I'm sorry, Pancho, but we're fresh out of lemons and limes," Lance said as he handed the man with the briefcase his drink. The man held the drink without taking a sip, his flat expression the opposite of its content, and Lance returned to his seat.

"The marker?" said the man.

Jack answered, "We have it."

"What's the problem?" Lance stood up, approached the man where he sat on the sofa, patted him on the shoulder, and, stumbling briefly, sat back down. "Don't you fellas trust us with your drug money?" Lance's laughter was not reciprocated.

The leader of the group stared at his shoulder as though it had grown a pair of antlers. Without looking at his partners, he said to Jack, "We would like to know who is this man?"

Jack acted confused for a moment. "Oh, I see. Well, he's you, in a sense." He hitched a thumb toward Lance and then pointed at the briefcase, saying, "That money had to come from somebody. Do you want us to say it came from you? Didn't think so."

Over the next fifteen minutes, Jack and the man had a conversation that, were Lance not in such low cotton and on his fifth glass of Kessler straight, he might have understood, at least enough for it to worry him. An agreement seemed to have been met when the man pushed the briefcase across the shag carpet like the shuttle of a loom. With the nonchalance of a gambler checking his hand, Jack picked up the case, unsnapped its hinges, and stared inside for a moment, whereas Lance, nonchalant in the way of a table bystander, stifled a yawn.

Lance's lack of concern owed a great deal, albeit obliquely, to his lack of a relationship with Susannah. Her birth mother's name was Patty, "not Patricia, just Patty, like the cake," a woman who, at a St. Louis hotel, had given him the short time. Nobody had heard anything from her since she signed the papers, took the check, had the baby, and said she could sometimes be reached through a cousin in Toledo. It felt appropriate to Lance that Susannah be raised by his twin sister, not least of all because Susannah made Ramsey so ridiculously happy. He simply wasn't the fatherly type.

"Ask anyone," Lance always said.

Over the years, he'd watched his daughter grow into a beautiful child—she had dimples, blue eyes, blond hair, and was perfect—but watching her grow up also proved a problem. Ever since he used the image to understand Newtonian physics in high school, Lance had imagined that, inside the part of his chest where a normal heart should have been, resided instead a row of metal spheres suspended from wires. When the sphere on the end swung and struck the row, the spheres in the middle remained stationary and the one at the opposite end swung out and back, repeating the pattern. Tick-tock, tick-tock. Being near his daughter caused the wires to snap and sent the metal spheres plummeting. On her first birthday he lied about an urgent phone call so no one would see the tears he could not hold back. *Snap.* The evening she played the piano for him he used allergies as an excuse. *Snap.* Her first dance recital? Her senior prom? Her high school graduation? *Snap, snap, snap.*

Lance wanted to tell her the truth but was worried about his sister. Who knew how Ramsey would take that? She'd probably consider it a betrayal. Eventually, after years of watching his daughter from afar, Lance had managed to overcome his feelings for her by burying them, so that Susannah, the baby in a crib wriggling her tiny fingers, the little girl curtsying to him by her piano, became an artifact of his subconscious. That solution generated, however, an even worse problem. For Lance, to stop caring about one thing was to stop caring about all things, just as to stop loving one person was to stop loving all people: he could only shut down the assembly line by blowing up the factory. The death of his wife in childbirth ten years ago had swept away whatever rubble that remained.

"Gentlemen, I want you to know that this money, it's not just an investment in some automobile manufacturer. Well then, *in what?* you ask. It's an investment in the American dream," Jack Moretti said to the three men in matching suits. According to a *Rolling Stone* article that would be published in September 1975, "Down and Out in the Paris of the West" by Lucinda Wong, he made the same speech to all potential investors. "I assume you know the name of our first model. The ADM-9. Advanced Development Moretti, ninth iteration since the prototype. I've always liked to think of those letters as standing for something else. The American Dream Machine. Ours is the sports car of the future, stronger, faster, and more beautiful than any before, the quintessence of this country. That's where your money's going. Toot?"

In his hand Jack held a vial of cocaine and offered it to Pancho Villa like a toast. The vial might as well have been a starter pistol. From the door to the hotel room, entering with a key obtained at the front desk, burst a line of six federal agents.

"Stay in your seats. You're under arrest."

Each of the agents carried a badge in one hand, a gun in the other, brandishing both around the room, holding them in the faces of those under arrest. Lance didn't mind the badges. "Would you please get that gun out of my face?" he said. "I don't like guns. I've got a thing about guns."

There was a story as to why.

. . .

Throughout the years following the incident in the woods, Lance would tell people about it, minus key points, as a funny, self-effacing way to illustrate "what a stubborn little shit I am." The story also served as an explanation for why he didn't hunt. "I haven't touched a gun since I was twelve years old," he would say to friends whenever they invited him on hunting trips. "Did I ever tell you the story about the time I jumped the creek?"

That morning it was cold even for February. Under a sky matted in gray, Lance and his father rode side by side on two mares— Peat and Repeat—their rifles tucked into scabbards. Lance was riding Peat. The horse was beautiful, her hair pale white with flecks of brown, milk at the bottom of a cereal bowl. She made for a much lovelier sight than the part of the estate they were now riding through, hoarfrost causing the trees to appear as though they were ghosts of themselves, ground a crosshatch of twigs, buttonbush turned into skeletons, the occasional hog wallow giving off ugly squishing noises when trod by hooves.

Neither father nor son said a word to the other. Lance didn't even know what they were hunting, whether deer or turkey, squirrel or duck, goose, bobcat, rabbit, or quail. Earlier that morning, when his father had woken him, all he'd said was, "Let's go shoot something." Afterward his father had tossed some nankeen trousers on the bed, made a let's-hop-to motion, and resituated on his shoulder a musette bag stocked with breakfast. An hour later they still had not shot a thing.

"How's school?" asked Houghton.

"Fine."

"Good."

Lance flicked his reins. "How's work?"

Much has been written, in other texts more so than this one, about Houghton Forster's willingness to discuss business with his children, no matter their age. He considered it training for their future work, a step toward his goal of creating the nation's quintessential family. So, without any hesitation, Houghton said to Lance, a boy whose face had yet to learn the need of a razor, "Governor Russell's not being particularly helpful with the plant we're about to build down in Biloxi." His son asked why not. "He thinks I've grown too big for my britches. And he's right."

"What does that mean?"

"Time to get bigger britches."

In Houghton's opinion the most overrated American virtue was honesty. His favorite type of person was someone who, if others would not be hurt, had no qualms about cheating. Consider his tactics during the onset of World War II. After the war began, the subcommittee chaired by Senator Edmund Ainsworth yielded its influence to a group as powerful in policy-making as it was innocuous in title, the War Production Boards' Sugar Section. The rivals of PanCola had already greased many of the WPB's members. Such information Houghton did not take well. "Coke and Pepsi? For the love of God. During a championship game, does the coach put in his number two and number three players? Don't fucking think so." He doubled the salaries for his team of lobbyists, assigned a new head of the Panola Cola Export Corporation, hired a Capitol Hill tax lawyer who people joked could escape death, and engaged in all manner of backroom politicking. His efforts were a success. Over the course of the war, seventy-five PanCola bottling plants and hundreds of "jungle fountain units" were constructed throughout the world, particularly in Europe, Africa, and the Pacific theater, a situation heralded back home in newsreels that began, "PanCola Spans the Globe!"

Houghton used similar methods when, decades before the war, his needs were not met by Governor Lee Russell, and he explained those methods, with the kind of detail many would deem improper, to his twelve-year-old son, Lance. Unfortunately, as he described how the governor could not pursue reelection this year because of term limits but that, nevertheless, campaign donations from various shell companies would ensure the next one would be a team player, his son internalized only part of the logic: that cheating to benefit one's self was an acceptable practice, but without the qualifier that others should not be hurt.

"Sounds like a smart plan," Lance said, one hand in the pocket of his shearling coat, balled for warmth. "Can I ask you something?"

"You know I hate that question. *Yes.* You can ask me something."

"What are we out here to hunt?"

"My friend Sam once told me golf is a good walk spoiled." Houghton chuckled. "I like to think of hunting as a pleasant stroll with protection."

"Har-har," said Lance.

Toward the western border of the estate, they reached an obstruction to their pleasant, protected stroll on horseback. The creek was roughly six feet deep. At its narrowest point it was over eight feet wide.

His sigh a cloud front moving across the creek, Houghton said, "I think the embankment's got a more manageable slope down the ways a bit," but his son, trying to eyeball the distance from one ledge to the other, would have none of that.

"I think I can jump it."

"What?"

"I can jump this thing."

Houghton told his son to stop speaking nonsense and get his fool self along down the property with him.

"Dad, I can jump over the creek," Lance said, his glance oscillating from the vocative expression to the direct object of his sentence, the orange clay on its bed, the clumps of dead leaves, its water turned the color of cola by tannins leached from tree roots. "How come you never trust me?"

"Okay then, have at, Quicksilver."

With that blessing from his dad, Lance tugged Peat's reins and guided her away from the creek. He turned her back around after thirty yards. They both faced the jump. Gently, Lance patted Peat's withers. *We can do this,* he hoped more than thought. *I know we can.* He figured it was a fitting day to take a leap of faith. Into Peat's ear Lance whispered the same thing that, on the schoolyard, he used to whisper in the ear of one girl to make another one jealous—nothing, just whisper sounds—and then he giddyapped her into a gallop.

Lance and the horse launched from the ledge of the creek in one strong and fluid motion, and for the briefest moment, floating high above the water, he thought they'd make it. Then reality and gravity set in. Peat landed in the creek bed pitched too far forward, so that when her front hoof hit a fallen tree trunk, she rolled to her side, hurling from her back the slingshot projectile that was Lance. It was only a matter of luck that, after he slammed into the wall of the creek and tumbled down its slope toward the bottom, he did not end up beneath the horse. Instead he ended up in the water.

"So there I am, soaked to the bone and it's freezing out. All I want to do is go home," Lance would conclude whenever he explained to people why he did not hunt. "And my dad says no. Because I was such a fool I'd have to go the rest of the day in wet clothes." At that point he would always pause for a beat. "We get home that night. My mom asks how it went. 'Terrible,' I said. 'I'm never hunting again.' And I never have."

Every time he told the story about jumping the creek, at charity benefits or over a business lunch, during squash games or in the waiting room, he always elided the part about what happened to Peat.

Lance came to his senses at the bottom of the creek, his shearling coat clinging to him like a second skin, the autumn cold mounting an attack on his wet body. Next to him lay Peat. Despite the ringing in his ears, the origin of which he did not know, he could hear the horse neighing, her pitch excruciatingly high, such that the pain causing the sound seemed to be transmitted with it, going from tactile to aural to tactile and back again. Lance got on his knees in the three feet of water. Near the edge of the creek, muddy and aching, he placed his hands on Peat's flanks, trying to calm her down, at which point he saw, first, the scabbard for his rifle, the tip of which was now confetti of torn leather, a sight followed immediately by Peat's foreleg, where, instead of a knee, there was a stump of blood, gristle, and bone.

"Goddamn it to hell. You stubborn little shit." His father worked his way down the bank of the creek until he was standing over the scene. "How many times have I told you not to pack it loaded?"

I'm sorry, Lance would have said if he had not, at that moment, spoiled the water of the creek with his breakfast. From the corner of his eye he watched his father tend to the horse.

On his knees Houghton urged Peat to keep still. "There, girl," he said. "Whoa now." After lifting her lid he studied her dilated pupil, and keeping a blank face he checked on the wound. Lance wrested himself to his feet, bits of sick around his mouth, just in time to hear the prognosis. "She's got to be put down," his father said.

"No."

"Yes."

The Colt Dragoon that Houghton removed from his holster had been a gift from Adolph Weil of Weil Bros. Cotton. The sight of the gun intensified the effects of the cold in Lance. His bottom molars knocked against the top ones, and his hands trembled so much they seemed to hum. Due to his lowering body heat, Lance began to resemble a piece of Delftware, white overlaid in a blue design. He just barely managed to articulate four simple words. "Y-ou ca-a-an't shoo-oot he-r!"

"I'm not," Houghton said, handing Lance the gun. "You are."

In spite of the cold the gun felt hot in his palm. Perhaps because of the increase in his heart rate that it brought about, Lance grew calm, shivering mitigated, as though his body were trying to torment his will, becoming better suited for using the Colt even as his mind screamed, over and over, for him to throw it away. He listened through the internal din of those pleas as his father explained that the revolver was loaded. The only thing he had to do was aim straight.

Lance stood looking down at Peat. With each second that passed, it seemed his organs developed organs of their own, a brain for his brain, a heart for his heart. He became an exponent of himself. Everything was amplified. He could hear the electricity snapping through his cells. *This isn't really happening,* he told himself. *Today isn't even a real day.* Somehow, pointing the gun at Peat's head where it lay in the mud, ignoring that look of animal panic born of sheer helplessness, Lance was able to hold back his tears. He held them back because of hope. Any second now his father would tell him to put down the gun. Any second now his father would tell him it had all been a test.

"Be careful, son. It's got a hair trig—"

One mile away, Jonah Dewberry, a square-bearded farmer puffing on an underslung pipe, asked his wife, "Is it deer season already?" Claire said it was probably the backfire of an automobile. Recent inquiries have revealed that the supposed backfire compelled her not to finish sewing the second elbow patch on a jacket that belonged to her son, Rocky Top Dewberry, whose death of galloping consumption she had, until that moment, refused to acknowledge. Two days later, while sharing a Pan float after church, Jonah convinced his wife to give the jacket to a drifter, John Reynolds, whose grandson, Burt, would wear it in his role as Peanut Griffin in *Killing Mr. Tiffee.* That film was seen eight times by the aptly yclept Samuel Betelhed, author of a novel, *The Elbow Patch,* which would never be published, due to its unwieldy narrative and authorial solipsism. Excerpts of the novel were being read on air by WKOS's shock-jock Eddie Lorenz as Harold Forster sat in a booth at the diner across the street from his apartment.

Harold liked the old 1950s-style tableside radios at the Batesville Diner. They were hard to find nowadays. On the morning of February 29, 1984, waiting for the person he was supposed to meet, Harold listened to but didn't understand the DJ saying, "Here's my advice, Betelhed. Don't quit your day job. Who in the world cares why some stupid jacket only had one elbow patch?" Harold was soon approached by a clean-shaven, bespectacled man in a navy sack suit.

"Mr. Forster? Frank Gavin."

Frank Gavin was the head of the technical division at Carol-Corp, a multinational food and beverage corporation formed in 1964 when Carol-Pinto, Inc., a manufacturer of grain-based snack products, merged with The Tropi-Cola Company. CarolCorp now owned the rights to PanCola. The acquisition was part of a corporate-wide marketing and product-integration strategy code-named Nostalgia, by which various once-popular but now-defunct products, including Knapp Crackers, Tart Twizzles, Smiley Pies, and Panola Cola, among others, would be introduced to the current generation of consumers.

At the Batesville Diner, after giving an abbreviated description of the new marketing campaign, Frank said to Harold, "Can I be frank with you? Ha-ha. Sorry, bad joke. The truth is I have a problem."

"I get it. Your name's Frank."

"Right." Frank had volunteered to speak with Harold Forster himself, rather than send the lawyers, because he had heard about the man's so-called limitations. He knew delicacy was of the order. "We're having trouble re-creating your father's formula."

"My father's formula."

Frank said, "I had a feeling you'd be quick on the uptake." From his coat pocket he removed a small sheet of laminated paper. He laid it on the table and slid it toward Harold. "This is the most definitive formula for PanCola we've been able to find in the company records. You may recognize your father's handwriting."

Unable to remember the look of his own handwriting, let alone that of his father, Harold nodded, examining the ancient, yellow, acidified sheet of paper trapped in plastic, its contents a list of ingredients such as "ext. vanilla 2. oz.," "lime juice 1 qt.," "sugar 40 lbs.," "water 3 ½ gal.," and "citrate caffeine 2 oz."

"Take a look at the item fourth from the bottom," Frank said, pointing it out. "'H.F. one point three grams.' Got any idea what that means?"

"H.F.?"

"We believe that's the secret ingredient. We've synthesized this formula, minus whatever H.F. is, and my senior psychometrician thinks we're close. The gas chromatography indicates we're off by as little as one point three grams of *something*."

"My father's initials were H.F.," said Harold, who nearly blushed when Frank responded, "Excellent observation, Mr. Forster."

A waitress placed menus in front of them and, notepad at the ready, asked if they would like anything to drink. Both men said they were fine with water.

"We think your father used his initials as a placeholder," Frank said once they were alone again. He went on to explain that it was not an uncommon practice. At Coca-Cola, for example, the "secret" part of their formula was referred to, within the company and with-out, as "Merchandise 7X." He added that basically everyone in the industry knew what those seven flavoring agents were. "I mean, taste McDonald's 'special sauce' and tell me that's not Thousand Island dressing."

So many odd-sounding words made Haddy feel as though he'd picked up a fever. "I'm sorry to own this to you, Mr. Frank, but I can't be of any help. I wouldn't be able to spot the secret ingredient if it was coming down the middle of a big road."

At dinner one night decades earlier, Harold, only ten years old and dressed in short pants and saddle shoes, had listened with his brothers and sister as their father told them about his creation of PanCola, mentioning how he chose white for the label because that had been the color of the show globe in Forster Rex-for-All. Sterling-silver flatware and lead-crystal stemware sat atop the can-dlelit and jacquard-clothed mahogany table.

"I couldn't have done it without an extra-special ingredient," their father had said. "And someday I'll tell one of you what that ingredient is. Maybe I'll tell you, Monty. Or maybe it'll be Lance.

But then again, what if it's Ramsey?" Harold had always figured his father must have accidentally forgotten to mention him.

"You have to remember something," said Frank, leaning forward in the diner booth.

"Nope."

"An offhand remark from your father?"

"Nuh-uh."

"Something he said over the phone?"

"I wish."

"Did he ever tell one of your siblings?"

Harold said, "He always planned to, but I think he passed on before he got the chance. I even asked them, back a long time ago. Each of them thought he'd told one of the others."

"We know for a fact your niece figured it out. She even mentioned it in her autobiography. Did she ever say anything? Do you think she may have told her brother?"

"I know for a fact Imogene wouldn't ever do Nicholas any favors."

Over the next few minutes, as Frank continued with his talk, saying he was authorized to issue a finder's fee of $75,000 for the secret ingredient, Harold studied the menu, trying to decide if he wanted oatmeal with raisins, pecan-crusted catfish, ginger-spiced chicken, or blueberry pancakes. He figured that either breakfast or lunch would work at this hour. Once he'd chosen, he looked around the diner, past someone plucking a parsley sprig from their bowl of chili, past someone eating a maraschino cherry from their milk shake, until, spotting the waitress, he flagged her over.

3.3

The Contents of an Urn—Owl Says What?— Next Stop, Italian Harlem—The Mineola Club

Nobody at The Coffee Urn on Forty-Third and Seventh was eating, not the two posttheater couples, one with an untouched slice of apple pie and cheddar sitting between them, the other busy studying *Playbill*s instead of the menu; not the lineup of smokers at the counter; not the businessmen reading the *Herald Tribune*'s late edition at various tables, tucking the paper in on itself as carefully as an army private would his bedsheets; not the cook sweating a ring into his white hat; not the young waitress with a finger twisting knots in her curly hair; and not Ramsey Forster, sitting alone in a corner booth, the salt of her dried tears like snail tracks down her cheeks.

She had told the cabdriver to drop her off anywhere, so long as it was far enough away from the Village. He'd told her she looked like she could use a cup of coffee.

"What can I get you?" asked the waitress.

With the heel of her palm swiping the corner of her eye, as it had been doing involuntarily for the past half hour, Ramsey said, "Coffee, please. And could you make it really strong?"

"You bet."

"I mean really strong. Strong as the Irish."

The waitress lowered her pen and pad and looked around the

coffee shop. "There's no need for that anymore," she whispered. "Haven't you heard? The world's sane again. We aren't even keeping any stocked these days. Not that we ever did."

"Please," Ramsey said. "Just one."

A twenty-year-old native of Jackson Heights, Queens, youngest of five sisters, daughter of an electrician with a drinking problem, and part-time student at the Michael Phipps School of Secretarial Studies, Angela Simmons, who waitressed at the coffee shop to help pay her tuition, had seen her share of women in distress. She noticed fog growing like an aura around Ramsey's hands where they lay flat on the steel tabletop. "The cook keeps a bottle in his locker. I'll sneak a splash from that."

"Thank you."

Angela Simmons, because of her place of birth, siblings, father, and vocational aspirations, wasn't entirely a soft touch. "Ten cents extra," she said over her shoulder while walking away.

Alone again, Ramsey recommenced her occupation of the past half hour: commanding her own body to continue to function. She told herself to breathe, and air swelled her lungs. She told her heart to beat, and blood charged through her veins. Was this going to be her life from now on? The notion frightened her even more than the thought she might someday run into *him* again.

It was almost eleven o'clock. Out the window, Ramsey could see a bright, gargantuan billboard for the radio program *Clara, Lu, 'n' Em,* on which was written, "You're in for a lot of laughs— There's never a dull moment in the lives of radio's most lovable housewives—Listen to them carry on every Mon., Wed., Fri." In the street below the billboard, steam rose from manholes in pavement that looked like dark liquid, as though the city itself, rather than some greasy spoon, were named The Coffee Urn. Pushcart men competed for sidewalk real estate with bag ladies. Tourists reeled in the false daylight of the Great White Way, on occasion shading their eyes from the glare, while pickpockets watched from the alleys between the Rialto, the Knickerbocker, the New Criterion, and the Paramount. "Just people trying to live." That was what Ramsey's father used to say, fancying himself a philosopher, when he looked at a candid public scene or was feeling particularly sentimental, situations that were often mutually inclusive. At the moment, looking at all the myriad people of New York through the window of a coffee shop, Ramsey tried to summon those words, to wish everyone in the city well as they went about their lives, but in truth, the only thing she wanted was for one of them to die.

He would in two years. On August 8, 1936, Ramsey, who had known from an early age that some emotions were so real they had a shape—love was a circle, hate was a square—would learn, while reading the paper, that the combination of hostility, relief, pain, and elation was a two-by-six-inch rectangular column, above which was printed in bold, RETAIL HEIR DROWNS IN SAILING ACCIDENT.

Onto the table chimed a cup of coffee, the reflection of its steam in the window overlaid against the steam outside in the street, a few spilt drops orbiting its saucer. "I'm grateful," Ramsey said, but the waitress had walked back to the counter, where with one hand she continued tangling her hair and with the other drank her own cup of coffee, most likely an Irish blend as well. Ramsey took an ample swallow.

The heat of the whiskey nicely accentuated the heat of the coffee. It felt good for an external sensation to match her internal one, temperature aligning with temperament, as though her whole body were a hall of mirrors, all the effects an illusion and their cause unidentifiable. Her hands slippery with sweat, her knees trembling beneath the table, the inside of her wrenched, pulsating, and coiled: not a single one of those was real. Ramsey didn't have to be herself.

She could be a reflection of a reflection of herself. She could be a trick of the light.

In the coffee shop, as she finished her cup, Ramsey was interrupted by the last thing she wanted to see or speak with, a man. "Hoot-hoot," he said from two tables away.

"Ex*cuse* me?"

"We're both night owls."

"Oh. Right."

This guy could go straight to hell, for all Ramsey cared. She didn't want to flirt. She wanted to be left alone. Why wouldn't this man, who kept staring at her, and the rest of the world, which kept interacting with her, just let her be invisible? Who did he think he was anyway?

On October 26, 1931, *The Hollywood Reporter* had run a profile titled, "Star Maker: How One Studio Head Is Remodeling the Heavens," in which its subject stated, "There's no science to finding the next Joan Crawford or Doug Fairbanks. I simply keep my eyes open. They're all out there. You just have to look. You have to be present." Those words would be confirmed years later when Ramsey, filing for a divorce, realized how, that night at the coffee shop, she hadn't fallen in love but rather out of shock, and Arthur Landau just happened to be there at the time.

. . .

One week, twenty showers, eight phone calls, twelve skipped meals, five long walks through the park, and two days after the night at the coffee shop, Ramsey accepted Arthur's offer of a cocktail.

He picked her up at eight o'clock in a chauffeured Delage. Ramsey's caplet-sleeved, town-tailored day dress was as disproportionate to Arthur's bespoke dinner suit as a buffalo robe would be to a pair of plus fours. On a normal occasion the discrepancy would have bothered her. Tonight she wore her hair down to hide the bald spot she'd unconsciously worn into her scalp near the nape of her neck. The gun in her ivory satin clutch seemed to radiate like the warming pan her nanny used to insist she sleep with on the rare cold nights in Mississippi.

"Jeffrey, take us to that speak I like. You know the one," Arthur said to the driver.

"At this time of night, sir, I believe we can catch it at One Hundred Twenty-Fifth."

"You're a titan among mortals, Jeffrey. How would I get by without you?"

The driver turned north onto Lexington Avenue. "The mind reels, sir."

Although she didn't know what kind of speakeasy would need to be "caught," Ramsey was comforted by the rapport between the driver and Arthur, as she had always believed the true nature of a person could be discerned in how he or she treats the help. But then again, she worried, perhaps the banter, which sounded suspiciously practiced, was all for show. Ramsey had no idea who or what or even how to trust anymore. She gripped her clutch.

It took less than ten minutes to reach 125th Street, the scenes outside the car, ailanthuses next to park entrances and silhouettes behind bay windows, passing by as quickly as clips in a newsreel theater.

"Careful of the curb," Arthur said after exiting the car, strolling around its hood, opening Ramsey's door, and offering the crook of his arm. Together they walked down the stairs into the subway station for the IRT East Side line. Over the years, Ramsey had heard of speakeasies hidden in secret, forgotten chambers of subway stations, a former control room that had become obsolete, an old platform that had closed because of underuse. Arthur guided Ramsey to the lower level of the bilevel station, its tiled walls echoing the rumble and screech of southbound local and express trains, gray-haired Italian men unabashedly singing as though they were wandering through a Neapolitan village, loaves of bread periscoping from grocery bags, the smell of olives, finocchio, razor clams, pomegranates, and cheese emanating from bins watched over by haggle-ready Sicilians.

The best goddamn armor against the most dangerous folk, Ramsey thought, enjoying the reversion to the Mississippi vernacular of her youth, *is a crowd of the most peaceful folk.*

At the north end of the station Arthur and Ramsey stopped in front of a closed door. It was nothing but a slab of black metal, no ornamentation or distinguishing marks, except for a tiny slot just above the knob. After looking around the platform, which was empty of people in that area, Arthur reached into his pocket, took out a small coin, and pushed it into the slot.

The door opened and then, almost immediately, began to close again. Arthur slipped through the opening and with a snatch pulled Ramsey in. "Easy there, damn it," she said, rubbing her forearm.

On the other side of the door, they stood on a subway platform just like the one they'd been standing on, a single island buttressed by tracks to each side, and they were not alone. Throughout the roughly fifteen-yard-long section of the platform—apparently the true northern-most end of the lower level, hidden from public use by the wall with the slot and door—men in tuxedos and women in furs lingered near the edges and next to the pillars, drinking cocktails provided by a waiter with a small bar cart. "Why do people still come to speaks after the repeal?" Ramsey asked Arthur.

"Suppose they like the secrecy. There's just one thing, though."

"What?"

Arthur smiled coyly. "The speakeasy isn't here yet."

In 1902, after an explosion that damaged a great deal of expensive property, construction of the IRT subway was halted, due to safety concerns, public outcry, and, most important, a lack of funding. August Belmont Jr., primary financier of the project, decided to raise the needed funds privately, offering lifelong access, for a substantial, one-time fee, to a private subway car, the *Mineola*. After the ratification of the Eighteenth Amendment, membership in the Mineola Club, as it came to be known, was expanded, and use of its subway car was repurposed for the consumption and enjoyment, legality notwithstanding, of alcoholic beverages.

"I'm just an annual member," Arthur said as he and Ramsey stepped onto the recently arrived *Mineola*.

New York Times columnist Meyer Berger would, many years later, describe the interior of the subway car: "mulberry silk drapes, knee-deep carpeting, sliding leatherette curtains, a kitchenette with kerosene stove and old-fashioned icebox, special subway-pattern china and glassware, overstuffed reclining couch, swivel chair and rolltop desk." Although, for the most part, Berger was accurate in his description, he failed to mention, being a former member himself, the features specific to the era of Prohibition, such as the Philippine mahogany bar stocked with a daily-newspaperman's best friend.

Sitting in leather chairs, Ramsey and Arthur were served a bourbon neat and vodka rocks, respectively. The train was passing 116th Street when Ramsey said, "Show-off."

Arthur sipped his drink. "I'm in pictures. It's my business to show off."

Until this moment, Ramsey realized, she had never really looked at Arthur, instead registering him like one is supposed to a solar eclipse, through the pinhole that her mind's perception of the world had become. He was handsome in the way men who are confident are handsome, and he was confident in the way men who have money are confident. His eyes were as murkily green as pot liquor. In the subway car, as the lights of the 110th and 103rd Street stations glided by, Arthur, with his pomaded black hair and his skin made ecru by the sun, turned into a constant for Ramsey, a fixed point where her gaze could settle as the train carried them toward lower Manhattan.

She could already feel her first drink. The past week of no alcohol and very little food had crippled her once impressive, if alarming, tolerance. She slowed down on the second.

"I've always wanted to meet a film mogul," said Ramsey.

"I've always wanted to meet a soda heiress."

From Ninety-Sixth Street onward, interrupted by the occasional stop to pick up waiting club members, Ramsey and Arthur discussed Vantage Pictures' upcoming films in 1934, the rumors of a shadow economy created by the robber barons at the turn of the century, how they both hated supper dancing, how they both loved miniature golf, and that Panola Cola maybe should consider signing an exclusive distribution contract with the Wichita Amusement Company, the country's fifth largest theater chain and a recently acquired, wholly owned subsidiary of Arthur's studio.

"Gripes. Is this Thirty-Third?" Arthur said as the train pulled into a station. "We missed our stop."

Ramsey drank the last sip of her third bourbon before following Arthur out of the upholstered confines of the *Mineola,* through the sepulchral walls of the station, and into the brick and metal and glass world of midtown Manhattan. A crumpled slip of paper doddered on the breeze down the sidewalk like a wounded bird. "Jeffrey always picks me up at Grand Central. I'll get us a taxicab." Arthur began to look north and south along Park Avenue.

"Don't be silly. What is it, nine blocks? Let's walk."

"Are you sure?"

Even though she told him, "Of course!" Ramsey was the opposite of sure. This was the first time in over a week she had been below Forty-Second Street. Staying above that imaginary line of demarcation had somehow made her feel safe. As she walked along the East Thirties, though, passing office buildings and the professional clubs attended by men who worked in those office buildings, passing residential homes and the social clubs attended by women who lived in those residential homes, Ramsey felt safe with Arthur, not because he could protect her, but rather because of something far more damaging to her self-respect. He seemed kind.

Forty-foot-high statues of Mercury, Hercules, and Minerva looked down on Arthur and Ramsey in their approach to Grand Central. A massive clock beneath the statues read the time as 9:55. Near Forty-Second Street and Vanderbilt, where Arthur said Jeffrey would be, Ramsey became, with each step, increasingly drawn to Grand Central, as though it exerted a force of gravity. Even shadows seemed to be stretching toward the building. Ramsey was musing about how the stars painted on the ceiling of the terminal could be the cause of the gravitational pull when one of the shadows that seemed to be subject to it changed shape.

"Your wallet, your watch. Her necklace. The rings, too."

In one hand the man who had stepped out of the alley held a flick blade. In the other hand, clinching it by the front brim as though he were greeting a society member, he held a hat. Sweat stippled his cheeks despite the cold. A widow's peak accentuated his raised eyebrows. "Okay, easy now," Arthur was saying as he took his wallet out of his pocket.

The loud pop had three effects on the man with the knife. First, his eyebrows grew even more raised, etching concentric wrinkles in his brow, like a drawing of radio waves. Second, he dropped his hat on the ground, where it wobbled for a moment and then stopped upside down, grimed with dirt from the sidewalk and marred on each side with a perfectly round bullet hole. Third, he screamed, "Jesus Christ, lady! You're a goddamn lunatic!"

After the man ran away, turning down the nearest cross street, Ramsey put the gun back in her clutch and turned to look at Arthur. "You should see your face," she said, unable to hold back an enormous grin.

3.4

The History of Narrative—
The Soap Opera Diatribe

Narrative weds individuals to history. On March 12, 1985, his twenty-third birthday, Robert Vaughn repeated those words in his head as he waited outside Leopold Marunga's office. They were as far as he had gotten in formulating how to express what he wanted to convey in his thesis. Narrative weds individuals to history. Pretty damn thin, he had to admit. If he wanted to avoid upsetting Marunga, whose fuse was not known for its ample length, Robert would have to lay the jargon on thick, intercutting references to McLaren and Spinetti with the occasional "dialectic," "gestalt," and "paradigm," all of which he would conclude were "in flux."

The door to Professor Marunga's office opened. Through it walked a girl who, with a pencil stuck in her Chrissie Hynde–style haircut and with a tattoo of Karl Marx jutting from her T-shirt sleeve, was a rarity not only for Millsaps but also for the entire state, an academic punk. She glared at Robert for a moment. Instead of meeting her gaze he felt an urgent need to check his watch. He wiped his hands against his pants, unsure if they were sweating because of his thesis meeting or because, since his senior year of high school, he'd had a crush on Chrissie Hynde.

"Get in here, Vaughn," called Professor Marunga.

Robert did as ordered. "Good to see you, sir."

A former renegade of the philosophy department who, after his insouciance had been mistaken for chutzpah once too often, not only received tenure but was also appointed chair, Leopold Marunga, Ph.D., was as eccentric as his own name, a collector of vintage golf clubs, frequent reciter of 1950s commercial jingles, and contributor, albeit indirectly, to the retirement funds of various farmers in Humboldt County. That day it seemed clear he had partaken on his ride to work.

"For Christ's sake, Vaughn, I know you're not the astrological type, but call me Leo already."

"Sorry, Leo." Robert took a seat across from Marunga. "How's Jane?"

"Upset she didn't get into the Junior Auxiliary. Auxiliary to what, you might ask. I've no clue."

"They're sort of a charity org—"

"Let me rephrase: I don't care."

Professor Marunga placed two sockless but shoed feet on his cluttered desk. The effect of mentioning the professor's wife, Robert knew, tended to be hit or miss for his mood, depending on what Marunga often euphemized as "cultural differences." Most people called them fights. On his arrival in Jackson, Mississippi, as an assistant professor, Leo Marunga of Christchurch, New Zealand, quickly met and fell for one Jane Gregory, debutante, belle, and daughter of the South. They liked each other's accents a great deal. Soon after their wedding it became apparent that was all they liked. Robert could tell as much the first time he met Jane, at a department mixer, when she introduced herself as Mrs. Cowabunga.

"Let's get down to it then. What, vis-à-vis a topic, do you have for me, thesis advisee? I'm in a rhyming mood today."

Robert's father used to say, "And remember, when you roll, roll high," a statement Robert would have considered somewhat profound if its author weren't a gambling addict. With that advice in mind, sitting across from Professor Marunga and surrounded by stacks of newspapers, obscure comp-lit texts, hardcover comic books, and issues of *Philosophia* and *People* magazine, Robert began what he would later think of as his "soap-opera diatribe." He started his argument with Theodor von Hedt's concept of external intratextuality. Then he began to riff. Aware of Marunga's penchant for invented terminology, lowbrow pop culture, and broad generalizations, Robert described the "will to narrative" found in *The Young and the Restless,* how *Days of Our Lives* could be described as a "dramopticon." He expounded on those concepts, applying them to society at large. "With this thesis I'd make the argument," he concluded, "that storytelling is the basis of all logic."

Marunga steepled his fingers. "Would you do me a favor? Go outside and check the sign out front. Does it still say 'Philosophy Department'?"

"I know it's a bit of a reach."

"Reach-around, more like."

"But I think I can pull it off."

By the way Professor Marunga rubbed his eyes, irritated but resigned, as though a film director had said, "This time, play it *begrudgingly,*" Robert could tell he had him. "Okay," his thesis adviser said, "write one chapter and then we'll see. But remember, you have to take this seriously, understood? This isn't some Intro to Lit Theory paper, five hundred words on how 'peanut butter and jelly sandwich' is a semiotic construction."

"Understood." Robert got up to leave. "Thank you."

"Just one suggestion. Cool it on the soap operas. Life's not like that."

Robert thanked him for the note, unable to look into those dilated pupils, before walking out of the office. His slowing pulse matched the reverb of his footsteps as he walked down the hallway. He was in the clear for now. Thank God. On the building's ground floor, Robert went into a wooden pay phone booth, called the woman he'd been seeing, and asked if they were still on for dinner. Jane Marunga told him she would rather they met for lunch.

3.5

Reflections of the Soda Business—Penelope the Friendly Ghost—The Magnolia Flower of Cambridge— Meditations in an Emergency

"Getting rich changes people," said one notable writer, an American in a Paris bar, to which another responded, "Sure. It makes them assholes."

Although that exchange would later be modified in various accounts, the character of men such as Nicholas Forster has proven that neither writer, Fitzgerald nor Hemingway, was correct in his assessment. People become assholes more often when they are born with rather than achieve wealth.

Throughout the entirety of his life Nicholas wanted for nothing but want itself. His spoilage began in the cradle. A beautiful child, with brown locks and the greenest eyes, he was given lenience by his mother, indulgence by his grandfather, and tolerance by his sister. It is his sister, in fact, whom we owe for the most personal information about Nicholas's early years, those details that led one person, arguably, to ruin a whole family.

"My brother's life began with the death of our father. That shadow hung over him from the day he was born," Imogene Forster writes in her internationally best-selling autobiography, *Ms. Panola Cola: Reflections of the Soda Business.* "Or so we would like to think. The truth is my brother would have been born rotten even if our father had lived."

One incident in particular illustrates the animosity between the two siblings.

In October 1949, a cold snap came to Panola County, rendering The Sweetest Thing an echo chamber of faucets dripping, dripping, dripping, as protection for its pipes. That year Imogene was sixteen, eleven years older than Nicholas. Following what was referred to among the family as "the accident," Houghton had insisted that the two children and their mother, Sarah, move into the house, where, he said, they wouldn't have to dwell on who was not there. Despite such good intentions, "who was not there" was very much there, hanging on a wall in the stairwell, framed in walnut on top of the Pleyel piano. The smell of his cologne seemed to linger around certain rooms. Yet, instead of upsetting Imogene and Nicholas, the presence of Montgomery comforted the two children. He served as a source of warmth, whether captured in oil paint or in sepia-toned photography, even when the temperature dropped to zero, as it did the night of October 22, 1949.

The two of them had separate rooms in the large house. Earlier that fall day, however, the fireplace in Nicholas's bedroom had begun belching soot into The Sweetest Thing's second floor, leaving its boiseries a fine mess. A chimney sweep couldn't stop by until the next day. So that evening the boy was set up on a spare bed in the room that belonged to his teenage sister. Their mother had thought nothing of the situation. To Sarah Forster, her daughter, perpetually four feet tall in her wheelchair, never grew older. To Sarah Forster, her daughter would always be the age, three years old, when she'd contracted polio.

"Just keep quiet, you little booger," Imogene said to Nicholas, both of them tucked in beds on opposite sides of the room.

"You're the only one talking."

Years had passed since the last time Imogene had someone's company as she tried to fall asleep. Penelope had first appeared, sitting on Imogene's thighs, one morning when Imogene was three years old. "Don't bother trying to get up, sleepyhead." After that day, the little girl was the only explanation Imogene could fathom for why she could no longer move her legs. Even when the doctors explained to her the medical cause, she clung to the notion of Penelope the ghost whenever people treated her like a pitiful child who would never walk again. "You're bothering Penelope," Imogene, in her wheelchair, would say to anyone who sympathetically touched her thigh during a conversation.

"Oh, don't worry," her parents would say to their guest. They'd laugh and add, "She's just Imogene's ghost!"

Imogene knew the girl was only a product of her imagination, but that did not keep her from relying on her make-believe friend. Penelope was brave when Imogene was scared. Penelope was bold when Imogene was timid. Even now, so many years after her ghost had faded from her life, long since relegated to the past the way thumb-sucking and bed-wetting were for other children, Imogene often wondered how Penelope would have responded in certain situations. She was doing just that when she heard a strange noise from the other side of the room.

"What was that?" Imogene asked, as confident as Penelope would have been.

Nicholas responded, "What was what?"

For the next few minutes, the only sounds in the bedroom were the wood crackling on top of the firedogs and the endlessly rhythmic plop, ping, plop, ping from the bathroom sink. Then Imogene heard a muffled, baritone rumbling the identity of which took her a moment to figure out.

Her brother was farting in bed.

Of course it would be just her luck to have to spend the night in a room stunk up by the flatulence of a four-year-old brat. A notoriously picky eater, Nicholas had been enamored, over the past year, with Van Camp's Beanee Weenees, straight from the can. Half his meals consisted of the stuff, and at dinner that night he'd had two helpings.

Imogene, getting assaulted by a smell so strong she imagined it curling her eyelashes, noticed another noise following each passing of gas, the sound of something being wafted. She looked over at Nicholas. He was lifting his bedsheets up and down over himself, as though they were tablecloths and his body the table. She asked, "What in the world are you doing?"

"I broke wind."

"So then fix it."

Again Nicholas started to waft the sheets over his body, prompting Imogene to ask about the more curious matter. "But what are you doing with your sheets?" When he told her the answer, the smell no longer bothered her, she found him so endearing. One part of her wanted to tease the little guy, and another part wanted to give him a great big hug.

The next day, while her brother was still asleep, Imogene took her breakfast, served by Miss Urquhart the cook, in the kitchen alcove used for informal meals. There were two Miss Urquharts in the household, mother and daughter, who, to avoid confusion among the staff, were often referred to with the suffix of their post, "Miss Urquhart the cook" and "Miss Urquhart the maid," the former of which was mother of the latter.

Imogene considered the suffixes demeaning. "Miss Urquhart," she said while stirring her bowl of chicken mull, "would you like to hear a funny story?"

"I've been known to enjoy them on occasion."

In the kitchen, Miss Urquhart, a coarse switch of hair atop a bald patch the only indication of her sixty years, scrubbed a Windsor pan as Imogene told the story, aided by sound effects, of Nicholas's bedtime flatulence.

"So when I asked him why he was flapping his sheets up and down like that, guess what he says? He looks at me and says, 'So my legs won't get stained brown'!"

The two of them broke down in laughter at the punch line, Imogene accidentally spilling some of her breakfast, Miss Urquhart accidentally dropping her wire sponge. They were both laughing so hard neither spotted Nicholas standing in the doorway, still dressed in his pajamas. He brought a quick end to their amusement when he finally saw fit to speak up.

"At least my legs aren't dead."

Until that moment, Imogene had always thought no one actually dropped their jaws when shocked, but on hearing Nicholas, that was what she did. She sat there, slack jawed, in the kitchen alcove, unable to stand because of her legs, unable to speak for that same reason.

Don't let him talk to you like that, Penelope would have told Imogene in this situation. *You know what to do to that little shit. Put him in his place. Go over and teach him he can't talk to you like that.*

It was almost as though Miss Urquhart heard Penelope's hypothetical command. Scottish in temperament as well as heritage, the elder Urquhart promptly traversed the kitchen and, with her hands still grimy, slapped Nicholas across his young cheek. "Shame on you," she told the boy.

His face bore a faint outline of fingers in sudsy grease. Throughout the rest of her life, Imogene felt enormous gratitude for Miss Urquhart—who was fired by Sarah Forster that evening but who the next morning Houghton Forster rehired—even when, years after the slap, Nicholas repaid it by taking over the Panola Cola Company.

. . .

Nicholas Forster, whom his sister describes as a "wolf in wolf's clothing" in her famous autobiography, never forgave himself for what he said that cold, gray morning in 1949. He also never forgave his sister for making him say it. "She sits in that chair like a queen," he once told his mother, "and everybody treats her like one."

He was a lonely child in the way children with too many friends are. Not smart enough to be self-conscious but self-aware enough to know he wasn't, Nicholas used that balance to win people over, alluring them with his handsome facade and charming them by taking it for granted. The result was friendship without intimacy. Later in life, when his career was on the rise, such general likability would serve him well, board members supporting his right to lead the company, trade journalists describing him as a savior of the industry, in much the same way and for similar reasons that, later still, those very people would turn on him, spreading rumors of a forced resignation, publishing headlines such as ADIOS, DIVIDENDS! SAYONARA, SPLITS! Future career aside, Nicholas's loneliness as a child was known only to him, exacerbated by his misunderstanding of the attention people gave his sister regarding her disability, and, much to his relief, cured by the advent in the household of his cousin Susannah.

Born four years apart, the two of them had, through the early part of their adolescence, been too different in age to get along. Nicholas knew her as the baby his aunt danced on her shoulder, as the toddler slinging handfuls of spaghetti from her high chair, as the preschooler who only visited on holidays, as the quiet little girl with a bow in her hair playing "Chopsticks." In 1956, though, Aunt Ramsey and her daughter, following the death of Nicholas's grandfather from a stroke, came to spend the summer at The Sweetest Thing. Nicholas was twelve. Susannah was eight.

Despite the pervasive gloom about the house—family members sweating through black fabric in the heat, a wife arguing with her mother-in-law about the desuetude of widows' bonnets, lawyers offering graceless condolences as they asked for a document to be signed, the dog waiting patiently by the door for his master's return—the two cousins had themselves a high time. Nicholas showed his relative from California what it was like to grow up in Mississippi. They ate pink popcorn next to heaps of rain-sogged cotton. They rode an abandoned kid hack down the spoil bank of a drainage canal. They trundled hoops with sticks along cedar-boarded roads.

Nicholas's favorite thing to do with Susannah was sit in the living room of The Sweetest Thing, a glass dish full of spoon-serve in each of their laps, listening to *Fort Laramie* or *Dragnet* or *X Minus One* on the Capehart.

"Imogene never listened to the radio with me," he once told his mother. "Why couldn't I have had a sister like Susie?" His mother wasn't paying attention to what he said; she was too focused on telling him something herself. Earlier that day, the company's chief in-house counsel, Connor Rolph, had informed Sarah about certain parts of Houghton Forster's will, particularly who'd inherited a controlling interest in PanCola. She did her best to explain the situation to her son. Nicholas, heartsick that his cousin would be leaving at the end of the summer, had just one question. "What's 'come of age' mean?"

...

A few months earlier, before the girl Nicholas wished were his sister came to stay in Batesville, his actual sister sat in a classroom at Radcliffe College, where she was a senior majoring in economics. That day was the last class. "In the future, what will be the most powerful, the most malleable type of entity in the world?" asked the professor, Elwood Ballantine, Ph.D., who'd never once received the correct answer to this question from his students in Economics 1308: World Economic History, a course he'd been teaching for the past five years. "Miss Powell?"

"Nation-states?"

"Wrong. Miss Rowe?"

"People?"

"No. Miss Forster?"

"Corporations?"

"Exactly right."

Professor Ballantine told the students he would let them stew on that one as they entered the world as "founding citizens of the corporate state." Class was dismissed.

Outside, slowly wheeling herself from Longfellow to Briggs Hall with a stack of books in her lap, Imogene took in the urban arboretum that was Garden Street, its red maples and hedge maples, its littleleaf linden and American linden, its ginkgo, ash, and sophora, all the while thinking, *Guess that's it, my last class as a college student, my last hour of not being an adult.* Birds whistled a rhythm to her thoughts like the bouncing ball on animated song lyrics, and young men decked out in crimson parted around her chair.

She reached her dorm at half past four. Imogene had just set aside her books, dried sweat from her face, and poured a glass of water when her roommate, Maggie Wyndham, burst into the room, yelling, "The time is right for getting tight!" In one hand she held an uncorked bottle of champagne, in the other a crisscrossed pair of flutes, wielding the panoply in the manner of a knight at arms.

The black sheep in a family that consisted solely of black sheep, Maggie had, over the two years they'd roomed together, acquainted Imogene with alcohol, jazz, cigarettes, poetry, and berets. She'd grown up privileged on the Upper East Side but came into her own below Fourteenth Street. During her teens, Maggie drank lowballs at San Remo, Chumley's, and the Minetta, accepted the occasional half ounce of primo grass from trust-funded, quasi-beatniks in exchange for correcting their grammar on term papers, went down on Jackson Pollock in a toilet stall, and made out with Lee Krasner behind a coatrack, activities she pursued under the auspice of what her parents called "a real education." Often in college Maggie took Imogene on weekend trips to her old haunts. Once, as they left a house party in the Village full of people wearing turtlenecks, Imogene said to a poet who worked as a curator at MoMA, "So nice meeting you, Frank. Let's have a Pan sometime!"

Years after they were roommates, Imogene, who in her autobiography writes, "Radcliffe gave me an education, but Maggie prepared me for the world," would pay for her friend's stint at Hazelden recovering from a heroin addiction and, later, introduce her to the editor who would publish her award-winning poetry collection, *Marching to the Beat of No Drummer*.

"I can't go out and get drunk with you tonight," Imogene said in the common room of their suite at Briggs Hall. "I need to work on my speech. I still don't have an ending."

"Valedictorian, shmaledictorian," Maggie said. "We're going out for drinks."

"No."

"Yes."

"Absolutely not."

They arrived at the bar half an hour later. In contrast to its name, Tops'l was furnished with unaerodynamic stools, tables, and chairs, all Shaker designs with sharp angles. Everything in it looked wooden. Imogene, whenever she came to the bar, always felt as though she'd entered a fairy tale, the kind with gnomes living in a giant tree trunk, each detail of their home, cups and lamps, plates and rugs, carved from the whole.

"Four rum and Pans," ordered Maggie, a chronic double-hand drinker. With marked reluctance the bartender placed two cocktails before each girl.

Maggie said to Imogene, "Feel like we should get these at half price, seeing as you kind of own half the ingredients."

"That's absurd."

The crowd was large even for five o'clock on the last day of classes. During her pointless attempt to keep up with Maggie, Imogene looked around the bar and, while sipping her drink, fell into a habit she had not yet managed to kick: ogling boys. She could have spent all night doing it. A veritable newspaper ad for J. Press sat reading a worn paperback in the far corner, and in the back, half a dozen members of the Porcellian toasted to their future good fortunes. Boys were carrying pitchers, boys were striking matches, boys were rattling ice cubes. They were the one experience Imogene had failed at throughout college. Over the past four years, she'd excelled in class and made all kinds of friends, but she had not lost the stupid, ridiculous burden of her virginity.

Many years later, purposely unmarried and unabashedly child-less, Imogene would disparage her former self, the dependence she'd once felt toward men. "They call us 'the better half' to make up for treating us like half a person," she writes in the part of *Ms. Panola Cola* excerpted in *Ms.* magazine's fourth issue. "I've only got one response to such reasoning: that dog don't hunt." On the evening of May 4, 1956, however, Imogene Forster still felt she was missing a key component in her life, especially as she watched, from her seat at the bar, a young man coming toward her through the crowd.

"I was going to ask if I could buy you a drink, but it looks like somebody beat me to it. Two somebodies. You must be quite the popular one."

He introduced himself as David. Dressed in gray slacks and a light pink sweater that, against his tan cheeks, threw his blue eyes into striking relief, David seemed a physical embodiment of the Stars and Stripes, a polychromatic anomaly of colors that were never supposed to run. "And what's your name?" he asked.

Imogene paused. "I'm Penelope."

"Pleasure to meet you, Penelope. Where're you from?"

"Batesville, Mississippi."

"Wow."

"Excuse me?"

"It's just, I love a good accent."

"Well then, butter my butt and call me a biscuit," Imogene said, playing up her twang, all the while thinking, *Please don't ask me to dance, please don't ask me to dance, please don't ask me to dance.*

Earlier, after helping Imogene climb onto a barstool, Maggie had parked her wheelchair in the broom closet. It was their stan-dard routine. For as long as she could keep from having to use the restroom, Imogene could hide her disability, a compulsion that, like her dependency on men, she would later regret.

She turned to where her roommate had been sitting but found an empty barstool. Maggie always knew when to make herself scarce. "Why don't you have a seat?" Imogene told David, hoping to curb his asking her the opposite.

"Thanks," he said. Imogene found the word oddly endearing. It wasn't as if she owned the stool.

"And where are you from?" she asked.

"Michigan, originally. But my fami—"

David's mouth fell open, his eyes refusing to blink. For a moment, Imogene worried he had noticed her legs, that he'd brushed against them and felt how unnaturally thin they were, but she changed her mind on realizing David was looking past her. His face, as though the psychosomatic manifestation of a racial cliché, paled. Soon the entire bar followed his lead. "The hush that comes across a room full of rich Ivy Leaguers on first seeing a six-foot-six, 250-pound Cherokee Indian in their midst is a truly remarkable thing to behold," begins the third chapter of Imogene's autobiography.

At the bar she turned around to ask Branchwater what on earth he was doing up north. "Is everything okay?" All it took was one glance into his eyes to know everything was not.

3.6

The Magnolia and the Mayflower—
Return of the Academic Punk

"Knew from day one I should have kept my maiden name. Right? I can't blame them for not giving a bid to Jane *Marunga*."

For the past twenty minutes she had talked of nothing but the Junior Auxiliary. Robert was only half listening. In a booth at the Magnolia, the second oldest restaurant in town, he tried to feign interest as his gaze drifted, from the photos of celebrities behind the counter to the house specials painted on the backsplash, from the framed magazine covers to the models of sailboats on shelves with collectible soft drinks, Archie Manning peering from a bottle of PanCola.

Jackson's oldest restaurant was the Mayflower. Established in 1935 by Greek immigrants, the café on West Capitol Street formed, along with the Magnolia across town, a binary of historical significance, particularly during the civil rights movement. John Doar supposedly quelled an angry mob by inviting them for lunch at the Mayflower, and Medgar Evers was said to have conducted secret meetings in the kitchen of the Magnolia. Both restaurants provided activists with boxed meals of fried catfish, bread pudding, collards, pork chops, coleslaw, and burgers doused in comeback sauce during the Freedom Summer. The Mayflower had once been the site of a sit-in held by the progressive students at Millsaps, and decades later it remained a popular hangout among undergrads. For that reason the more logical place for a tryst with the wife of one's thesis adviser was clearly the other half of the historical binary.

I may be an idiot but I'm damn sure smart enough to know that much, thought Robert at the same time as Jane asked, "Are you even paying attention to what I'm trying to tell you right now?"

"Of course!"

"It's just, with all that's going on, I need to think about me, not others. I need to center myself."

"Right."

"I'm so glad you understand."

Jane grabbed her oversize purse and began to slide out of the booth. "Where are you going?" said Robert, his mental recording of their conversation fast-forwarding through his head. "Are we breaking up?"

"Of course you were paying attention. Of course."

Unable to respond, Robert watched Jane march out of the restaurant, purposeful as Dukas's broomstick. Was that it? They may have only been dating for the past four months, but he figured their relationship deserved a more climactic ending. It felt like she had gotten up to use the ladies' room. Jane hadn't even seemed sad. Robert was trying to think of a word to describe her when someone in the next booth gave it to him.

"Got to say, that was cold."

The girl from earlier that day turned around to face him. Karl Marx's beard poked out from her sleeve, and the bangs of Chrissie Hynde hung in front of her eyes. Robert said, "You." Never had a pronoun made him feel like such an idiot.

The girl grabbed her plate and stood up from her booth. She sat down across from him and took a bite of her po'boy. "Me Molly Allen," she said after swallowing. "You Robert Vaughn."

"How do you know my—"

"Leo's right, you know. You really should cool it on the soap opera shit." Molly nodded in the direction where Jane had swept her way through the Magnolia. "Though at least now I see why you're interested in it."

"Nobody saw you pressing your ear against his office door?"

"Didn't have to, loud as you talk."

That got a smile out of him. In response, Robert took a fry from Molly's plate, trying to initiate a kind of intimacy. The move didn't faze her. "Want to know the worst part?" he asked, chewing the fry for effect.

"Sure."

"Today's my birthday."

Molly, giving him a sloe-eyed, blank facial expression, pushed her plate toward Robert and said, "Have another fry. You deserve it."

Over the next half hour, while Molly played a dollar's worth of heartbreak songs on the booth's Seeburg Wall-O-Matic jukebox, each one prompting an impish grin from her, Robert found out she was originally from Kentucky, that her parents had died within a year of each other when she was ten, that she was a senior at Millsaps majoring in English literature, and, "most important," her best friend as a child had been a sock monkey named Sydney Carton, whom she still slept with every night because he helped her find "a far, far better rest" than she'd ever known.

Robert's half of the conversation was a series of statements he did not tell her about himself. He did not tell her he wished he had grown up without parents. He did not tell her that when he was younger he'd wanted to produce what she was now studying, nor did he tell her that in high school he'd written a collection of modern-day updates to the work of Flannery O'Connor, *O'Connor*

Stories and Other Stories, the latter category of which included "The Lucky Star Is Always Open" and "Sipping Suicide after a Double-Header." He did not tell her that *in no way* were those stories based on his own life, despite the fact that his father, a frequent patron of a dive called the Lucky Star, used to buy him suicides— all the fountain sodas mixed together—from the concession stand after his Little League games. Robert, who once wrote an unauto-biographical short story titled "My Flammable Heart," especially did not mention that looking at her, Molly, made him feel as though a match had been struck inside his chest.

"So why were you at Marunga's office this morning?" he asked as they stood at the counter, each of their checks in hand.

"I was asking him a few questions had to do with my thesis."

From the side of his eye Robert noticed Molly's lips briefly curl upward. It was the first time since they'd met less than an hour ago, he realized, she had emoted rather than performed emotion, the difference being that she didn't know he was watching her.

So you're his dealer, he decided not to say. Instead he thought of a line he had read somewhere, probably in a novel, though he could not for his life remember which one. "Nothing exists in this world that is more beautiful and destructive than the smile of a woman with a secret."

3.7

Significant Monkey—*Les Colporteurs*—
Ash Wednesday—Sick [*sic*] Transit—*Belle de Jour*—
Easter Sunday—Photo Finish

The line is actually from a work of nonfiction. In her controversial book, *Significant Monkey,* the noted literary theorist Elsa Rankin-Smith frequently references the "beautiful and destructive" smile of her titular subject, Josephine Baker. "She smiled on the world, and the world smiled back." "At times her face seemed to smile even when it was covered in tears." "Hers was a smile that knew, thought, and felt with an accord of its own."

On February 9, 1937, Ramsey Forster, who had recently arrived in Paris to recuperate from her "losses," the term her therapist used for her miscarriages, among the French landmarks that had populated so many of her childhood fantasies, saw firsthand the famous smile of La Baker.

Ramsey was at the music hall Folies-Bergère. All around her the crowd bustled, people leaving early, people arriving late, but none distracted her from the show. On the stage, what E. E. Cummings called a "plotless drama" played out: sixteen showgirls, ten chorus boys, and sixteen nudes, in addition to a chorus line of dancers, all of whom were centered, spiritually if not physically, around the show's *vedette*. Cummings wrote of the Folies-Bergère and its starlet, "The revue is a use of ideas, smells, colours, Irving Berlin, nudes, tactility, collapsible stairs, three dimensions, and fireworks to intensify Mlle. Josephine Baker." Ramsey would have agreed. She could not look away from the intense figure onstage.

"A weird cross between a kangaroo, a bicyclist, and a machine gun," as the biographer Phyllis Rose would later write, the woman variably known as the Black Pearl, the Creole Goddess, and the Bronze Venus had skin nearly the color of squash and hair that "looked as if it had been plastered down on her head with caviar." She danced around the stage with a sort of jagged fluidity. In her fox and feathers, each body part appearing to have not just a mind but also a soul of its own, Josephine typified *le diable au corps* so much that Ramsey, watching from the audience, thought she was to traditional dancing what soda water was to wine. Her frenetic movements seemed to be powered by air trying to escape her bones. Rather than dance to the music she roiled with its rhythm. Ramsey figured that must be what attracted her to the woman, how she was like a physical embodiment of her family's signature product. At the conclusion of her set—after doing such dance moves as the Mess Around, which reminded Ramsey of her twin brother, and Through the Trenches, which reminded Ramsey of her older brother—Josephine Baker sang what had become a sort of theme song, her syrupy voice matched perfectly to her effervescent body:

> *J'ai deux amours,*
> *Mon pays et Paris.*
> *Par eux toujours,*
> *Mon coeur est ravi.*

"Rumzee! Rumzee!" someone yelled into Ramsey's ear, grabbing her by the elbow, pulling her toward the doors of the music hall. "*C'est parti! Vite fait!*"

It was the girl with whom she had come to the revue, a part-time nude model who posed in an atelier beneath Ramsey's apartment, often wore blue *salopettes* with nothing else, and, after they crossed paths a few times in the elevator, had invited Ramsey for *une nuit de folie*.

"Where are we going," Ramsey said in broken French, "and why all the rush?"

"*Quoi?*"

The language was still somewhat of a barrier for Ramsey. She attempted to truncate her turn of phrase, searching through memories of the bedtime stories her mother had read to her as a child. Annabelle Forster had considered it an absolute necessity that none of her children be unilingual, as "only guttersnipe make do with their native tongue when they could have any in the world." To that end, she'd put her children to sleep by reading them Charles Perrault's *Les Contes de Ma Mère l'Oye* in the original French. For Ramsey, the tales of Sleeping Beauty, Cinderella, Bluebeard, and Little Red Riding Hood had turned her into more of a Francophile than a Francophone, inculcating her with the desire to live a life of sophistication in the city of lights. Her felicity with the language hadn't lasted as long as that desire. On her way out of the music hall, Ramsey ran through the vocabulary left over from her lessons with Monsieur Perrault and, finally, settled on two vowels.

"*Où?*" she asked the girl, whose name she still wasn't quite sure she knew.

"*Les colporteurs!*"

"Street vendors?" said Ramsey. She felt reasonably certain that was what that word meant. Instead of giving an answer, the part-time nude model grabbed her hand, guiding them both through the nighttime dwellers of Paris—charwomen whose dirty aprons smelled of cabbage soup, young gangsters in flat caps milling near the *pissotières,* page boys gathered around a dice box, and repairmen carrying acetylene torches down streetcar tracks. Finally Ramsey and the girl reached what the latter had meant by *"les colporteurs."*

Mr. and Mrs. Cole Porter lived at 13 rue Monsieur. Inside the *maison de ville,* where the girl led Ramsey by her pinkie finger, members of the smart set lingered in rooms with platinum wallpaper, on top of zebra-skin rugs, and in chairs painted mandarin red. Comely servant girls, their pupils dilated by belladonna, wandered the room, carrying trays of champagne dyed various colors, green and red and violet and orange and blue, while guests decked out in tuxedos, smelling of hair oil, cloves, mint, jasmine, sweat, and antiseptics, mingled around the piano, which was momentarily quiet as the host of the party, in a checkered scarf, concluded the irreverent tale of a wealthy, clubfooted widow from Lyon. Anaïs Nin switched which leg she leaned on each time she took a drag of her cigarette. Henry Miller rearranged his crotch by hand whenever he thought nobody would notice.

"Papillons d'amour," said an effete man in a green suit that looked to have been crafted from the felt of a billiards table. He was standing by Ramsey's side, where the part-time model had been, directing his gaze toward the couple, Henry and Anaïs, who didn't seem to be on speaking terms. "Such a lovely phrase. 'Butterflies of love.' Far more pleasant than 'crabs,'" the man said before his attention was suddenly redirected to another point in the room. "Wallis! I am in *love* with that bolero jacket!"

He disappeared the same way he had appeared, mysterious and nameless, prompting Ramsey to think, *Now this is what I've been looking for,* a smile inching across her face for the first time in she couldn't say how long.

Throughout the two weeks since her arrival, she had been trying, with little avail, to find "her people," Americans hoping to suck the marrow out of Paris, proving correct that old Harold Stearns line describing the city as "the greatest testing ground of character in the world." Ramsey frequented the Coupole, the Dome, the Rotonde, and the Select. She took her meals at Maxim's, Les Trianons, and Drouant over by l'Opera. All those places, however, were so prosaic. The feast had moved on. So for those first two weeks, Ramsey, walking along the quays at night, applying a heart hook to her bangs, squeezing fruit at the greengrocer, felt more alone than she had back in the States. Not just alone but empty. A failure at Paris's character test, she could not get rid of the void that remained after her miscarriages, the hollowness, the excavation, a sense that within her body were four cavernous, echoing, amorphous spaces that had once been her children.

Ramsey sampled every color of champagne served at the party. She was on her fourth one, blue this time, when the person she was speaking with, an aggressively pleasant woman *d'un certain age* whose *robe de soir* shimmered in the dim lamplight, said, "Looks as though Josephine made it after all. Have you had a chance to meet her?"

"In fact, I have not."

"My dear, oh my dear, but you simply must!" the woman said, switching to French, as if the force of her sentiment were too great for one language. "She is going to love you!"

That the woman had used the verb *adorer* instead of *aimer* sent an odd thrill through Ramsey. Wasn't *adorer* the stronger of the two words for *love*? During her time in L.A. prior to her losses, Ramsey had been captivated by the world of matinee idols and budding ingénues, and now, after so many months of trying to overcome her depression, it was comforting to allow herself the superficiality of being starstruck. Ramsey imagined becoming best friends with Josephine. She could see it perfectly, the two of them reading *Le Figaro* on a bench in the Tuileries, the two of them spending *une petite fortune* at Place Vendôme.

On being introduced that night, though, Josephine Baker exchanged only mild pleasantries with Ramsey. Every one of Ramsey's attempts at friendly flirtation with the Creole Goddess was met by strait lace. "This is some party" elicited the response "Isn't it wonderful?" "I'd love to know where you learned to dance" elicited the response "Watching the kangaroos at the St. Louis Zoo." "Your body is very intelligent" elicited the response "If only my head were as well." "I enjoyed the show tonight. You're such a talent" elicited the response "I have no talent. I have only friends. I like people."

"Could have fooled me."

Although Ramsey immediately regretted saying them, those last words, however impertinent, managed to unleash the famously "beautiful and destructive" smile. Josephine finished her champagne, called for her coat, and said, "Come along, *chèrie,* you wicked little thing. Some place I want to show you." The party soon turned into nothing but a low rumble on the other side of a closed door.

. . .

Ramsey woke to the sight of a parakeet spitting seeds at a bust of Louis XIV. In the spacious, loft-style apartment, piles of clothes dotted the wood floors, the needle of a phonograph blipped over and over at the end of some recording, a coromandel screen blocked the sunlight from a sooty window, and, next to Ramsey in bed, an impossibly long, impossibly smooth leg the color of caramel lay across red silk sheets.

"*Pauvre oiseau,*" said Josephine.

Instead of looking at the parakeet, which continued to assault the Sun King from its cage hanging by the bed, Josephine was looking at Ramsey, circling her ring finger around an exposed nipple. Ramsey pulled the sheets high up her chest, the previous night coming back to her in pieces, each made ragged by too much champagne.

They had left the Porters' party around one. After being questioned by *cyclos,* black-caped police officers on bicycles, about whether they'd seen a *sans domicile fixe* running down the street with a homburg hat far too luxurious for a bum, Josephine and Ramsey had walked, hand in hand, to Notre Dame. "*Mademoiselle Baker!*" cried the woman who watched over the cathedral at night. "*Vous avez revenu.*" She unlocked a heavy door and motioned for them to enter. At the top of a spiral staircase, Ramsey and Josephine reached the roof of the Notre Dame, their view from its balustrade a painter's dream, heavy fog situated between the Hôtel-Dieu, the Sorbonne, the Eiffel Tower, and Sacré-Cœur, wrapping itself around them like cotton balls in an expensive package. Ramsey, while growing up in the rural South, had so often fantasized she'd one day see Paris, France, in perfect repose, as though it had been waiting patiently, over decades, over centuries, for the boon of her presence. She took in the nearly mystical view of a nearly mythic city without realizing her mouth was hanging open. It was pushed shut by Josephine, who, using the crook of her index finger, pulled Ramsey toward her by the chin. With the city of Paris spread out before them, they kissed, lightly at first and then urgently, just as they found themselves doing the next day in Josephine's apartment, moments after waking up.

"The bourgeois way is to save and accumulate. Sexual potential is a woman's capital," Phyllis Rose writes in her book *Jazz Cleopatra.* "[Josephine's] promiscuity was very likely a mask for a deep-seated distrust of intimacy."

In the expatriate heiress Ramsey Forster she had met her match. Ramsey had distrusted intimacy since the night she'd been invited into the coatroom of an apartment in Greenwich Village. Ramsey had trusted intimacy even less since the series of nights she'd woken her husband by whispering, uneasy and confused and fearful, *"Something's wrong."*

But this, here and now, felt right. Although she had never been with another woman, Ramsey had always believed in the elasticity of love, as cognizant of other types of sexuality as she was of the fact that in various parts of the world people ate with two sticks instead of cutlery, wore wigs in open court, had dozens of words for *snow,* and rode through jungles on the backs of elephants. Until now she had not thought to try the other types the same way she had not thought to dance the hula. Ramsey's experience with Josephine that morning made her regret her previous self's lack of enterprise. On top of silk sheets, a type so often described as being like a second skin, the two of them felt each other's own, Ramsey drawing her palm down a midriff often rubbed with lemon in an attempt to lighten its complexion, Josephine walking her fingers up a thigh still striped where a bathing suit had encountered the California sun. They coincided halfway.

"Josephine was always, always, always dominant in bed," writes Elsa Rankin-Smith, whose flagrant claims about the inaccuracy of Phyllis Rose's biography were themselves found to be inaccurate in the *Columbia Journalism Review*'s investigative report, "Follies of Truth: Josephine Baker and Two Biographers."

The consummate performer, onstage as well as in life, Josephine proved, while lying next to Ramsey in the cool morning air, that Rankin-Smith was right about one thing at least. She was in control. All those years abroad had given her the advantage as she reached down through the sheets. Shocked at first by the new sensation, Ramsey gradually settled into it, allowing herself to be handled, clutched, hefted, until the moment Josephine grew even bolder, at which point Ramsey thought, with a gasp, *Sweet Jesus, she's double-jointed.*

"I should be getting to the theater soon," Josephine said an hour later, the afternoon sun breaking through a western window. She was methodically placing petit fours on Ramsey's tongue like some kind of Eucharist.

"Can I ask you something?" said Ramsey between swallows.

"*Bien sûr.*"

"When did you know, I mean, when did you know you were, uh, interested in, well, um."

"*Les femmes?*"

"Yes."

Josephine rolled over so that she was lying flat on her back. "My first two husbands were named Willie. Willie Wells and Willie Baker." She hoisted her penciled eyebrow. "Took two divorces for me to realize I don't need a willie in my life."

Ramsey reached across Josephine to get to the plate of petit fours, her forearm glancing against a body molted of its theatrical feathers and fur, her nose filling with the scent of hair unleashed by restless sleep from the slick grip of pomade. "When can I see you again?" Ramsey asked, chewing on a *glacé.*

"Tomorrow we go on tour."

"How long?"

"A month."

"Where'll you be touring?"

In a sudden but unsurprising reversal of demeanor, Josephine sprang from the bed, saying, "Can't remember. *Ne t'inquiète pas.* I'll be in touch." She wrapped herself in a kimono printed with butterflies. "Jo-Jo will show you out."

"Who?"

Josephine's bodyguard was named Jo-Jo Chowdhury. "I may have twice her name," he was fond of saying in regard to his boss, "yet I am but half that woman." Formerly a security guard at the Galeries Lafayette, Jo-Jo was a stout man roughly five feet in height, with a neck as thick as some men's thighs. His pulse strained against the top button of his shirt as he stood next to Ramsey in the elevator's hydraulic cage. She wondered how many times throughout the tenure of his position the button had been rocketed into flight by some fearsome display of strength.

"If you tell me your address, *mademoiselle,* I'd be delighted to give you the directions on how to get home," Jo-Jo said to Ramsey, leading her out of the elevator and opening the front door to the building.

"I think I can manage. Have a lovely day."

Despite Josephine's about-face earlier, Ramsey was having a lovely day. A smile began to take hold as she looked onto the Avenue Pierre 1er de Serbie and tried to figure out the best route to her apartment. Who cared if she had gotten brushed aside? She was in Paris! At this very moment, with the city spread out before her, anything was possible. She could hop onto the zinc *comptoir* at the Falstaff and scissor her legs for a crowd of whistling sailors. She could steal the hat right off a police officer's head and lob it on top of a Metro station's glass canopy. She could get her hair shingled at one of the most fashionable salons, go skipping down a lime avenue, and let a windswept strand hang over one eye as a stranger lit her cigarette. In the middle of the sidewalk, Ramsey was considering how best to enjoy such a beautiful afternoon when, suddenly, she found herself surrounded by the vibrant, giggling bodies of four children.

They seemed to be playing a game of tag. Two boys and two girls, all toddlers of varying age, the children ran circles around Ramsey, one chasing the other, as though she were a maypole, slowly being wrapped in ribbons. The girls were twins.

Ramsey knew without doubt who all of them were, not only because of those eyebrows on one, that mouth on another, but also because of the soot on their foreheads, which she believed had to have been placed there so that, on a Parisian street, she could more easily spot them in the crowd.

"*Les enfants! Venez ici! Onyva!*" said a young woman, corralling the children into a cluster. She guided them down the sidewalk. "*Dépêchez-vous. Votre mère vous attend.*"

Her joints going loose in her body, Ramsey watched as the four children were taken away. She didn't know what to do. She had no idea what to say. Finally, after the children and their nanny had rounded a corner and were out of sight, Ramsey took a long breath, flexed her hands, and stumbled toward the curb, where she was sick into a refuse cart.

. . .

Two weeks after Ash Wednesday, Ramsey sat in a café on Boulevard St.-Michel, trying to think about her husband, Arthur, but instead thinking only of Josephine.

They had not spoken since the first time they had been together. Over the past two weeks, Ramsey had relived that night and the subsequent morning in her mind, concentrating on the taste, the aroma, the sound, the touch—sheer physicality combined with a sense of being unmoored from the physical world. If Ramsey's life had begun as three-dimensional, she considered in the quiet café, and if the events from the last few years had left her as two, even one, then making love with Josephine slung-shot her past three-dimensions and into four, six, ten, a hundred.

Ramsey chose to focus on the pleasure of that night as a means of avoiding, often without success, the memory of what had happened outside Josephine's apartment building the next day. Those four children weren't really hers, Ramsey knew, but she couldn't shake the feeling they were. Was she going crazy? Ever since that day on the sidewalk she'd been seeing other incarnations of them all over the city—her daughters asleep in a double pram while being strolled through the quartier, her sons chasing after a pigeon around the parterres in a municipal garden. The sight of them deboned her like a fish.

"*Excusez-moi,*" Ramsey said to the waiter. She then asked him to bring her some stationery, a request whose diligent, unquestioning, routine fulfillment was one of Ramsey's favorite aspects of Parisian cafés. Seconds later, the waiter placed pen and paper on the table. Ramsey began with "Dear Arthur."

> Do you ever think about what we would have named them? I do. Perhaps a family name, from yours or mine. In the South we have an odd but fair tradition of giving children their mother's maiden name. I think "Forster Landau" would have been a wonderful name for a firstborn son. Fitting, too, as it sounds so much like that of a movie star. The star maker's son with a movie star's name. For our daughters, the twins, I would have liked to have named one of them Fiona, after my grandmother. She would have liked that.

At her table in the café, Ramsey stopped writing, unable to see past those names, Forster and Fiona. She set the pen down and took a sip of coffee. The cup rattled as she placed it back in the saucer.

That drew the attention of the man sitting a few tables away. For him the sound of a coffee cup rattling was similar to a siren going off in the night. It meant the person holding the cup needed his help. The other things that drew the man's attention were, though he was not aware of them as such, matters of chance's intrusion in the trajectory of a life. Over the past two weeks, Ramsey had not managed to keep down much food, which had left her cheeks gaunt, and earlier that morning, she'd been too distracted to notice the *pull paysan* she'd put on had a hole in its sleeve. The man followed the apparently near-starving, near-penniless woman as she walked out of the café.

"*Mademoiselle,* is this your necklace?" he asked her after one block. From his fingers dangled a gold necklace with a sapphire gemstone. "I believe it fell off back there at your table."

"Do I know you?"

Vincent de la Baume, besides being a gifted mythomane, was the son of Sephardic Jews and a member of the Camelots du Roi who, after a twelve-year stint in La Santé prison, would become known as Vinnie the Bomb. Presently, he worked as a "wholesaler" or "meat man" for more than half a dozen "hump houses" throughout Paris. It was his job to keep them stocked with girls. On his daily hunts, whenever he came across a desperate character, Vincent would claim to have found her necklace, which, if she said it wasn't hers, he would insist that she keep, thus ensuring loyalty from the soon-to-be *fille de joie* with a subconscious advance of wages.

This woman now was not a typical one. She steadfastly refused the necklace. "*D'accord,*" Vincent said to Ramsey. He offered her one of his brand, and she heartened him by taking it. Together they walked down the boulevard smoking Gauloises Blues.

"Please excuse me for the frankness I have, *mademoiselle,* but you seem to be someone in need of assistance."

"Assistance?"

"There is a phrase for which I am now searching my mind. 'Wit's end.' Yes. You seem to be someone who is at her wit's end."

"So, I'm that obvious, huh?"

"What luck you are now finding yourself in! There exist in this city men who specialize in helping women like yourself. I am such a man."

Ramsey had no doubt he was a pimp. It only took one glance at the guy. Nobody but *un maquereau* would wear a scarf made of Valenciennes bobbin lace.

Still, he was a welcome distraction, from the children singing in a school playground across the street and from the note in her pocket that would never be sent. Ramsey was almost thankful. The least she could do was listen to what this man had to say.

. . .

"Another round?" asked the bartender at Summer Solstice just outside Los Angeles on the night of November 2, 1975. The old woman, his last customer, shook her head. She could barely keep her eyes open. "Want me to call you a cab?" the bartender said. "I think I should call you a cab."

"No, thanks."

The old woman laid a hundred-dollar bill on the countertop. She staggered outside, got in her car, and cranked the engine. After the wreck there would barely be enough of a body left to test for alcohol.

"She was really impressed by some car in the parking lot," the bartender told a police officer the next day. "Last thing she said, while she was walking out the door, was 'sick transit.' I remember exactly. Sick transit. It must have been the Chevy Camaro one of our regulars drives."

Nearly four decades prior to that incident, during her Paris sabbatical, Ramsey Forster whispered the first two words of the Latin phrase that meant "thus passes the glory of the world" as she walked into the parlor of Le Chabanais. All around her stood young women in varying degrees of undress. Tapestries hung along the walls next to oil paintings that wouldn't have been out of place in The Sweetest Thing. Chandeliers twinkled overhead like those in the lobby of the Memphis Peabody. Built on the site of the Hôtel Chabanais Saint-Ponges, the brothel known as Le Chabanais was considered the epitome of Parisian grandeur and elegance. Vincent de la Baume thought it would be just the right sort of venue for a woman like Ramsey Forster.

A particularly strong dose of Veronal helped her acclimate that night. The drug reminded Ramsey of *Alice's Adventures in Wonderland,* a book that had played almost as large a role as Perrault's fairy tales in her childhood desire to escape the confines of her home state, her family name, her entire country. Rather than make her larger or smaller, though, the drug gave her a sense of being at once present and absent, quantum and infinite, similar to how she'd felt during her too-brief time with Josephine. The drug made Ramsey extradimensional. Only in that condition could she consider accepting the universe's refusal to apologize.

What does anything matter? she thought, gazing around the parlor. Nothing mattered. That was the key. For the person Ramsey was right then, it did not matter that she had lost four children in two years, nor did it matter that Josephine hadn't sent her so much as a *petit-bleu* in over a month. Was she still on tour? Was she already back? Had she used Ramsey as a body, a goddamned receptacle in which to expend a moment's pleasure as oblivious morons discussed *Anything Goes* in the background and the stench of filthy, sweaty coats engulfed the room? The answers to those questions didn't matter to the woman draping herself across a chaise longue while getting browsed by a group of tuxedoed men.

"Would you please join me for the evening?" one of them asked her.

"*Non,*" Ramsey said, causing a girl across the room to chirp in shock. Ramsey stood from the chaise longue and walked through the customers, those sentient tuxedos, all of whom grew, as she'd hoped, obediently still and quiet. She'd be damned if she'd let them have all the fun. Insouciant yet deliberate, as if she were choosing jewelry to wear for an evening out, Ramsey studied the men, dragging her fingers across their shoulders, tugging at their cuffs, rubbing their lapels, pondering the relative pertness of their butts. "You'll do," she said to one with hair in the style of a Roman emperor.

The man said, "*Merci,*" and as he led Ramsey from the parlor, he glanced back at those who were not chosen and beamed at their dejection.

Le Chabanais was famous for its theme rooms. Replete with furniture of the *Ancien Régime,* the Louis XVI boudoir was decorated in homage to Marie Antoinette and the Louis XV boudoir in homage to Madame de Pompadour. There was a Moorish room. There was a Pompeian room. The Torture Chamber included all manner of whips, gags, flails, handcuffs, crops, clamps, and leather blindfolds. The Chinese Pagoda featured a variety of Oriental rugs, bamboo screens, lamps, fans, stools, and a platform bed. At the 1900 World Fair, the Japanese Room won a prize for its exemplary "French refinement and taste."

On Ramsey's evening at Le Chabanais, the tuxedoed man led her to the Hindu Room, which had once been the favorite of the future King Edward VII. "Does this room meet your satisfaction?" the man asked Ramsey.

"I suppose."

She pushed her arms into his jacket, helping him slide out of it, and began to loosen his bow tie. Ramsey thought of herself as an actress playing a role. No longer was she the girl from Mississippi who had married up, or the woman who could not do the one thing only women could, or the girl at a party in New York following a man into the coatroom. She was a lady of the evening, someone whose daily expenses were clothes, hair set, manicure, and drinks, someone for whom the bidet was the most vital bathroom fixture, the corset drawer the most necessary in the bureau.

Judging by the man's English, not just the way but also the fact he spoke it, Ramsey guessed he was Hungarian. He seemed more nervous than she was. Most likely in his late thirties, the man did not appear to Ramsey, as she guided his hands up her body, the type who would have never visited a *maison close,* not too young and not too old. She found a possible answer in the wedding ring on his finger.

"Please excuse me for that," he said, wrenching the ring off and placing it in his pocket. "I should have remembered."

In an attempt at playfulness, Ramsey said, "And what will the missus think of your being in a place such as this?" looking up at him through her eyelashes.

"Nothing."

"*Pourqui?*"

"She died three months ago."

He blinked away the tears that had briefly welled. What a strange thing. Ramsey had no idea how to respond to such naked emotion from a person whose name she did not even know. Until that moment he had simply been the Hungarian.

That he would reveal a matter so personal unhinged something inside her. Near the foot of the rococo four-poster bed, kissing the man on his mouth and then turning her back to him and wrapping his arms around her and then swiveling her neck and kissing the man on his mouth again, Ramsey misremembered one of the lessons her mother had taught her when she was growing up. "Sometimes the world can get so biting you have to start biting back" became in her memory "When the world gets too biting, just hold out your hand."

Ramsey loosened the grasp of the Hungarian. She leaned over the bed, pressed her cheek into it, and spread her arms wide.

. . .

Ramsey's evening at Le Chabanais concluded with an "accidental" spillage of wine on her dress and mumbled comments from the staff that she and her fancy manners should go slum somewhere else. She couldn't say she blamed them. Women who worked there out of necessity had a right to hate those who only pretended to. Still, Ramsey was disappointed, because of how much she had enjoyed her encounter with the Hungarian. It had made her feel whole again. The ounce of pleasure had outweighed the pound of pain. She'd regained control by relinquishing it. If she couldn't replenish that sense of control, satisfaction, and wholeness at Le Chabanais, Ramsey decided, then who the hell cared? She'd find it somewhere else.

At the *boîtes de nuit* patronized by the café-terrace set, Ramsey convinced everyone she was a Russian aristocrat waiting for her Nansen passport, stateless and destitute, and she did not refuse when they offered to pick up her check. She got blind drunk with rag pickers, *vidangeurs,* navvies, and Zouaves on leave from their regiment. She invited clochards to join her for Vouvray and escargots at the city's most upscale restaurants. In the restroom of a Coq d'Or dance hall, she snorted the white powder a waitress had said would "bring the universe into submission," and at a street fair in the Place d'Italie, while the trainers were distracted, she opened the cages for the exotic birds and filled the Parisian sky with streaks of emerald-green, ocean-blue, fire-red, and lemon-yellow. One night, driving through the city in a stolen Renault with a dancer named Artemis the Heathen, she hit a slick spot in the road caused by a leaking Richer pump, and after bringing the spinning-out car to a curbside stop, she winked at her startled passenger and said, "Always turn into the skid."

Seldom during those few weeks did Ramsey spend the night at her own apartment, a result, though she would never admit it, of her eternal struggle to rout convention and her utter distaste for sleeping alone. On the evening of March 22, 1937, after "puffing bamboo" with a hurdy-gurdy who had a crush on her, she returned to the apartment for, as far as she cared or could recall, the first time that month. Ramsey wandered down the sidewalk and through the entrance to her building, whistling some erratic melody, unaware she was being watched by two men across the street, one in a parked car and one by a lamppost, neither of whom was yet aware of the other.

"*Mademoiselle!* So good you return!" yelled the concierge from his loge. He reached under his desk and held up a stack of envelopes. "*Votre courier.* Please, I give to you, yes? *Tellement de courier!*"

Ramsey mumbled, "Later, okay?" before getting on the elevator.

In her apartment, ignoring the pervasive scent of withered flowers, she poured herself a glass of Malaga, turned on the radio, and sank into the crushed-velvet cushions of a settee. She disappeared into an absence of thought, the voice from the radio merely a backdrop of sound. ". . . an encyclical of Pope Pious XI against the German Reich . . . *Mit brennender Sorge* . . . document condemns the exaltation of any one race over another . . . idolatry of State is still idolatry . . . Herr Hitler . . . but national pride does not absolve hatred or the . . ."

A knock at the door pulled Ramsey back into unwanted thought. Through the green translucence shed by the Venetian-glass globe hanging above her head, she walked across the room, her intoxication, though in its descent, slowing each step to a subaquatic pace. Ripples and currents feathered the air as she reached for and opened the door.

"*Bonsoir, mademoiselle,*" said Vincent de la Baume.

At first Ramsey couldn't place him, so much had happened since her one night at Le Chabanais. The bobbin-lace scarf that only a pimp could pull off triggered her memory. What did he want? Ramsey studied his deckle-edged stubble, those teeth as misshapen and blotchy as freshwater pearls, that lank, greasy hair, and knew this wasn't a social call. Despite the temperate weather, Vincent wore a black leather overcoat, double-breasted, with a wrap-across front and a belt buckled at the waist. Ramsey didn't have to go near the coat to know exactly what it smelled like. Her hands shriveled into fists.

"Hello, Vincent. To what do I owe the pleasure?"

He walked past Ramsey into the apartment, and with his back turned to her, he said, "You are a difficult woman to find. I have been in search of you everywhere. Many weeks *sans* success. Until now."

"Congratulations."

Vincent turned to Ramsey. "Why have you not been back to Le Chabanais?"

After she closed the door and strolled past Vincent, attempting to keep her trepidation hidden, Ramsey picked up her wineglass, drank all that was left, and said, "I've been busy."

"Busy."

"*Oui.*"

"Your hands. What is the word? They are quivering." Vincent picked up the bottle of Malaga from the bar alcove. As he refilled Ramsey's glass, he whispered, "Say when."

"When."

But it was too late. A large drop of red wine overflowed onto the wood floor. "*Merde,*" Ramsey said before siphoning off an inch from the glass to keep it from spilling further. While retrieving a rag from the bathroom, she made the mistake of looking in the mirror, where she saw the collateral damage of the past few weeks. Dark lines crosshatched her skin like a journeyman cartoonist's approximation of shadows. Her eyeliner did little to distract from the bags under it, and skipped meals had imploded her cheeks.

"The Romanian admired you very much," Vincent said, standing near the bar while Ramsey draped a white rag over the puddle of wine. A red moon waxed within the terry cloth sky.

"I figured he was Hungarian."

"Day after day he returns. '*Où est la femme?*' '*Où est ma belle?*' He would appreciate very much if you return to Le Chabanais. I would appreciate if you return as well."

"No, thank you."

Vincent walked toward Ramsey. "'Thank you,' she says, but she refuses my special generosity. *Quelle fille bête.*" He tried to touch Ramsey's hair, but she drew back. "Do not be afraid, Miss Forster."

His use of her name made Ramsey realize that, in this situation, speaking with some repulsive thug in a foreign country, she was no longer protected by the aegis of it. The name of "Forster" was like the Louis Vuitton luggage stacked in her bedroom closet: prestigious to certain people but right now nothing more than Damier-checkered boxes.

"The Romanian would pay a great deal," said Vincent. "*Tu seras riche.*"

"Do I look like I need money?" Ramsey gestured around her, at the palatial apartment and its lavish decor. The momentary flair of snobbery gave her a momentary sense of power. If this son of a bitch *tutoyered* her again, Ramsey thought, she'd scream until everyone on the street came rushing up to the apartment. With a careless wave of her hand, the motion of which was regaining normal speed, she asked Vincent to leave.

"One last thing," said de la Baume.

For someone new to the experience, a punch in the face can seem, however briefly, more exhilarating than it is painful, more surprising than it is frightening. The key word, conceded Ramsey afterward, was *briefly*. After she crashed to the floor, Vincent said, "You seem to have lost your footing, my dear. Is something wrong?"

Ramsey's pulse rippled through the spot where the punch had landed. Her ears chimed. Her eyes flooded. Her lips shook. Was this it then? It couldn't be. She wouldn't let it be. The world's glory was *not* going to pass. Ramsey ordered herself to stand, but her body refused to obey. From the window, she heard car horns, shouted expletives, and somebody telling someone else, in a creole accent, to get the hell out of the way. Across the apartment, she did not see the door slowly open.

Crouched in front of Ramsey, Vincent pushed a strand of hair out of her eyes, stale tobacco and heeltaps riding his breath. "You shall return to Le Chabanais tomorrow night, and you shall not leave until I say you can leave. If you don't do as I say, I'll—"

Jo-Jo Chowdhury wrapped his thick hands around Vincent's neck and lifted him into the air. His feet dangled inches above the floor. In the subsequent fray, Vincent de la Baume proved that the nickname he would be given in prison, Vinnie the Bomb, did not concern his explosive fighting skills, but rather his proficiency at failure. Jo-Jo had him in a choke hold against the wall when he said to Ramsey, "You will find her waiting outside, Mademoiselle Forster." His words were underscored by the patter of a button bouncing past where Ramsey lay on the floor, one that she knew had, in a recent, previous life, held together the collar of Jo-Jo's shirt.

Even though she wanted to run, Ramsey forced herself to walk as she left the apartment, passing through the floral-wallpapered hall and stepping into the elevator. The different floors rose in front of her eyes like an emery board sloughing off a callus. Ninth floor, eighth floor, scrape, scrape. Seventh floor, sixth floor, scrape, scrape. Fifth floor, fourth floor, third, second, first. In the lobby, the concierge asked Ramsey if everything was all right. "Never been better," she said, holding a hand over the red, swelling side of her face.

Outside, the air smelled of powdered sugar and fried potatoes—circus food. Workmen in red sashes tilted their heads at Ramsey as she peered into the dim evening twilight. Josephine, her cosmetics by Rubinstein and hair by Antoine and jewelry by Van Cleef and apparel by Schiaparelli, sat in the leopard-printed passenger seat of a Ballot, parked on the street in front of the building. She hopped out of the car just in time for Ramsey to stumble on a gap in the pavement and fall theatrically into her outstretched arms. "And they say I'm the one starved for attention," Josephine said. She then scolded Ramsey for not replying to any of the messages she had sent over the past few days via the *pneumatique*.

• • •

Two years later, Ramsey woke from a dream on the morning of April 9, 1939, after being tapped on the shoulder by Boonwell, a chimpanzee. He held an orange in one hand. "Hello there. What's for breakfast today?" she asked him as he placed the orange on her pillow. "Thank you, Boonwell. Where's your mama?"

The château Les Milandes was a haven for Josephine's myriad pets. "Originally a run-down house on a hilltop in a beautiful part of France known for its rivers, its foie gras, and its cave paintings," Phyllis Rose notes in *Jazz Cleopatra,* the château and its surrounding estate, bought by Josephine in 1936 for a song, would eventually become home to hundreds of cows, pigs, chickens, dogs, and peacocks, their head counts fluctuating by the dozen, as well as "two hotels, three restaurants, a miniature golf course, tennis, volleyball, and basketball courts, a wax museum of scenes from Josephine Baker's life, stables, a patisserie, a foie gras factory, a gas station, and a post office," not to mention three monkeys, two white mice, and a Great Dane named Bonzo. Ramsey had been living there ever since the short period she referred to as her "bad times."

That morning she got out of bed, took Boonwell's hand, and walked with him downstairs. In the airy, sunlit kitchen, Josephine was having coffee and, for breakfast, eating a plate of spaghetti, her favorite food, the idea of which always tickled Ramsey. Breakfast, lunch, and dinner: spaghetti, spaghetti, spaghetti. You can take the girl out of America, give her unimaginable fame and fortune, but she'd still be little "Tumpie" from St. Louis, Missouri, wearing shoes made of coal sacking, considering noodles and ketchup a special treat for Sunday dinner. Those were the things Ramsey loved most about her, the tiny threads of her past that constituted the fabric of her present, everything that went into making this woman who always rode in the front seat of taxis, despised the telephone, adored the cinema, and wanted to write a fairy tale about her romance with Ramsey entitled, in reference to the tool commonly used for sipping soda pop, *The Straw Princess*.

"Good morning, Tumpie."

"Happy Easter."

"It's Easter?"

"You need to get out more," Josephine said while Ramsey walked her fingers along her shoulder and kissed her on the cheek. In return, Josephine took Ramsey's hand and, as was her habit, anointed the inside of her wrist with her lips.

On the other side of the kitchen, Ramsey poured herself a cup of coffee, thinking Jo was right; she did need to get out more, though, point of fact, she was hardly some recluse. Over the two years she'd been at Les Milandes, Ramsey usually made the trip to Paris at least once a month, going to a party or doing some shopping or taking in a show, altogether the type of life that she and Josephine, as they discovered in one of their late-night, wine-charged conversations, had both dreamed of during their respective childhoods in Mississippi and Missouri. To both of them, Paris had represented not only a way out but a way up, a path to worldliness, class, style, and elegance via masterpiece-filled museums and snail-based cuisine.

With the rest of her time at the château Ramsey had been training herself as a writer, an undertaking for which she had far more ambition than she ever did for the, in her opinion, incredibly boring soft-drink business. She'd even had a minor success last year.

Under the pen name Ptolemy Brown, Ramsey had published her first novel, *Rebel Yell Down Under,* part bodice ripper and part dime western, about a Confederate major who moves to the Australian outback, where, aside from running a cattle station, he defends the natives, woos damsels, beds wenches, and triumphs in many a drunken brawl. The reviews were mixed. Sales were modest. Recently, though, she had finished a children's book about a dog that lives at a French zoo owned by two elderly friends, Auntie Rue and Gram Magog, whose personalities were not unlike the current residents of Les Milandes. Its subtitle included a made-up term of venery, except in reverse. The animals at the zoo named humans collectively the way humans in the real world usually did animals. Although it wouldn't be published for another decade— the outbreak of war would soon leave the manuscript forgotten at the bottom of a trunk—*The Adventures of Catfish the Dog: A Discombobulation of Philosophers* would spawn many additional volumes, including "A Remainder of Novelists," "An Imbalance of Accountants," "A Yodel of Swiss," "A Gossip of Seamstresses," "A Shuffle of Gamblers," and "An Independence of Americans." Just yesterday Ramsey had decided on a dedication for the first adventure of Catfish the dog.

> *J'ai deux amours,*
> *Mon pays et quelqu'un d'autre.*
> *Par eux toujours,*
> *Mon coeur est ravi.*

"Tonight our old friend *colporteur* is throwing a party at the Ritz," said Josephine, carrying her empty plate to the sink. "Want to make a quick trip to the city?"

Ramsey thought the same thing Neville Chamberlain might

have while negotiating the Munich Agreement half a year earlier: *What's the worst that could happen?* "Sounds lovely," she told Josephine.

They drove instead of taking the train. Branches reticulated overhead, gossamer clouds visible beyond them like stuffing in threadbare upholstery, the couple passed through the French countryside in Josephine's new Voisin, which she'd bought in brown to match her own coloring and whose seats she'd had lined in snakeskin, "to match my soul!" Villagers shielded their eyes from the sun as if in salute as the two women zoomed past their farmhouses.

In the July 22, 1939, issue of *The New Yorker,* Janet Flanner would describe Paris as having "a fit of prosperity, gaiety, and hospitality" unheard of since the trouble in Munich the previous year. She would add, "It has taken the threat of war to make the French loosen up and have a really swell and civilized good time." Ramsey could already see that atmosphere burgeoning everywhere. Washerwomen nearly danced a jig in their sabots as they carried bundles of wrapped laundry. Young men who were clearly *dans le milieu* tried to race the milk train. Even people outside the *bureau de contentieux,* waiting in line to express their grievances, had smiles on all their jolie laide faces, crooked teeth disguised by dimples, scars disguised by batting eyelashes. After a quick stop at Josephine's apartment to freshen up, she and Ramsey headed for the Ritz on foot, carrying the invitation that read, near the bottom, ICNW rather than RSVP: "In Case No War."

At the party things took a turn for the surreal. Beneath a banner that read PAS DE HISTOIRES, PAS DES PROVOCATIONS, PAS DE BRUIT, or NO FUSS, NO PROVOCATIONS, NO NOISE, a slogan for the French policy toward German military buildup, people of all nationalities and nary a geopolitical creed, British and American and French, stood around drinking cocktails, making jokes, telling stories, and playing with jewel-encrusted, gold-leafed yo-yos from Cartier. Yo-yos were popular that season. "Germany can *have* Czechoslovakia!" a man with an eye patch said as he "Walked the Dog" and then performed a poor version of an "Around the World." He almost broke one of the six white globes in the electrolier hanging above his head.

"Are you feeling okay?" Ramsey asked Josephine as they ordered a drink from Claude, the Ritz's barman.

"But of course, *chèrie*. Why?"

"You were quiet the whole ride up."

Josephine swatted the air. "Pfftt! Think nothing of it." It was all Ramsey could think about as she followed Josephine into the crowd.

The first people they ran into were what Jo's friends liked to call the Lavender Element. Noël Coward, currently in town for some "security detail" he loved being coy about, was playing straight man to Cole Porter, who, at the moment, was telling the story of how he'd won a Croix de Guerre in the Great War. "My fellow soldiers lifted me to their shoulders and cheered, I tell you, cheered as they carried me out of those beastly trenches."

"I'm sure you enjoyed some beastly behavior in those trenches, Porter."

"Oh, shut it, Noël. I was at war, which, you know, *does* things to a man."

Everyone laughed obligingly except Josephine. What had her so upset? Ramsey spent the next few hours trying to pry an answer loose, but all she received was the usual meaningless exclamation. "Isn't it wonderful?" These funks of Jo's were common. The main difference with this one was that she seemed to be trying to hide it.

Around four in the morning, Ramsey finally got an idea of its cause when, on a makeshift runway atop the bar, models from Lelong, a couturier, began an impromptu fashion show.

On their bodies the models wore dresses, exquisitely tailored and obviously expensive, but on their heads they wore gas masks, military-grade, operational, and painted in gold. They looked like giant humanoid insects strutting on the bar top. "You have to leave," Josephine whispered in Ramsey's ear as the crowd applauded.

"What?"

"You must go home."

"Shouldn't we sleep it off before driving back to Les Milandes?"

"Not that home."

Josephine took her by the sleeve and guided them both out of the party. As they walked through the city, passing apartment buildings in front of which sandbags would soon be piled to protect against fire from incendiary bombs, stepping on bits of newspapers in which crossword puzzles would soon be discontinued for fear they contained code, passing cafés in which waiters would soon require customers to pay up front in case an air-raid siren emptied all their tables, Josephine told Ramsey she had to go back to America.

"It's no longer safe for you here. Any day now that pudgy little man with the mustache will come stomping into the city," she said. "I know his kind. They don't give up. And when he's here, do you think he'll simply open the gates for you? 'Run along home, child'?"

"But what about you? America's home for you, too."

Josephine smiled halfheartedly. She raised the inside of Ramsey's wrist to her lips, as though telling it a secret. "*Mon pays c'est Paris.*"

It was almost seven o'clock. The sun was creeping into the sky behind their backs, shedding a honeyed glow on the Arc de Triomphe a short ways up the avenue, while shopkeepers drowsily began to open their doors. Only a few tourists were milling along the Champs-Élysées. "If it's yours, it's mine, you damn fool," Ramsey said, tears halfway down her cheeks and a seam running jagged through her voice, as she wiped her thumbs across the bags Jo always had under her eyes. She would stand by those words until the day after September 1, 1939.

Five months before that day, however, the two of them pulled their hips close, not bothering to ensure they were unwatched. "The famous photograph of Josephine Baker and Ramsey Forster kissing in front of the Arc de Triomphe was undoubtedly staged," Elsa Rankin-Smith writes in *Significant Monkey,* one of many libelous comments that would lead her publisher to have all unsold copies of the book pulped. In truth neither woman knew their picture was being taken by a man sitting on a bench across the street.

"A colored," said the photographer, Franklin Scarlatti of Vantage Pictures, lowering his camera from his expressionless face.

3.8

True Delta—A Phonetic Reminder of an Old Friend—
Struck Pond—*Caste and Class in a Southern Town*—
Three-Card Monty

"This here's cotton country," Montgomery's driver, Push Lloyd, was saying as they entered the Mississippi Delta. "Miles around everything you can lay eyes on used to be swamp. Pestiferous swamp. Full of panthers and bears and 'squitoes big as fists. Then you white folks took care of all that. By likes of which I mean you had us take care of it."

It was the night of June 21, 1939, two months before Ramsey witnessed the famous smile of Josephine Baker for what she thought would be the last time, forty-nine years since the day Houghton kissed Annabelle for the first time beneath a walnut tree, thirty-seven years before the United States Bicentennial and three hundred and nineteen years after the Pilgrims landed, seventy-five years after Tewksbury's adoption by Dr. McAllister, five years before the birth of Nicholas, thirty-eight years before the death of the last Forster to run the Panola Cola Company, twenty-one years after the end of World War I and ten weeks before the start of World War II, and four months, two weeks, and three days before the Mississippi gubernatorial election. Montgomery was on his way that night to fund-raise in the Delta.

Despite the privilege of his upbringing, Monty was unaccustomed to being chauffeured, to the extent that, when Paul had insisted he hire an aide for the weekend—"the folks we'll be dealing with expect it"—Monty had blanched, partly due to the terminology. "What do you mean, 'a man'?" he'd asked, to which Paul had answered, unhelpfully, "Monty, please. Don't act dumb."

The "man" Monty had hired as a driver through a temp agency in Jackson continued speaking like a tour guide as they drove up Highway 49. "What I'm saying is you got to take your mind to the 1850s, hop into your way-back machine and picture this place as it used to be, and you know what you got in front of you? Hell on earth," Push Lloyd said, motioning toward the open window, where cotton fields that were made silver with moonlight passed by, their perimeters a wall of mammoth trees, hickory and poplar and sycamore, an infrequent stump in a turnrow crowned with a smoldering rubber tire. The air suddenly grew cool when they drove past a cane brake. Although Monty could only see it in silhouette, a pelican at the top of a cypress dilated its wingspan and flailed once or twice against the inky-blue night sky, an athlete shaking it out. The tree beneath the bird stood on the spindly stilts of its roots, as though tiptoeing through the marshy water on the ground, keeping its limbs, unruly with moss, raised high so they wouldn't get wet. "Hell. On. Earth," said Push Lloyd, turning down a dirt road. "Once she got tamed, though, hoo boy, this place offered up soil so dark, so sweet you want to eat it à la mode. Cotton stalks shorter than a man were scarce as chicken teeth. The Delta's actually two deltas, you know, the Mississippi Bottoms and the Yazoo Bottoms, and shaped like a diamond, not a delta. I believe that's what my schoolteacher Mr. Perkins used to mean by 'enigma.'"

In the backseat, checking his timepiece, Monty wanted to say, *You know I'm from Mississippi, right? You don't need to explain the Delta to me.* He could have told Push Lloyd that historian Michael Thomas Griffin once described the region as "the taproot of all Southern history." He could have claimed that, because its soil was enriched by alluvium drained from roughly 40 percent of the continental United States, there was more of America in the Delta's seven thousand square miles than anywhere else on earth. Instead, Monty asked, "Why do they call you Push Lloyd?"

"Can't you see what size I am," said the man Monty guessed must be over 250 pounds. "Out in the fields, a tractor gets stuck in mud, a wagon, even the miss's automobile, they'll send me out behind it and say, 'Push, Lloyd!' That name's only thing I can't get unstuck."

The dirt road lined with sweet gum trees, ancient barbed wire running straight through their trunks because they'd grown around it over the decades, gave way to an absurdly expansive cotton field, at the far end of which, barely within squinting distance, stood the outline of a house. On their way toward the structure—which, with each tenth of a mile passed, took on the appearance, square foot by square foot, not of a house but a mansion—Montgomery and Push Lloyd kept quiet, both in awe of the vast, flat acreage of Bluest Heaven. Crown jewel in a crown full of jewels, the plantation was one of many owned by Maximilian Everard IV, the others including Struck Pond, Pilgrim's Progress, Astrolabe, Sextant, Moon of the Plains, and Fox Grey, named so, Monty had learned in his research, as a purposeful inversion of the nickname for General Lee.

Nine cars were parked in the circular driveway. "I shouldn't be more than an hour," Monty said after they stopped behind a Cadillac with Yalobusha County plates. Push Lloyd chuckled.

Even though he'd assumed the cars were empty, Monty noticed, as he walked toward the house seat of Bluest Heaven, that each was occupied by a single black man, all nine of the men asleep on top of pillows made from jackets, all nine of them with at least a day's growth of beard. "Couple hours," Monty called back to Push Lloyd, who chuckled again. The backseat of one car was covered in what must have been a dozen wrappers for MoonPies; a paperback novel, its dog ears dog-eared, lay open like a hymnal, flat on its back amid the plastic. "Maybe three," Monty said over his shoulder. "Three or four."

A servant opened the front door before Monty had a chance to give it even a single rap. "Hello, my name is—" Montgomery said before the servant, a woman in her fifties with a gold tooth, interrupted him.

"I'd soon as not know. Go on join the others. Main parlor."

Earlier that week, when he was explaining that Maximilian Everard controlled more than a fifth of the votes in the state via his sway over his white friends who in turn held sway over the Negro tenants farming their land, Paul Johnson had warned Montgomery about the evening they were going to spend at Bluest Heaven, noting, "Those boys there will be *true Delta*." Monty had understood the phrase to refer to any white plantation owner from the "Valley of the Lower Mississippi" who was socially entitled, financially comfortable, and, as if Zeno had devised a paradox concerning Kentucky bourbon, perpetually fixed halfway between sober and drunk. He knew those weren't the only paradoxes to their breed. True Deltans were also, simultaneously, ostentatious and genteel, careful of debt but careless with risk, patrician planters and rugged frontiersmen, as hedonistically liberal as they were politically conservative—the most Mississippian of Mississippians. In the main parlor, a semicircular room with ceilings eighteen feet high and alcoves built into the walls to exhibit marble statuary, Monty was introduced to a group of men who made him realize he'd barely understood the half of it.

All of them remained seated at the poker table on his entrance. "Montgomery Forster, man of the hour," said Maximilian Everard IV. "Max Everard. Friends call me 'Four.'"

The curtains, noses, rugs, wallpaper, and cheeks throughout the room were varying shades, whether from expensive dyes or dilation in the blood vessels, of red. Cigar smoke hung in the air like fine lint in a cotton gin. The round poker table's green felt cast the players' faces in sickly undertones. Still seated, a cigar wedged in the crook of his mouth, Max Everard introduced his friends to Montgomery: Theodore Wimberley of the Cleveland, Mississippi, Wimberleys; Bartholomew Peterson of the Philadelphia, Mississippi, Petersons; Peter Crydenwise Anselm and Hernando de Soto Money; Hugh Dair, whose first name everyone pronounced like "who"; Patrick Doohickey, which was his actual name; and John Dollard, who was not, despite his claims, a cotton factor from New York City.

On Four's order—Max Everard's deceased father had been known as "Three"—Monty pulled a chair up to the table and took a seat between John Dollard and a man whose name he'd already forgotten. The man seemed to intuit his own lack of memorableness. "Hugh Dair," he offered.

"Who dere?! Who dere?!" shouted everyone at the table. "Who dere?! Who dere?!"

Monty took the exclamations, so routine the players barely looked away from their cards to make them, as a sign these men had known each other for many years, had been playing poker for a very long time, or both. "How long have y'all been at it?" he asked. "The drivers out front looked like they've been here awhile."

"Drivers?" Four's eyebrows neared each other. "Oh, you mean the hands. Surely all yours does for you isn't drive?"

"Well."

"It is late, though. Let me have a sandwich taken out to him. Delia, baby! Take a sandwich out to Mr. Forster's hand."

From behind the heavy, thick door on the other side of the room appeared a beautiful black woman whose skin had the subtle, creamy tint of a boniato. Montgomery wouldn't have been surprised if she were the daughter of the woman with the gold tooth who had let him into the house. "Kind of sandwich?" yelled the young woman.

"The hell do I care? Throw some ham on a beaten. Use your head, girl," Four said, making a what-can-you-do face at Monty. "Apologies, Mr. Forster. Here at Bluest Heaven I've a poor tendency to let the help go undisciplined." In Four's accent, which had apparently never met a postvocalic *r* it gave a damn for, the word *bluest* became a single syllable. "After freedom they just never were the same. Delia gets it from Big Delia. I'm in for two hundred."

Throughout the time Monty and Four had been discussing one type of hand, Theodore Wimberley had dealt another type to each player at the table, two hold cards facedown. All but John Dollard called Four Everard's bet. Over the next few rounds of betting, Monty tried to memorize everyone's name—Patrick Doohickey was the one with a face so pockmarked it looked like a cathead biscuit; Bart Peterson was the one who complained that his maid had been "totin' the good silver"—so he could more effectively coerce their vote. At fifth street Monty's three sixes lost to Four's three sevens.

"Paul certainly is running late," Monty said, trying not to sound irked that his backroom running mate had not yet arrived. This whole evening was his idea.

"Didn't you hear? He's not coming." Four stacked his chips. "Telephoned a few hours ago to say he was feeling peaked."

That lazy son of a bitch, thought Monty, unaware that Paul Johnson was at home with blurred vision, chest pains, and general fatigue, symptoms of the heart condition that four years later would end his life.

In front of Montgomery the woman he assumed was called Big Delia placed a drink. She left before he could thank her. "Given Paul's absence, I'm eager to hear what you gentlemen are looking for in a governor." The Four Roses sour mash burned off the bad taste in Monty's mouth.

"Aren't you running for *lieutenant* governor?" asked Hernando Money while dealing the next hand.

Monty raised his chin but not his eyes; his jack of clubs looked so much like Nicholas. "Did y'all know in England they pronounce the first syllable 'left'? *Leftenant*. But you're correct. I am indeed running for lieutenant governor."

"*Left*-enant?" said Peter Anselm.

"Left-*enant*?" said Hugh Dair.

"*Left in it*?" said Patrick Doohickey.

"Are you running for lieutenant governor of England, Monty?" Four asked. "Then what in God's name does how they pronounce the word got to do with the price of cotton in China? My mother was an Anglophile. Ruined her life. Please don't tell me you're in love with the English, too."

"In love? Christ, no. In love. What?" Monty tried to convince himself it was the bourbon coloring his cheeks. "It's just I find language fascinating."

Monty's subsequent laugh wasn't desperate. It was as robust and warm as the cigar smoke that whirled and dispersed in its wake. At least he tried to believe as much.

"I agree. Language can be very fascinating." After staring intently at his cards, John Dollard looked up to address the entire room, not only the players but also Delia, the younger one, who was

lighting her employer's cigar. "Take the Delta," he said, betting a hundred.

"Already have!"

Once Four had finished laughing at his own joke, John Dollard continued. "All around the Delta," he said, "people have a unique language, I've noticed in my short time here. People don't 'spend too much money' in the Delta. They 'go on a spree.' One could argue the colorful language this region is admired for has become a means to absolve the conspicuous consumption for which it is criticized."

"Those're awful fancy words for a cotton factor." Theodore Wimberley took a long, dramatic swallow of his whiskey. "I swear I've never consumed conspicuously my whole life."

Everyone chuckled except John Dollard. Instead, he stared at the three cards in the center of the table, a queen of spades and a nine of clubs and a king of spades, with what Monty considered an anthropological demeanor, as though the cards were not slips of paper stamped with numbers and symbols but actual people. Haddy looked at cards the same way.

After the turn, a king of hearts, John Dollard raised the bet by two hundred. "Consider your economic model. The very structure of it has its own language. You've got cash-renting, share-renting, and share-cropping," he said as everyone but the host of the evening folded. "And now consider the language within that language. In my recent travels around the South, I've heard how sharecroppers will 'light a shuck' or 'hit the grit' after payday on a plantation, despite whether they 'came out ahead,' 'just lived,' or 'went in the hole,'" he said as the river was revealed to be a nine of spades. "And that brings me to the Negro Question."

"Do you have it?"

John Dollard slowly lifted his head, as though nudged from a dream, to stare droop-eyed at Four Everard. "Have what?" he said, oblivious to the heap of chips at the center of the table, red discs intermingled with white discs, green discs intermingled with blue discs, leftovers of a disintegrated, grass-stained American flag.

"'Have what?' he says," said Four. "Monty, is that your ear on the table? I imagine the fellow sitting next to you must've talked it off by now, with his 'economic models' and 'conspicuous consumptions.'"

"I'm sorry to have offended you with my vocabulary."

"Just answer my question." If a cigar, burned down to the length of a big toe, weren't stuck in the corner of his mouth, Four's teeth would have been clenched. "Do you have anything better than kings over nines?"

"Oh." Despite his obvious talent for poking up a fire in his host, John Dollard, looking at the cards in his hands as if they had appeared there by magic, showed no signs of possessing any innate skill at poker. Luck was a different story. "My, it seems that I do have something better," he said, laying down a ten of spades and a jack of spades at the two junctures between the king, queen, and nine of spades on the table.

"What do you have, Four?" asked Bart Peterson.

"I was playing the board. Goddamn it." Four threw his cards facedown at the community cards. "Should've known better than to try and bluff a fool."

Ever since he was young, Monty had not taken kindly to what his grandfather Tewksbury used to describe as people who "did not uphold the chivalry." Landowners and managers who mistreated hoe hands and plowmen, kickers of dogs, hitters of women, rich whites who looked down on poor whites, poor whites who looked down on rich blacks, scalawags, scamps, scoundrels, and anyone who ate all the cashews from a jar of mixed nuts: Monty had trouble letting trash be trash. As such, in spite of his goal of winning votes that night, he chose to jeopardize his political career by saying, after Four Everard had called John Dollard a fool, "Says the man who just got taken for one."

Silence is often thought of as the absence of sound, just as white is thought of as the absence of color. Monty understood neither to be true. White is the combination of all colors, and silence is the presence of one emotion. Although that one emotion varies among situations—library-quiet is full of anxiety, bookstore-quiet is full of pride—the silence that followed Monty's remark at the poker table consisted, unequivocally, of pure, authentic, utter joy.

"Oysters!" yelled Four, a grin chiseled into his face. "What say we take a half hour and get something in our stomachs? Delia, bring out seven dozen! We're famished!"

Their yawns muffled by invisible, broken microphones in their fists, the players stood from the table, stretched their arms, tucked their shirts, and began to stroll about the room. Four gestured his drink toward Monty.

"Mr. Forster, looks as though we're both on empty. Let's refill our cocktails."

Here we go, thought Monty. Four's joyful smile must have just been a ruse, something to distract everyone from his anger. Monty wouldn't have been shocked if he took one of the servants aside and whispered, "Fetch my knife."

At the bar, however, Four remained cheerful as he tipped bourbon from a crystal decanter into Monty's cocktail glass. "You showed me something just now." He filled his own glass. "Did you know not a single parcel of my family's estate ever once appeared in *Debow's Review.* Everards acquire, Mr. Forster. We don't sell." Four rotated his cocktail glass on the rosewood counter. "Three things allowed us and our fellow Delta gentry to prosper: the crop-lien law, Illinois Central's acquisition of the LNO&T, and the blessed Mississippi constitution of 1890." He finished his drink in one gulp. "All those combined made me perhaps the greatest cotton planter in creation, only possible exception being the Khedive of Egypt."

Montgomery, who knew the crop-lien law guaranteed a lien on crops to landowners but not to laborers, who knew the formation of the Yazoo and Mississippi Valley Railroad had modernized the farming economy, who knew the 1890 constitution instituted poll taxes that deprived the vote from black citizens, said, "What is it again I showed you just now?"

"That you've got a pair."

"Not sure I follow."

Whiskey sloshed on the bar as Four refilled each of the cocktails. "Past forty years it's been difficult for a Deltan to win the governorship. But that's where the 1890 constitution is the gift keeps on giving. We've got the legislature. Ways and Means? Ours. Appropriations? Ours. Tell me something, Mr. Forster. How do you feel about the sales tax?"

Monty believed it was abhorrently regressive taxation. "I love it," he said.

"And how do you feel about the income and ad valorem tax?"

They were progressive, equitable tax structures. "I hate them," said Monty.

While Four said, "Do you think Paul would agree?" Montgomery watched the other players wander around the parlor, their bodies leaving person-shaped tunnels in the cigar smoke, like ants digging through sand. Should he tell the truth? Monty figured that was the only way to respect Paul.

"There's no chance in hell he would agree."

Four grinned the same way he had earlier at the poker table. "Smartest thing you've said all night. Paul Johnson, 'Champion of the Runt Pig People,'" he told Monty, incredulity adding a carnival barker's bombast to his voice. "You and I both know *our* people are not the kind to own runt pigs. Question is, time comes, can you convince Paul to agree?"

"And that's why you need someone with a pair."

"And that's why I need someone with a pair."

So then this was politics. Promise to betray your friend so that you'll have the opportunity to betray your friend. Of course Monty knew what Paul would say. He'd say these people were not part of an aristocracy but a slavocracy. He'd say landowners in this region used phrases like fiscal responsibility, economic modernization, and corporate expansion when what they really meant was racial subjugation. He'd say these people were trying to reestablish their cotton kingdom. What Paul would never say, though Monty would, was that promises only have meaning when they're given it. "Four, you have my word," Monty said, his gut pitching with the lie.

"You're truly a gentleman and scholar." Four clinked glasses with Monty. "I don't know about you, but I could use some sustenance. Delia! Bring that tray over here."

From across the room, carrying a tray of ice studded with plump oysters on the half shell, walked the light-skinned girl. "Lemon?" asked Delia.

"Oh, come now, sugar," Four said. "You know a proper oyster needs a lemon squeezed over it. That's the secret ingredient. Have at."

Delia did as she was told, rills of juice tracing the valleys between veins in her wrist, the occasional seed wedging itself among chips of ice. "There's a good girl," said Four. "Guests first, Mr. Forster." Monty reached for an oyster, aiming for a small one because of the fracas that had recently begun in his stomach, but Four stopped him. "I said 'guests,' Mr. Forster. As my guest you should be treated as such. Delia, feed Mr. Forster."

A night that so far had been a good example of odd behavior became an even better one when Delia, acquiescing to the order with a look of annoyance, lifted an oyster from the tray, sighed through her nose, pressed her lips together, and held the oyster up to Monty's mouth. Blank-faced with alarm, Monty shifted his gaze from the oyster to Four, who, consequently, opened his mouth as one would in an effort to get a baby to eat.

"Think I can handle that myself," Monty said as he took the oyster from Delia. He sucked it into his mouth and replaced the shell on the tray. "But thank you nonetheless."

After glaring at Four one more time, Delia nodded at Monty, turned away with such a smooth pivot she could have been standing on a lazy Susan, and walked through the room, stopping occasionally to offer the tray to the other guests. Four giggled to himself while he watched her work.

"You two have an unusual rapport," Monty said.

"We've known each other a long time. And she is my sister, after all."

In the pursuant silence, Monty had no idea what to say or think, other than to think he had no idea what to say or think. Four, still watching his apparent sister across the room, glanced at Monty and, in his almost English-sounding southern accent, said, "Father was known for committing depredations with the help."

Montgomery supposed that gave new, loathsome meaning to "perquisites." He'd have been tempted to say something to that effect if Four had not announced to the room, "Gentlemen, are y'all ready to begin again?" in response to which everyone started to lumber toward the poker table.

Grabbing Monty's shoulder, Four leaned into him and whispered, "One more thing. Call me a fool again in front of my friends and I'll remove your kidneys via your esophagus with a pair of fire tongs I special-ordered from a blacksmith in Liverpool." He kept his arm wrapped around Monty's shoulder and walked him back to the table like a prom date who'd had five too many and was liable to fall out.

"Who's on the button?" Four asked.

Peter Anselm said, "The left-in-it."

Over the next two hours, the hillocks of chips in front of each player rising and falling like time-lapsed photographs of soil erosion, Monty, who in college never had to write home for extra cash because he won more than enough in the basement of his eating club, kept his stack of chips level. He tried to distract from the threat he had just received as well as the pain in his stomach by listening to the other men talk. Practitioners of the sporting lie as much as the sporting life, southerners are only as good as their ability to tell a story, and the players that night, Monty learned, were excellent southerners. Patrick Doohickey, recalling an event from when he was thirteen, described how his uncle hired a remarkably affordable lady of the night to make his favorite nephew a man, only for said nephew to discover the lady's affordability was due to an equally remarkable case of dysentery. "My sheets. Ruined." Theodore Wimberley told a story about his youngest daughter, who, the first time they made breakfast together, said, "The pancakes are learning!" in reference to the fact each one cooked better than the last. All throughout the conversation, most of the hands were won by either John Dollard or Hernando Money—fitting names, Monty thought—to the obvious annoyance of Four.

"Did I tell you, Mr. Forster, I knew your wife at the University?"

Monty had not been expecting to hear mention of Sarah. "No, I was not aware," he said to Four.

"We even went on a few dates."

"That so."

"Yes, it's true."

"Small world."

"We had fun. She was good."

In the middle of dealing a round, Hugh Dair froze, his hand hovering over the table with a card clutched in it, and two chairs down from him, a nugget of ash fell from Bart Peterson's cigar, crumbling unnoticed on the felt. If everyone else hadn't been so noticeably stunned, Monty might not have registered what Four had just said about Sarah. This was a silence full of alarm. "Come again?" Monty asked.

"She was a good person, your wife. Always doing charitable deeds."

Hugh Dair dealt the rest of the round. Bart Peterson brushed at his spilt ash. During their courtship, a process that began when Sarah was a senior psychology major at the W attending a Junior Auxiliary ball on her mother's orders, Monty appreciated his future wife for what she was not. She was not charming. She was not bright. She was not witty. Put in a different way, she was not Nicholas. On their wedding day, reciting vows that were so in name only, Montgomery stared at his bride and recalled a quip from her antithesis. "'I just want you to be happy,' chaps say when they're trying to convince a lover not to end it," Nicholas had said, "but they really mean, 'I'm the one person on the bloody earth who can make you happy.'" As Monty lifted his bride's veil, he understood he'd long ago lost his "one person on the bloody earth."

For that reason Four's words about Sarah didn't upset Monty.

What upset him was how he could ever hope to control, or rather, not be controlled by, someone so small, petty, and cheap. The sound of the answer was the sound of chips tinkling across felt.

Hit the man's pocketbook.

"Believe I'm like to pass out if I don't get some shut-eye," Peter Anselm said while standing from the table and collecting what remained from his losses. "I'll be in the guest room with those creepy dolls. Y'all give a holler when it's time for eggs and ale."

Each of the cards dealt to Monty calmed his upset stomach. What better way to keep tabs on Four than to keep tabs on Four's tabs! Planters throughout the Delta, it was a commonly known if not fully comprehensible fact, took pride in being in debt. The fools considered it a status symbol. Therefore, Monty figured as he studied his hand, a jack of clubs and nine of hearts, he could stop Four from extorting him to break faith with Paul simply by asking his associates at the Bank of Greenwood, Unions Planters, and Citizens Bank & Trust to take a hard look at their exposure.

John Dollard said, "In for a thousand."

Even though he'd been drifting in a slipstream of thoughts, calculating as they were nostalgic, Monty had remained completely aware of the table. The flop gave up an ace of clubs, a ten of hearts, and a ten of clubs; Four raised by two thousand; and Hugh Dair, Patrick Doohickey, Hernando Money, and Theodore Wimberley folded, leaving John Dollard, Four, and Montgomery as the only players still in. The pot had climbed to $13,000.

"King of clubs," John Dollard said on fourth street, dealing the card. Monty studied his hand: club, club, club, club, ace high, ten low, queen of clubs shy of a royal flush. It was a long shot, he figured, ridiculously long, but to hell with it.

"Is there anybody still in," said Monty, digging through his coat pocket, "who doesn't trust a personal check from me?" He unfolded a blank check onto the table. Both John Dollard and Four shrugged. Monty asked, "Any y'all got a pen?"

Four took a fountain pen from his pocket and slid it across the ashy green felt to Monty. The lacquered brass barrel of the pen felt as sickeningly warm as a toilet seat shortly after someone else had been sitting on it. Monty filled out the check, dropped it in the pot, and said, "I'm in for five thousand," which brought a new kind of silence to the room.

After calling the bet, John Dollard still had a sizable stake left, at least seven thousand, according to Monty's quick count, but Four, with his two-finger-high stack of chips, would have to go all-in or fold.

"I ever tell y'all how Struck Pond got its name?" Four said, dribbling his chips onto the table, over and again. He told the story of how his great-grandfather, surveying the future plantation, got caught in a thunderstorm, and after a bolt of lightning struck a nearby cow pond, he watched in his soaked clothes as dozens of dead fish slowly bobbed to the surface. "Man took it as a sign of luck. And he was right. We've never had a short crop on that place. I'm telling you it's a thousand acres of ice cream land." Four paused. "Struck Pond is my call and my raise."

Montgomery had already gone all-in, so everyone turned to John Dollard. The cotton factor from New York City no longer studied the community cards but instead was staring at Four Everard in his tailored dress shirt. "'Ice cream land,'" he said, shoving his chips into the pot with the thick side of his palm. "That's another good one. I swear, you fellows. Language is fasc-in-a-ting."

Tilting back in his chair, exhaling loudly, pointing his thumb at John Dollard, Four shared a look with Monty, as if to say, *This guy*. Monty had to agree. Something was earnestly askew with John Dollard. Nobody at the table was able to give the odd man further thought, however, because the river had just been dealt, and there on her back lay the queen of clubs.

What beautiful crown molding, Monty imagined her majesty saying.

He studied the two people who were about to lose. John Dollard still had the bemused, childish expression of someone who didn't comprehend serious money was at stake, whereas Four, who let a faint smile slip upon seeing the card that had been dealt, arranged his features into a hard grimace after noticing the bemused, childish expression on John Dollard. Monty knew what he had to do.

"Four of one suit on the table," said Four. "This'll be interesting. Excuse me. This'll be fasc-in-a-ting." With his gaze fixed on John Dollard, Four laid down his cards, so gingerly he could have been placing them on top of a house made of fifty other ones, first a ten of diamonds, then a king of spades. He told John Dollard directly, "Tens full of kings."

The tension in the moment barely lasted a second, because John Dollard, while Four was proudly announcing his hand, had laid down his own: a ten of spades and an ace of diamonds.

Monty figured Four's heart must be located, half to each one, in his shoulders, because they sank dramatically at the sight of John Dollard's hand, tens full of aces. Despite wanting to relish Four's loss a few moments longer, Monty, realizing he was now under scrutiny, laid down his own cards. "All I've got's a pair," he said, nodding at his nine of hearts and nine of spades.

"Does that mean I win?" John Dollard said. "Suppose that means I win."

As John Dollard reached over the table, his arms hooped to rake in the chips, Four, whose grimace now included arched eyebrows, providing his facial arrangement with a touch of the sinister, said, "Don't you dare touch that pot."

John Dollard withdrew his outstretched arms, placing them in his lap, a third-grader reprimanded by his teacher. He looked around the table, from one face to another, but found on each the blank, obedient look of a good check dog. "I knew it was a bad idea to play a group of farmers," he said, to which everyone at the table, in nearly perfect unison, responded, "*Planters.*"

"Big Delia!" Four yelled. "The book!"

How he said those last two words led Monty to surmise he was referring to the Holy Bible. Perhaps the hypocrite wanted to read scripture on the sins of gambling to the man who had just beaten him at poker. The book Big Delia handed Four, though, was a typical hardback, the kind Monty had often, while growing up, checked out from the Batesville library. The book was much thicker than the ones he used to read. On the dust jacket, too, there was no rendering of Magwitch raising his shackled fist at young Pip or Oliver carrying an empty bowl toward Mr. Bumble.

Four turned to the first page. "*Caste and Class in a Southern Town,* by John Dollard," he read aloud. He stared at the author for a moment and then flipped through a few more pages. "'They say the only thing richer than the history of a person's life is the history of their imagination. I say the only thing richer than the history of a region is the history of its people. The Mississippi Delta taught me that.' Decent opening. Let's try a little further on, shall we? 'Wealth, whether one strives for it, runs away from it, or stays aristocratically, obnoxiously complacent with it, is the defining American characteristic, the first two varieties more than the last. Americans require the struggle to be different from and on occasion identical to their heritage. The Mississippi Delta is America the Beautiful, America the Ugly, America the Great, and America the Weak, embodied by the beautiful, ugly, great, weak Mississippi

Deltans.'" After closing the book and tossing it on the table, Four looked at John Dollard, scrunched one side of his face, and said, "Bit purple, don't you think?"

"Eh," John Dollard said. "Er."

With the approaching dawn, all the windows in the room slowly turned from mirrors back into windows, their prospect a navy sky hanging over ivory cotton bolls coruscating with dew.

"Gentlemen," Four said to everyone except John Dollard and Monty, "you all owe my family in some way or another. I'll have you repay part of that debt with two deeds. One, please support the estimable Paul Johnson and Montgomery Forster in the coming election. I mean *full-staff* support. Two, remove this scum from my house. Pistols may be drawn at no offense to the propriety of your host."

The others appeared to assume, as Monty did, the second deed had been in reference to one of the subjects of the first, but after double-taking between speaker and supposed subject, they soon realized, as Monty did, the man Four had been referring to was John Dollard. Pistols were drawn.

Once the guest had been removed—he showed newly discovered skills at the quiet game on his way out—Monty and Four were left alone at the table. Both of them sipped their drinks. "Mr. Forster, as an honorable man, I'm sure you understand that the triumphs of a dishonorable man are null and void."

"What do you mean?"

"John Dollard did not win Struck Pond."

"He didn't win Struck Pond."

"That's what I'm saying."

Monty raised both of his hands with his palms toward Four. Slowly, exhibiting the patience of a magician, he slipped two fingers down his shirt cuff, removed a jack of clubs, and placed it next to the ace, king, queen, and ten of clubs on the table. He said, "I did," then stood up.

Before leaving Bluest Heaven, his blood muddied with just enough booze, Montgomery turned around in the doorway of the parlor and told Four that if he ever spoke ill of his wife again he'd yank out his kidneys through his esophagus and that he wouldn't need a fancy instrument from England to do it.

3.9

Highway 16 Revisited—Turtle Soup Surprise

At the Millsaps library, where he attempted unsuccessfully to finish a bit of research for his thesis, Robert started to understand, crouched in a carrel that had become his second home over the past few years, the reality of what had happened at the Magnolia earlier that day. His affair with Jane Marunga was officially over.

Not that he wasn't used to this sort of thing. Sometimes it seemed he was only whole when his heart was broken. In high school and college, regardless of the length of the relationship, every time a girl told him it was over, Natalie Stewart writing her reasons on a slip of loose-leaf from her Trapper Keeper, Beth Helmsley shrugging at him after he spotted her making out with a guy at KA, Robert would feel almost relieved by how much it hurt, as though brooding were his natural mental state, sulking his natural physical one. He'd often wondered if he sought out the pain as a subconscious way of proving he was capable of it. Did he push away Natalie, Beth, and all the others as some masochistic attempt at confirming he had a functional, breakable heart? It hurt to even consider the possibility, which he supposed might be the point.

Then again, this instance was different from the others, wasn't it? Instead of heartbroken he felt angry.

Robert pulled a book from a nearby shelf. As he flipped through it, he didn't consider the words there, but rather the ones Jane had used. The more he thought about them the angrier he got. He could hardly believe the audacity of Jane. Only the most selfish people in the world said things like "I need to think about me." Everybody always thought about themselves! It took a truly self-centered person not to realize how self-centered everyone was each second of their lives. "I've thought about me too much" was what someone *ending an affair* should say. Jesus Christ. Robert jammed the book back into its place on the shelf, grabbed his bag, and, fully aware he was throwing his own little tantrum, marched out of the stacks self-consciously and self-satisfyingly clomping his feet.

Not until he was outside, climbing into his car, did he register the title of the book he'd been looking at, *Kant and the Problem of Metaphysics* by Martin Heidegger. On his drive home, Interstate 55 to Highway 16, Robert repeated the words *Heidegger Kant* in his mind until they morphed into two different ones, "high-digging cunt," their lack of sense matched only by his shame in thinking them. It was the kind of thing his father would have said.

A man prone to violence, against himself as well as others, Jimmy Vaughn had been born with that perennial southern handicap: pride in circumstances undeserving of it. He took pride in the color of his skin. He took pride in his lack of education. "The only break I got in life was when my father snapped my arm for leaving the back door unlocked," he once told his son. "Your cunt of a mother running off after you showed was the best thing ever happened to you."

The only advantage to his father's undue pride was that Robert grew up not realizing how disadvantaged he was in life. Pride in one generation became dignity in the next. At school, he routinely breached the unspoken caste strata represented by the different colored lockers, kids whose families owned land congregated by the yellow ones and kids whose families worked that land congregated by the blue ones, with the various gradations of class demarcated by the green, red, purple, and orange lockers in between. Whenever townsfolk called his father "nothinbutadronk" he figured it for praise in the local slang. Robert and his father were Vaughns. Why would anybody ridicule someone descended from the town founder? It would take years for him to begin to see his life as a "shadow box of degeneration," the last line of a poem he published in a literary magazine at Millsaps, where he became, as far as he knew, the first person in his family to attend college. His father would have considered the poem—correctly, in Robert's current opinion—awful, but to do that he would've, of course, had to have cared enough to read it. Sometimes Robert wondered if he chose such an impractical major as a way to spite his father. Philosophy, after all, couldn't win a lawsuit, fix a car, cure a disease, or build a house.

By now the flip-book animated scenery that was Robert's drive home had transitioned from urban to rural. Cotton modules studded the edges of cotton fields. A rusted tractor sat stuck in the same ditch it had been stuck in for the past ten years. A country mile down a country road called Fugates, so haphazardly paved its asphalt looked as though it had been smeared on with a giant butter knife, he turned into his driveway, Hellion's barking detectable by the time he'd parked.

Robert considered it a shame the trailer's heater had not magically fixed itself. "You cold, buddy row?" he said to Hellion, who jumped on him, propping his one front paw on Robert's thigh. "Let's get your supper."

In the kitchen, he filled Hellion's dog bowl and then opened the fridge. Robert took out a pint of turtle soup his neighbor had given him last week as thanks for filling in when her bridge club was a player light. *Guess the hare won this race,* he thought, taking a whiff of the soup. Aesop must have put in a fix. Robert poured half the pint in a bowl and placed it in the microwave. Due to the noise of a golden retriever scarfing kibble and a microwave nuking turtle soup, Robert almost didn't notice the knock at the door.

He checked his watch. Who'd be stopping by at six in the evening? Folks from Yazoo County respected dinnertime nearly as much as the Sabbath. Although he'd been too embarrassed to bring Jane to the trailer, Robert thought for a moment it might be her—that she'd looked up his address and had come to say she wanted him back. Yeah, right. Of course it wasn't her, he told himself as he ran a hand through his hair, wiped off the kitchen counter, closed the silverware drawer, and tucked in his shirt before yelling what he hoped was a not too hopeful, "Coming!"

Robert opened the door to the sight of a man who seemed oddly familiar. He must have been in his eighties, dressed in a suit that looked new, his hands shoved in the pockets. With a nervous smile the man cleared his throat.

"You've never met me," Harold Forster said to Robert Vaughn, "but I'm your grandfather."

PART 4

4.1

Prairie Burial—A Noise That Would Never Come— Arabian Sand

A sixteen-inch blade made of tempered steel, long and narrow, with a rolled top edge for foot placement, D-grip, and twenty-four-inch North American ash handle: the garden spade was just right for digging a child-size hole.

Charles Culp had found it hanging from a peg in the barn. On his walk back to the house that night, he held the spade in one hand and, with the other, clenched the front of his jacket shut. March was always cold in Kansas.

Inside the house, which Charles's grandfather had built shortly after his emancipation, the scene had not changed. His mother, Tabitha, was still boiling water on the stove, her pinafore stained red near the waist, and his father, Arnold, was still pacing in front of the icebox, swigging at a glass of bonded bourbon. Two cousins from his mother's side, Katherine and Selma, had gathered medicinal substances, flake tar camphor and Epsom salt and milk of magnesia, on top of the Florentine cabinet set, ready to be distributed when called upon. A cousin from his father's side, Timmy, six years old, peeked out from a door across the room, where he'd been sent to shield his virtue. In the middle of the scene, atop a thin mattress that had been pulled from one of the beds, lay Charles's sister, Lurlene, sweat coursing down her face, knees raised, legs spread, nothing but a sheet covering her underthings. The man in front of her, looking beneath the sheet and calling out orders, was Dr. Henry Blair.

Everyone called him the Angel Maker. On his arrival at the house earlier that day, Dr. Blair had told the Culp family that, due to the fact Lurlene was so far along, the operation would cost double, a sum of a hundred dollars. "The fetus is crowning," he said now, hours after he had administered an injection. "I need another towel."

The next few moments passed like many another stressful time Charles had been through during his short eighteen years in the world. Sounds grew loud and quiet all at once. The held breath of each person in the room seemed to be holding its own breath. On the ground, Lurlene, following Dr. Blair's request, pushed so hard the veins rose in her arms, forehead, and neck. Every member of the family, standing as though in vigil, listened for a noise they understood would never come—the crying of a newborn.

Instead, they heard the doctor's muted voice say, "It is done," as he held a small body, pink-skinned and grime-covered, as lifeless as a washbasin.

He began to swaddle it in a blanket. Once finished, Dr. Blair set the body aside and checked on Lurlene, who had passed out. He appeared satisfied with the rate of her pulse. As he prepared to leave, toweling blood from his hands and gathering up his instruments, the doctor casually asked why he had not been informed the child's father was white, a question that drew blank stares from the family.

"Up until then, you see, they had no idea the father was white. The Culp family was strangely respectful of their girl Lurlene," Tom Branchwater would later tell Harold Forster, who would repeat the story to Robert Vaughn. "They never asked about how she got pregnant. They never asked why she changed her mind and wanted to get rid of it so late."

Dr. Blair took the lack of a response as indication the family had not been aware of the father's race. He glanced under the swaddles to confirm that, yes indeed, the baby had a complexion so fair, ruddy white, it had to have been the result of miscegenation. His plans would have to be adjusted. In his distracted state, the doctor gave the family instructions on how to care for the patient—"She'll be out for at least another few hours," he said, "so I suggest tidying up before she wakes"—until he noticed a young man across the room with a shovel in his hands.

"What is that you have there?"

"It's for the, uh"—Charles coughed—"for the burial, sir."

"Entirely out of the question!"

His color rising in the soft light of the prairie house, Dr. Blair turned to the parents of his patient and explained that, given the legalities of the operation he had just performed, the "by-product" had to remain with him. He assured them it would receive a proper burial. In addition to keeping both the family and himself safe from legal repercussions, the doctor noted, the lack of a reminder of the ordeal often mitigated the emotional toll on patients, consequently aiding their physical recovery. Did they understand?

One parent did. To keep his sobbing wife from snatching the bundle away from the doctor, Arnold Culp wrapped his arms around her, making hush-now sounds and giving Dr. Blair a look that asked, *Can you blame her?* He nodded in the direction of the door.

Outside was dark as a cellar. Dr. Blair figured it must be close to midnight. He shuffled down the split-log porch steps, tossed his medical kit in the back of his automobile, placed the bundle in the passenger seat, and started the engine by turning the hand crank, each action underscored by howls of "That's my *grandchild*!" echoing out of the house like the sound of the ocean from a shell.

Even though he kept the gas pedal to the floor, it took almost an hour for him to reach the highway, his car, nothing but a flivver, dawdling through the countryside at twenty miles an hour. The doctor would soon be able to afford a new car. Yes indeed. He was considering what type he would buy, a Lexington or a Briscoe, a Templar or a Maxwell, when something moved in the seat next to him. The swaddling cloth began to unravel. Without taking his eyes from the road, Dr. Henry Blair, maker of angels, reached across the seat and, humming a lullaby, stroked the baby's twitching face, all while trying to decide what color his new car should be, Arabian sand or Niagara blue.

4.2

Heir to a Dynasty That Was—A Mythic Trinket Finds Its Way Home—The Linchpin of a Downfall

In a trailer near Vaughan, Mississippi, sitting across from a strange man who claimed to be his grandfather, their breaths visible because of the broken heater and a dog with three legs panting at their feet, Robert asked, "So the doctor only *pretended* to give her an abortion?"

"Uh-huh."

"What'd he do with the baby?"

"Sold him to a family named Vaughn."

Harold took a sip of the tea he'd been given by his grandson. In contrast to the relaxation he felt as the tea's warmth seeped throughout his chest, he grew upset thinking that this young man, heir to a family name that had once been synonymous with wealth, could not afford to heat his own home. The trailer was freezing cold. Harold's lips dipped toward his mug like divining rods. For how long had he stood by doing nothing as his only grandson shivered to sleep each night? He should have been here to help the boy. If only he'd known.

The story Harold had just told Robert had first been told to him in his least favorite place: a hospital. Five months earlier, during a particularly slow afternoon at the museum, Harold had received a call from Branchwater's niece, Portia, saying her uncle had suffered a heart attack and, though he would pull through, wanted to see him. Not even locking the door, Harold ran out of the museum, got in his truck, and drove the fifty-minute trip to Memphis's Baptist Memorial in just over half an hour.

"That you, George?" Branchwater had asked on first seeing Harold. "Come here closer."

"Branchwater, it's Haddy."

"Haddy?"

"Yes."

"There's something you need to know."

From his white-sheeted hospital bed, tubes coming out of his arms and nose, Branchwater, looking suddenly every bit of his nearly one hundred years, told Harold what had happened to Lurlene Culp. "I never said a word about the day your mother had me take that girl to the train station," he said. "The reason I finally tracked down the truth was so you wouldn't be alone when I'm gone."

In the trailer months after that day at the hospital, Harold sat on the couch across from Robert, and on the ground between them lounged Hellion, periodically thumping his tail for some love. The day had by now eased off into night, leaving the trailer to be lit by two lamps in the living area, so cluttered it could hardly be called that. Harold watched his grandson as he took in all he had just told him. The only part of the story Harold had left out was how, a few years before either of them died, Branchwater had spoken with Robert's father, telling him not only the truth of who he was, but also why Robert had not known till then.

"Get the hell out of my house!" Jimmy Vaughn had yelled immediately after asking Branchwater, "You're telling me I'm part nigger?"

There were a thousand things Harold wanted to say to his grandson, that he was sorry the boy's father had passed away, that he wished he could have met Jimmy despite what he'd been told of him. He wanted to say how he'd always dreamed of having a child or grandchild to call his own. He wanted to say he would've been there for Robert if only he had known about him. He wanted to say nothing in the whole entire world could have made him prouder. But instead of those true sentiments, he told his grandson one that wasn't.

"Your grandmother was a kind woman."

Robert crossed his legs. "Lurlene Culp," he said to himself, thinking, *Now there's a name that can't be said in anything but a southern accent.*

He'd always found it helpful to make jokes in difficult situations, and this was most definitely a situation that could be called difficult. Was this guy for real? Robert couldn't tell. In his suit, which appeared to have been bought for the occasion, speaking so deliberately it was like the words were slow to come, Harold Forster seemed legitimate out of sheer awkwardness, but then again, now could be the time he'd mention an expensive operation he needed. "I'm short just a couple thousand dollars," he'd probably say, or he might go with, "If only there were a viable kidney donor."

Despite Robert's concerns, Harold behaved, throughout their conversation, suspicious of him, Robert, instead of the other way around. He even mentioned that a month ago, on the advice of a retired lawyer who was an old family friend, he had hired a private investigator.

"That was probably rude of me. I'm sorry. With my situation, folks tell me, some people might try and take advantage. Can't never be too safe."

"Your situation?"

"Good news is the investigator said you came across trustworthy."

"What situation?"

"He gave me a great big file on you. Copy of your birth certificate. Yearbook pictures. Your dad's police record. Your mom's coronary report."

So overwhelmed with the information—birth certificate? yearbook pictures?—Robert nearly missed the last bit of it. "My mother's dead?" he asked Harold, who immediately looked down at his lap, as though he'd been scolded.

"Yes."

"Good."

The aggregate number of fucks Robert gave about Tonya would hardly fill a marble bag. That was how he usually put it when people asked about her. Less than a month after she gave birth to him, Tonya Nichols, who never married his father, left town without explanation, abandoning Robert to be raised by a "man" unworthy of the handle. Fiend was a better fit. On rare occasions, when he hated himself for hating his mother, Robert would go back to the time, twelve years ago, his father had tree'd him like a squirrel. He was in third grade. In spite of his father's repeated warnings, he had taken his car for a joyride on Scotland Road and accidentally clipped an eight-row planter, leaving the front bumper behind as somebody's lawn ornament, and after his father saw the car, Robert had run out of the trailer, climbed a tree on a farm called Three Oaks owned by one of their neighbors, and tried to stay quiet, ignoring the sound of a trunk strap getting popped. "Come on down, son," Robert's father said on finding him six limbs high in a mockernut hickory. "Promise I won't hurt you." He continued making that promise for half an hour. So, eventually and reluctantly and hopefully, Robert climbed down from the tree, at which point, with the trunk strap that had never been used for travel, Jimmy Vaughn whipped his back until the skin broke.

Over the years to come, Robert would remember that day not

because it had been the first time his father had beat him, which it wasn't, nor because it had been the last time he had trusted his father, which it was, but because the half hour he spent in the tree that day had been the only time in his life he did not worry that, should he fall, somebody would be there to catch him.

"I want to believe you, sir, but you have to understand, this sounds, well, it's a bit hard to swallow," Robert said to the man claiming to be his grandfather.

"Fair point."

"What is it you want from me?"

Harold said to the young man he knew to be his only heir, "You've got it all wrong. I don't want anything from you. It's what I'll be leaving behi—"

It was the weirdest thing. One second, the old man was talking to Robert, making eye contact like a normal person; the next, his mouth dropped open, forehead striating, his gaze fixed on something past Robert's shoulder, his hand latched onto his ear.

Robert worried he was having some kind of stroke. "You okay, mister?"

"Where'd you get that?" The man stood from the couch and walked to a shelf on the wall. Placed along it was a row of knick-knacks from the old feedlot out back, rusty horseshoes, a dirty soda bottle, broken locks, empty frames, the antique type of clothing iron that had to be heated on top of the stove. Gently as plucking a flower, Harold picked up one of the items, a metal figurine shaped like, from what Robert could tell, some kind of bird.

· · ·

"So, the thing's called the Mockingbird, right? It's a figurine from Houghton Forster's soda fountain," Robert told Molly over drinks three weeks later, "and somehow, after being lost for years, it wound up sitting on my shelf! I mean, can you believe?"

"Talk about freaky."

They were at Robert's favorite bar. Zebra Stripes was a juke joint of the first water. Built in a former dry-cleaning facility on Bridge Street in Yazoo City, Mississippi, "the place where nothing's black and white" served coffee for a quarter in the morning, screened cult films for fifty cents in the afternoon, and, at night, poured dollar beers for a sundry clientele, including southern apologetics and southern sentimentalists, northern trash looking for the "Real South," blues musicians, country musicians, folk musicians, and certain unlawful types who'd migrated north from Tangipahoa Parish. The Rotary Club once destroyed half the barstools in a brawl with the Knights of Columbus. Although it was lit with old railroad lanterns, used a hokey-pokey cart as a beer cooler, and featured signs for such obsolete brands as Old Settler tobacco and Tube Rose snuff, Zebra Stripes was a relatively new establishment, owned and operated by Hank Collingham, the photographer best known for his black-and-white shots of run-down liquor stores, compiled in a popular coffee table book, *Packie,* published by Blue Highway Press in 1972.

The evening Robert brought Molly to the bar, Collingham, sitting by the door with his double-plaited beard hooked behind his ears, looked as anachronistic as his surroundings, mute except for the occasional "You broke-dick motherfucker" grumbled at friends asking if he'd had too many.

"This place is absolutely insane," Molly said, her elbows on the bar top. She turned to Robert and added, "Thank you for bringing me here."

"You sure? We could still catch the nine o'clock *Killing Mr. Tiffee.*"

"Screw Burt Reynolds. This is the real shit."

That night was their fourth date in half as many weeks. On the first three, Robert had kept matters typical, taking her out for dinner around the Jackson metropolitan area. Tonight, though, he had suggested they drive up U.S. 49, where, in a small town called the Gateway to the Delta and said to have a witch problem, they could drink cold ones next to addlepated septuagenarians dealing freezeout poker, use the bathroom behind doors labeled POINTERS and SETTERS instead of MEN and WOMEN, stand on stray bits of silage, and, if they felt the need, soak up the beer with a few tamales kept steaming hot in a Playmate behind the bar. He ordered two Budweisers at the place he had promised Molly was like a movie poster by Jack Davis sprung to life.

"Heard any more from the long-lost relative who may or may not be trying to con you out of your vast fortunes?"

"We've talked a few times," Robert said. "Guy seems kind of lonely."

In fact, over the past month, he had not only talked to but seen his supposed grandfather, and more than a few times. They had taken to meeting for coffee at a gas station in Duck Hill, a town almost exactly halfway between their two homes. Aside from their favorite topic—whether the town had a hill shaped like a duck or one where ducks had a fondness for congregating—the two of them spoke most often about the Forsters, who they were, what they did. Any question Robert asked about the family Harold would answer. It didn't matter how personal, which was to say, it didn't matter how utterly sad. The old guy was the only one left.

Robert was most curious about this grandmother. Apparently, she was a "dear, sweet" woman who worked as a housemaid for the family and with whom Harold and his brother Lance were "hopping mad in love." Lurlene ran away in order to keep the peace between the two brothers whom she loved equally. Nobody knew she had been pregnant. When Robert asked how Harold knew that he, rather than his brother, had gotten her pregnant, Harold mumbled, "Lance said he 'always used lambskin with the help,'" and even though that answer seemed to hint at darker, untold elements of the story, Harold gave it with a look of affectionate nostalgia.

"Of course he's lonely. Why else would he reach out?" Molly finished her beer and ordered another round. "So I take it there's no inheritance coming your way?"

"Not a single red cent," Robert said. Aside from his Social Security benefits, Harold had told Robert, he lived on the small amount of proceeds from the Panola Cola Historical Museum, housed in the A-frame built by Robert's great-grandfather, the contents of which Harold said would be left to Robert when he was "on the other side of the grass."

"Nothing? Then why the hell am I sleeping with you?" Molly asked, putting on a show of flabbergast.

"But we haven't yet."

"We haven't?"

"Think I'd remember."

She gently chucked Robert's chin with her fist, saying, "Guess I figured I probably wouldn't."

He smiled at her. It was true. So far they hadn't done anything but kiss. Still, that had been enough for him, her floral scent, as though they were lying beneath a shade tree on a warm summer day, combining with her taste, honeyed and delicate, so that he could not keep from thinking, *Jane* who? Robert remembered that look Harold had when talking about Lurlene, and wondered if he, Robert, were already feeling nostalgic for Molly, a woman he still barely knew. That's what nostalgia does, he supposed, warp the present and shatter the past.

On their fifth round Robert considered asking Molly about her parents. What had the two of them been like? How did she manage without them? Ever since she mentioned their deaths the first time he talked to her, brushing it off as carelessly as the salt joggled from her fries, he had been wondering about that aspect of her life, a curiosity compounded even more when he learned about his mother. Robert was an orphan the same as Molly. It felt like some kind of bond between them, a connection by way of disconnection, solving the problem by making it a paradox. Two people couldn't be alone together.

Before he could ask Molly about her parents, though, a crunching sound came from the front door. The sound was as loud and metallic as it was quick. Everyone at the bar turned in unison to its source. "Here we go again," muttered one person. "Third time this month."

"What happened?" Molly asked Robert.

"Are you ready to leave?"

"No."

"Good. We're going to be here awhile."

A woman prone to drink, jealousy, and innumerable acts of rage, Hank Collingham's wife, Margot, had recently taken to suspecting him of "stepping out in his own joint." Thus, on the frequent occasion she had a few under her belt, she would drive by the bar and, convinced whatever car parked in front of the door belonged to her husband's mistress, ram it from behind with her own car until the door was blocked shut. Due to a zoning irregularity Zebra Stripes had no other means of egress.

"Sigh," said Molly, propping her temple against her fist. She looked at Robert with a half-smile slivering the corners of her green, green eyes. "Thank God I'm having a great time."

Those words sent a pleasant jolt through the stripped wires of

Robert's nervous system. "The nice thing is we'll get a free movie out of the whole ordeal," he said. "They always put on a movie till the fire department gets here."

The films screened at the bar over the past month included *Drop-Top's Last Rodeo, Zardoz, Dark Star, The Alabama Switchblade Murder Gang, Pink Flamingos, Two-Lane Blacktop, Golem 4,* and *Sic 'Em with That Crisp Wit, Mark Twain!* the titles of which were scrawled in chalk on the back wall. That evening the crowd temporarily held captive at the bar was treated to the exploits of a knife-wielding rabble of nuthouse escapees on a rampage in a small backwoods township.

Although he did not know it yet, Robert would learn, during his research over the coming weeks, that the film they watched that night, *The Alabama Switchblade Murder Gang,* had been partly financed by his cousin, one of the many poor investments made by the man who, according to most historians, was the linchpin of the Forster family's rapid fall from prominence.

4.3

Can't Never Could—News from Connor Rolph Is Seldom Good News—A Secret Proposition— The Cola Wars Begin

Years later, a *Harper's Magazine* review of her famous autobiography would describe Imogene Forster as "fearless and indomitable," but on May 8, 1956, she lay in the bathtub on the second floor of her family home, crying into the lukewarm water, afraid to get out because she had no idea what to say in the eulogy for her grandfather, Houghton Forster. The funeral was scheduled for that afternoon. Following the death of Imogene's father when she was ten, Houghton had raised her as if she were his daughter rather than his granddaughter, acting the part of a much younger man. He took her for piggyback rides and taught her how to play catch. He helped her with homework and never missed a single recital. In those years, he often said one important thing to her. "Can't never could." Whenever Imogene felt helpless, saying she *just couldn't* reach the jar of preserves on a shelf, or she *just couldn't* make it to the end of the driveway in time to catch the bus, or she *just couldn't* go to the school dance with the other kids, her grandfather would respond with those three words. "Can't never could." Now, soon to graduate at the top of her class from Radcliffe, Imogene knew she had her grandfather to thank for everything she'd managed to accomplish in her life, which made her fear about giving his eulogy all the worse. She unplugged the bath, waited for the water to drain, grabbed the pulley above her head, and, lifting herself in one smooth motion, sat down in her wheelchair.

Imogene recited possible openings in her head—"Stories are the ultimate retribution of the powerless," "Stories are the ultimate crutch of the powerful"—while she dressed in her bedroom. *I've heard it said that the difference between the past, present, and future is merely an illusion.* Ugh. *The South isn't real. America isn't real. There's just the world. And my grandfather was a man of it.* Nuh-uh. Imogene's black dress made every sentence she thought of seem too bleak.

Downstairs she was greeted by a sound typical of the past few days, her grandmother saying into the telephone, "No, he did not tell anyone! Please don't call here again. Secret ingredient? Grow up, you fool," and slamming the receiver on whatever reporter had most recently procured their number. Annabelle turned around and took notice of Imogene. "I swear," she said, "if one more of them calls, just one more, I'm involving the authorities."

"It'll taper off. People don't care anymore."

But Imogene did. Later that day, shortly after the burial, she was scheduled to meet with Connor Rolph, the company's chief in-house counsel and the executor of her grandfather's estate, who would inform her, she knew, of what her grandfather had promised years ago: that she, Imogene Forster, had inherited control of the Panola Cola Company. It felt only proper that the new CEO should know the "secret ingredient" for the company's main product. Her grandfather had never told her before he died.

"Darling, have you seen your brother around?" Imogene's mother, Sarah, asked while pushing Imogene's wheelchair past her grandmother and into the kitchen. Imogene hated it when people pushed her chair without permission. Her arms worked just fine, thank you and good day.

"He was following Susannah like a puppy earlier."

"That boy will be the death of us all. He's got ten minutes to get his suit on."

Without further explanation, Sarah left the kitchen yelling, "*Niiiick!*" leaving Imogene alone, as though in a holding pen. Imogene had no clue how that woman could possibly be her mother. She was the epitome of a Southern Frantic. Sarah Forster laughed when she was upset, cried when she was happy, was constantly saying she was at her "wit's end" despite the obvious lack of a beginning, and had not once, to her daughter's knowledge, allowed a beverage to sit on a dinner table, side table, or coffee table without a coaster.

Then again, being a single mother certainly hadn't made things easy for her, Imogene thought as she looked out the window. The odd configuration of panes split the light so that two sun dogs stood vigilant on both sides of their source. From her chair, Imogene calmed herself by studying the light as it reflected off a metal bread safe, lit up a row of cruets, ewers, vases, and flagons in a cellarette, and reflected again off a display of apostle spoons. She watched dust swirl through each beam, creating paisley patterns in the air. It felt as if she were looking at the bubbles in a glass of soda. Everything these days reminded her of the business. Imogene had big plans for PanCola. In the kitchen, she was thinking about the sugar problem, how constant fluctuations in the price of sugar destabilized their profit margin, and about a conversation she'd recently had with a chemistry major at school, who mentioned it might soon be possible, even scalable, to change the glucose from corn starch into fructose, the result of which, a sort of corn "syrup," could potentially replace sugar in certain products. Imogene was considering the costs and benefits of funding a research institute to investigate such a possibility when she was interrupted by the sight of Branchwater standing at the door.

"Come on in, you big oaf."

Branchwater entered the kitchen, hat clenched in his giant hands. "Thought I'd check on y'all before I head to the church."

"Mother's about to wring Nick's neck and I'm about to wring Mother's neck. That sound about typical?"

"Suppose I'll just mosey on then."

They both laughed, naturally at first and then awkwardly, as the purpose of the day, the weight of the occasion, sank in. From the second floor came the sound of Sarah Forster yelling at Nicholas Forster that it wasn't *her* fault nobody had ever taught him how to tie a tie. "Branchwater?" said Imogene.

"Yes."

"Will you drive me to my grandfather's funeral?"

"Don't you want to ride in the limousine?"

"No."

Throughout Imogene's childhood, her grandfather used to spend at least one Saturday a month with her and her alone. Each time, he'd start by asking, "Want to act rich today?" She always smiled rather than nodded. The two of them would then head to Memphis, where they'd have steak for lunch, shop at dozens of stores, get tutti-frutti ice cream, and listen to blues music on Beale Street. Imogene's favorite part was always the ride back, sitting next to her grandfather in his car, drowsy and content, packages jostling in the trunk. Sometimes, when they were getting close to home, he'd yell, "Tree bear!"

"I've been thinking," Imogene said, neither drowsy nor content, sitting next to Branchwater in his pickup truck. Its recently simonized paint job shone blue as Barbicide.

"So that's what you've been up to at college."

"I've been thinking about the future. I know the kind of things you did for my grandfather. Things that required, let's say things that required a forceful hand."

"Imo, that was a long time ago."

"Save it," she said, less gently than she'd intended. "I've got plans for the company, now that I'm in charge. And I need your help. I don't like that Coke and Pepsi are so close to us in sales."

"We've always been number one."

"Present perfect doesn't last forever."

"What'd you have in mind?"

She wasn't sure yet, but it didn't bother her. Somehow being the one chosen by her grandfather made her feel capable of anything. He'd picked her! From all the possible choices—Annabelle or Sarah; Lance or Ramsey or Harold; Susannah or Nicholas—her grandfather had picked her, Imogene. She wanted to flip somersaults down the road. She wanted to do high-kicks on the sidewalk. So capable did she feel that not even the church up ahead could lower her spirits, or the fact she still had no idea how to eulogize the man who'd raised her.

. . .

After the funeral Imogene skipped the reception and went directly to Panola Cola's central office. She'd thought it would be closed that day, out of respect for the passing of the company's founder, but the place was as busy as usual. She entered the nineteen-story building at One PanCola Square alone that afternoon, having refused Branchwater's offer of assistance, and nearly tripped an electrician as he hurried to fix a flickering light above the entrance's revolving doors, which had apparently replaced the doorman Imogene's grandfather had hired for aiding visitors in wheelchairs. At the front desk, Imogene said to the severely eyelined receptionist, "I'm here to see Connor Rolph."

"And do you have an appointment with Mr. Rolph?"

"He has one with me, yes."

The receptionist asked for Imogene's name, didn't blink a demarcated eye at it, and ran her finger down a sheet of paper, stopping a third of the way from the bottom. She turned to a gray-suited man who it seemed to Imogene had nothing more productive to do than sit in a club chair, staring at a closed folder. "James, will you take this young woman to Mr. Rolph's office?"

"That's all right," Imogene said. "I know my way around."

Exploring the building had been one of her favorite pastimes as a little girl, discovering closets full of office supplies that were more fun to play with than any dress-up doll, eavesdropping on gossip whispered among the secretaries. She first learned about sex after hearing how so-and-so had gotten tight and spent the evening with you-know-who after the office party last week. In the cafeteria she had drunk her first cup of coffee, and when a busboy warned it could stunt her growth, she'd laughed, saying she didn't have to worry about getting taller.

On the top floor, Imogene exited the elevator. She took a moment to assess her bearings, looking both ways down the hall. Connor's office was at the end, if she recalled correctly, across from a small kitchenette. Her wheels made chipmunk sounds against the linoleum as she made her way down the empty hall.

Connor wasn't in his office, though his door was open, a library lamp turned on. His secretary wasn't at her desk either. Not sure whether to wait, Imogene headed in the opposite direction, looking in each open door she passed. She found Connor in room 1901.

"Imogene! The prodigal daughter returneth!" The firstborn son of German immigrants who'd settled in the Pinch District of

Memphis, Tennessee, Connor Rolph graduated at the top of his class from Ole Miss, where, in reference to Tintin's wire fox terrier, his fraternity pledge name had been Snowy. Not only was he similar to the dog in appearance, his blond hair almost white in a certain light, his eyebrows two slightly raised semicircles, but he was also similar in demeanor: affable, curious, energetic, and, above all, facile with occasionally dopey comic asides. While sitting in the doorway to room 1901, however, Imogene didn't give a damn about Connor Rolph's personality, but rather his location.

"This's my grandfather's office."

Connor allowed smile lines to trim his eyes. They failed to disguise his obvious embarrassment at Imogene's obvious annoyance. "Good memory. With all this new work on my plate, I thought I could use a bit more room to spread out." He straightened a stack of paper.

"That's my grandfather's chair."

In one swift motion, as though he had been sitting on an ejector seat, Connor sprang from behind the leather-topped, ash-veneered desk and walked toward Imogene. "Come in, come in! Can I help you? No, you don't like that. I remember."

Imogene wheeled herself into the office, stopping beside the coffee table where she used to doodle pictures of robots, unicorns, and flowers while her grandfather worked at his desk. Connor pulled up a chair catty-cornered to her. "I'm sorry I had to leave in such a hurry after the funeral. All this work, like I mentioned. But what a turnout! And I loved your eulogy. Did Houghton really say, 'Do you want to *act* rich?'"

"Every time."

In attendance at the funeral had been three former Mississippi governors, one former United States president, John D. Rockefeller Jr., Martha Baird, Charles Chaplin, Edward R. Murrow, eight ambassadors of foreign nations, twelve CEOs of Fortune 500 companies, Tallulah Bankhead, William Shawn, Ella Fitzgerald, and four presiding chancellors of state universities. So of course Imogene had felt *completely* unfazed while approaching the podium at Batesville First Presbyterian. Up onstage, she recovered by turning her grandfather into what he'd always wanted to be, a character.

"I sure did love that man. He was my mentor, really. Taught me everything," Connor said. "But hey, listen to me, getting emotional. This tree's got a lot of sap to it."

Imogene laced her fingers together. "I wanted to discuss with you a few of the plans I have for the company going forward."

"Right, but—"

"My grandfather always said you were one of his most trusted advisers, his former protégé, as you put it, so obviously I'd like your feedback. I could use people who are honest."

"Before that, we really need to—"

"I want my transition into leadership to be as smooth as possible. I realize the fact I'm a wo—"

"Imogene," said Connor. "We should really discuss the will first."

In that moment, Imogene was stunned speechless, not because of what Connor had said, but because he had emphasized it by touching her thigh. Her horrific, withered, spindly, disgusting thigh. Imogene couldn't even manage to look down as a way to show she was upset. Connor drew his hand back in seeming response to her silence. Thank the damn Lord.

"What about the will?" Imogene asked.

"I want you to know your grandfather loved you very much. Personally, and please don't repeat this to Nick or Susannah, but I think you were his favorite."

"What. About. The will."

"Your grandfather"—*can't never could, can't never could*—
"left the company"—*can't never could, can't never could*—"to
your brother."

...

Two years later, Imogene Forster appeared on the cover of the
June 30, 1958, issue of *Time,* beneath the headline, COLA NATION.
She exhibited the same determined stare she'd once given Connor
Rolph after he'd told her news that sent brine through her veins. Her
only visible accessory was a magnolia flower pinned to the lapel of
her jacket. She did not smile. In the article, Imogene responded to
the question of what was next for the company by saying, with the
verbal equivalent of a shrug, "We're going to war."

Thus the neologism "cola warfare" entered the lexicon. The
phrase appears numerous times throughout *Ms. Panola Cola,* in
reference to, for example, the constant struggle with Pepsi and Coke
for the title of best-selling soda, the controversy over the Ameri-
canization of foreign economies for which PanCola was held up
as a token, the so-called arms race for a diet cola, and the diffi-
culties winning over the peace-loving countercultural youth of the
1960s. Then came the year Imogene's brother came of age. Although she never speculated in public about Nicholas's actions—
"All's fair in a cola war" is the only thing she writes of them in her
autobiography—the reason he took over the Panola Cola Company
was not, as many believe, a desire for wealth, power, and fame.
Somewhat ironically, his mother, Sarah Forster, who had exhibited
such a lack of discernment in her naming of him, correctly guessed
Nicholas's motives when, believing her son to have met someone in
college, she remarked to her mother-in-law, "The things a young
man will do to impress the woman he loves."

The Harrington Limit—Like Brother, Like Sister—
Candy's Dandy—Pre-Post-Imperialism

Montgomery was dressed to make an impression. On the train from London to a small village south of Birmingham, he wore a three-piece suit of fine glen plaid wool, a silk tie with a tie bar, polished Oxford wing tips, and a gray trilby pitched at a spry angle, its Petersham band matched perfectly with the houndstooth of his cashmere dress socks. He focused on the countryside out the window in the hopes of calming his nerves. To the other passengers on the train, Monty seemed as though he were about to meet his lover after a long absence—"He's giddy as a schoolboy," a commuter on holiday whispered to her husband, "just like you were with me"—an observation that, for the American trying to appreciate the English landscape, was at least partly accurate. It wasn't his lover he was about to meet but his lover's family.

One month earlier, a letter had arrived for him at the PanCola headquarters, where, during any time he had to spare from his campaign for district attorney, he served as head legal counsel. "April 28, 1934," was its first line, and its last read, "William Harrington." Between those two was a formal offer to develop, produce, and market a hard candy based on the flavor of Panola Cola. Monty hardly took a breath during the short time it took him to read the letter.

"I suppose you may be wondering why I'm writing to you about this matter instead of your father," wrote the owner of Harrington Limited, a British confectionery manufacturer. "I believe you were acquainted with my son during the war. Nicholas mentioned you in his correspondence."

Ni-cho-las, Ni-cho-las. The syllables stole into Monty's mind as if on a winter gale. They drifted in the air before his eyes, six little clouds of condensed breath, offering hope and relief, a glimmer of deliverance from a life of measured desperation. *"Name's Nicholas. These chaps call me Nick, but to my friends I'm Nicholas."*

Although it took a great deal of persuasion, Montgomery convinced his father that, no matter if they chose to accept the deal, a company representative should visit the Harrington facilities, to get a sense of their operation. Monty volunteered to be that representative. In answer to the request for a visit, William Harrington not only agreed to one but also, just as Monty'd hoped, insisted he stay with the family at their home. "Any friend of my son's is a friend of mine." So, roughly a month after the negotiations began, Montgomery Forster made the third voyage in his life across the Atlantic Ocean, the first of which had led to falling in love with a man, the second of which had helped in letting him go, and the third of which, Montgomery suspected as his train inched north toward Birmingham, would be some combination of the two.

"Paisley Street and Ashbrook! Paisley Street and Ashbrook!"

That was his stop. Once the conductor had passed by, still hollering, "Paisley Street and Ashbrook," like a folk song, Monty gathered his luggage, waited at the train doors, and, after they opened, stepped out onto the platform. The bright sun was a shock to him. He had to blink for a few seconds in order to draw focus on the village that, despite being just five miles south of a major city, looked as though it had been preserved in a jar for the past hundred years. The streets were unpaved and the cottages mossed over. A cow munched on grass in the middle of an alley. Monty had to scatter chickens as he walked down to the lane that ran parallel with the station.

"Mr. Forster," called a man standing beside a lustrous beetle-black Bentley. Mustachioed and bespectacled, he kept his thumbs and index fingers tucked into the pockets of his waistcoat, part of an ensemble of Harris Tweed. The admirable tailoring of his suit did little to disguise a portliness one might expect in the owner of a multinational candy company. Montgomery's heart, which he had felt expanding with each mile he'd gotten closer to Nicholas's home, shrank like a snail touched with salt to see that the father bore little resemblance to the son.

"William Harrington," the man said. "Your trip enjoyable?"

"Very. Thanks."

His tight collar reminiscent of an overdone coddled egg, Mr. Harrington placed Monty's luggage in the Bentley, refusing any help by modestly insisting that he had it. The man even doffed his cap. "Let's be off then, shall we? Do accept my apologies for picking you up myself. My daughter insists it's improper not to send the chauffeur," Mr. Harrington said. "But I'm eager to show you our little village. The not-necessarily-grand tour."

Named for a local stream that, due to a glacial deposit of boulder clay, appeared the color of soot, Ashbrook was originally a farming community but, Mr. Harrington explained to Montgomery, had taken a moderately industrial turn fifty years ago. That was when Mr. Harrington's father, George, chose it for the new, expanded premises of their company, believing its access to canals and the railway would give Harrington Limited an advantage over their main rival, a company Mr. Harrington referred to, over the course of their drive through the village, as "the chicken coop," "fowl chocolate," and "the egg layers."

The small village became, as they drove farther into it, a sort of economic model. Farmsteads gave way to commissaries. Barnyards were replaced by living quarters. Country lanes turned into paved roads. "When my father purchased these three hundred acres, he wanted it to become an idealized village for our employees," Mr. Harrington said to Montgomery. "You'll notice there are no pubs. Father advocated temperance. Just beyond this knoll here is an outdoor swimming lido." Despite being on a wholly different continent, Ashbrook reminded Monty of plantations in the Delta, how they were self-contained systems in many ways, a thought that, in turn, reminded him of the joke Nicholas had made whenever Monty pronounced his rank. "Who is this Lou Tenant," he would say, "a farmer from Mississippi?"

"To your right is the factory," Mr. Harrington said, nodding toward the last still in the time-lapse slide show of capitalist progression that was the village of Ashbrook. The confectionery factory was mammoth, at least twelve floors, steepled by smokestacks, with an oval perimeter, like a giant royal crown built of red brick. Its proprietor said, "We'll visit the old girl tomorrow. I'm sure you must be dashed tired from your trip."

Fifteen minutes later they reached Ashbrook Hall, a building just as impressive as the factory. Even more so, thought Monty. Previously owned by Edmund James Lowsley, 3rd Baron Atwell, the country house was a square block of seven quarters and three floors, its exterior constructed of Runcorn sandstone in ashlar blocks, Welsh slate on the roof. The south front included a pedimented porch with a balustrade, and the north front featured a portico with two monolithic columns. Marble steps approached an imposing doorway. Nicholas must have crossed that threshold a thousand times. Monty could see him now: seven years old, hair in want of a comb and a smudge of marmalade at the corner of his mouth; fifteen years old, dressed in cricket whites; sixteen years old, dressed in boating flannels; eighteen years old, army cap tucked under his arm, freshly shaved, effortlessly handsome, a young man strutting out a doorway through which he would never enter again.

Inside the house, where Montgomery was led by the butler, Samuel, whom Mr. Harrington spoke of like family, the drawing and dining rooms were to the east, smoking room and library to the west, all of which could be reached from the entrance hall, a rare early example, the butler said regarding its decoration scheme, of the "Wrenaissance style, the one with a W."

"Is there anything I or the staff can get you? A batch of rock buns was baked this morning," said Mr. Harrington, half his digits nestled, once again, in his waistcoat.

"No, but thank you. Your home is lovely."

Mr. Harrington placed a hand on Monty's shoulder, saying, "You're more than welcome. Like I said, a friend of Nicholas's. Samuel will show you to your room."

Once he was alone, Monty loosened his tie, yawned, removed his shoes, yawned again, and plopped himself on top of the billowy, soft eiderdown covering the bed in what, he assumed, must be one of at least twenty rooms in Ashbrook Hall. Talk about to the manor born. During their short time together, Monty had known the phrase "well-off" certainly applied to Nicholas, but this was at a different level.

He took a deep breath through his nose. The smells of an early English summer came to him—hints of peppermint creams from the kitchen, outside the window a Bourbon rose heavy with buds, furniture polish, apple charlotte, mildewed wicker, a new bar of carbolic sitting in a bathroom soap dish—all of which Nicholas must have known growing up. With his eyes closed, Monty tried to conjure his friend, to feel and see him, to taste and hear him, by focusing on these new additions to his senses and trying to ignore his memories of the war, that smell of the harvest on distant farms, freshly bloomed gunfire, ready to be reaped by chests, arms, legs, and heads.

Forgetting the war while also remembering Nicholas had been Monty's most difficult struggle over the past sixteen years. He practiced the trick every night before bed. Seeing and not seeing. Hearing and not hearing. Tasting and not tasting. Feeling and not feeling. If you want to get better at anything, Monty had learned, you push yourself until the point of no return, and then you return.

It was almost cocktail hour when he woke up. Monty splashed some water on his face and reestablished the part in his hair before venturing downstairs and getting understandably lost on his way to the parlor. He wandered into it by the mercy of luck.

From a carved Victorian armchair Mr. Harrington rose to greet him. "May I offer you an aperitif?" he said, lifting a preprandial decanter from the bar cart.

"That would be wonderful."

Drinks in hand, the two men sat down crosswise to each other, each putting ankle to knee. "Afraid we're going to be a light party this evening," said Mr. Harrington. "The boys still have a few more weeks left in the term." Monty knew he was referring to Nicholas's brothers, Baxter and Rupert, both of whom, according to their father, were at present living a life that would make Riley himself say, "Those two chaps certainly do have it easy." One was at Cambridge, the other at Oxford. Monty also knew from his many conversations with Nicholas that their mother had passed away giving birth to Rupert.

"Shame they're not here. I would have liked to've met them."

Could have sworn Nicholas mentioned he had a— Monty was thinking when a woman entered the drawing room, saying, "So this is the man who fought alongside my brother."

Sophie Harrington was essentially the female version of Nicholas Harrington. Two years junior to her deceased sibling, roughly an inch shorter, with the same chestnut hair marked by a slight bit of curl, the same tawny complexion, not to mention the same casual, proud disregard for social niceties, she bore the resemblance to her brother Monty had been expecting to find in their father. Monty had a difficult time getting down his last sip of cordial in order to introduce himself. "Nicholas told me so much about you," he finally managed.

"I highly doubt that."

"Don't be rude, Sophie." Mr. Harrington turned to Montgomery. "She and her brother were very close. So close it was as though neither liked to share the other."

"Please refrain from analyzing me in front of strangers."

In Sophie's emphasis on that last word, *strangers*, Monty thought he detected a provocation, some dig at his friendship with Nicholas. What had he done to make her so angry with him? During the war, Nicholas had rarely spoken of Sophie, it was true, focusing instead on his brothers, Baxter and Rupert, in nursery school at the time. It had seemed perfectly normal that a pair of rambunctious boys would make for better stories to tell.

"Dinner is ready." The butler stood in the doorway to the drawing room. "If you please."

Ashbrook Hall's dining room, where the three members of the party took a seat at the table, featured a white-oak wainscot, giving it a yellowish lambency. The room looked as though it had been dripped from a tallow candle. "Before I forget," said Mr. Harrington, cast in a light similar to his own skin tone, as he reached into his pocket. "The prototype."

He slid a small item across the table toward Monty. The hard candy was oval-shaped, light brown, and not covered by any wrapper. "May I?" asked Monty.

"Please, go ahead," Mr. Harrington said as two uniformed women served a course of vichyssoise. "Give us the verdict."

Although he was trying to appear enthusiastic, Montgomery, while holding the candy in his hand, worried that his fingers would start to shake. He had not touched or tasted a hard candy since the wrapper for one saved his life and sanity in the war. Over the past sixteen years, he had often woken up at night, brow rimed with sweat, an odd sugary taste in his mouth. More than once he'd had to excuse himself from office meetings because of a lozenge-size knot that had inexplicably formed in his throat. He unfailingly grew nauseated whenever he took medicine whose flavor, to make it more palatable, had been masked with a cloyingly sweet imitation of some fruit, cough syrup that went down like sour cherry, antacids that turned electric orange in water.

"Here goes," Monty said, lifting the candy to his mouth. He had to pry it loose with his teeth because it was stuck to his palm.

In his seat at the table, rolling the candy around his mouth, Monty had a feeling not of *déjà vu* but rather of *presque vu,* a sense that he could almost remember this taste. It was literally on the tip of his tongue.

All the elements of Panola Cola's flavor were present, a little nutmeg, some vanilla, a little citrus, some caramel, a subtle trace of the coca plant's sui generis extract. The difference was a sensation that, years later, would come to be known as mouthfeel. Soda involved the sense of touch as much as it did the sense of taste. This candy lacked the tactility of carbonation, that feel, exhilarating in its strangeness, of bubbles zooming all throughout the mouth. This was PanCola gone flat.

Montgomery told Mr. Harrington, "Spot on, in my opinion. I'm of course more used to it being aerated, but the flavor's all there, despite no carbon dioxide." He placed the glistening candy on the edge of his soup saucer.

"Thank you, Mr. Forster. I thought so myself. Indeed, I do feel there's one flavor missing, but I don't presume you're willing to reveal the notorious secret ingredient."

"Would if I could. The old man's never even told me."

"'Upon this rock,' I suppose. And sympathize," said Mr. Harrington. "I'd rather like to meet your father. He sounds of my own mold."

"I'm sure the two of you will meet soon enough."

"Can I take that to mean you'll agree to the contract?"

Monty demurred. "I should see the factory before reaching a decision. Didn't come all the way over here just for the fine company." With a smile he raised his glass.

Despite his objection that night, Monty knew he was going to agree to the contract with Harrington Limited, no matter the state of its factory. The agreement would prove lucrative for both parties. In the decade to come, Panola Cola would be introduced to Europe by way of Harrington Limited's best-selling candy Pan-Tics®, an introduction that would be augmented when America entered a war lurching into motion that very night, June 5, 1934, as Adolf Hitler, less than a thousand miles to the east, decided Operation Hummingbird had a nice ring to it. Fate would inevitably show her unmerciful side. The prosperity that both the Harrington licensing agreement and the Second World War brought to the Forster family, turning them into royalty in a nation that had foresworn the system of estates, would create a sense of invincibility in the last Forster to run the Panola Cola Company, a character flaw made all the more tragic by the fact that it belonged to the accidental namesake of one Nicholas Harrington.

As servants placed dishes of stargazy pie, fish heads protruding from the crust, before each diner, Sophie Harrington said, "Now that we've dispensed with business, shall we move on to topics a bit more pleasant? Tell us about my brother's death in the war, Mr. Forster."

"Sophie, honestly," said Mr. Harrington.

"No, no. I'd very much like to hear about it. Couldn't have been as *sanitary* as the Home Office would have us believe."

"Please accept my apologies, Mr. Forster. Sophie can be—"

"It's all right. Really, it is," Monty said. He set down his fork, drank a long swallow of wine, filled his lungs with air, and turned toward Sophie. "Bullet to the base of his skull. German sniper. Hardly any pain. No spasms. Very little blood," said Monty, somehow defying his legion impulses to break down. "I was looking into his eyes when he went. Before that moment, I thought we were doing the right thing over there, making the world a better place. Before that moment, I didn't believe in the human soul."

Seconds passed. Monty caught up with his breath, chest rising and then falling, while staring at Sophie. "Good enough?" he asked.

From his plate, the head of a pilchard, eyes cloudy, mouth agape, stared at Montgomery, as though in dumbfound, weary, justified reprehension of his conduct. Even without the fish he knew he had gone too far. How could he have been so cruel? This wasn't the campaign trail. He wasn't trying to win some debate.

Sophie, barely moving her face that so closely resembled her brother's, said, "I thank you for your candor," her voice as impassive as her powdered cheeks, her smooth brow, her colorless lips, her fixed stare. She asked her father if she might be excused and did not bother to wait for an answer.

"Now it's my turn to beg your pardon," Montgomery said once he was alone with Mr. Harrington. "There's no excuse for my behavior just now."

"My daughter's a willful young woman. Her mother was the same way—more so—thus my forbearing nature. Shall we retire to the smoking room? I don't think I can eat a bite of this pie. I've no idea what the kitchen was thinking. Collywobble would be a more suitable name than stargazy."

Monty gave a mental tip of the hat to God. He had not been looking forward to pretending to enjoy that particular dish. In the smoking room, which lay just beyond an overdoor on the opposite side of the main hall, he accepted a glass of what tasted like liquid peat and, refusing a cigar, settled into the vegetable-tanned sheep's leather of a club chair. "Good Scotch," he said, thinking of his grandfather, who could distinguish, by smell alone, between the Highlands, Lowlands, Islay, Speyside, and Campbeltown, most of which tasted the same to Monty.

"I'm pleased you like it," Mr. Harrington said, swirling the amber contents of his glass. "It was a birthday present I gave myself last year."

"The bottle?"

"The distillery."

Over the next hour, Mr. Harrington showed his investment to be financially prudent by drinking, as he pontificated on the confectionery trade, five glasses of Scotch. Monty kept himself to half that number, barely listening to the man, instead looking around the smoking room. On the mantel an ormolu timepiece struck ten o'clock. Spangled colors poured from a leadlight. In the corner a globe atop its floor stand collected dust.

"But I'll tell you why my daughter's so unhappy," Mr. Harrington said, apropos of nothing in their conversation, as far as Monty could tell. "She was raised among the haut monde, wanted for nothing, and yet, because she's just three generations from working class, because her lineage does not have any 'Right Honorables,' she'll always be an outsider. 'So sorry. Back of the line for you, little woman.' And your mother has a brother called Robert."

"That's unfortunate."

"Your people had the right idea. No lordships. No peerage. You are what you make of yourself." Mr. Harrington took a gulp of his sixth whisky. "Yes, Mr. Forster, the world belongs to America now. Hope you take better care of it than we did."

Monty thought of disagreeing in order to be polite, but his host chose that moment to fall soundly asleep. His glass tumbler remained clutched in his hand. Just as Monty was about to relieve Mr. Harrington of it, careful not to spill what little whisky remained, a voice on the other side of the room said, "If you please, sir, I'll see to him."

The butler, Samuel, stood in the doorway, a folded blanket in his arms. *Don't worry,* the look on his face said. *This happens all the time.* Samuel walked across the room, removed the tumbler, placed it on a side table, unfolded the blanket, and situated it over Mr. Harrington. "Is there anything I can offer you, sir?" he said to Monty while placing a pillow behind his employer's head.

"No, thank you. Don't mind me. I'll find my room on my own. Good night."

In the main hall of the house, Monty got his bearings, turning from the fire burning in an ornate hearth—which back home would have been odd, given the time of year—to the Aubusson carpet in front of the staircase. He felt that lingering here would be inappropriate while the rest of the household was asleep. On his way toward the stairs, though, Monty came to an abrupt stop because, with a suddenness that sent a tremor through his body, he found himself in the presence of a ghost.

The portrait of Nicholas must have been painted shortly before Britain entered the war. It was given pride of place on the wall between a watercolor of indeterminate provenance and a landscape by one of the lesser Romanticists. In the half-length portrait, composed from a seated position, with oil paint, and framed in a detailed hardwood, Nicholas disproved a famous line from Dickens, how there were only two styles of portraits, "the serious and the smirk," by coupling sealed lips with mischievous eyes. Monty could remember that same look from so many occasions, the morning they first met, the night they first kissed, but not from the one occasion he would never forget, when those lips were riven by shock, those eyes opening wide and then blinking slowly in disbelief.

Monty's vision melted the portrait of Nicholas. That mustache slicked with brilliantine became a dark streak of smutch, and those cheeks doused in sandalwood oil became two hazy daubs of yellow. He had only just managed to wipe away the tears when someone cleared their throat behind him.

"Warm milk helps me get to sleep," Sophie said, holding up a glass as proof. She was wearing a silver peignoir over a nightgown trimmed in tulle. "I take it Father passed out again?"

"He may have had one too many."

"Would you believe he used to be a teetotaler?" She took a sip of milk, turning her lips, momentarily and disarmingly, a bluish-beige. "He only started after."

To end her sentence Sophie nodded at the portrait of Nicholas hanging on the wall. Although he was worried how he might react, Monty allowed himself to look at it again, those lips that had so often been puckered around a hard candy, that mustache like stove black, those eyes that hinted at what he had liked to call "ease of virtue."

"Listen, Miss Harrington. About dinner, I really would like to apol—"

"Do see that you get a good night's rest, Mr. Forster. Father has a busy day planned for the two of you."

Already halfway up the lengthy staircase, she was speaking to him over her shoulder. She had vanished into the upper floors before Monty thought to wish her a good night of rest as well. He walked across the hall to the fire. In front of it, he rubbed his hands together and then folded his arms across his chest, squeezing tightly, even though he wasn't the least bit cold.

4.5

Robert in the Library with the Wrench—
The Stuff That Dreams Are Made Of

The cover of the July 3, 1964, issue of *Life* magazine featured an American flag made out of soda cans—red Coca-Cola and white PanCola and blue Pepsi-Cola—superimposed on which was the headline, FOR GOD, COUNTRY, FAMILY, AND SODA POP.

Robert studied the cover on microfiche at the school library. It was late April. For the past month, instead of working on the first chapter of his thesis, he had been researching the history of the Panola Cola Company, its mythic origin and unprecedented growth, its unequivocal reign and tragic demise, an activity that tempted, he was aware, Leo Marunga's very possible, very dangerous wrath. Robert couldn't help himself. Something about the company gave him the thrill he used to get from schoolwork. The inherent qualities of its product, that dramatically Manichean life span of soda, fizzy to flat, delicious to awful, in combination with the qualities inherent to historical records, the beauty of factuality, the authority of details, the poetry of specificity, allowed Robert to lose hours and even days at a time inside the narrative of PanCola. His imagination gave flesh to the bones of his research, enabling him to meet people he'd never known, to visit places he'd never been.

Robert was particularly intrigued by the mystery of the secret ingredient. Trying to solve it felt like playing a game of Clue.

All throughout his research, he'd been keeping a notebook on PanCola, replete with information he thought could help identify the ingredient, essentially a list of the potential suspects, rooms, and murder weapons. Perhaps one of the Panhandlers might know the secret. Called "drummers" in other industries because they drummed up trade, Panhandlers were salesmen who, indoctrinated by the "PanCola Bible" on company policies, traveled the railways across the nation, passing out coupons for free samples, overseeing advertisements, contracting soda fountain proprietors, and, according to the bible, "routing any venue that dares sell imitation or adulterated PanCola." That last duty interested Robert. Panhandlers were trained to know the flavor of their product so well they could detect if even one ingredient had been substituted with an inferior version. The problem was only a few of them were left alive, and with each day those who remained dwindled further.

What if the key lay in one of the buildings Houghton Forster erected in nearly every major city of the United States? With the Forster Investment Company, created in the early part of the twentieth century for procuring real estate, Houghton put his name on skyscrapers in Chicago, Tampa, Memphis, and Seattle. The Forster Building overlooked Bryant Park in midtown New York. Forster Hall on Peachtree Street enraged the company's rival in Atlanta. The Forster Center became a tourist attraction in downtown Baltimore. In each building, like in the reliquary of a church, Houghton designated an area for displaying artifacts from the history of PanCola, such as the first bottle produced, early streetcar placards, signs made of steel and muslin and tin and oilcloth gone ragged, change trays, posters, calendars, the first church key bearing the company name, and even a life-size reproduction of Forster Rex-for-All. The relics were sold at auction when the company was liquidated. So now, Robert figured, evidence of the secret ingredient might be in an antique shop on a backstreet of Podunk, USA, collecting dust in a display case, situated between T. Nash Buckingham's legendary twelve-gauge, Bo Whoop, and a Honus Wagner card some kid would buy for a dime and wedge into the spokes of his Schwinn.

Then again maybe the ingredient's identity was already in his notes. It could be the magnolia flower. In the *Harvard Crimson*, following her graduation, Imogene Forster was referred to as the Magnolia Flower of Cambridge, though Robert suspected that was a result of the crush the article's author, Barry Rojas, clearly had on her. "It had been right under my nose the whole time," Imogene wrote in *Ms. Panola Cola* regarding her deduction, four months into her tenure as the company president, of the ingredient's identity. What if it were bay leaves? In an interview for the *Ladies' Home Journal,* Annabelle Forster was quoted as saying, "I remember the moment I fell in love with Houghton. He wrote in a letter, 'I want to be the bay leaf in your gumbo.' Sounds silly, I know, but it worked, mostly because he didn't say he wanted *me* to be the bay leaf in *his* gumbo." The ingredient could even be hidden in plain sight, referenced, perhaps, in one of Ramsey Forster's last books, *A Tumbler of Kentuckians* or *An Anecdote of Pub Dwellers,* both of which seemed, after the fact, to foretell the plunge from sobriety that led to her death.

At the library that day, going over his research, Robert was struck less by the clues, each suspect, room, and weapon, than by how they all fit together so well, creating a network of causality, an entanglement of chance and fate unbelievable but true, each coincidence, he thought, proving a fool of anyone who says, "You can't make this stuff up," because of course you could. The mystery no longer felt like a board game but rather like another form of entertainment. Robert didn't know what form exactly until he looked at his notes on PanCola Too. He suspected, based on the animosity Imogene Forster held toward her brother, that she had refused to tell him the identity of the secret ingredient, which meant PanCola Too had been a product of necessity rather than foolishness. When Imogene regained control of the company after Nicholas's death, she changed Panola Cola back to the original, labeling it the Heritage Formula—the abbreviation for which Robert wrote off as a red herring—and using a new catchphrase, "Tastes Classic!" Hundreds of articles were published on the situation, but a line from one in particular stood out from the rest.

"Why read fiction? Why go to movies?" Jesse Meyers noted in a special edition of *Beverage Digest*. "[The] soft drink industry has enough roller-coaster plot-dips to make novelists drool."

4.6

The Member(s) of the Wedding—How to Catch a Doodlebug—The Un-Cola—Cotton's a Good Boy— *Die Freizeit-Klasse in Amerika*—Royal Teague's Funeral—(A Not Quite the) Delta Wedding

On a back road of Panola County, Lance Forster told his father about his fiancée, Karen DeWitt, whom the two men, father in the driver's seat and son in the passenger's seat, were on their way to pick up at the Batesville train station. He concluded, "Petite little thing, Protestant, but she's got those big, floppy, Jewish-girl boobs, you know?"

Houghton's face remained deadpan. "Be sure to put that in your vows."

Few people close to the family would have guessed that, of all the Forster marriages, excluding the first two—Tewksbury to Fiona, Houghton to Annabelle—the one to last the longest and feature a reasonable facsimile of love would turn out to be Lance's. The marriage of Ramsey and Arthur lasted only five years. Monty never actually loved Sarah. Neither Harold, Imogene, nor Nicholas ever married. Even though he would not stay faithful to her, being nearly incapable of such a thing, Lance did, in his own way, love Karen, remaining monogamous in that emotion throughout all eight years of their marriage. He was genuinely looking forward to having her as his wife the afternoon he and his father drove to the train station to meet the 3:27 from Memphis. The wedding, to be held on May 21, 1955, was three days away.

"My darling love!" yelled Karen as she jumped into Lance's arms. Her feet were two inches off the platform, strands of her brown hair stuck to his lips. "My Lancelot!"

"As you live and breathe."

"I'm finally here."

"There's someone I'd like you to meet," Lance said as he loosened her arms from his neck. During the time it took a porter to secure her luggage in the trunk, Karen exchanged pleasantries with Houghton Forster, whom Lance had told her "dangerously little about." Yet, despite her claim to want to know everything about her future father-in-law, it was Karen who, on the ride home, commanded the conversation, talking mostly of how she'd met the "lovely, darling man" to whom she was now engaged.

"'Lovely, darling man,'" Houghton said, feigning confusion. "I thought you were engaged to Lance?"

"Oh, you hush up, Mr. Forster!"

"Call me Houghton."

"Houghton, let me tell you how your lovely, darling son swept me off my feet."

An actress by desire more than talent, Karen had been living in Los Angeles for two years, auditioning with little success, when she went to an open call for a creature feature, *The Dawn Breaks at Midnight*. The film was being produced by Five Olde Entertainment. In the mid-1940s, sensing the possible fall of the studios, Lance had founded the production company, supposedly to diversify his portfolio, though the actual reason was so that he could ruin Arthur Landau, the man who, during his divorce from Ramsey a couple of years earlier, had sent a picture of her kissing

Josephine Baker to every major tabloid in the country. The 1948 federal antitrust suit against the Big Five hastened the accomplishment of Lance's goal. Over the years that followed the verdict, Five Olde set its sights on Vantage Pictures, using the fleetness of its smaller operation to undercut the lumbering studio, producing knockoffs of Vantage's forthcoming slate of films and then releasing said knockoffs a month before their originals. *See You at the Beach* took in ticket sales that would have gone to *Countdown on D-Day*. *Oil! Oil! Oil!* preempted *A Texas Saga*. *Riviera Rendezvous* outstripped *My French Summer*.

Lance met Karen at the auditions for Five Olde's version of the space-alien picture *They Came from the Sky*. Not wanting to tell her she was as wooden as Howdy Doody, he said, "We can't have someone pretty as you in a horror flick. Nobody in the audience would ever look at the monster."

"Then he asked me out to dinner," Karen said to Houghton. "Is that not the sweetest thing?"

"Certainly is." Houghton nodded at the mansion creeping into view on the horizon, fully aware that was not what she had meant but, nonetheless, enjoying the coincidence. He was surprised at how much he liked the girl. Given Lance's age—he and Ramsey must be, what, forty-four years old by now?—Houghton and the rest of the family had resigned themselves to his remaining a bachelor for life, dating ingénues and eating takeout, most important *not* continuing the Forster name with a child. Houghton would have pretended to like the girl even if she had rubbed him wrong. He worried that, when his children were young, he'd been too hard on them, and now, almost in his eighties, he hoped to course-correct any past mistakes. Lord knew he never forgave himself for the frostbite Monty got on his toe the night Houghton sent him to chop firewood in an ice storm. Most of all he regretted the incident with the horse. How could he have forced his own son to shoot Peat?

Some part of him had always known the answer. Houghton had worked hard throughout his entire life not so his children could live easily but so they could work even harder. He often worried he'd only succeeded in creating a bed of laurels for them to rest on. That worry, coupled with the sense that a tremble in the bloodline can become a tidal wave generations later, pushed him to push them. Houghton wanted his children to know the taste of sweat as well as they knew the taste of PanCola. Unfortunately, he sometimes couldn't tell when he had breached the line between rigor and cruelty, and he now knew he'd done so with Lance that day in the woods, especially when, on their ride home, he'd answered Lance's question about whether Peat would go to heaven. "There's no heaven for horses, son. There isn't even one for people."

. . .

"Ladybug, where's your gentlemanbug?" whispered Susannah.

She was sitting on the back lawn of the main house, the hem of her batik dress billowing around her, the scent of false dragonhead and yucca bells carried on the breeze. Her hand was raised in front of her face. Along her fingers, weaving in and out, crawled a ladybug, which she had named Elizabeth Bennet. The strong-willed Miss Bennet was a fretful mess. Susannah supposed it must be all the preparations that were in order for the ceremonies. Her uncle was getting married this week. Even there in the yard, far enough from the main house to allow for some quiet, she could hear her family greeting the bride, who'd just arrived from the train station. "I think I'm going to get along with her splendidly. Don't you, Miss Bennet? Yes, I daresay, she's likely to be an agreeable wife."

Seven years old, a native of California who came to Mississippi but rarely, Susannah Forster had been raised a fan of Jane Austen by accident. From the time she was a baby her mother had read to her from *Mansfield Park, Sense and Sensibility, Pride and Prejudice,* and *Emma,* always planning to switch to more traditional fare as soon as the child could understand the words. Her mother, Ramsey, realized she had postponed the switch too long when Susannah began to say, "More, pwease!" at the end of story time. Soon it became apparent she had created a monster: a young girl in tune to and obsessed with courtship, who used "dear" as an adjective and for whom walks were nearly a sport.

Years later, Ramsey would refer to the man her daughter was seeing in secret as "Mr. Darcy," and after the prop plane he was piloting with Susannah as his passenger experienced sudden engine failure on a flight to Los Angeles in good weather, it was noted among certain friends and family that "books sold the poor girl out."

"Your mother told me to tell you not to get your dress dirty," Nicholas said to Susannah, purposefully giving his voice the tone of boredom. He livened up on noticing the dot of red crawling on her hand. "Want me to show you how to catch a doodlebug?"

"A *what*le bug?"

"Doodle."

"You're making that up."

Susannah squinted at her cousin Nicholas. He was tall for an eleven-year-old. His blond, side-parted hair held a natural wave, like a still shot of a pennant in a light offshore breeze. Since her arrival at the house, Susannah had noticed that everyone acted different around Nicholas, treating him, it seemed, like the reincarnation of his father, whose death Susannah knew about from her mother. People acted as if saying anything harsh in front of the boy would make him disappear in a puff of smoke.

"Just watch," said Nicholas. He walked in an expanding circle around her, staring at the ground, until he found a bald patch of dirt that seemed to satisfy him. He motioned for her to come look. "See the tiny little hole right there? That's where a tiger beetle laid an egg." After plucking a long, sturdy blade of grass, Nicholas spit on the end of it and then slowly lowered the blade into the hole, inch by inch, making sure Susannah was watching the procedure closely. He let go of the grass when there was only the length of a finger still above ground. Situating his legs Indian-style, he said to her, "Tell me when you see it move."

"Move how?"

As though on command the finger's length of grass began to twitch. Surgically, being careful not to move too fast, Nicholas took hold of the grass and began to pull it from the ground, stopping on occasion and then restarting even slower. Dangling at the end of the blade when it emerged was a tiny white grub with a brown head and three pairs of legs, its wriggling body splotched with dirt.

"Susannah, you can keep playing out there for another ten minutes," her mother called from a door to the house. "Then you have to come back in here and pretend you're having a good time."

Ramsey closed the door behind her, walked back through the kitchen, and reentered the crowded living room. Despite what she had said to her daughter, she wasn't pretending to have a good time but, surprisingly, having an actual one. She hadn't expected much from her brother's fiancée. The surprising part was that she liked the girl. Lighthearted, funny, self-deprecating, and genuine, Karen seemed just what was needed among the Forsters, someone who hadn't been raised under the scrutiny of the world. Just yesterday, Ramsey had read a profile of her family in the *Chicago Tribune* that began, "The Forsters aren't the type of people who won't take 'no' for an answer. They are the type of people who don't even bother to ask permission." How could you not feel self-important with statements like that floating around?

In the living room, another round of cocktails was being served, tumblers glinting with perspiration, their contents mostly liquor and ice and, despite how the family product was often used, little to no amount of mixers. A wedding wasn't a time for watering things down. "No, thank you," Ramsey said to the house servant who offered her one.

"Still on that kick?" asked Annabelle.

"Not drinking isn't a kick, Mother. I don't need alcohol in my life."

"What you need is a man."

Ramsey said, "Get some new material already."

The absolute truth was Ramsey sometimes worried her mother was right about the need for a man in her life, not for her sake, but so that Susannah could have a father figure. Over the past seven years, Susannah hadn't seemed to mind not having one around, let alone not knowing who her father even was—Ramsey already had a heartfelt speech on love and "the timing was just wrong for us" ready in the hopper—nor did Susannah seem bothered by her mother's social life. Ramsey still dated. The people she went out with, though, be they men or women, old or young, working in pictures or not, had trouble getting over either her past marriage to a notoriously vicious studio head, the fact she was in her forties and had a daughter, or the rumors, confirmed by a famous photograph, of the actual person with whom the timing had been wrong.

Ramsey took a seat near an open window, getting some azalea-laced air as she looked on the happy couple. She had seen Josephine only once since the war. In 1951, visiting her book publisher in New York to discuss merchandising rights, Ramsey was having dinner at the Stork Club when someone calling herself "Gracie Walker" was refused service because of her skin color. Ramsey immediately recognized Josephine, and throughout the rest of the night, after paying off the maître d' to let Josephine's party dine at her table, she did her best to tolerate Josephine's girlfriend, as gut-wrenchingly young as she was gut-wrenchingly beautiful.

According to the conversation that evening, the two had worked together during the war, Josephine as an "honorable correspondent" for the Deuxieme Bureau, her girlfriend as a covert operative for the OSS. "Love is an elastic sort of art," concluded the former in a way that sounded rehearsed, a suspicion confirmed when the latter responded, "Same goes for espionage." Despite how much it hurt to see her past lover, Ramsey was so elated to be in her company again that, at the end of the night, she repeated the first of three things Josephine had said to her the last time they were together.

"Don't drink too much."

Josephine smiled. "Sleep a lot."

"Work evenly over time."

At home for the wedding Ramsey wanted to give her brother Lance the same pieces of advice. He was clearly drinking too much. Not that the other Forsters were so different. Thus far, even though it was still early in the evening, most everybody in the house was on the fourth or fifth round of whatever flavor suited them, such that they were now starting to dance. Over by the plantation desk, Imogene and Nicholas and Susannah were clapping to the beat coming from the Capehart, some fast-paced number, while Lance and Karen flung each other around, bobbing side to side with grins, all of which was watched over by Houghton and Annabelle, whispering near the china closet. To Ramsey the entire scene looked like a delightful if tame Rabbit's Foot Minstrel. She forgot what had been on her mind.

"Sister-in-law!" Karen said as she and Lance swung close to

Ramsey. "You're next!" On turning loose her intended, she grabbed her not-yet sister-in-law's forearm, hauling her onto the makeshift dance floor. They began to twirl about the room. Karen pulled Ramsey close and whispered, "I never had a sister. Always wanted one."

"Me, too."

"I just know we're going to be close. You wouldn't believe how much Lance cares about you."

"Really?"

"And here I always heard twins could read each other's minds."

The next song was slower paced. In a corner of the room, watching Karen and Ramsey dance, Lance turned to see Nicholas and Susannah, seated on the couch, deep in an adorably grown-up-looking conversation. "Mind if I cut in, buddy row?" he asked his nephew.

"Ew! Think I'd dance with *her*!"

Lance held out his hand to Susannah. "Well, then I will."

She let him guide her into the middle of the room, where, instead of simply beginning to dance, she curtsied as if they were in a novel of manners. Lance bowed in return. The factory of his emotions not yet demolished, he took Susannah's perfect little hands into his own and waltzed her around an imaginary ballroom, the faces of their family, Ramsey and Nicholas, Houghton and Annabelle—did Karen count yet? Lance wondered—becoming images from a shadow lamp thrown against the wall.

Currently in his forties, he had figured any more children were no longer an option for him, but now, about to wed a woman in her late twenties, he thought he could not allow himself to die without a child to call his own, though he would. Karen was too afraid to tell him about her thyroid disorder.

At the end of the song, Susannah said, "Thank you ever so

kindly, sir," and curtsied once again. Lance told her not to be silly. She didn't have to call her uncle "sir."

. . .

Dinner finished and the dishes cleared, nightcaps served, drunk, refilled, and drunk again, Houghton sat in his study taking a cigar, listening to the sounds from upstairs of people settling into bed. He went up himself when everything was quiet. In front of the door to his bedroom, he stopped for a moment to look across the hall at the door to his wife's bedroom, wondering if she was still awake.

She wasn't, but Lance was. In his bedroom, he stood by the door and, after hearing the creak of floorboards outside in the hall, paused with his hand on the knob. Somebody was out there. He waited, listening for any further movement.

Having to sneak around this way made him feel like a fool. Lance wasn't a teenager anymore. If he wanted to sleep with his fiancée, he should damn well be allowed to, *propriety shmopriety,* no matter if his parents insisted he and Karen couldn't stay in the same room until after they were married. He slowly opened the door, centimeter by excruciating centimeter, until he just managed to fit.

While sliding through the ten-inch berth, he heard a strange sound coming from the hallway, something animalistic and definitely unkind. He turned his head to see Cotton, the family's white Labrador, growling with hackles raised. Dogs had never liked Lance. He closed the door, went back to bed, and stared at the ceiling.

Ramsey couldn't sleep either. In the room next to Lance's, she lay in her bed worrying about her daughter, who'd insisted she spend the night on the sleeping porch, surrounded by moon vine and the berceuse of crickets, the very possibility of which was wholly exotic to a girl unfamiliar with country living. Did she really need a father figure? That was the question worrying Ramsey. Then again, she thought, maybe that wasn't it at all. What if she, Ramsey, were just lonely, raising Susannah by herself? Best not to worry about it right now. Methodically, almost by habit, she lifted her arm from the bed, slid it under the covers, and helped herself fall asleep.

. . .

In the South, males are "boys" until death. Only after their funerals, whether at eighteen or eighty-five, are they referred to as men. Imogene figured that was why she had never really dated when she was growing up in Mississippi. She wanted a man, not a good old boy. The wheelchair didn't help, obviously, even though none of the boys in school, around town, or at the club ever said anything rude about it. In fact they were perfectly polite. The problem was they didn't actually see her as an option. She was just the poor crippled girl.

On the second-floor gallery of The Sweetest Thing, cup of coffee in hand, Imogene chastised herself for thinking that way. She wasn't just a disability. She wasn't even just a girl. She didn't "want" anyone. Want implied need, and need was weakness. Her uncle's wedding, two days from then, must have put her in mind of such things, though, she thought, that wasn't an excuse.

Years later she would be called the Virgin CEO. Despite welcoming the title—"Strong women don't resort to clichés" was her response when pundits defended her by asking people who used it, "Would you call a male executive that?"—Imogene knew it was a lie, one she affirmed as such repeatedly throughout her career, and always with the same person. Her lifelong, secret affair with

"Barry from the *Crimson*," as she thought of him in college, when they were only friends, began around the time she took over the Panola Cola Company following her grandfather's death. For many years his ascent in journalism mirrored hers in the soda industry. He was a beat reporter when she first introduced cans to the soda market and he was a managing editor when her worldwide sales became more than a third of the company revenue and he was a bureau chief when she reinvigorated the industry with diet cola. Barry Rojas was editor in chief of the *Wall Street Journal* at the time Imogene was ousted from PanCola. On Imogene's return to the company after her brother's accident, Barry was the only person she confided in, about her newfound lack of enthusiasm, about her overwhelming fear of failure, and throughout the next year, the *Journal* was the only major newspaper in the country not to run coverage of how "PanCola Goes Flat!" when the introduction of new products, Vanilla Pan and Pan with Lime, failed to right the company.

Imogene was still an actual virgin the week of her uncle's wedding. On the second-floor gallery, she watched as cars filled up the driveway, looking for boys—*men,* she reminded herself, *men*—her own age, college students whose parents made them come.

Unfortunately, most of the somewhat few people invited to the wedding were distant relatives, Teagues or cousins of Teagues, Wadsworths or cousins of Wadsworths, people Imogene often thought of as the Un-Forsters, a formalism she would later modify in an ad campaign for CitraPan. They were mainly there to kiss the proverbial ring. Although Houghton had rented out three floors of the recently refurbished Batesville Inn, he'd offered The Sweetest Thing as an informal place of congregation, noting in the invitations that guests should come by for cocktails and food once they had settled into their rooms. Lunch was close to being ready. From the back lawn Imogene could smell a Pan-basted hog roasting on a spit.

"Where y'all going?" she yelled at her grandfather and Nicholas, who had emerged from the house and were walking toward the garage.

"Ride around the place," Houghton called back. "We won't be long."

"Can I come?"

"Sorry, honey, but I still haven't gotten seat belts put in the Jeep yet."

The U.S. military had given Houghton the Willys MB as a gift following World War II. It had been used by the company's "technical observers," employees assigned to set up bottling plants behind the lines, who were better known to most soldiers as Panola PFCs. Houghton loved it more than any of his other vehicles, using it to survey the estate as a planter would his farmland.

Today he wanted to talk with his grandson about the meaning of a birthright. They were driving down a rutted dirt road that cut at a diagonal through the property, passing open fields that looked like golf links, shallow ponds girded by overgrown thickets, rolling hills, dried creeks, and all kinds of trees throwing shadows along their route. Houghton pointed them out to Nicholas—pecan and water oak and cypress and walnut and maple and sweet gum. "What's that one there?" he asked, pointing ahead.

"Ash?"

"Elm."

"Why are we out here, Granddaddy?"

Nicholas wished he were back at home, watching as the guests, all those different types of people like these different types of trees, showed up for the festivities. Instead he had to ride around in this awful heat surrounded by a whole bunch of nothing.

"We're out here because one day this will all be yours."

"Really?"

"And not just this. The company, too. Yours and yours alone." After downshifting, Houghton turned onto the trail that ran along the perimeter of Eden, defining its border. "I want to be sure you deserve it. Understand? It's a lot of responsibility. Think you can live up to that kind of standard?"

"Uh-huh."

"*Yes, sir.*"

"Yes, sir."

The rest of Nicholas's life would fall decidedly short of the standard Houghton had in mind. Ask any gossip columnist from that era. Middling in academics but socially popular, Nicholas attended Phillips Exeter, where he was president of the student council, captain of the squash team, captain of the baseball team, and a film critic for *The Exonian*. Then, like most people who didn't get into Harvard, Yale, or Princeton, he pretended Dartmouth had always been his first choice. He enrolled in 1962, the same year his unknown cousin, Robert Vaughn, was born. After college, Nicholas held a number of positions, interning for a Mississippi senator, acting in an Off-Broadway play, but none were more important than his role as, to use his blind-item name, "The Soda Jerk." British model Penelope Tree became his on-off girlfriend after they met at Capote's Black and White Ball. The car he sponsored placed respectably at Le Mans. His polo team defeated Cibao-La Pampa in an overtime chukker. Such playboy antics, however, were relatively brief. In 1967, over a year after he had come of proper age, Nicholas decided to replace his sister at the head of PanCola, proving himself, as Imogene would later put it in a section of her autobiography that her editor at Penguin insisted she cut, "the very embodiment of deceit, a man whose conception had been unwanted by his father and was only made possible when his mother, from what I've heard, started using her diaphragm as a pincushion."

"You know, you look like him," Houghton said to Nicholas as they rode around Eden. It was an old joke between them. "Have I told you that yet?"

"Nope. Never."

Nicholas's grandfather told him he looked like his father just about every single day. It was difficult for Nicholas to see a resemblance. He considered the old guy in the portraits and photos around the house to be just that, an old guy, not the magical preincarnation of himself that his grandfather seemed to see in them. "What would've been his is going to be yours," Nicholas's grandfather said as they took a dogleg south.

"Neat."

From where they were now riding, an old game trail next to a long meadow, it was possible to see the main house off in the distance, smoke rising from the cookout in its backyard. Annabelle watched them through the kitchen window. Sunlight flickered off the jeep's windshield like Morse code as they drove along.

She looked down and realized the whiskey she had been pouring into her lemonade was overflowing the glass. Damn. She had only meant to float a tiny bit on top. So far the day had been its own kind of hell, welcoming guests for the wedding, getting them fed, trying to remember all their names, such that a top-off was just what she needed. While taking a hand towel to the spilled whiskey, Annabelle looked back out the window, wondering if Houghton was trying to avoid dealing with their guests, or trying to avoid her.

They had been losing touch ever since the day, fifteen years ago, when he told her he wanted an open marriage. Although Houghton never admitted it, Annabelle had always figured it must have been another woman that prompted his request, that he had met some young piece in Los Angeles, where he'd been spending a lot of time for work, and, thinking it would somehow be fairer, wanted her, Annabelle, to have a lover as well. What a coward's move. A real man would have asked for a divorce. Instead, a sort of truce had settled into their marriage, one in which the two of them, Houghton and Annabelle, remained faithful in infidelity, neither of them asking the other about their dalliances. Throughout all fifteen years of their open marriage, though, she hadn't been able to bring herself to flirt, let alone sleep, with another man.

Annabelle set aside the towel, looked away from the window, and took a sip of her lemonade. The problem was she loved her husband. God damn him to hell, but she loved the bastard! Despite the usual, fixable problems—his long hours spent with work and her difficulty showing affection—the closed version of their marriage had been wonderful, the kind other couples, much of the media, some of the public, and their own relatives thought to be a ruse. Even their sex life had been great. After the unhinged lustfulness of their early years, when their locales veered toward the semipublic, a new position was attempted each day, and they often accessorized more than their attire. Annabelle and Houghton successfully made the transition, one other married couples frequently failed at, into sex that was not just fun but playful. The routine they liked best started with her singing him a lullaby. "Sleep My Baby" was a favorite, as was "Toora Loora Loora." In bed, while she sang, he would slowly undress her, both of them grinning at the childish words, their debauched intent, or a combination of both, and then they would attempt to make, grinning and giggling, the very thing for which the lullaby was intended.

"We're running low on champagne for the mimosas, Mrs. Forster," said one of the house servants, standing in the doorway to the kitchen. "Shall I get another case from the cellar?"

"Yes, please. Go ahead and make it two. Is Mr. Forster's mother here yet?"

"She arrived fifteen minutes ago."

"Better bring up a case of Beefeater as well."

In the other room, coincidentally if not fortuitously, Fiona was drinking the last sip of her second gin rickey and looking for somebody to bring her a third. She couldn't find anyone. Houghton must be understaffed. Closing in on a hundred years old, still upright but only with the help of a blackthorn stick, Fiona had a mind to give her son a what-for—just as Tewksbury's had before he put in, her vocabulary had turned fully southern—but, thank heavens, a server appeared by her side with a fresh rickey.

Beneath a triad of palm-leaf fans in heavy rotation, she wandered through the crowd of relatives she barely knew, brushing against watered silk, overwhelmed by the smell of rice powder on cheeks. Many of the guests were distant Wadsworths, Fiona's name before she married Tewksbury. Although she had not grown up particularly well-off, it seemed the family store, Wadsworth Confections, had become a success, with branches throughout England and other parts of the continent, selling products from its two main suppliers, Cadbury and Harrington. Her so-called cousins kept coming up and asking where they might find Houghton, mentioning they wanted his "impartial advice" in expanding the business to the States.

"Grandmother," said Lance as he walked over. "Like you to meet my fiancée."

Fiona, glad to be near someone who was a direct rather than an extended part of her blood, said hello to her grandson and his fiancée, Karen. "Such a beautiful girl."

"Thank you," said Karen.

"And young. Shouldn't have any trouble making a grandchild."

Lance laughed awkwardly. "Now, Grandmother."

"I'd love to have another girl in the family," said Fiona, leaning in conspiratorially. "Tell me, Karen, have you heard about the rhythm method?"

"Okay, it was good visiting with you, Grandmother."

With his arm like a shepherd's crook around her waist, Lance dragged Karen off the vaudeville stage that was his grandmother's presence. "Sorry about that," he said as they bobbed through the crowd, accepting handshakes, giving handshakes, telling people it was lovely to see them.

"Don't be sorry." Karen gripped his elbow. "I thought she was a hoot!"

In fact she thought this whole ordeal was a hoot. Her family back in Toronto hadn't been much of one. They had all but disowned her when she moved to Los Angeles, her father saying she would be taken advantage of, her mother saying she would be broke in a month. Neither of them was completely right. True, she had gone to a number of "private casting sessions" in order to get some part, but in Karen's opinion, she was the one taking advantage of those producers, not the other way around. She had always wanted and needed people to like her. Didn't most actresses? Here at Lance's home, surrounded by his family, Karen felt a similar want and need except for something else, for the bond that seemed to exist among all the Forsters. What that bond was she could not quite say because it had been so scarce among her own family.

Decades later, in a short obituary for his grandfather, Robert Vaughn would expound on the bond Karen was trying to identify when he wrote, "One emotion twined his family members together, the same one that led to the creation of a product that made them famous, and that emotion wasn't hatred."

. . .

Near ten o'clock, after all the guests had gone back to their rooms at the hotel, Lance sat on the edge of his bed, waiting for the house to go to sleep. He was prepared this time. At half past, he crept to his bedroom door, turned the knob, and carefully began to open it.

Cotton growled.

"Who's a good boy? Cotton. That's who's a good boy. Aren't you, you little shit?" Lance whispered as he reached into his pocket, where he had placed a hunk of pork wrapped in a napkin. He tossed the pork a short ways down the hall. The dog glanced at it but then turned back to Lance, lips curling up, ears going stiff on top of its head. "I take back what I said. You are the worst boy."

. . .

Across the hall, Ramsey tiptoed out of her daughter's bedroom, thinking what a good girl she'd been this entire trip. It was the oddest thing. Back in California, Susannah took forever to fall asleep, asking for a glass of water, her night-light to be turned on, or one last bedtime story, which, in Susannah's case, meant a chapter of Austen. Tonight, though, she had drifted off almost immediately, the scent of bougainvillea and hum of crickets drifting in from the window and filling her room, a swath of moonlight touching her pillow. Ramsey, as she closed the door behind her, thought this wouldn't be such a bad place for a girl to grow up.

. . .

Houghton, whose death a year from that night would prompt his daughter to bring her daughter to live for a summer at the house, sat on the edge of his bed, horny as all hell. It didn't seem particularly natural for a man who was almost eighty to want to have sex this bad. He was alone in the master bedroom. Fifteen years ago, despite his objections, Annabelle had insisted he keep their room, and she would take a smaller one across the hall. They had not had sex since then. Houghton had not had sex at all, with anyone, since that day.

Even though the open marriage had been his idea, he would hold up his hand there, not a day passed that he didn't consider it a terrible one. He had thought it was the only thing that would save their marriage after he found out she was cheating on him.

The only actual proof of Annabelle's infidelity came about a month before Houghton asked for an open marriage. Around that time, he had been traveling more than usual for work, stopping unionization among his bottlers, creating low-interest loan plans for vending-machine owners, signing contracts with airlines, learning how to enter the age of the refrigerator. While he was away Annabelle started making frequent trips to New Orleans for no apparent reason. Her father had died five years earlier. She had not stayed close with her childhood friends. Houghton could not think of any reason his wife would have for going to Louisiana. On a day when he was back home, he discovered one when, by accident, he overheard her talking on the phone.

"I told you not to call me here. I told you not to call me at all," Annabelle was saying into the receiver when Houghton happened to walk past the study of The Sweetest Thing. "Yes, yes. I know. I'll come down next week. Okay. I love you, too."

Near the bottom of the stairs, Houghton Forster, CEO of one of the most successful companies in the United States, had to sit down because the universe had just cracked apart. His wife was cheating on him. Not only the love of whatever accounted for his life, nor simply the mother of his children, she was the woman whose approval he always sought, whose touch sent a ripple through his entire body, the one person in the world who could make him think, *All you have to do is ask*. Without her Houghton never would have even discovered PanCola's secret ingredient.

Was it possible to let her go? The concept of a divorce felt as foreign to him as a trip to the moon. He could not imagine being without the love he had leaned on all these years. She was his Annabelle constellation. He'd be lost if she weren't there to show him the way home. For those reasons, Houghton decided to let his wife be with whomever she wanted, to be happy without guilt, in the hope, desperate and unspoken, that an open marriage would keep her from leaving him.

Fifteen years after that decision and two nights before the wedding, Houghton sat alone in his room, wondering if Annabelle was still awake over there in her own. Probably not. He told himself to get some sleep. Tomorrow was going to be a madhouse.

. . .

In her bedroom Ramsey was helping Karen try on her dress, downstairs Annabelle was asking Miss Urquhart for coffee, behind the stables Susannah was giving Nicholas unwanted dance lessons, on the porch Imogene was telling Branchwater about college, scattered throughout the front lawn florists were decorating chairs with smilax and a carpenter was erecting a small altar and waiters in plainclothes were situating epergnes on tables beneath a party tent, and back inside, sitting at the top of the staircase, Harold was in a state. His hand latched onto his ear. He rocked back and forth on his heels. All the commotion recently was just too much for him. Over the past few decades, as his brothers and sister left, Harold had been the only one to stay behind at The Sweetest Thing, and during that time, he'd come to think of himself as its caretaker. The quiet suited him. With the approach of the wedding, though, his world had been flipped topsy-turvy, the house overrun with relatives, strangers actually, people asking him what he did for a living, whether he was married, how many children did he have. The kitchen staff was too busy to fix him his usual clabber with nutmeg for breakfast. Branchwater kept saying he didn't have time to play a game of "Running Water, Still Pond." Even his own father forgot to give him his tobacco tags for his collection. Haddy had to find them in the trash among all the half-eaten hors d'oeuvres and lipstick-stained napkins thrown away by the wedding guests who had invaded his home.

"Calm down, buddy row," said a muffled voice by his side. A big hand gently pulled Haddy's own away from his ear. "Sssh. You're all right."

Haddy was shocked to see the hand didn't belong to Branchwater. "What do you want?" Tears trembled in his eyes, as though he were underwater and his brother Lance stood looking at him from above the surface.

"Just checking on you."

"I'm okay."

"I know you are," Lance said. "I know you're okay." He sat down on the stairs next to Haddy. Making amends. Was that not how people foolishly put it? Lance wanted to make amends with his brother. *Build* seemed a more apt word: nail by nail, board by board.

"Has Mother told you about how the wedding's going to work yet?"

"Nuh-uh."

"Remember when Monty got married? How the groom had groomsmen and the bride had bridesmaids? Instead of doing it that way Karen and I are going to have one special person up there with each of us. Ramsey's going to be Karen's maid of honor, and I want you to be my best man. Think you can do that? Be my one special person up there?"

The knots in his back loosening, Harold said that yes, he thought he could.

"Thank you." Lance checked his wrist for the time, but he must have forgotten to put on his watch. "You don't really have much reason to ever want to do me any favors. I know that. It's just, well, people change, you know? Like butterflies. Or moths, in my case. I'm not the same as I used to be. I'm not angry like back then. I don't let anger or spite or whatever control me."

Lance, unable to look at his brother, stared at his shoes. A pair of white bucks with red rubber soles, a style he'd worried he was too old for when he'd bought them, they seemed even more garish here in the South than they had in L.A. To make matters worse, the left one had a long, black scuff mark on the inside of the heel. Lance resisted the urge to lick his thumb and scrub and scratch and scour the goddamn thing.

"It's eleven," said Harold.

"What?"

"You were looking for your watch. It's eleven o'clock." Harold held up his wrist, on which, one link too tight, hung Lance's sixteen-year-old Rolex.

"Where'd you get that?" Lance said.

"You left it on the mantel downstairs last night."

On her way up the stairs, Miss Urquhart, with a drink tray in her arms, asked, "What's so funny?" as she approached the two chuckling brothers.

"Oh, Haddy's just giving me the time of day," Lance said, his laughter winding down. He squeezed his brother's shoulder for emphasis.

"That's nice," Miss Urquhart said. "Excuse me, gentlemen." She wove her way between the two of them, walked down the hall, and, announcing herself at the door to prove she was not the groom and therefore stood no risk of breaking an old wedding superstition, entered the room where the dress was being tried on. Karen stood before a long mirror, and Ramsey sat in a chair behind her. In Miss Urquhart's opinion, which she formulated while setting the tray on an end table, the bride looked magnificent—standing there in her A-line dress of ivory tulle, with its natural waist, court train length, delicate beading, floral embroidery, and illusion lace sleeves. The maid of honor, on the other hand, looked annoyed.

"The waist is *perfect* like it is," Ramsey said. "It does *not* need to be taken in."

Seasoned bartender and amateur therapist, the latter an indirect result of the former, Miss Urquhart announced, "I've brought the makings for juleps. Thought you two could use one."

Karen turned around. "But it's not even noon."

"It's the eve of your wedding day, my dear." Into silver beakers Miss Urquhart dropped mint leaves. She spooned in two teaspoons of sugar from a Weck jar, crushed the contents with a muddler, packed each beaker with cracked ice, filled them with Kentucky bourbon, and added a mint sprig for garnish. "There now," she said, handing the drinks to Ramsey and Karen.

"Thank you." Karen sipped. "Think everyone will like my dress, Miss Urquhart?"

"Of course."

"Think they'll like me?"

"Beg pardon?"

"I want everyone to like me. Houghton and Annabelle and Fiona and Harold and Branchwater and Sarah and Imogene and Susannah and Nicholas. And you, Ramsey. And you, Miss Urquhart. Do you like me?"

"Well, I—"

"Of course she does," Ramsey interrupted, trying to save poor Miss Urquhart. Over the entire morning, Karen had been teetering on the border between unhinged and awkward, continually asking Ramsey if she really did like her. It was weird if nothing else. Apparently, from what Karen rambled on to Ramsey about, her family in Canada had been extremely religious, the kind to pound the Bible instead of thumping it, and after she moved to what they called Hollow Wood, they refused to take her calls, telling the operator, "We don't know anyone named Karen DeWitt." That last bit was true. She had changed her name from Clop to DeWitt in the hope it would help her career. Karen's family told the operator they didn't know her even when she used her old name.

Ramsey wasn't sure which part made her feel worse for the girl: that she had come from such a horrible family or that she had spent her entire childhood named *Karen Clop*.

After reordering her mixology tools on the tray, Miss Urquhart told the two women to send for her if they needed anything and then, satisfied that they appeared to be enjoying their cocktails, left the room. Downstairs she set the tray on the bar counter. While emptying the ice bucket, she glanced out the window and noticed Mrs. Forster in the side garden, tangled up in crepe myrtles, passionflowers, and trumpet vines the colors of rainbow sherbet. *That woman and her gardening*, thought Miss Urquhart, sneaking a quick nip of bourbon.

Annabelle took enormous pride in her garden. It soothed her. Not once since moving in to this house so many years ago had she allowed a gardener to tend it without her presence. Mulch season? She was there. Time to weed? She was there. Rarely did her plants even get watered without her supervision from a house window. Today, hoping to distract herself from the impending nuptials, Annabelle was pinching back her roses, deadheading her petunias, and gathering a few bouquets' worth of the season's best to use as centerpieces.

"Tend your own garden," her father had always told her, a saying he meant figuratively but one she took the other way as well. She'd had that saying in mind when she planned out the lie about his death. Twenty years ago, her father's drinking reached the point where he could no longer even feed himself, so she had to put him in a rest home, one she paid for with a private bank account. Rather than let her family name get besmirched, she told everyone, including her husband, that her father had died. She insisted on overseeing the burial alone, telling people he had not wanted a funeral. That her father had by then alienated every one of his friends and his only family left were distant relations helped her subterfuge. Until his actual death ten years ago, Annabelle often came close to getting caught in her lie about Royal, who would somehow gain access to a phone, call the house, and plead with her to let him see his grandchildren. He always ended the phone calls by saying how much he loved her.

Along her neck sweat trickled in the blazing sun, just as it had the first time she kissed Houghton. She could use something cool to drink. On deciding that was enough work for today, Annabelle picked up her flower basket and, trying to ignore her throbbing joints, went back inside to get ready for the rehearsal dinner that evening at the country club.

. . .

"Every small town in America has a Country Club Road," writes Theodor von Hedt in his classic book *Die Freizeit-Klasse in Amerika,* part travelogue, part social history, part manifesto. Although its name would change to "Old Country Club" when Pine Grove's new facilities opened a decade later, the road where the club was located on May 20, 1955, still proved the German philosopher's comment regarding the American leisure class.

Not since the Moonglade Serenade her junior year of high school had Imogene been to Pine Grove. In the ballroom, a large octagon with limestone pillars at each corner, spoked beams overhead like the stripes of a circus top, and floor-to-ceiling glass for every other of the eight walls, she sat at one of the nearly two dozen dining tables, trying not to seem bored while listening to some third cousin once-removed talk about how "for toy shops, it's Christmas, but for us, it's Easter through and through." Over the chattering crowd in the room the band began to play.

"Mind if I distract Imogene from you?" her grandfather, taking a seat at the table, said to the third cousin once-removed, who answered, "Not at all. I've love to chat with you later about—"

"Sure. We'll figure out a time."

Once they were alone, Houghton said to Imogene, "Why did the chicken cross the road?"

"Why?"

"Because this party was boring him half to death."

"Think about going professional," said Imogene. "You're a really funny guy."

Houghton smiled rather than laughed aloud. His granddaughter had always reminded him of both Annabelle and his mother, incapable of settling for anything, saucy when needed, sympathetic when necessary, the type of person who could become someone great with the tiniest, tiniest push. Wasn't competition the basis of capitalism?

"I need to have a serious talk with you, Imo."

"Okay?"

"It's about the company. One day it will be yours. Yours and yours alone." Houghton leaned forward, tilting his head at Imogene. "I want to be sure you deserve it. Understand. It's a lot of responsibility. Think you can live up to that kind of standard?"

Ding! Ding! rapped a piece of silverware against a glass. Ding! Ding!

Across the ballroom, as the band came to a halt, Ramsey stood at a table next to Harold, setting down the fork she had just used to strike her champagne flute. "Ladies and gentlemen!" she yelled. "My brother and I would like to make a toast!" On the other side of her at the table sat Susannah, who wasn't listening to a word her mother said. Susannah was busy planning how to make her Big Escape.

Earlier that evening, she and Nicholas had promised that, if the party wasn't fun, they would sneak away to the golf course, and Susannah had now decided this party was not the kind of fun she had been expecting. She'd wanted to see women in lilac evening gowns of ribbons and netting and accented by long white gloves, men with fluffy cravats at their necks and pleated frills poking from their cuffs, all of them dancing an ever-so-splendid Scottish reel around the ballroom. Instead, the men wore baggy slacks and sports coats with fat ties, the women, though gloved, wore dresses of only one fabric, and none of them were so much as tapping their feet. Someone could have at least sat in the corner playing a pianoforte.

Susannah's mother was still making a speech about her uncle Lance. Trying to make it appear an accident, Susannah knocked her napkin, balled next to her dinner plate, off the table and onto the floor. She feigned a look of concern. In order to pick it up, she slid from her chair, knelt to the floor, and, leaving the napkin behind, started to crawl away.

Banquet tables along the walls of the ballroom kept her hidden from sight as she worked her way toward the exit. The knees of her white stockings looked bruised from all the dirt on them by the time she ran into Nicholas. "Did anyone see you?" she asked.

"No. You?"

"Uh-uh."

"The doors are right there. We could make a run for it, but I think it'd be better if we just walk right to them, act natural."

Acting natural, Nicholas and Susannah rose from their hiding spot at the same time, their reappearance camouflaged by the sudden bout of applause from the crowd as Susannah's mother finished her speech. Waiters bobbed around the tables, refilling water glasses, carrying away empty plates. A few guests stood and headed for the bathroom.

The two fugitives reached the doors, on the other side of which, viewable through glass panels, lay acres on acres of green-grassed, rolling-hilled freedom. Unfortunately the doors were locked for the evening. Nicholas twisted them hard, but the knobs would not budge.

"What are you two criminals doing?"

Drink in hand, Houghton stood smiling at his two grandchildren, wondering why they were so comically wide-eyed, their mouths shaped into perfect Os.

"Nothing," they said in unison.

"That's for sure." He sipped his cocktail without taking his gaze off them. "Nicholas, I think your mother's looking for you. Susannah, maybe go tell yours you enjoyed her lovely toast. 'I enjoyed your lovely toast, Momma!' Practice it on your way over."

What cookie jar had they been trying to stick their hands in? Houghton was thinking as he watched Susannah and Nicholas weave a set of paths to their respective mothers. He edited the turn of phrase: "respective *single* mothers." Years ago, nobody would have imagined a child could be raised properly without two parents, but now, here were two children who had been raised exceptionally well in just that scenario. Houghton had to hand it to Ramsey, and he especially had to hand it to Sarah. After Monty's accident, Houghton had worried that Sarah, a dry wit without the wit, more pageant queen than world-beater, would have problems raising Nicholas on her own. But she had done it. He supposed it shouldn't have surprised him all that much. The two strongest people he knew were women; one had given birth to him and the other had said, "Obviously," when he proposed.

Into Houghton's view of his grandchildren appeared Truitt the pastor. Resident of Belzoni, Mississippi, where he presided over a Black Jack church, Truitt Baumgartner had been brought in to officiate tomorrow's ceremony because of his expertise in the traditions and customs of a "genuine southern wedding." For his son's big day Houghton wanted the circumstantial pomp by which the Delta had come to be known. Not having met the pastor till now, he was surprised at the man's age. He doubted if Truitt was even thirty.

"Mr. Forster, I presume," said the pastor, taking Houghton's hand.

Houghton said it was a pleasure to meet him and asked if he had settled into his room all right. "Thank you again for agreeing to officiate. I realize it was short notice."

"My pleasure." The fair-complexioned Truitt nodded mechanically. His hair, the mottled color of a fox squirrel's tail, fluttered. "It's the least I could do, given my history with your family."

"History?" asked Houghton.

"Did Mrs. Forster not mention it? I gave the service for her father's burial. Of course, she was the only one in attendance, but she still felt someone from the church should be there."

Houghton laughed. "Think you've got the wrong Teague. If you gave the service, you'd have been—how old are you?"

"Thirty-one."

"You'd have been eleven years old."

With a tilt of his head, Truitt said, "I was twenty-one at the time. I remember because it was my very first burial. Yes, though, I can see your point. I was indeed young. Felt the calling at an early age, Mr. Forster. My father had a saying about that, in fact."

For the next few minutes Truitt continued, but Houghton could no longer hear him. He was looking through the crowd that filled the ballroom at Pine Grove, past the waiters bringing out dishes of syllabub for dessert, on a few occasions and by request leaving and returning with banana ice cream; past the club manager standing like a drugstore loafer in the back; past bowls of pickled peaches congealing in syrup and plates smeared with watermelon-rind preserve; past the local guests who were attired on the cocktail-hour side of formal, voile dresses on the women, planter's boots on the men, and middy blouses on the children; past the bride; past the groom; until he spotted Annabelle sitting by herself at their table.

...

That night, Ramsey went quietly to her room after putting Susannah to bed. She closed the door behind her. In front of the mirror, she was about to undress, taking down her hair, sliding off her rings, when in a corner on the opposite side of the room a shadow moved.

"Jesus Christ!" Ramsey said, half scream and half whisper, on noticing Karen. She turned around to face her. "What are you doing in here? You scared me about half to death!"

Karen, sitting in a chair, shrank into herself. Her only verbal response was a distinct rhythm, low sobbing as the flat notes, infrequent sniffles as the sharp. She was dressed in a nightgown. Her hands cradled her face.

"Hey. Hey there." Ramsey knelt in front of Karen. "What's wrong?"

"They're not coming."

"What? Who? What?"

"Never mind," said Karen, standing up. "I shouldn't be in here." With hesitant determination she marched toward the door, not making any noise because she had taken off her shoes. Ramsey, still on her knees, didn't have time to grab her before she reached the door, so she gave her a command, accidentally putting more force into it than she had intended.

"STOP RIGHT THERE."

Like a reprimanded child Karen did as she'd been ordered. Her fingers hung frozen midair, reaching for the doorknob. After getting on her feet, Ramsey guided the stunned girl to a seat on the edge of the bed, squeezing her hand to get it to relax. Next, on the second floor of a house quiet as a bookstore, in a bedroom colored by the noncolor of moonlight, blue but not blue, white but not white, Ramsey sat beside Karen, looked directly into her eyes, and, trying for the gentlest tone she could muster, asked, "Who's not coming?"

"My family."

"Aw, honey, I'm so sorry. Were they supposed to? Didn't Lance say—"

"They told me they weren't coming. But I thought." Karen's voice crumpled in on itself. "I was hoping they might try and surprise me."

"Ssssh, ssssh," Ramsey said when the sobbing started up again. She put her arm around Karen's shoulder and pressed her face against her chest, letting her make a damp outline of her eyes, nose, and mouth on the front of her dress. "They could always show up tomorrow, a last-minute surprise."

"No."

"How do you know?"

"Because their wedding present came today." From a pocket of her nightgown, Karen removed an envelope, The Sweetest Thing's address written on its front, below the name "Karen Clop." She handed it to Ramsey. Inside the envelope was a single, one-way train ticket to Toronto, nontransferable, third class, "Fair Weather Route."

For years after that night, anytime Ramsey and Karen saw each other, they'd exchange a look, the flattened expression of trying to suppress a smile, in remembrance of the moment Ramsey considered the entire situation, how it explained why she had been so anxious that day for everyone to like her, and, while ripping the ticket to pieces, said, "Third class? You're about to be a Forster. We don't travel third class."

Karen looked almost angry for a moment, watching wide-eyed as the pieces fluttered to the floor. Then, quietly at first but gaining in volume, she began to giggle, like a spit-take in slow motion, culminating with a burst of breath exhaled through closed lips: "*Pffffffffffft!*" Ramsey joined in herself.

"I bet Lance would have done the same thing," Karen said once their laughter had quieted. Her eyes were still sodden with tears.

"See? Now your head's going in the right direction. Think of Lance."

"Yeah."

"You've got him now. Tomorrow you'll be a part of this family, and everybody will love you like one."

"I've got him now," Karen repeated flatly.

"You've got us now."

Both of them stood, and Ramsey told Karen that, if she felt like it, maybe she should check in on Lance, superstitions be damned. Karen wiped the tears away with the heel of her palm. "Ramsey?" she said on reaching the door.

Without needing to hear the request, Ramsey twisted an imaginary key into an imaginary lock on her lips and then tossed the key across the room, where, rattling for a brief moment, it would never be found.

. . .

Afterward, as they both lay naked in bed, Lance couldn't remember the surprise he had felt when Karen snuck into his room, the confusion when she began to kiss him, or even the pleasure when they made love. Instead there was simply a giant blank spot of happiness in his brain. Cotton must have fallen asleep on duty.

. . .

A feeling of weightlessness woke Annabelle as Houghton gently lifted her body from the bed. "Hush, little baby, don't say a word," he sang while carrying her across the hall to their old bedroom. "Daddy's going to buy you a mockingbird."

"Oh, you," she said.

. . .

The day of the wedding! The day of the wedding! The day of the wedding!

Although Harold hadn't actually heard anybody use those exact words, they seemed to be on everyone's mind, taking physical form in the baby Louis heels and piled hair on so many women around the house, the tuxedos worn by so many men, the butts of Fatima cigarettes scrunched into ashtrays, the handkerchiefs being wiped across sweaty brows, and the polished wing tips beating a tattoo against the polished floorboards.

Everyone looked excited. In the back garden, Harold's mother watered a flower bed she had recently planted in an old Louisiana sugar kettle, an activity Harold knew she used as an easement of nerves. On the front porch, Harold's father, who that morning had allowed himself the luxury of being shaved with a leather strop and straight razor by a barber he had paid extra to make a house call, waved hello to guests as they were seated by staff in the chairs lined up across the lawn. Lance's posture was so stiff while he stared out the living room window it appeared as if a shoe last shaped like a person had been wedged inside him. Nicholas sat at the dining room table sharing a coffee mug of tutti-frutti ice cream with Susannah. And in the kitchen, Harold's grandmother was saying to Miss Urquhart, "Taste this. Is that Gibson's? God help the bartender if he gave me *Gibson's*."

"Here, Haddy," said Ramsey, her arms raised to adjust her brother's bow tie. "You've got a talent for getting these things skewed. Though you are getting better at it, have to say."

"How is it outside? There a big crowd?"

Satisfied with the tie, Ramsey took a step back. "It's Pandemonium out there. Get it? *Pan*demonium. Oh, Lord. I just kill me."

"What's Pande . . . that word mean?"

Before Ramsey could respond to Haddy's question, an illustration of its answer materialized when two staff members, carrying a five-tiered wedding cake, said, "Excuse us, folks!" before walking the cake between Haddy and Ramsey and then careening out the front door.

They almost tripped four times while carrying the cake to the reception tent. Branchwater counted. For the past hour, while chewing a piece of orris root, he'd been overseeing the final touches on the event, walking between the tents, giving orders to the staff, detaching beggar's lice from a waiter's pant cuff, all despite his boss's insistence that today he was a guest only. Branchwater couldn't help himself. "Careful, fellas, easy now," he said to the two men as they slid the cake onto its table, distracting himself from the potential disaster by wondering whether wedding cakes evolved to look like wedding dresses or wedding dresses evolved to look like wedding cakes.

"Thank you for your help, Mr. Branchwater, but I can handle it from here," said the person actually in charge, Philomena Kirkland, local wedding coordinator, baker, florist, and seamstress. "If you'll please take your seat. Ceremony's about to begin."

"But I—"

"If you'll please."

Aware he could not win an argument with a woman known for being a cottage industry of matrimony unto herself—not to mention her obviously being a complete bitch—Branchwater, who would start dating Miss Kirkland less than a week later, exited the reception tent and took a seat on the groom's side.

The fluttering of hand fans throughout the crowd gave everything the blurry, jittery look of television programs when reception is not particularly good. Sweat began to make world atlases of suit backs. On a platform to one side of the altar, a pianist warmed up, his fingers wobbling, tinkling, stretching through notes, as though scoring a child's first time on a bicycle. Overhead the bright sunshine could not be contained by one sense and seemed to drum against the tom-tom clouds floating within its reach. The occasional fascinator listed woozily in the breeze.

Once Wagner's "Bridal Chorus" began, the members of the wedding Branchwater had been waiting for arrived, the groom standing near the altar by himself, the best man escorting the maid of honor down the aisle, until the front area was a Forster chess set ready for play, Lance at the center and to either side of him Ramsey and Harold. They were so beautiful all dressed up. Throughout years past, whenever he regarded that generation of the family, Branchwater would have three thoughts in a specific, unvarying order—"Look at those children" followed by "only thing I ever did right in my life" followed by "and they aren't even mine"—but now, watching one of them about to get married, only the middle thought occurred to him, the first negated by their age, the last by his lack of regret.

To end the procession Houghton escorted Karen to her place at the altar. He took a seat beside his wife. "Dearly beloved," Pastor Baumgartner said, "today we gather for a joyous celebration."

4.7

The Malediction Returns—"See Rock City"—
An Unexpected Package

The last few of the Forsters were felled by the Malediction in quick succession. On June 22, 1966, ten years after the death of her husband, Annabelle Forster stood in her garden and wondered why the flowers had no smell. She died of a stroke that night. On March 10, 1972, after extensive questioning by the FBI regarding his recent business ventures, Lance Forster was found hanging by his belt in a suite at the Jacobs-Allen. The Wayne County coroner declared it a suicide in spite of the cigarette burns that were known to be a trademark of a certain South American group. Nicholas Forster lived six years past the death of his mother in a house fire. Susannah Forster lived eight weeks past the death of her mother in a car accident. On January 25, 1958, Fiona Forster was running a seed-pearl comb through her hair when she asked her live-in nursemaid to fetch her husband's old medical bag because "It seems I'm having a heart attack." On November 14, 1963, neither Karen Forster nor her child survived the birth. On March 5, 1977, little over a year after her unceremonious return to the company from which she had been ousted, Imogene Forster passed away of an illness few people knew she had. "Cancer may have killed her," Barry Rojas wrote in the *Wall Street Journal*, "but she died of a broken will."

Decades before those tragedies, Montgomery Forster set the

precedent for them with his own death, an event put irrevocably in motion on December 24, 1943.

He arrived home late that night. In the kitchen, he flipped through the mail, not noticing a package next to the bread box. He poured himself a full glass of whiskey and carried it through the first floor of the house. The family had been living there since they moved to the state capital following the election three years earlier. On his walk through the house—passing tinseled holly draped along the cabinetry, a wooden swan placed at the center of the dining table, wreaths, garlands, a tree heavy with homemade ornaments and from beneath which presents spilled out, tiny wise men kneeling before a tiny manger, and a single patchwork stocking hung from the mantel—Monty took long gulps of his drink. The glass was empty by the time he reached the second floor.

"How's Paul?" asked his wife from where she lay in bed, a magazine facedown on the comforter.

Monty stood by the dresser, wrenching loose his necktie. "Not good."

That evening he had visited the home of his boss, Governor Paul B. Johnson Sr., who'd been in poor health for a while and who, a few weeks ago, had taken a hard turn. His face the color and texture of paper, eyes sunken, cheeks deflated, and arms barely strong enough to lift a spoon, Paul had lain in bed, lecturing Monty on what, despite a recent, hopeful prognosis, he insisted would soon be his lieutenant's job. "Don't worry about me. I've had a big life," he said, smiling through obvious pain. "Let's put it this way. I've seen Rock City." Monty would become acting governor two days later.

In their bedroom, Monty told Sarah, "I just hope he makes it through Christmas. Be a shame for his family to always have that memory." He placed his watch, keys, and wallet on the dresser.

"I'll telephone Corrine tomorrow."

"That'd be kind of you." Monty sat on the edge of the bed. He asked, "How's Imogene? She upset the presents have to wait?" referring to their family tradition of opening gifts on Christmas Eve.

"She'll survive."

"I'll make it up to her."

He stood from the bed. Near the closet door, Monty was unbuttoning his cuffs when Sarah, having returned to reading her magazine, asked, "Did you see the package in the kitchen? Came for you this afternoon."

"Who's it from?"

"Somebody Harrington, I think," she said, turning a page. "Hey, where are you going?"

Back in the kitchen, standing by the bread box with one cuff of his shirt still buttoned, Monty stared at the package's address label, the sender portion of which read, "Sophie Harrington."

Monty held the package like a rare artifact. Wrapped in brown paper, it was roughly the size of a shoe box, weighing a couple of pounds. Methodically he began to remove the paper, starting with each corner and working toward the middle. Did Sophie send him a Christmas gift? Monty had not spoken with her since the one time he'd visited her family home in England. He lifted the cardboard lid.

The package contained three items: a sealed envelope, a bundle of folded paper wrapped in twine, and a bottle of Scotch. After setting aside the Scotch, which he recognized as being from the distillery owned by William Harrington, Monty took out the envelope. He read the letter it contained with the deliberation of someone learning a new language.

Dear Mr. Forster,

Nicholas often referred to you as his little Oliver Twist. That he did so worried me, as my brother had a poor tendency to romanticize the world, not merely its people but also their intentions. I always considered it my duty to protect him from that habit.

Did he tell you what happened to him near the end of fifth form? My brother was caught with another boy. Although such an occurrence is not uncommon in public schools—hormones, et cetera—this particular one turned pernicious, due in whole part to the other boy, he of Norman blood, whose family filled a sizable number of pages in Debrett's. The boy accused Nicholas of molestation. With great effort, Father succeeded in resolving the matter, but my brother's reputation was tarnished.

Yet worse still, throughout the horrid affair, he continually professed to love the boy. For that reason, I was leery when, in his letters to me during the war, he professed to love you.

Only halfway through the letter, Monty stopped reading in order to take a glass out of the cupboard, fill it with the Scotch from the package, and belt a third of the drink before starting again.

When we first met, I had in many ways already met you, having been told, with meticulous, excruciating detail, about your every freckle and fancy. He wrote incessantly of his new American friend. Until Nicholas's death, I did not think highly of you, I must admit, in part from concern my brother would be hurt again, in part from sheer jealousy.

You were the love of his life, which upset me, for he was the love of mine.

Please accept my apologies for my ghastly behavior during your visit to Ashbrook. I was suspicious and resentful of the man for whom my brother cared so much, and only after seeing you overcome while looking at his portrait did I understand how much you cared for him as well.

With this parcel, I've included the letters he wrote me during the war, fewer one or two in which you are not mentioned. I believe you'll appreciate them more than I ever can.

Sincerely,

Sophie Harrington

PS. The whisky is from Father.

Although he couldn't remember drinking more than a sip, Monty's glass sat empty on the tile countertop. He wiped a trembling hand across his lips. Without daring to look at the stack of letters in the box, he refilled his glass, drank it, refilled the glass again, drank it, and then, waiting for the hinges of his brain to loosen, stared out the window. Two pickets were missing from a fence across the street. Four birds were perched on a power line.

Monty picked up the letters. They felt strangely light for being the weight of the entire world. Not yet undoing the twine around them, he held the letters in one hand and with the other grabbed his glass and the bottle. The kiln created by the whisky in his stomach reached a pleasant burn as he walked up the stairs. On the second floor, Monty turned down a hallway, headed for the balcony that overlooked the front yard, but he was interrupted by two syllables, both as groggily spoken as they were impossible to ignore.

"Daddy?" said Imogene.

In the hallway, Montgomery paused for a moment, not because he was debating whether to answer his daughter, but so he could decide what to do with the bottle, glass, and letters. He placed them gently on a side table draped in damask. "You should be asleep, young lady," he said to the ten-year-old Imogene as he stepped into her room. "Santa won't stop by unless you're asleep."

"Ho-Ho no come?" she whispered.

Monty chuckled. "Ho-Ho no come."

Years ago, when she was four, Imogene had stumbled across the closet where her mother had stored the presents that would be from Santa Claus. It was early December. Sarah, arriving home after running some errands, found her daughter sitting in the closet playing with the toys, dress-up dolls and a rocking horse and jacks and a pinwheel and stuffed animals, oblivious to the fact they weren't supposed to be seen until Christmas. "What're you doing? Those presents are from Santa! What's he going to bring you now? He'll just have to skip our house this year!" she yelled at Imogene, who poked out her bottom lip and, as her eyes welled in tears, whispered, "Ho-Ho no come?"

The story as well as its punch line had since become a mainstay of family lore. Only on occasion did Monty regret that his daughter learned the truth about Santa at such an early age.

"I'm sorry about tonight." He knelt beside her bed.

"It's okay."

"Uncle Paul's very sick. I needed to be there."

Imogene rolled over to face him. "I said it's okay."

How'd you get so tough? Monty wanted to ask her. Instead, he tucked a strand of hair behind her ear and said, "We'll do presents tomorrow."

He tugged the covers up to her chin, leaned over, and placed a kiss on her forehead. They both wished each other a good night before he closed the door to her room.

From the hall side table Monty collected his three items. He tucked the letters in his armpit and resituated the glass and bottle in order to open a glass door and walk onto the front balcony. Outside, the air smelled of cedar-chip potpourri, frost flowers bloomed on car windows along the street, the sky hung dark as blackberry vinegar, and somewhere near the service station a few blocks away, two cats were rutting, their yowls like a soogan quilt keeping out the winter cold. Monty sat in a rocking chair. He choked down one more glassful of whisky to brace himself. His eyes watered and his face reddened while he coughed into his fist and breathed through his nose. In the cold nighttime air, Monty began to read the stack of letters, one after the other, which he would do every day over the next few weeks, until the moment he decided, for all and at last, never to read them again.

PART 5

PART 5

A Death in the Family—Nyva Adanvdo, Part One—The Lion, the Witch, and the Cotton Gin—Nyva Adanvdo, Part Two—Molly Carmichael's Will to Narrative

Branchwater died on a Friday. That was how Harold took the news. At the Panola Cola Historical Museum, after hanging up the phone, he tried without success to stanch his tears by thinking, *Today is Friday, today is Friday, today is Friday, today is Friday.*

Up until that day, things had been going so well, what with slowly getting to know his grandson, spending time with the young man, both of them starting to feel like family. The stories were the best part. Robert seemed to love hearing them, and Harold surely did love telling them: the one about when he saw the king of the tree bears, the one about how his mother and father met because his grandfather had the gout, that humongous party one year at the Peabody when he made friends with the ducks, how he was his brother's best man at his wedding, all those times his mother let him pretend to teach her how to play solitaire.

How did Branchwater know that a grandson, someone to listen, someone to understand, would be just what Harold needed after he, Branchwater, had passed away? Harold supposed Robert was his parting gift.

The burial service took place at a garden cemetery a dozen

miles outside of Batesville. Under the hot summer sun, a preacher so thin he appeared liable to fall out and with a face like a boiled ham read from a worn Bible, giving the verses a decent amount of flair, despite how poorly he looked to be handling the conditions. Not even Harold knew all of Branchwater's relatives. There must have been some twenty folks in attendance with the name.

Once the service was over, Harold shook hands with Branchwater's longtime girlfriend, Philomena Kirkland, followed by Jeremiah Branchwater, Alfred Branchwater, Peggy Branchwater, Alice Branchwater, and Portia Branchwater, the last three of whom were Tom's nieces, all of them now over fifty. Harold had watched them grow up, the same way their uncle had watched him. "Remember, you call me if I can help out with anything," he told Portia, who'd been the one to call him with the news. "How much do funerals cost? Daddy always said numbers weren't my strong suit."

"You be shush about that. Your father took good care of Uncle Tommy."

"I don't mind paying."

"Not another word about it." She nodded past his shoulder. "Those young folks belong to you?"

Harold turned around to see Robert. He was wearing a suit that looked good on him, one of those high-booted navy-pinstripe numbers, and by his side was some girl with an oddball haircut, as though she'd done it herself with a mirror and some house scissors. Flushed in the cheeks, either from the heat or the moment at hand—it was hard for Harold to be sure which—Robert said, "I know you said I shouldn't come, especially since I never met him, but I figured you could use some company."

"I'm happy you did."

"Hello," said the girl.

"I'm sorry. This is my friend Molly."

Portia had returned to the fold of her kinfolk, so the three of them, Harold and Molly and Robert, stood on the outskirts of the cemetery, as stoic as the Confederate generals chiseled into a number of gravestones around them. Harold asked, "A girlfriend friend?"

"Well, she, uh—"

"That's right," Molly said, smiling, her hand like a blood-pressure cuff on Robert's arm. "A girlfriend friend."

"Don't that beat all." With a smile Harold shook the one hand of the girl's that wasn't presently hooking its way through Robert's bent elbow. She certainly was a pretty one, with sorrel eyes and a mouth like a tiny bow. *I never had a girlfriend,* Harold considered saying, and then grew embarrassed at the subsequent thought, *No girl ever would have me as a boyfriend.* Passing a quick look back toward the Branchwaters, at the freshly stirred dirt of the grave, at the half dozen jars of local blooms, he asked his grandson and his grandson's girlfriend if they'd like to go for a ride. Maybe they could stop by the Jr. Food Mart for an orange push-up. "And I can tell y'all some good stories about Branchwater. Lord knows there are plenty."

. . .

Although they had not been part of a tribe for many years—whether having left for employment opportunities, to attend school, to avoid jail time, or because a white man once took a liking to their mother—the people of Branchwater's community still spoke a few words of Cherokee on occasion. Branchwater was in an awful period of what would turn out to be a very long life when they started calling him Nyva Adanvdo.

His older brother, George, had been "wrong in the head" going on ten years. George did not seem to be getting any better. The hope that he might was mitigated each time he got lost on his way home, put his trousers on inside out, held a spoon with a fist, woke with wet sheets, or forgot the word for those square panes of glass in the side of a house. Sometimes, though, a faint glimmer of the person he used to be would show, his eyes holding steady for a moment, his voice taking on the decisive tone of an adult. That version of George appeared briefly one morning when Branchwater was headed out.

"I'm late for work, buddy. Can't take you fishing right now," Branchwater said, tucking in his shirt as he walked toward the door. "Maybe when I get home."

"That's all right, Tom. I appreciate the thought. I appreciate everything you've done for me. Have a nice day at work. You've been a good brother."

In the doorway, Branchwater turned around. "How are you feeling today?" he asked, enunciating each word purposefully, trying to keep himself from looking startled.

"Fine as a fiddler. Right as raindrops."

"George?"

"Think I may take a bath. Yeah, uh-huh. I'm going to take me a bath." George lodged his thumb in his mouth, the switch having flipped back to off, and shuffled away from the door.

Branchwater had taken the role of his brother's guardian after their father had passed on, in part because he knew his mother was getting too old to take care of a child cursed with a man's body, in part because of something his father had told him years ago. At that time, everybody in town knew the truth about the two young Branchwater boys, a conclusion drawn from their relatively light skin, the fact their father had been working an oil field in another state at the time they were conceived, and the frequent occasions a circuit judge from Oxford had been seen tipping his hat toward their mother. The gossip wore at Branchwater, a pestle to his mortar, until he'd finally had enough. "How can you keep going about your life knowing what she did?" he yelled at his father. "We're not even *yours*." His cheeks grew damp. "How come you treat us like we're your children when you know we're not?!"

His father pulled Branchwater into his arms and pressed his cheek against his son's hair. "Because both of you *are* my children. You and your brother. Don't you know that?" he said. "You can't choose who you love and neither can blood." He pushed his son's head back so he could look him directly in the eyes. "Blood doesn't make a family. Love does."

Years later, as he got home from work, Branchwater could still remember the look of absolute conviction on his father's wrinkle-mapped, sun-hardened face. "George, I'm home," he called out while placing his hat on a hook by the door. "You think we got enough day left to catch a few whoppers at the pond?"

No answer came from anywhere in the house. The only sound was a horsefly repeatedly crashing into a windowpane, tap, tap, tap, tap, trying to reach the freedom of the outside world. "George?" Branchwater had checked the kitchen and the bedrooms before he noticed the bathroom door was closed. "Two baths in one day?" he asked, opening the door. Because the bathroom shutters were closed, blocking out the daylight, the water in the tub looked brown instead of red. "I guess somebody got themselves awful dirty today. Did you roll around in a bunch of mud?" In the dark, Branchwater could just barely see his brother's vacant face. His open eyes did not blink. His open mouth did not speak.

"No. No, no, no, no, no, no, no, no, no, no, no, no, no, no, no. No. No."

With the same desperation, resolve, and obstinacy he would one day have when putting a snake-bit Harold Forster on the back of his horse, Branchwater lifted George, a marionette unstrung, from the cold, pink bathwater. He knew it was too late as he carried his brother out of the house, across the patchwork lawn, and, with the help of Semper Fi, recently purchased at auction, over miles of North Mississippi hill country. His suspicion was confirmed when he reached the town doctor, Al Phelps, who smelled nauseatingly of liquor and charged double for the visit, citing what he called his "racial sufferance." He refused to assist in the burial preparations.

After the funeral, people began referring to Branchwater by a Cherokee phrase that translates loosely as "Stone Heart."

. . .

His grandfather wasn't kidding about the orange push-ups. On the threadbare bench seat of Harold's old truck, Robert sat pressed next to Molly, both of them licking at the nearly fluorescent sherbet rising from cardboard cylinders coated with frost. Two notions occurred to Robert at once: this moment was the first he had thought of Harold as his "grandfather" without putting quotes around it in his mind, and today was the first time either he or Molly had referred to their "relationship" in terms of it being an actual thing.

Even though they'd been dating for three months and rarely spent more than a single night apart—he would sleep at her place in Rooney Heights, a condo complex near campus, or she would make the drive to his place, claiming it was to see Hellion rather than him—neither of them had spoken of the other as a boyfriend or girlfriend until earlier that afternoon in the cemetery. Molly seemed to enjoy how much it had surprised Robert.

"Ever seen a real live cotton gin?" Robert asked her as they passed one. The building consisted mainly of steel beams and cor-

rugated metal siding, unremarkable as sheet cake from a grocery store, except, through an open hanging door, a different world could be glimpsed. Cotton lint, wispy and fine, seemed to grow from every surface like barnacles. It clung to the roof beams, the sturdy columns holding them up, the floor, the walls, even the giant machinery modules, with their fan belts and ginning ribs.

Molly said, "Feels like I'm catching a glimpse of Narnia."

After considering it, Robert decided the comparison was more apt than Molly realized, because he, too, felt as if he were giving her a tour of some mystical storybook world. The South had just the right blend of strangeness and darkness to fascinate and frighten children, didn't it? It was similar enough to the real world to make a child think, *I know this place,* yet also different enough for them to go to sleep at night knowing it was only make-believe. Over the next few miles of the ride, as they passed a juke joint named C. Barrett's Snack Shack, a fried-peanut stand, tin one-sheets for Red Coon and Wild Goose chewing tobacco, a former plantation commissary, a deer-processing center, a hot-tamale stand, and two "undercover" revenue agents staking out a moonshine operation, Robert felt that he was showing Molly not only a world from a children's book but also the world of his own childhood, the strangeness, darkness, and altogether fucked-up-ness that made him the incredibly well-adjusted person he was today.

"Look it!" said Harold.

He pointed up ahead. On a billboard next to the highway, a silhouette of the classic "southern belle" bottle, so named because of its bonnet-like cap, its slim neck, its corseted midsection, and its lower half shaped similar to a hoop skirt, appeared against a simple white backdrop. REMEMBER THE ORIGINAL? was printed to one side of it, and to the other, WE'VE BOTTLED NOSTALGIA. Near the bottom corner of the billboard could be seen the logo for Panola Cola.

"I thought you said they weren't going to roll it out till they knew the secret ingredient?" Robert asked his grandfather.

"Guess they got antsy."

Molly said, "There was a secret ingredient?"

As Robert told her about the H.F. issue, how those initials had been a placeholder in the formula, how the engineers at CarolCorp were convinced Harold must know its identity, how the corporate lawyers had even threatened litigation, he struck at a thought, one so simple it seemed crazy he was only putting it together now.

"Harold, have you ever noticed that H.F. aren't just your father's initials? They're yours, too."

"And?"

"And, well, I don't know. Just feels like something. Like maybe you know what the ingredient is without knowing you know what the ingredient is. You know?"

"Not really."

Harold was exhausted from thinking about the ingredient. What did it matter? PanCola was just a memory, something he used to cherish, true, but now he had his grandson, a part of himself that extended into the future rather than the past. Robert wasn't a memory. He was sitting right there, holding his pretty girlfriend's pretty little hand.

"Are you in college, too?" Harold asked Molly.

"Yes, sir."

"Parents must be proud."

"Uh-huh."

Robert said, "Both her parents passed away."

Before Harold could tell her he was sorry, the girl said, "Did you grow up around here?" then licked the last of her push-up. Harold said he sure did. He added that they could stop by the house he'd grown up in, if only it hadn't burned down back when she was just a baby.

. . .

"Nyva Adanvdo," whispered Mother Shumate in the dream. "Let it burn."

Even though Branchwater didn't believe in premonitions, he still felt, on waking, a sense of the uncanny at what the hoodoo woman had told him in his dream, perhaps because in real life she'd been the last person ever to address him as Nyva Adanvdo. He despised the name. Coined because of his refusal to cry for his brother—Branchwater wouldn't give a damn thing, especially not tears, to the world that had taken George—the name had faded away around the time he'd become part of a surrogate family, one that helped replace what he had lost. Life always keeps the balance in check: he believed something could only be gained by the loss of something else. And vice versa.

It was for this reason Branchwater worried, on the morning of November 12, 1969, as he got out of bed, that his dream had something to do with the Forsters.

The family had been falling apart for a while. Branchwater had stood by helpless as Houghton and Annabelle took up acreage beside each other at Batesville Cemetery. He had stood by helpless as Nicholas steered PanCola toward complete financial ruin. He had stood by helpless as Ramsey, divorced from her husband, was derided for her "bedmate druthers" by the media, and briefly lost her daughter, Susannah, to a radical branch of the New Left. He had stood by helpless as Monty left his little girl without a father. He had stood by helpless as Lance sank steadily deeper into the bottle.

What else might befall the family? How else might it burn down? Branchwater realized he had been thinking too metaphorically when he heard sirens in the distance.

He ran outside and climbed into his pickup, but the worthless thing refused to start. Down the road, a pair of headlights approached—two circles of yellow that, inch by inch, materialized into a long, black hearse. The sight of it caused Branchwater to wonder, in all seriousness, if he was still asleep, trapped inside his dream. His father used to tease him as a boy by speaking of such maladies.

"Know where the Forster place is?" he asked the driver after flagging him down and getting inside the hearse.

"Bet your fern."

The driver was a teenage boy with a lopsided flattop. Half a dozen empty beer bottles clattered on the floorboard. A small calendar with tear-away months, roughly the size and shape of a cigarette pack, was stuck to the center of the dashboard, a promotional product, Branchwater judged by the name printed along the bottom, for BENTONIA FARM SUPPLY. Each month on the calendar featured a Bible verse. Branchwater was reading the one for October, thinking about how "fishers of men" was such an odd phrase, when the driver, noticing the calendar was a month out of date, tore off the top sheet to reveal November's verse: Ecclesiastes 1:4.

Wake up right now if this is a dream. Wake up right now if this is a dream.

If this had begun as a dream, Branchwater thought as they pulled up to The Sweetest Thing, roiling in flames and erupting smoke, it had now become a nightmare. A small crowd had gathered on the front lawn. Firemen aimed hoses at the house, their cheeks coppered by the glare, their suits shimmering from the water misted back on them by the morning breeze.

"I figure you don't know my daddy," the boy with a haircut like a tilted mortarboard said to Branchwater, who was stepping out of the hearse, "but if you do, please don't tell him I borrowed the company car last night."

Branchwater was in too much of a hurry to answer. He scrambled through the crowd of gawking neighbors, searching for the face of Sarah, Montgomery's widow and the only person still living in The Sweetest Thing. He screamed her name, but everyone shook their heads. Branchwater turned toward the house, the heat so palpable it was like being swallowed by a huge, invisible creature. There was still time. Plenty of time. He began to run toward the front door, plotting the quickest way through the house to the master bedroom, ignoring the screams from the firemen to stop.

The first fireman to tackle him registered as only a mild pressure on his lower back. Gradually, the pressure spread to his thighs, his knees, and his calves. Five firemen were dragging behind him by the time he fell to the ground.

From where he lay pinned to the wet grass, Branchwater watched in disbelief as flames ate away the house. It was impossible for him to have dreamed this would happen. He must have heard the sirens in his sleep. Despite the roar of the fire as it took down the shiplap siding on which Houghton had marked Monty's height while he was growing up, then the roof constructed of cedar shingles Annabelle had spent weeks selecting from two dozen available options, then the porch where Branchwater and Imogene used to sit and talk about her day, he could hear in his mind those five words from Mother Shumate. "Nyva Adanvdo, let it burn." He could also hear the last thing she had said to him before he woke up.

"Ain't no way to rebuild a house unless it's ash on the ground."

...

In the kitchen of her condo, Molly, while she chopped a bell pepper, asked Robert, who was adding rice to a pot on the stove, "What's an Estate Heatrola anyway?"

"It's a kind of heater they had back then. Ran on coal."

She was referring to what his grandfather had told them caused the fire that burned down The Sweetest Thing. Her question was the first thing Molly had said about the ride they'd taken with Harold since they got back an hour ago. She seemed to have liked him. Robert looked at her as she stirred the red beans. Although it hadn't occurred to him until this moment, he'd never in his life cooked food with another person, not a single pancake breakfast with his dad, no licking the cake batter off a spoon handed to him by his mom. Now here he was playing house with his girlfriend, and the strangest thing was how comfortable it all felt.

Was he in love? Robert had no idea. The way he saw it, being in love was like walking in a fog bank: you only knew you were in it before and after you were in it; the middle part was an indeterminable haze.

Into a pan Robert placed two links of andouille sausage. Sure, their relationship wasn't perfect domestic bliss, okay. She thought he spent too much time obsessing over his research into the history of his family. He thought she was an idiot for selling the occasional dime bag to make extra spending cash. Overall, though, at least they were honest about their faults, each of them aware that past relationships had left dents in the other, a fact they didn't ignore or criticize but accepted, tacitly if not gladly, as proof that neither of them was at an advantage.

"Are you going to get that?" Robert said, hearing the phone, located in a hallway that connected the kitchen with the foyer, start to ring. He turned around to see that Molly was looking in the refrigerator. She must not have been able to hear it.

The answering machine clicked on. Fascinated with the device—he didn't know anybody else who had one—Robert always liked to listen to it work, Molly's voice saying, "Please record your name and number into this contraption and later on I will return your call," followed by a robotic screech. That was why, in the weeks to come, he didn't think of himself as having eavesdropped, at least not with ill intent. He'd just been curious about the technology.

"Honey, it's Mom," a voice blared from the machine. "Give me a call."

Robert became so aware of his reactions it felt as though he were performing them: a stiffening of his back, his eyebrows making M-shapes across his forehead, a tilt of his chin, then the slow swivel of his body until he faced Molly. She held a bunch of green onions, the refrigerator open at her back. She looked at him with what he thought of as her muscadine eyes, preposterously large, exaggeratedly round.

"But I thought . . ." he said.

"I was going to tell you, I swear."

"But you said . . ." he said.

"When I told you they died, I mean, how could I know we'd start dating?" Her voice rippled with the kind of panic that sounded like laughter. "You were just some guy I was talking to in some diner!"

"They're both alive?"

"Divorced, but yeah."

Not the type of person to pace, Robert began to pace. Not the type of person to yell, Robert began to yell. His awareness that he'd become a yelling, pacing cliché only made him more of one as he asked of her, demanded of her, begged of her, *How could you?* "Lie to me" was the implied second half of that question, but the actual one easily could have been "have parents." It was absurd of him, and he damn well knew it. Molly said he was taking the whole thing out of proportion. So, of course, he took the whole thing further out of proportion.

"You're the most morally corrupt person I've ever met."

A pot of beans gurgled on the stove. In the frying pan a link of sausage spat grease. "I'd like you to leave," Molly said, pointing the way with an inherently furious, belittling, and accusatory calm. Robert did as ordered, not telling her the recipe for red beans and rice he had claimed was an old family secret he'd actually gotten from page 172 of the cookbook *Southern Sideboards*.

5.2

Thesis—Antithesis—Synthesis

Fate only exists in stories, and stories only exist in the past: one of those statements is true. Robert was trying to decide if that would make a good first line for his thesis as he walked into the office of Leo Marunga.

It was the morning of September 2, 1985. Campus was quiet due to Labor Day.

From behind his desk, acting more formal than usual, Leo said, "Take a seat, Vaughn," between sips of coffee. His eyes were bloodshot, not in the smudged scribble pot tended to give them, but from what looked like, given the bags underneath, a lack of sleep. He kept his feet on the ground rather than atop his desk. "Thanks for coming in on the holiday," he said. "I figured it's best we get things squared up before classes start."

"No problem."

"How've you been? Everything dandy in your personal life?"

So it was that obvious. Almost a month had passed since the incident with the answering machine, when Robert stood in Molly's kitchen, flushed with anger and absolute shame, experiencing a moment he figured was common in most relationships, a moment when you think, *What the fuck did I just do?* He'd always considered himself so much less volatile than that. How could he have let go of the one person who'd managed to disinter what years of heartbreak had buried? Throughout the past month, maybe because he and Molly had been cooking dinner when the incident occurred, Robert hadn't had much of an appetite, only managing to keep down a sleeve of cashews every so often. He hadn't been outside much either. His rolled sleeves revealed the fluorescently pale skin of his forearms.

"Everything's going great. Just been spending a lot of time at the library. You know, grinding away."

"Okay, then." Leo leaned back in his chair. "What have you got for me?"

Despite his claim to have been working, Robert hadn't made a great deal of progress on his thesis, focusing instead on his research into the Forsters. The notebook he began flipping through bore the proof. It was a veritable *Bartlett's* of the soda industry. In the November 21, 1891, issue of *Harper's Weekly*, for example, Mary Gay Humphreys wrote, "Soda water is an American drink. It is as essentially American as porter, Rhine wine, and claret are distinctly English, German, and French. The millionaire may drink champagne while the poor man drinks beer, but they both drink soda water." Beneath that quotation Robert had scrawled another:

What's great about this country is that America started the tradition where the richest consumers buy essentially the same things as the poorest. You can be watching TV and see PanCola, and you know that the president drinks Pan, Liz Taylor drinks Pan, and just think, you can drink Pan, too. A Pan is a Pan, and no amount of money can get you a better Pan than the one the bum on the corner is drinking. All the Pans are the same and all the Pans are good. Liz Taylor knows it, the president knows it, the bum knows it, and you know it.
—ANDY WARHOL

Robert began to talk while he stared at the quote by Warhol. "Lately I've been thinking about the South. I've been thinking about the people down here." He resituated himself in his chair. "Southerners don't lie. They *tell* lies. Have you noticed that yet? Our instances of not being truthful have a performative aspect."

"You've got my tail wagging."

"Remember that Didion line 'We tell ourselves stories in order to live'?"

"Oh God, that woman," said Marunga. "It's hard for me to take seriously anyone who takes themselves that seriously."

"Sure, okay. But that line of hers. People love, love, love to quote it, which is idiotic, because Didion immediately refutes it. It's basically, 'We tell ourselves stories in order to live, but we shouldn't.' And she's right. The truth of it is we tell ourselves *lies* in order to live."

"This sounds in complete opposition to the sample chapter you gave me."

"I think it is."

The fight with Molly had given Robert the new idea. After he asked her why she'd lied about her parents, she looked at him in a way that meant, *Because you wanted a story.*

Leo clasped his hands together with his index fingers pointed upward. He bounced them against his lips. "Then I've got just one question," he said. "Was my wife a good fuck?"

Over the next few seconds, while his blood thickened from the sudden loss of hydration through sweat, Robert became something of an antiunion capitalist. If today were not the first Monday in September, the hallways and offices of the philosophy department would be bustling with professors, secretaries, teaching assistants, students, janitors, and security guards. If today weren't Labor Day, there would be dozens of potential witnesses to the

murder of Robert Vaughn at the hands of his thesis adviser, Leopold Marunga.

"I don't know what she told you," Robert said, trying to keep
his voice calm.

"Calling my wife a liar is not the way to go."

In the middle of Leo's office, watching his adviser struggle to
keep himself from openly weeping, Robert came to a realization.
He was the bad guy here. He wasn't the victim; he was the culprit.
It all made sense now, the bloodshot eyes, the staid manner: this
man was in grief.

"I believe it goes without saying you'll have to find someone
else to work with on your thesis."

"Okay."

"Jane tells me the two of you haven't seen each other for some
time. It's going to stay that way."

"Sure."

"I'd like to throw you out that window. Ruin your entire academic career? Nothing would make me happier in the whole goddamn world." Leo's chest deflated. "You aren't to mention this to
anyone. It ends here. Am I being understood? Lovely. Now get the
fuck out."

The hallway was as eerily quiet as it had been when he arrived.
All down the length of it, suggestive of the approaching season,
everything was ochre-tinted, the leather chairs by the reception
area, the wood panels on the walls, the linoleum floors, the drop
ceiling tiles, even the ancient, faded sign that read FALLOUT SHELTER.
Robert walked toward the stairwell. Because of his echoing footsteps, it was difficult to tell, by sound alone, whether he was coming
or going.

5.3

Long Way Down, One Last Thing—Caesar's Harem—
The Lemurian Confederated Militia—
Sic Transit Gloria Mundi

On the set of *Boogie into the Night* (Five Olde Entertainment, 1975), a roller-skate picture in which a teenager hopes to parlay her skills at the rink into big-time movie stardom, Nicholas Forster damn near had a fit. They were overbudget by more than a quarter million dollars. The script's third act needed a punch-up. His lead actress was clearly ten years older than her character. Worst of all, craft services had stocked Coke and Pepsi products but nothing from PanCola. The hell did they think was bankrolling this whole thing?

Nicholas walked toward the trailers, passing a group of PAs who looked bored, most of them smoking cigarettes rather than working because set-decs couldn't get the disco ball to spin. He was in a particularly bad mood because the latest earnings report had come in that morning. The company was not doing well. Despite positive results from consumer tests, their most recent product to launch, water that came in a bottle, had failed to gain a foothold in the market. More than just Nick's brainchild, an idea whose research and development he oversaw, $PanH_2O$ had been his Hail Mary.

In a parking lot blanched by sunlight, the heat shimmer transforming it into impressionist art, Nick wandered through columns and rows of trailers until he found Havermeyer Dunn, the director, who was "advising" a slight, blond actress half his age.

"Action!" yelled Nicholas. "Cut!"

After whispering something to the actress, who blushed, nodded, and walked away, Havermeyer turned around to face Nicholas, extending his arms in greeting, hands low and palms up, as though he were carrying a giant pumpkin. "Nicky, my man."

"Quiet on the set! Roll sound! Roll camera!" Nick crossed his arms. "Uh-oh. Did I interrupt you by *doing your job?*"

He knew it was a mistake to have hired this guy. A regular at Five Olde, the production company Nicholas had scavenged after his uncle Lance died two years ago, Havermeyer Dunn hadn't directed a picture since *Caesar's Harem*, the subtitle of which Nick liked to joke should have been, "He Conquered, He Saw, He Came." Dunn had begged him for a job, saying, "Your uncle and me had a verbal agreement. He promised I'd always have work with the Forsters."

Like hell he did, Nick had thought, and then asked, "Can you roller-skate?"

"Nicky, my man, this is just a snag. We'll be up and running in an hour. I mean, it's a disco ball, not the Hoover Dam."

"One hour."

"Swear on my life."

"Wonderful," Nick said. "That should give you just enough time to talk with craft services. I want nothing but Pan on offer. Throw out all the Coke and Pepsi."

"Isn't that something the PM should handle?"

"Havermeyer."

"Okay, I'm on it."

"I've got a lunch in the hills. This parade better be marching by the time I'm back."

Nicholas looked at his watch. It was 12:30. He had half an

hour to make it to a restaurant that for most people was twenty minutes away. Nick needed the extra time. His friends were often surprised he was such a cautious driver, never exceeding the speed limit, always using his turn signals, interpreting yellow lights as stop rather than caution. He supposed it was the pilot in him.

"Welcome back, Mr. Forster," said Lagniappe's valet when Nicholas pulled up at 12:58. Although the restaurant had, over the past few years, lost favor with the younger crowd, Nicholas still went there, primarily due to his girlfriend, who liked Lagniappe for the food, the staff, and because it had, over the past few years, lost favor with the younger crowd. She was as cautious in their relationship as he was on the road. Lagniappe's hostess, after telling him his guest had already arrived, led Nicholas through a dining room planked with barge board from demolished Louisiana creole cottages, down a stuccoed-brick hallway, past a trompe l'oeil veranda, and onto a patio terrace shaded by fake Spanish moss hanging from real palm trees, where, at a table near one corner, sat his girlfriend. The hostess handed him a menu, said their server would be with them shortly, and walked back through the restaurant. Nicholas leaned in and kissed Susannah.

"Damn it, Nick. We're in public. How many times do I have to tell you?"

He made an exaggerated frowny face. "So-rry."

"Fuck off, okay?"

"You and your mother." Nicholas chuckled, shaking his head. "The language."

It drove Susannah crazy how flippant Nick could be. Ever since they had started seeing each other three years ago, a consummation made possible only after her mother confessed about the adoption, Susannah had been more of the adult in her relationship with Nicholas, constantly worried a tabloid reporter was lurking nearby, steno pad ready. Nick didn't worry about a single thing, which, if she were being honest with herself, was part of why she loved the little shit. People like him were allowed to be children their entire lives. He had that movie star quality, exuding a sense that the country, the world, the cosmos had been authored into existence for him and him alone, with everyone else, in their normally progressing lives, happy to oblige his stunted one.

Take his travel habit. Susannah understood all too well that Nick, like most beautiful people with means, loved to travel, ostensibly so that he could experience new cultures, but really so that he could be seen by new people and in new settings. Unlike most others of his kind, at least, he was never trite or clueless or plain silly enough to say, "I love to travel." Who didn't?

"I'll have the jambalaya flatbread," Susannah said when their waiter arrived, headlines scrolling through her mind. INCEST COLA! one read. FORSTER FAMILY CONFIRMS MISSISSIPPI ROOTS.

"And I'll go with the risotto étouffée," said Nicholas.

Susannah said, "No onions in his. He can't do onions."

Even if they told everyone they weren't related by blood, she figured only a few people in the world would believe them, the rest seeing nothing but two rich, entitled cousins who, besides committing the sin of being rich and entitled, committed the one of sleeping together. Susannah blamed herself for the necessity of discretion when going out in public with Nicholas—herself and the LCM.

The Lemurian Confederated Militia was a cross between the Merry Pranksters and the Black Panthers. It was founded on the philosophical underpinnings of Maoism, Marxism, vaudeville, Scientology, and pre-Atlantean occult, in particular the theory of a "third root race." Prior to joining the group, Susannah had been just another student at Stanford, deputy editor of the literary magazine, British lit major, occasional lifeguard at the campus pool.

Afterward, however, she became Susannah Forster, famed heiress and brainwash victim. Whether robbing a convenience store by claiming a jar of baby oil was nitroglycerin, setting free animals from a pet shelter, tossing red paint on police vehicles, or holding the school president hostage with a banana wrapped in a paper bag, all while wearing a T-shirt on which was printed I AM ANDY DEVINE, GOD OF DEATH, DESTROYER OF WORLDS, she was omnipresent in security-camera footage shown on every major-network news program. Reproductions of the T-shirt sold out nationwide. Although Susannah was eventually found not guilty—her lawyers used "coercive persuasion through involuntary intoxication" as her defense—the public celebrated her as an outlaw provocateur. She'd had to learn to handle being recognized, by shop clerks letting her into the dressing room, by people in the car across from her during a traffic jam, and by, she suspected, the waiter placing a dish in front of her at Lagniappe.

To distract from her suspicions, Susannah focused on her food, an example of a new culinary style described as Marigny Mélange. *So that's how you make something new,* she thought while taking a bite, *combine at least two things that are old.*

"Yours good?" she asked Nicholas.

"Uh-huh. Basically a creamier version of regular étouffée. You?"

Susannah swallowed. "They should just call it Chicken, Sausage, and Shrimp Pizza."

"Everybody's afraid to sound too California."

"Tell that to Alice Waters . . . Yes, please."

The waiter, holding a carafe of iced tea shawled in a napkin, refilled Susannah's glass. She was still suspicious of the guy. Lingering near their table for too long, spilling some of the tea because he was distracted, and tilting his head to listen to their conversation: he had eyes blue as toilet blocks and a nose stuck in business not his own. Susannah remained silent until he had left their vicinity. "How's the new toy?"

Nicholas wiped his mouth. "She flies smooth as red velvet. Plus, the throttle doesn't jam up like on the last one. I've been trying to think of a name for her. Too bad PanAm's taken."

"We should make another trip up to San Francisco."

"I can't right this minute. Business. The bottled water's not selling."

"Told you no one would pay for what they get for free at a fountain down the hall." Susannah took the last bite of her jambalaya flatbread. "Hey, remember when we were kids, in the summer, drinking water from the hose? Tasted kind of rubbery but also kind of perfect? That's what you should bottle. Remind people of their childhood."

"Hose water. Hmm. Good idea."

Hose water was just about the dumbest idea he had ever heard. Who would want to drink the kind of water they sprayed on their lawns? Nicholas nodded anyway, because of Susannah. She liked to think of herself as the wise adult in their relationship. Truth be told, however, without actual adults watching over her she would be lost, and most likely in prison. Following her arrest for robbery, vandalism, and kidnapping, among other charges, Susannah would have surely been convicted, were it not for the help of the rest of her family. They hired Roy Cohn, who promptly discredited the toxicology reports that had come back clean and paid a well-known psychiatrist with a not well-known gambling problem to say Susannah's IQ had dropped twenty points during her time with the LCM, a common side effect of coercive persuasion. Throughout the entirety of the trial, Susannah maintained she hadn't done anything wrong, continually saying, "Can nobody take a joke?" The unamused court ordered her into therapy.

Once their plates had been cleared, Nick asked, "Are you coming over tonight?" but Susannah wasn't paying attention to him. For
some reason she kept staring at their waiter. Instead of repeating the
question, Nick decided to ask it another way, slipping off his loafer,
reaching his foot across the floor, and, obscured from view by the
tablecloth, running his toe up Susannah's calf.

"*Niiiiiick.*"

"Yes?"

"Quit."

"Quit what?"

He had almost worked his way to her inner thigh when the
waiter suddenly appeared by his side. "Whenever you're ready!"
the guy said, laying the bill on the table as Nick, ruddy-cheeked
and half-smiling, tried to maneuver his foot back into his shoe.

Inside the black leather billfold were two items, one that required a mental calculation of the tip and another that brought
about a mental groan in Nicholas. Five by three inches was an odd
size for a head shot. The waiter must have had a bunch of them
printed up specifically for this ploy.

"Looks like our guy is an aspiring actor," Nicholas said, tossing
the photo to Susannah. "Want something to remember him by?"

On their walk out of Lagniappe, having managed to avoid further awkwardness with the waiter by leaving exact change, Nicholas
noticed a mild shift in Susannah, how she seemed more at ease than
she had been earlier. She briefly put her arm around his lower back
and pressed her head to his shoulder, telling him thank you, thank
you, thank you for the lovely lunch. She smelled of flowers, but not
any known kind. She smelled of her own kind of flower. *Susannah
Incarnata.* Outside, waiting for the valet to bring their cars around,
Nick, encouraged by her change in demeanor, pulled Susannah toward him and kissed her.

"Damn it, Susannah. We're in public," he said after she playfully batted him away. "How many times do I have to tell you?"

"Smart-ass."

"We can't have anybody seeing us."

"You're telling me."

They were too late. Down the street, in a parked car, sat Ramsey Forster. She couldn't believe what she had just seen. Her eyes hidden behind oversize sunglasses, tufts of hair strewn across the console, she stared at what she knew was her fault. If only she'd told Susannah the whole truth! Once her daughter and nephew were gone—"*We're not* actually *related, Mother*"—Ramsey began to drive, taking mindless turns, a left here and a right there, until she saw, ahead in the distance, the sign for a bar named Summer Solstice.

5.4

Ecclesiastes 1:4—A Sudden Downpour
of Men's Apparel—Rosebud

In high school, Robert had written a terrible short story named "An Autumnal Passage"—about an elderly woman who thinks a stray cat is the reincarnation of her dead husband—and throughout it he had used the word *especially* nineteen times; he could still remember the exact number because the carelessness of his writing had embarrassed him so much. On the afternoon of May 2, 1986, that story came to mind, not because its plot was *especially* relevant, nor because he was in such an *especially* nostalgic mood, but simply because of its title, how it seemed the exact opposite of this bright, warm spring day.

He stood on the front porch of the Panola Cola Historical Museum. Today was the first time he had visited it since his grandfather had passed away three months ago.

The floorboards inside were so scuffed they had the appearance of suede. Shadows from the window grilles created games of tic-tac-toe along the countertop in the front part of the museum. At the foot of the counter lay an eight of clubs. Robert picked it up, stared at it for a moment, and put it in his pocket.

As he walked around the room, going from one wall to the next with the slow, uneven gait of a librarian searching for a title, he saw the history not only of a company but also of his family.

Everything was so tangible; he wanted to touch it all. On a wooden shelf, wrapped in plastic sleeves like the kind used for baseball cards, sat two tickets for a one-way trip, New Orleans to Memphis, on the transport steamer *Fortune's Hostage*. Next to the tickets, also wrapped in plastic, was one of the hundreds of thousands of coupons for a free sample that the Panola Cola Company, hoping to create lifelong customers, gave away during its first few decades in operation. In the year 1895 alone 130,000 were given out. Under glass in a display case perpendicular to the main counter lay a paper bag from Wadsworth Confections; a specimen of the *Erythroxylon coca* plant, withered and dead; two dusty bottles of Vin Mariani, a coca wine, the ancestor of PanCola; promotional matchbooks, doilies, pencils, blotters, pocket mirrors, pendants, and baseball score cards; a bowl of Harrington candies in moon-white wrappers; and the rusting license plate from a Whippet Roadster that Robert knew from his research had been nicknamed Volstead. A large bookcase stood in one corner of the room. Among its contents, warped by the heat and discolored by the sun, were copies of the Dickens novels Monty had read as a child, copies of the Austen novels Susannah had read as a child, a first edition of *Ms. Panola Cola: Reflections of the Soda Business,* Ramsey's notebook for her apparently unfinished memoir, and a complete set, volumes one through twelve, of *The Adventures of Catfish the Dog.*

Robert checked his watch. He had to be back by seven o'clock, when Molly's parents, in town for her graduation, were coming by the apartment for dinner. They wanted to meet the guy they still referred to as just her "roommate," even though he and Molly had been dating for over a year, minus that one horrible month after their big fight. It was two o'clock. Robert had plenty of time.

Upstairs in the attic, he encountered a hoard of ad materials, from point-of-purchase to "premiums." PanCola wall hangers and bottle hangers were piled next to fountain festoons, window trims, and seashore cutouts. Branded scales, chairs, serving urns, and cabinets were loaded with soda trays and sheet music for the Panola Cola song. On a far wall, varicolored by the ambient light refracted through a stained-glass chandelier, hung an illustration of the back of a man's head, an unfinished painting on an easel in front of him, and, just past the painting, the model whose image he was trying to capture on canvas. "One of our artists working on next year's PanCola Girl," read the first caption. The girl posing, unlike the version of her in the painting, was a brunette. So the second caption read, "A gentleman, he CLEARLY prefers blondes!" The attic included ads from other companies as well. Between two posters for the movies *Catch a Tiger by the Toe* and *Boogie into the Night* was situated a one-sheet for the Folies-Bergère, creating a triptych of musical tastes from the 1920s, 1930s, and 1970s. Against the wall beneath the posters leaned a placard for Moretti Motors' ADM-9.

On his way back downstairs, Robert passed a rare photograph from 1910's notorious "PanCola Summit," a weeklong motivational sales meeting. The photo featured hundreds of Panhandlers crowded in front of a platform. According to the exposé "The Church of Pan, or the Cult of Pan?" written by a British reporter who infiltrated the event, it was less of a pep rally and more of an indoctrination, creating mindless automatons whose only goal in life was to sell sugar water. "This wasn't the country I'd envisioned," began the exposé, if Robert remembered correctly. "It was the South, a country within a country. But which was more real, the exterior one or the interior, the body or its soul?" Robert tapped the photo with his finger before continuing down the stairs.

"No need for us to go in that room," Harold had said the one time he'd taken Robert on a brief tour around the PanCola museum. He'd been talking about a room in the back part of the ground floor. "It's just where I store the records and other leftovers."

The room was locked. Robert ran his fingers along the top of the door casing but had no luck. He then walked over to the cash register and, while he tried to determine how to open the damn thing, noticed the key sitting on its bottom ledge. A key-shaped clean spot was left in the dust after he picked it up.

Inside the back room he saw his grandfather had told the truth about it being a place for storage. Marble-print boxes were stacked in haphazard columns throughout the room like stalagmites of cardboard. Robert took the lid off one to find it full of registration ledgers. "August 26 1984. 10:37 morning time. Maitland Family," he read on a page he turned to at random. "Peter, Claire, Jones, Rose, Brooks. Austin Texas." Such detail! There must have been a record of every single person who had visited the museum. At first, Robert felt proud of Harold, imagining the unwavering, monkish dedication required for him to spend time every day noting dates, hours, minutes, names, and places, but then Robert remembered that, until his grandfather had learned he had a grandson, he thought he was the only Forster left. Harold had spent all that effort taking notes while thinking nobody would ever care enough to read them. Robert, picturing his grandfather hunched over a desk, eyes squinted and pen in hand, the singular embodiment of an institutional memory, promised himself he would read every single page.

Around the rest of the room, he found plastic crates and wicker baskets and even coffee cans full of PanCola memorabilia: Diamond Bert Farwell scowling on the cover of *The Shadow Magazine*, a Peabody duck in silhouette on an invitation for a New Year's Eve gala, the No. 2 House catching a light rain in a photograph of Ashley Down. Newspaper clippings were spread everywhere, freezing time via the permanence of linotype. Houghton Forster was forever defeating the federal government in *The United States vs. Fifty Barrels of Panola Cola,* and Royal Teague was always losing to a poor cotton farmer in an election for the Louisiana House of Representatives. In an ice cream pail overflowing with bottle caps Robert discovered a share certificate for the Panola Cola Company. "Incorporated Under the Laws of the State of Mississippi" printed at the top and scrawled at the bottom the nearly illegible signature of Houghton Forster, the slip of paper reminded Robert of a time he'd only read about, when the origin of many family fortunes in the South could be explained with the remark, whispered over tea, across church pews, or between rounds, "They bought Pan stock early."

He balled up the certificate and dropped it on the ground before leaving the room and walking out of the museum. Again he checked his watch. He had just enough time to take a look around Eden.

On the fifteen-minute drive there, Robert gripped the door handle in his old navy Buick, his knuckles nearly going numb with the strain, because that morning the latching mechanism had broken. Although he had, over the past few months, convinced himself wealth wasn't important, not being able to afford a decent car, he had to admit, was a big regret about inheriting nothing but an old museum.

Not that he was destitute. Freelance gigs were working well enough, a book review here, an op-ed there, to the extent that he had looked into building a house in the pecan grove, right where the trailer had been before he'd sold it for scrap. Unfortunately, even a modest house, as little as 1,600 square feet, would cost upward of $70,000. His father had never even had the imagination to consider building a house on the property. Robert had to admit, though, he'd never had the imagination either, not until Molly came along, not until there was someone in his life to build the house for.

He turned onto the long dirt road that led to Eden. A wrought iron swing gate blocked his way. In spite of the POSTED signs everywhere, Robert hopped out of his car, climbed the gate, and walked up the road, toward the spot where The Sweetest Thing had once stood. On his forehead drops of sweat began to fatten. Dust kicked up by his shoes revealed spiderwebs in a ditch alongside the road. The blowfly wind blew blowflies, and woodpeckers pecked wood.

At the crest of a gently sloping hill, next to a pair of magnolia trees in bloom, Robert located what had to be the former site of the house, a smooth rectangle of grass beneath which, like a wound seen through gauze, the soil was a shade darker than normal because it had been leavened with ash. Four concrete blocks flush with the ground gave the rectangle its shape, yellow ragwort providing the only relief from the overwhelming green. In the middle of what must have been the front lawn, Robert was looking around, at the barn where Rocket the Miracle Horse must have once lived, at the clearing where Lance and Karen had likely gotten married, when, reality giving way to memory, he found himself in a sudden downpour of men's apparel. Suit jackets and dress shirts and neckties drifted through the air, landing in the grass beside pants and suspenders and undershirts. Crooked pillars of sunlight flashed through armless sleeves flailing in their slow descent.

One Sunday afternoon in the early 1920s, according to the story Robert's grandfather had told him, Houghton Forster lay on a sofa in the living room, hungover from having spent the previous night at a local juke trying to keep up with Branchwater. Annabelle was cleaning the house and cooking dinner herself because, at that time, they couldn't afford a full staff and the help they had took off on Sundays. In no mood, her cheeks comically streaked with flour and her hair a caricature of frazzled disarray, she was going to order her husband to give a hand, if only he hadn't preempted her by saying, oblivious to her condition, "Make sure my blue shirt is pressed. I'm going to need it tomorrow." That was it for her. Annabelle marched up to their bedroom, retrieved an armful of her husband's clothes, including his blue shirt, marched out to the second-floor gallery, and proceeded to fling the clothes, one piece at a time, onto the front lawn. The ten-year-old twins stood barefoot and giggling in the middle of the downpour. An hour later, Fiona, having arrived for dinner, gathered up a few items of clothing as she made her way into the house, where Houghton asked if she'd seen what his crazy wife had done. Annabelle then explained her side of the story. So, immediately grasping who was justified in the situation, Fiona walked out to the second-floor gallery and, like flicking cards into an upturned hat, returned the clothes to their rightful place on the lawn.

Robert, picturing a pair of socks caught on a tree branch above his head, chuckled. He decided to add that story to the project he had been working on since dropping out of school—*temporary leave of absence,* he corrected himself—a project that'd begun with his thesis but, over the past few months, had evolved into something more personal than academic.

He walked along a path extending from the barn, stepping over the occasional terrapin in sluggish, persistent transit between duck ponds. When he looked back up after plucking a cocklebur from his pant cuff a strange thing occurred. Robert found himself caught in a maelstrom of Forsters. Timelines unraveled and so too did sensations. Near a thicket of brambles, the child version of Susannah was picking blackberries, her fingers dyed purple by the juice, while in a stand of slash pines, Cotton barked at a squirrel as it clamored through fragrant needles, some of them falling onto a rusted tin bathtub, inside of which stood Harold at seventeen years old, pretending he was captaining a pirate ship, its prow overlooking a short ridge where Montgomery, dressed in the plug hat of a young man on the make, was going for a morning stroll, Bear-Wolf trotting tongue-out by his side. Suddenly the air shifted, quivered, as if the channel had been flipped, the antenna adjusted. Now Susannah had been joined by Nicholas, who told her he knew a secret trick for picking blackberries, and now Montgomery, much older, marched across the ridge alone, a shotgun cradled against his shoulder, and now, instead of standing in a tin bathtub, Harold sat on Rocket, whispering in its ear that a horse who could do miracles was its own miracle.

Lost in those impossible memories, each so vivid it felt as though he'd actually been there, Robert came upon a field covered in wild rye. He recognized it not only as the place where his great-grandfather used to harvest drinking straws but also where he had first kissed the girl who would become his wife.

With his hands outstretched, Robert wandered through the field, letting the rye stalks brush against his open palms, all the while trying to conjure what that day almost a hundred years ago must have been like: a breeze evaporating the sweat from his great-grandfather's collar, a parasol keeping the sun off his great-grandmother's shoulders. Beside a walnut tree Robert sat down in the grass. He closed his eyes. In the stillness of the afternoon, he allowed his mind to clear for a brief moment, wrapping his arms around his knees, loosening his shoulders, taking a long breath through his nose. The world grew so quiet he could hear the ticking of his watch. That reminded him it was time to head back.

Robert stood to leave Eden, and only then did he notice the smell of honeysuckle flowers.

ACKNOWLEDGMENTS

Over the years, the saying "All stories are true, and some actually happened" has been attributed, in various forms, to Thomas Jefferson, Mark Twain, and an anonymous octogenarian quoted in the *Washington Post*. That nobody knows for certain who coined the saying testifies to its accuracy.

I owe a great deal of thanks for this "true" story.

Thank you, Wendy Flanagan, Tom Treanor, Kimberly King Parsons, C. J. Hauser, Ruth Curry, Nadja Spiegelman, Chandler Klang Smith, Michelle Conroy, Thom Blaylock, Caitlin McNally, Alexandra Rose Chase, and Matt Burgess. Y'all know how to shake the hot sauce into a bowl of gumbo. I'm grateful for the generous support of everyone involved with the Stone Court Writer-in-Residence program in Stockbridge, Massachusetts, where part of this novel was written, and to the students and faculty of the 2012 Summer Literary Seminar in Lithuania, where part of this novel was workshopped. Everyone at William Morris Endeavor (Laura Bonner, Matilda Forbes Watson, and Haley Heidemann) and William Morrow (Ryan Cury, Eliza Rosenberry, Julia Elliott, Lynn Grady, Liate Stehlik, and Ploy Siripant) who worked on this book is, in my unwavering and thankful opinion, the bee's knees, calves, ankles, and toes. Until the end of my days, I'll be in spiritual hock to Eve Attermann, literary agent and human being extraordinaire. Thanks especially to Jessica Williams—brilliant editor, honest reader, masterful critic—for never hesitating to say, "It's almost there, but . . ." and for always having faith when I responded, more or less, "Aye aye, Cap'n."

In addition to the books and articles noted within the novel, I'm indebted to the following sources for research: Mark Pendergrast's *For God, Country and Coca-Cola: The Definitive History of the Great American Soft Drink and the Company That Makes It*; Edward M. Coffman's *The War to End All Wars: The American Military Experience in World War I*; Lizzie Collingham's *The Taste of War: World War II and the Battle for Food*; Brassaï's *The Secret Paris of the '30s*; Vera Petrov's *Carb-o-Nation*; Lawrence Dietz's *Soda Pop: The History, Advertising, Art, and Memorabilia of Soft Drinks in America*; A. N. Wilson's *Burt Reynolds*; Scott Faragher and Katherine Harrington's *Images of America: The Peabody Hotel*; Anne Cooper Funderburg's *Sundae Best: A History of Soda Fountains*; Fiorella Grayson's "The Lion's Roar: An Oral History of 'The Pride'" from *Annals of Organized Crime*; William Alexander Percy's *Lanterns on the Levee: Recollections of a Planter's Son*; William Wiser's *The Twilight Years: Paris in the 1930s*; *The WPA Guide to New York City: The Federal Writers' Project Guide to 1930s New York*; the diary and correspondence of Pearl Ledbetter; and James C. Cobb's *The Most Southern Place on Earth: The Mississippi Delta and the Roots of Regional Identity*.

Above all, I'm thankful for my family, in particular my parents, Charles and Becky Wright, and my grandfather Fred Snowden, to whom this book is dedicated. I wish he were still here to read it.